The King's Archer

A Medieval Adventure of The Wars of the Roses

Francis Lecane

authorHOUSE®

AuthorHouse™ UK Ltd.
500 Avebury Boulevard
Central Milton Keynes, MK9 2BE
www.authorhouse.co.uk
Phone: 08001974150

Published by AuthorHouse 12/7/2011

ISBN: 978-1-4678-8694-9 (sc)
ISBN: 978-1-4678-8695-6 (e)

Chapter One

Christmas 1460 was bitterly cold. The snow lay thick upon the countryside and the stock in the fields huddled together against the cutting wind that seemed to blow unceasingly across the Welsh Marches.

In the Three Tuns, Shrewsbury, the sound of yuletide merriment reached a crescendo as a serving wench carried a tray of ale and wine to a group of liveried soldiers sitting with their backs to the roaring log fire.

"God's blood Diccon, I reckon you could swive 'er. "

"Yer, and the rest" Diccon's laughter was interuppted by the huge belch that erupted from his mouth along with a dribble of vomit"

"The whoreson pig never could hold his ale" shouted the third man in the group as he nimbly twisted out of the way of the avalanche of ale and half digested food that shot out of Diccon's mouth.

"You are more disgusting than Owen Tudor on his welsh privy, and that is saying something.!" This last comment was delivered by the youngest man in the group. A muscular fair haired man of eighteen to twenty years with the calloused fingers of his right hand clasping the bowl of an ale pot.. He was dressed in the padded doublet and wool hose of the period and on his feet a fine pair of leather boots that much to his delight had still not started to let in water ever since he had liberated them from the body of a footpad who had tried to rob him on his way from Presteigne to Ludford Bridge.

Having made his way north to Shrewsbury to join with his friends and fellow indentured archers and foot soldiers who gave alliegance to The Marcher Lordship of Stapleton. In all there were several score of these marches men and they tended to keep together as much as was practicable. They all fought under the banner of the young Earl Of March, Edward Plantagenet.

"More ale, Thomas, get us more ale" shouted Diccon at the fair haired yougster.

"With what, you drunk pig, my purse is as empty as a priest's charity. And any wayI,m off back to my bed."

"Cannot keep up with the likes of us"Diccon's head slumped down upon the ale covered table and seconds later a huge snore reverberated across the room. His companions looked at one another and after a quick divvy up of coins from each purse which amounted to hardly enough to pay for a single jug of ale they set off into the bitter cold of the Christmas night.

Thomas pulled his cloak around him, partially for the warmth but also to protect the yew wood of his most precious possession. His bow. He had made it himself from the seasoned heartwood of the old yew that had been cut in Lingen Churchyard back in the days of King Henry. It was a rare thing to have a bow made from a churchyard yew. It imbued the weapon with something special,a spirituality, an acknowledgement that God was looking out for him. For sure most good bows were made of yew, but supplies were fast becoming scare and many staves were now being imported from Italy and Spain,.

and God only knew what dubious quality that inferred. He had heard of laburnam wood being used,but he didn't trust it, also wych or hazel bows that he had seen on Ludlow market, but surely nothing could beat the tried and tested good old English yew bow.He thought back to the days when the Lingen yew had been felled and how lucky he had been to get hold of two ells of the heartwood and the softwood,the combination of which ha d eventually given him the makings of 'sweet slayer' as he fondly named his bow.He reached up under his leather sallet to touch the bowstrings he kept wound there to avoid damp.

A trader on Ludlow market had told him that the price of imported staves was coming down. From an all time high five years ago of five shillings a bow they w ere now around two shillings each. Arrows on the other hand had gone through the roof, and a sheaf was fetching two shillings. Anyway Thomas preferred to make his own if possible selecting the straightest ash stems and trimming and gluing the goose feather flights in place, then getting the local smith to fashion the bodkin tips that he preferred.. With these pleasant thoughts swirling round his head he made his way back to wards the large tithe barn that had been allocated to the Marches soldiers. Up to one hundred men and a good few women, dogs and some horses were crammed into this space. At least it kept the sleepers warm.

Suddenly, ahead he saw three or four figures struggling in the snow. Male shouts and the piercing scream of a woman in distress. As he drew closer it became apparent that three men,soldiers in a distinctive livery were molesting a young woman.

"Hold her down,you two, and after, she'll be yours."A leering black haired youth of about Thomas' age commanded the other two who had the women's arms pinioned and her face pushed up against the wall of the feotid alley through which she had been walking.He ripped the back of the woman's dress and proceeded to pull savagely at her undergarments until he had exposed her white and naked buttocks."Bend over my lady and see how you likes this" he fumbled with his hose and proceeded to move in on the woman. His companions were absorbed with what was happening and were watching their young master within tense delight Too late delight turned to fear as Thomas drew his rondel dagger and launched himself onto the three. He stabbed one through the upper arm and he reeled away with a bitter cry,the next had by now pulled his own dagger.Thomas and his assailant cirled one another whilst the rapist instigator tried to recover his balance whilst still keeping hold of the woman who was kicking and scratching at his eyes and his exposed genitals

" Prithee Sir, do you know who you are stopping having his fun?"

"This is no fun I know" snapped Thomas and he lunged forward through the guard of the second assailant piercing him to the heart. Swift as one of his arrows he pivoted on his left foot and threw the rondel. Hours of idle practice had made him an accurate expert at knife throwing and the dagger spun through the air and stabbed the black haired youth through the eye. He sank to the floor with barely a whimper, dead.

"Are you hurt" He turned to the woman.

"No, praise be to God, though two minutes later I should have been. "She pulled the tattered remnants of her dress around her and gave Thomas a grateful smile.

"I am a ward of the Earl of March and he will reward you for saving me."

Thomas noticed that through the tears and grime on her face she was the most beautiful woman he had seen in a long time.

"What brings you out alone my lady" he asked..

"My lap dog, Cyrus, ran off from the castle and I vowed to get him back. None of my companions would venture out on this cold night so I thought to go myself. It was a foolish move!"

"Aye my lady happen it was. Take this cloak now, and I shall walk you home to your companions."He slung his cloak around her torn dress. She shivered and lent against his body heat with a greatful sigh..

"What is your name ?"

"Thomas of Lingen, I am an archer in the service of the Earl of March.

"And you my lady, what shall I call thee?"

"I am the Countess of Hambye in Normandy, I am a ward of the Ealf of March.

"But you speak good English yet you say you are French."

"Only by marriage,my husband the count was French,, but I am from the Griffiths family of Carew in Pembrokeshire.My husband was killed fighting for the Earl of March in a skirmish near Calais,and when the Earl discovered what had happened and who I was he made me his ward and now I live where he does"

"My Lady, dost you know who it was attacked you.?The Countess looked Thomas straight in the eye. "Yes. I do.That reptile was the son of one of the Earl's battle commanders Lord Grey of Wilton, and I fear killing his son will make a mortal enemy of him."

Thomas felt sick. He knew that the power of the aristocracy stretch ed like tentacles into every corner of life.If he was arrained for the death of this young man he had virtualy no chance of escaping the hangman.The strict hierarchy would never allow his reasons or excuses to be heard and he was as good as dead. H e shivered.

"You are cold without your cloak Thomas ?

"Nay my lady, I am thinking how best to avoid any trouble from the killing of your molester."

"Never fear, I shall intercede on your part with the Earl and he is an honest and fair man and when he hears the truth you will be exonerated"She gave him a smile.

Ahead of them at the top of Castle Street loomed the forbidding bulk of Shrewsbury Castle.Built of red sandstone the bulk of the castle straddled the only dry route through the town.

"Wait in the courtyard Thomas.I shall send for you."The countess disappeared through the massive oak doors that fronted the keep.Thomas looked around him. In the courtyayd various groups of soldiers warmed themselves at fires, playing dice and passing leather flasks of wine back and forth.. Against the rear wall about twenty horses were tethered and stooks of weapons pikes and pole axes rested against the wall. A huge siege cannon on wooden wheels was pulled up against the wall and Thomas wandered over to look at it. He had heard much about this new innovation in weaponry but had never seen one.This gun was approx 18 feet long with a diameter of seven to nine feet bound over its length with reinforcing straps of metal to stop it exploding when the deadly force of its charge was let off. It lay upon a large wooden cradle the base of which was a sledge with huge wooden wheels. The act of dragging the thing into the castle courtyard had gouged out two furrows through the cobblestones. Thomas could only marvel at the sheer weight and ugly evil of the weapon.

"What thinks thee of that cully?" a squat soldier in a leather apron patted the bulk of the gun.

"God's Destroyer we calls her and she do."

"Do what "asked Thomas.

"Why, you whoreson, destroy. Ain't you never seen a thing like that afore I bet. Where you from any road not to know of God's Destroyer." He laughed to himself and took a swig from the leather flask that hung at his waist.

"She be off on the next saints day, Earl of March wants her to be part of the next battle he fights, and I'll be in charge of getting her there."

"So the gun needs a few oxen to pull her" said Thomas

"Team of eight oxen and a back up team of twelve horses. They'll move her anywhere."

"And do you fire her?"

Why bless ye no. That's the job of they bastard Italians. They think they're the only folk knows how to operate one of these. But I could do it as easy. Pack in the powder, make sure 'tis nicely mixed and not damp. Add the round stone and the wet earth. Let ee dry off and when all is done, pierce the touch hole with nice mealed powder and touch ee off with the linstock. Boom" He capered round the cannon with a maniacal grin on his weathed old face.

Thomas laughed. " I should give a groat to see that "

"Give it here now and when next we comes to fire it you'll be the first to know."

"What do you take me for, I ain't just come up the brook"

"Aye, mayhap, but you looks like you might" The gunner spat a gob of foul smelling phlegm at Thomas' feet.

"Whom do you fight for Cully I ain't never seen you afore?"

"The Earl of March is my liege lord and I'm an archer in his battle." Suddenly there came the sound of horses hooves into the courtyard, a priest on a palfrey with half a dozen soldiers also mounted,swept into the keep of the castle.Casting his eye around the priest pointed at Thomas.

"That's him, that's the villain. Hold him" before he could move or even register that he was surrounded he felt himself pinioned and held in an armlock.

"I have done nowt" He cried.

"Nowt but murder" replied the priest "He killed Guy son of Lord Grey of Wilton in front of witnesses and unprovoked."

"That's a lie" screamed Thomas" the dog was raping a woman"

"That's not what we heard,and we have a witness who can prove it. Step up my son and tell what you saw." To Thomas' horror, from behind the priests horse the figure of the third man from the melee his arm roughly bandaged stepped forward.

"Aye that's him" he spat. "came on us from behind as we walked home minding our own business. Stabbed Johno and the maister robbed them of their silver and then stabbed I.Then he ran off leaving us to God's mercy"

"That's not true and ye know it, what of the woman, what of the Countess?"

The priest laughed," there is no woman never was a woman. Throw him in the dungeon till we have time to hang him"

Thomas' captors hustled him across the yard down some stone steps in to the feotid dank of the undercroft. There they threw him into a tiny windowless cell and slammed and locked the door.

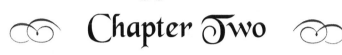

Chapter Two

In the large solar at the rear of the castle in front of a cherry log fire stood three or four well dressed and fed men.

"What do you suggest My lord.?"

"We need reliable intellignce.How many men how many horses, whence they ride,when they will be near here, in fact every goddamned thing which up to now we have not had notice of."

"Well my lord,it is a notoriously difficult task to obtain such facts. Prisioners do not tell truth as you know, and there are no good men able to infiltrate the enemy."

"Lord Grey you always were a dissembler, for sure we can find some good men to go into Tudor's camp and get this information I shall find some myself." The young Earl of March turned his back to the fire.and warmed his nether regions.

The door to the solar opened and a servant hurried in he whispered something in the ear of Lord Grey of Wilton whose ruddy facial look drained away to grey. He staggered back and sank onto a chair.

"Why whatever is wrong my lord?" cried the Earl of March.You look as if a ghost has passed your grave."

"It might as well have, my son is slain....Killed by one of your archers in an unprovoked attack......."

"If this is true, the villain will be caught and hung." "They have him already in the dungeon."

The Earl of March turned to his steward." Find out what is happening and put the prisoner to the torture to see what truth he tells.For now this meeting is closed we will talk again on strategy to contain Pembroke and Tudor. "He waved dismissal to his nobles who led the disconsolate Lord Grey of Wilton out of the solar.

In a warm bed chamber in the south tower of Shrewsbury castle the Contess of Hambye had just finished telling her tale of rape and her saviour to one of the Queen's ladies in waiting.

"You must be examined for hurt " Nay, I have but a few scratches on my arse, if Thomas of Lingen hadn't passed by when he did It would have been much worse."

"Where is this paragon of virtue?

"He waits in the courtyard." "Bring him in so I may thank him,"She turned to a servant and gave orders that Thomas should be brought forwith.

Some time passed and the servant returned. "He is gone my lady, there is no archer by the name of Thomas in the yard."

"What none, Oh well, I shall have to find him in the archer's camp to thank him.On the morn, go to the camp and seek out this man and have him brought here to the castle"

"Aye my lady, " the servant bowed and left the room.

"He must be a humble man your saviour not to have waited for your summons Elenor.Most churls would be hoping for monetry reward," "Not this one I think, there was something different about him" "Art smitten with the youth I find" said the older woman as she gave the Countess of Hambye a broad smile.

"Not at all my lady" though a strong blush suffused her throat as she thought about Thomas.

The door to the cell banged open.

"Out you whoreson".A hugefat man over six foot tall dressed in a leather jerkin and leather trews with manacles hanging from his waist band stood in the door way. He grabbed Thomas by the arm and manhandled him out into the fresher air of the courtyard.

"Now 'tis time to see if you tell the truth or no." He hustled Thomas across the yard and down some stone steps that led into the underparts of the castle through dank corridors they went past thick oak doors with tiny barred windows.Moans and groans of despair could be heard from the inmates behind the doors and Thomas felt fear for the first time. He thought he would never get back up to the pure fresh air of the English countryside again but would be forever incarcerated amongst the sordid smells of damp and human excrement that lingered in these foul halls.

At last they came to a large chamber. Windowless but lit by a circular iron candle sconce in the centre of the room. On the walls hung manacles and a rack stood in the centre of the room Two iron braziers glowed red whist the instuments of torture that were in them heated up to red hot. Two squat and ugly henchman dressed In similar fashion to the one that had brought Thomas to this place waited.

"On the water board with this one first, something nice and gentle to get ee in the mood."The first jail;er chuckled.

The other two men pinioned his arms an forced him head downwards upon a long elm board that was pivoted on a wood stand so it could move up and down.In the down position his head would be immersed in a tub of rancid water.

"Down you go my cully "Thomas felt his head and shoulders become immersed in the cold stagnant water of the wooden tub. He tried to take a deep breath but the jailer seeing this punched him hard in the kidneys which expelled any breath he might have taken. He felt the water flood around his mouth and nose he gagged for air, but there was none, in a panic he thrashed and tried to tear himself free from his bonds.

"We got a strong 'un here Jake," "Aye right enough, but they all weaken in the end."

Thomas felt he was drowning and there was nothing he could do to stop it he swallowed the sordid filthy water gagging and spluttering. Suddenly the elm board was lifted up and blessed fresh air flooded back into his lungs. " "Did ye like that then my cully, plenty more where that came from. "

Once more the board was tilted down and once more his head was filled with the stink of the rancid water.. After the third immersion, each one slightly longer than the one before Thomas' will was close to being broken. "Now we puts the question" Jake laughed as he looked down onto the bedraggled head and shoulders of his prisioner.

"Did you, unprovoked kill the son of theEarl of Wilton and his companion and rob them of their silver.?

Thomas shook his head. "Under you go again cully, 'cos that aint the right answer" He tlted the board down and this time kept it there until the bubbles that flowed up from Thomas' mouth had virtually ceased. The board was swung back into the level position, but by now Thomas was unconscious.

"You've killed 'ee you daft bugger"

Nay, we'll bring 'un back with a hot iron, never fails".

The third torturer stepped over to the nearest brasier and pulled out a pair of red hot pliers.

"This'll wake the bugger, he's an archer ain't he, well he aint ever gonna pull a bow string again" so saying he took hold of Thomas first and index finger of his right hand and squeezed down with the pliers trapping the two fingers. A smell like roasting pork and a thin line ofsmoke. Thomas sceamed. "Told you that'd bring him back"Jake looked round triumphantly at his companions.

The third torturer shook his head in admiration."You're the one for sure Jake, you knows a few tricks"

"Yes I do God be praised, and this bastard has yet to talk, or at least talk like I want him to."

More immersions followed and more touching with hot irons to bring him round.But Thomas' strong will would not allow him to give in. It would have been so esy to admit to what his torturers wanted him to say, so easy to have just gvien up so the pain would stop. After some time and whilst Thomas hung from the elm board in a state of extreme pain and rolling in and out of conciousness, Jake the head jailor called a stop and Thomas was taken back to his cell his feet dragging on the ground behind him. He was thrown down onto the floor and he crawled over to the stinking pile of damp straw that was all there was that constituted a bed and fell into an uneasy sleep half way between waking and unconciousness.

In the great Hall of Shrewsbury Castle on the day after twelth night the young Earl of March convened a King's court to try offenders who had been arrained before him for offences committed during the festive period. Mostly these consisted of thefts from the good citizens of Shrewsbury and they weredealt with in the summery way if found guilty by the use of a branding iron.Branded on the thumb if a first offence so that the perpertrator would be known to the authorities another time, or if the thief was there for a second offence branding on the forehead so all could see their shame. There were several more important cases to be dealt with and one of those was the murder of Guy Wilton.

"Bring forward the accused"The steward of the Earl of March cried. Seated on a raised dias in front of an oak refectory table with a clerk beside him the Earl of March looked bored. These courts took up valuable time which he could ill afford to give, but his inherent fairness to all men ensured that he was always willing to do his duty to his citizens.

From the rear of the hall two soldiers dragged Thomas of Lingen forward. He was in a filthy state. His doublet and hose dirty and torn and his tortured hand hanging uselessly beside him. Three or four days growth of beard covered his face from which his haunted eyes gazed out at his accusers.

"You are Thomas of Lingen?" demanded the steward.. Thomas nodded.

You are accused that on the last Tuesday after Christmas tide you did foully murder and rob one Guy of Wilton and his companion Jono of Boldre.How do you plead.?"

"Not guilty my Lord"

"Are there any witnesses to this crime"

From the back of the hall the third man involved in the melee stepped forward

"What say you of this?" demanded the steward.

"On the Tuesday night as we walked home with God's grace upon us and no bad thing in the air. This man "pointing in the direction of Thomas "Came up behind us and attacked us in an unprovoked manner he stabbed me in the arm and killed both my master Guy and my companion Jono.He stole our silver and ran."

"Are there any witnesses to speak for the accused." The steward looked around the hall.

Suddenly from the back there came the sound of raised voices and into the hall came three elegantly dressed women. One was Elenor Countess of Hambye one was the lady in waiting to the Queen and the third her companion.. The Earl of March gave a start and sat up, his boredom vanishing.

"What do you here my ladies, this is the King's court and it is unusual to see members of your gender here before us."

"my Lord, we are citizens of the king and have a right to be heard, and what I have to say may save an innocent man from an unjust punishment.Your ward the Countess of Hambye was brutally attacked by three men whilst innocently looking for her dog that had escaped here. If it had not been for Thomas of Lingen she would have been brutally used and maybe even murdered by the villains.

He came upon them and by his prowess at arms he was able to save her."

"How is it that this man accuses him of murder and theft?"

"A calumny and a lie said to hide the truth from you."The Earl of March beckoned the countess forward. "What say you of this Elenor"

"All is true as my lady has said my Lord. Had it not been for the bravery and skill of Thomas of Lingen my virtue would be as nought and even my life might have been forfit."

"How is it then that the accused has been tortured and kept in a cell for so many days before you came forward to plead for him." ""Twas only this morning that we discovered that he was being held in the cells. We asked amongst his companions and none of them had seen him for several days. By pure chance we heard of a prisoner charged with murder due to come before the court today and upon investigation it turned out to be Thomas."

The Earl of march stood up."Step forward Thomas of Lingen" Thomas squared his shoulders his useless right hand hanging down beside him and took a step forward.

"There are not many cases that come before me which have such an interesting story to them. My ward the Countess of Hambye is a devout lady whose truth I trust. Therefore you are exonerated from any crimes you are accused of and you are a free man.Release him".

Thomas stood unable to believe the vagaries of chance that had propelled him one moment from certain death to being free once more. He looked with gratitude towards the Countess who acknowledged him with a smile.

"This case is not finished." The Earl of March cried." For bearing false witness and causing an innocent man such trouble you"pointing at Thomas' accuser" you shall be hanged forthwith. Take him out. " Turning towards Thomas he said "Thomas of Lingen,you may be able to do me a great service. When you are recovered from your ordeal I shall ask you to attend upon me where I shall have a task for you to undertake. By noon tomorrow should be time enough from the look of you. Steward, make clothes available for this man and attend to his injuries." Thomas was led from the great hall to a small room where in stood a wooden tub filled with hot water. After complete immersion and washing with scented soap, an apothecary of the court attended to his injuries smearing salves upon his burns and minor scratches. A complete new outfit of doublet and hose in the livery of the Earl of March was given to him. Luckily his old boots werestill quite serviceable.

To crown all this he settled down to a meal of pottage and mutton stew washed down with ale. For the first time in several days he began to feel his old self and felt his confidence return.

∽ Chapter Three ∽

Thomas came awake and for a moment was at a loss to remember where he was, the memories of yesterday flooded back into his mind. He stretched luxuriously amongst the sheepskins he had wrapped himself in on the floor of the great hall of Shrewsbury castle. His burnt hand throbbed, but the salve the countess had provided was doing some good for he could flex the fingers and there was no sign of pus or poisin. He rose from his bed and made his way to the privy hole in the wall where he relieved himself then back to the great hall where morning activity was well under way. Finding some fresh baked bread and new brewed ale on the great refectory table Thomas made his breakfast He wandered out into the courtyard. It was a beautiful crisp January morning. Steam was rising from some horses thethered against the wall and the familiar face of the castle sergeant grinned at him.

"Back with us then babba, you was lucky she stood up for you, there's not many would have done " "Aye, and God's praise, I'm greatful.Tell me, what became of my bow stave and cloak.?" "Oh they got taken to the armory, you'm best be asking Hugo, he's the boy for all things armory" "Where's that then?" "Down through the undercroft and first door you comes too" Thomas thanked him and went to find his precious bow.

In the armory Hugo was tallying the number of fletched arrows available to the Earl's battles and after a wait of some time came over to see what Thomas wanted. Explaining the circumstances of his loss he was shown where new staves and odd armour was kept.Immeaditely he saw "sweet slayer " propped up on its own against the wall. "That's the one "he said

"Oh, that 'un, she's a beauty, English yew if I'm not mistook, I was thinking of keeping that one for myself. " "Over my dead body, that's yew from a five hundred year old tree in Lingen churchyard I cut and made myself. Its like a part of me, I'd rather lose a leg than lose that."

"That's a groat to get that back and this was with it"He scuffed his foot around Thomas' cloak which lay in a heap beside the wall."What of my rondel and sallet?"

"No idea cully, but I can let you have a nice dagger and helmet for a few pence, here they be." Hugo pointed to a long table covered with weapons of all sorts and leather hats and steel helmets.Thomas went over and inspected what was on offer.He pulled out a 15 inch long rondel dagger with a nicely worked bone handle. The dagger was encased in a strong leather scabbard. He also choose a leather sallet to replace the one he had lost. "I shall need some bow strings and some arrows if you please Hugo" "What the fuck do ye take me for, some sort of shopkeeper"Shouted Hugo.

"You takes what I gives you and be well pleased and you fucking pays me."

"A groat you said and a groat I'll give"He tossed the small silver coin onto the table.Hugo scooped it up in a ham like fist. "Taint enough cully." "Prehaps this will be then" Thomas leapt forward and pinned Hugo to the wall holding his new dagger dangerously close to the armorourer's eye. "You bring me four best bow srtrings and two dozen arrows, this dagger and this sallet and the rest of my stuff, and you keeps the sight in your left eye, oh and you keeps

the groat.Good exchange no robbery?" Tomas chuckled as Hugo's bravado deflated like a pigs bladder. Five minutes later equipped anew with all he wanted a happy Thomas strolled out of the armoury and set off in the direction of the tithe barn to speak with his earstwhile companions.

He took the path that led down to the river Severn that passed through Shrewsbury in a great meandering curve. The river was in full flood after all the heavy rain and snow melt that had come off the Shopshire hills in the last month or so. Pieces of debris and logs of wood flowed past his eye. He saw a barrel float past, and what looked like the body of a calf. Then in the distance something moved on the surface of the water flowing towards him and right in the middle of the river a small wood pallet bobbed past, on top of the pallet stood a bedraggled six month old puppy. From where Thomas stood he saw that the dog was a mongrel mix of sheepdog, wolf and hunting dog.The dog was looking piteously toward Thomas and its wet bedraggled tail thumped once agaist its scrawny back legs.

"Jump you little bugger>Swim over to me "He exorted the puppy, but the dog was too mesmerised by the rushing water to help itself. Running alongside the river Thomas noticed that the current swept close to his bank where the next curve started. Unslinging his bow stave he pushed it out into the path of the puppy. with a great yawning bite the dog clamped his theeth around the horn nook on the end of "sweet slayer", and with one long heave Thomas delivered the soaking creature to the river bank.

"Well that's a horrid place you found yourself then,aint it. "He towelled the puppy dry on the edge of his cloak and was rewarded with ecstatic licks to the face.Tail thumping and rear end moving back and forth the puppy gave a few whines and then lay down exhausted on the bank of the river.

"That's what I'll call 'ee then. Orrid, cos that was ahorrid place for you to be. He ruffled the dog's head and sat beside it to regain his breath.

After a few moments the dog had started to dry out in the sun and it rose to its feet and gave a hearty shake and looked up at Thomas as much as to say. Now come on my saviour its time to go. Thomas took one of his new bow srtings and fashioned atemporary coller and lead for Orrid, and man and dog set off in the direction of the tithe barn.

Ahead of them now stood the ancient barn the yard in front littered with the remains of cooking fires and lines of clothing drying in the breeze. Several women were preparing food for their men folk and a number of small children were running back and forth.An ox cart with the side let down was being used as an impromptu ale house having several barrels of ale side on with their spigots readily available to the red faced inn keeper dispensing the ale to a constant stream of liveried soldiers.The smell of wood fires, ale, human excrement and animal dung permeated the air.

Ahuge shout came from near the ale bar."ThomasWhere be ye at my boy,We'm nearly given you up for dead."It was

Diccon, closely followed by John the two close friends that Thomas had come to see. He quickly told them what had befallen him since their meeting in the tavern and a schocked look of concrn came over their faces.

"We'm thought you'd found yourself a woman and you'd be back in you'r own time. Never thought it ud be like this though.

"I have to see the Earl of March at midday, maybe for a special job of some sort and I reckons I can get you two in on it. What say you. Up for a bit of adventure away from the army, who knows might be a bit of plunder and silver found if it's a right 'un. "

Diccon's eyes lit up "Oh ar, God's truth I could do with a bit of extra silver, 'tis so pricey living in this town." "That's cos you drinks to much you dog. So I'm to ask for you then?

The two of his friends nodded and wishing them well he turned and made his way back towards the castle and his meeting with the Earl of March. As he walked up towards the castle the midday bell for mass tolled out from the church. At least he was on time. Entering the castle courtyard he saw the sergeant ahead of him and stating his business he was shown into a guard room in the lower keep. After some time a castle steward dressed in the livery of the Earl came in and escorted him back to the solar deep in the heart of the castle. Knocking on the heavy studded oak door they were admitted to the large sunlight room furnished simply with a table some upholstered chairs and with the walls covered in colourful tapestries depicting scenes from bible stories. Sitting at the table with a parchment map unfurled before him was the Earl, beside him stood several middle aged advisors, as Thomas was shown in the buzz of their voices fell away. Thomas bowed.

"Ah, Thomas of Lingen "The Earl said.

"Sir" acknowledged Thomas.

"Tell me Thomas, can you read and write?""

"Aye Sir I can. My father was rector of lingen Church and he taught me " "A useful skill and makes my choice of you for this task much easier. Come over to the table " Thomas moved forward and stood beside the Earl looking down on to the map.He saw it was of the Marches of England and Wales with some small detail of roads andtowns imposed upon it.

"Our enemies The Earl of Pembroke and that devil Jasper Tudor have got 5000 men,Welsh beserkers and foreign mercenaries from Italy and the Low countries and they are heading this way."His hand stabbed down onto the map. "The last intellegence we had was that they were north of Carmarthen and would be here near Shrewsbury within the next sennight.I need thorough new information accurate numbers and details of what makes up his army. Something I can rely on and I believe you are the man to get it for me." Thomas looked schocked. This was a major task he was being given. First he had to find the Welsh army then infiltrate it and then deliver the intellegance back to the Earl. "I shall do my best My lord"

"Good man, now is there anything you require for this task." "Yes Sir, I would like my two companions Diccon of Knighton and Jon Stapleton to come with me. Also horses and pack animals and any weapons we think we'll need." "Granted, when can you leave ?" "At first light tomorrow My Lord" "Good, may God go with you and I shall expect some news 'ere long."The Earl waved his hand in dismissal and Thomas bowed himself out of the solar.

Back in the courtyard he untied Orrid from the ring bolt and they set off back to the tithe barn.

Next morning just as dawn was breaking, Thomas,Diccon and Jon with Orrid running free beside them,mounted on strong chestnut horses and with two sturdy pack animals to carry their equipment left the town of Shrewsbury by the main town gate heading south.

Already there was a group of villains and serfs gathered on the outside of the town gates waiting for entry, some carrying baskets of vegetables others with goods to sell on the daily market. Even one or two unfortunates who had missed the curfew bell the night before and had had to sleep up against the town wall. Mostly these folks were serfs from the surrounding countryside taking advantage of the opportunities a vibrant market could bring.

"We need to head south down the turnpike till Hereford,then west into Wales, no doubt we 'll hear of Pembrokes army before long. 5000 welshmen make a big enough stink. "Thomas laughed.

"And what then Tom, whats to do when we do find em."Diccon said with trepidatiopn.

"Oh I'll think of summat" Thomas airily waved his hand "Don't I always" "Aye, so you do "Broke in Jon," and its usually some scrape we have to help you out of." "Ah, but now I've got Orrid, he's worth a couple of you idle tossers" Laughing he touched his heels to the side of his horse and trotted ahead.

Jon looked after him and shook his head ruefully."He don't know he's born that 'un."

Three or four miles out of Shrewsbury where the old roman road passes through the village of Dorrington Thomas called a halt and the three of them went into to the village tavern for some much needed breakfast.Through the smokey atmospherethey were able to see they weren't the only customers. Sitting at a rough table were a group of travellers enjoying bread and ale and a bowl of hot pottage. Amonst them was a Scisterian monk in a light coloured wool robe, another priest and two burly looking serfs who had a stout wood box bound with steel straps on the floor at their feet.

"Good morrow, fathers, may we join you at table ?" asked Thomas politely.

The priest looked up. Thomas could see that his face was badly disfigured is if from a sword slash and that he had a black silk patch over one eye.His right arm hung uselessly beside his body and he had to spoon up his pottage with his left.hand.

"We are on the lord's business and God be praised we are leaving now, so my son, the table is all yours. " So saying he gestured to the two villains to pick up the wooden box and the small party left the inn.

"Not the friendliest of priests that's for sure" said Diccon.

"And not the prettiest neither" guaffawed Jon.

They sat down and called for ale bread and pottage. It was brought over by a pretty serving wench in a low cut blouse who gave Diccon a suggestive look as she placed the food on the table. "Quick one is it then my lovely" he said slapping her rump as she passed.

"Twopence" came the reply.

Diccon looked schocked. "Two pennies!, why I could have half of the whores in Shrewsbury for tuppence...at once.

"Best go back to Shrewsbury then my Babba."Shetossed her head defiantly and disappeared in the direction of the kitchen. "Oh well, better luck next time eh Dick. Now I need to talk about what is the best direction to take to find these Welshmen. We need to strike west into Wales, but as you know the going ain't too pretty round Radnor way, lots of forests and one or two heavy robbers and outlaws to contend with. On the other hand if we stays on this road all the way to Hereford we may well miss sight of the whole army." "Well what about going south to Ludlow and then up to Knighton and on into the wastelands beyond." "What Wastelands beyond? That's God's own country that is up round Knighton, that's my homeland you'm maligning"said Diccon.

"Sorry, I forgot you're from those parts and anyway 'tis wastelands further on Llandovery way, why I've heard they've got three legs each up there and they only drink rain cos that's all the wet they have.And they got Dragons"

"Ah, they got Dragons all right, and anyway I ain't never been as far west as Llandovery,and I must say I don't relish the idea."Diccon took a huge swig from his tankard.

"Well, that's the direction the army'll be coming from and I think it best if we try for it" "Well, you're in charge this time, so we'll come with ye"

Thomas left a few copper coins on the table to pay for their breakfast and the three of them mounted up and trotted off in the direction of the Long Mynd.

The day was a beautiful early January day with the sparkle of unfrozen frost across the fields and shrub land that they were passing through.On either side of the old roman road down which they travelled huge ruts were evident where previous carts and wagons had passed one another, so much so that for twenty yards on either side of the cobbled surface the edges were churned up and macerated with deep ruts.

"Look at this"" said Diccon," you 'd best not let your mount get in amongst that, for sure she'd break a leg"

"Aye, keep well off those sides boys" almost as soon as he'd said this up ahead they could see a huge barrel wagon drawn by a team of eight oxen, the teamster flicking his whip and calling out encouagement to his oxen in the time honoured hypnotic way of such folk. One either side of the wagon two or three burly men were walking, occasionally giving a shoulder heave to the wagon to help it over a sticky patch on the road.

"Make way cullly" shouted Thomas"We'm coming past" The ox cart came to a halt amidst clouds of steam from the animals'nostrils.Thomas and his horses moved slowly round to the side onto the edge of the churned up road and past the massive wagon.

"Where are you going then "He shouted in a friendly manner to the teamster.

"Huh"came the gruff reply"Nowheres fast if'n we have to keep stopping."But as you ask maister we'm on our way to Ludlow, be there day after tomorrow. Bring a good bit of wine and ale to those thirsty buggers in the town."

"Good luck then, have you heard anything of some welshmen on the rampage up from Carmarthen," "No way, we've been on the road from Chester this last sennight, aint seen hide nor hair of nuthin' cept the arse end of this 'un. " so saying the teamster flicked his whip over the leading oxen and the huge rig lumbered into motion again.

Thomas and his friends trotted on leaving the barrel cart in the distance. Talking and laughing amongst themselves. By midday they had covered another five miles and were coming into the deep defile that that was made by the Long Mynd as it's steep hillside swept down to the road. In places the bottom of the valley was liitle more than ten yards wide and the shadows cast by the hillside never allowed the frost to clear away. So steep was the Long Mynd at this point that Thomas looking up could see red kites wheeling high above him as they looked for prey on the sunnier uplands of the Mynd.

"This be a dark and damp old hole " said Jon"Lets get out of here, " and he dug heels into his mount. Trotting on, they rounded a sharp corner, ahead of them in the road they could see the bodies of two or three men lying like sacks upon the ground.

"Shit and God's blood, what's this" Thomas dismounted and pulling his bow off his back quickly nocked a bowstring on to it and an arrow. Running forward he crouched low beside an outcrop of rock that half obscured the trackway. He could see that the bodies were those of the priest and his two retainers that they had met in the tavern earlier that day, but of the Cistercian monk and the heavy iron box there was no sign. Diccon and Jon came running over and looked down at the bodies. Jon knelt down beside the priest. "Thomas," he cried "He breathes" They turned towards the priest who gave a weak groan. They could see that the front of his cassock was stained with his blood, when Thomas gently moved the priest's hand from his stomach they could see that the poor man had been eviscerated and it was a wonder he had lasted as long as he had.

"Not much we can do for him I'n afraid"said Thomas"Just make his last moments comfortable.'

Suddenly the priest gave a great groan and then grasping Thomas' wrist he moaned "Father Ignatus, a traitor, in league with who did this"he gasped and took a shallow breath".In God's sweet name, you must get the box back, take it to the Prior at Llananthony, you'll be rewarded" so saying he gave a gasping moan as he drew in his last breath and with a death rattle he expired..

Thomas rocked back on his heels and looked at the others. Orrid bounded over and sniffed at the corpse, then giving a whine he cast about as if he could pick up the scent of the murderers than he made off up a track leading upwards towards the top of the Mynd.

"Follow the dog" cried Thomas and mounting they followed Orrid upwards and upwards through dense shrubland which pressed in on either side to make the path all but invisible.After climbing for some minutes the shrubland started to give way to bare outcrops of rock interspersed with short cropped grass. And the track on which they stood came out at the top of the Mynd. The dog was standing alertly looking across a large expanse of upland moorland,interspersed here and there with dense outcrops of low stunted oak trees almost as if the creator had thrown them down to make something more interesting than bare uplands.No habitation or human kind could be seen anywhere. The trail had gone cold.

Thomas looked down at the dog. "Good boy, Orrid, but now we want to know where they went next"He dug his heels into the side of his horse and trotted forward to an outcrop of rock a hundred yards away.Dismounting he climbed the mound and cast his eye across the countryside. In the distance and almost invisible in its surroundings, nestling with its back towards a larger outcrop of rock lay an isolated turf roofed farmhouse and two or three mean turf buildings around a yard. A thin spiral of woodsmoke drifted up into the air, it was that that had caught Thomas' eye..

He called the other two over. " I think,boys the answer may lie in yonder farm we need to get closer, but not be seen, if it is their den they will have a guard.Diccon, you skirt round to the left, Jon you go right and I'll crawl up from the front.Have a good look and we come back here and talk about what were going to do. I'll take Orrid."He grabbed the dog and slipped a lead on him then set off across the moorland towards the farm.The short grass was easy going but Thomas felt exposed to any one who might be keeping a lookout and so he moved carefully from one outcrop of stones or shrubs to another. Within ten minutes he had got as close as it was possible to be without going right into the yard. He could see that there were six to eight horses tethered and hobbled in the yard. Two of them looked similar to the packhorses the priests had had in their party. There didn't seem to be a sentry or anyone keeping watch, these outlaws were so complacent in their isolated stronghold that they didn't think it worthwhile.

The door to the turfed hovel opened and a gust of smoke eddied out. Father Ignatus came out into the yard and relieved himself against the stone wall of one of the buildings. A roar of male laughter erupted from the house.

"Shut the fucking door, you barstard priest, do you want me to freeze my bollocks off?"

"I don't care my son" said The Cistercian as he went back indoors pulling the crude wooden door shut behind him.

Proof enough thought Tomas as he gently eased himself and the dog back to where the others were waiting for him.

"Well, I saw the monk and I saw some horses and this is where they are, no doubt of it" "Aye, both Jon and myself seen the priest. But we don't know how many is in there. " "With six horses outside could be as many as a dozen" "Or as few as six. Plus the priest." Thomas looked up at the sky." Dark soon" he said." We could attack them now and take a chance there's only a few in there, or we can wait till morning and have them in the dawn whilst they are still half asleep and the light's better.What say you Diccon, Jon ?" He looked questioningly at his friends.

"Wait till morning, they are not expecting anything, they think they got away with it and the surprise will be greater" "I agree, and I have a plan that will make sure they all come out of the farm"Thomas grinned. The three friends moved further back into the more dense undergrowth right on the edge of the Mynd and settled down for the night. They had sheepskin coats and spare fleeces with which they wrapped themselves. Thomas organised them into three four hour watch shifts and whilst one watched the other two slept.When Thomas was shaken awake by Diccon for his shift he had had a good few hours sleep and he felt rested and able to start preparing his plan of attack.Casting his eye around their camp he found some dead long grasses and tinder like leaves which he gathered together.Going to one of the pack horses he extracted the linen bag that held the arrow fletching equipment, spilling it out on the turf he pulled out the goose greese pot and started to smear the grasses and leaves with the grease until he had a conglomerate mess of stuff which he stuck around the end of a bodkin point on two or three arrows. Tearing a piece of linen from a shirt he tightly wound the strip around the arrow shaft, making sure as he did so that the addition to the arrow was not too unbalanced and that it could still fly true. Laying the fire arrows beside him, he took up his tinder box and struck a spark.All seemed in orderHe glanced up at the sky Still some time till dawn. The other two were fast asleep on the ground and Orrid was curled up beside Diccon sharing his sheepskin.Thomas checked the horses one gave a whinney as he approached

He soothed the animal and pulled out some provisions for their breakfast from one of the saddlebags.

A gentle lightening of the sky in the east heralded the dawning day and he shook his companions awake. He explained his plan with the fire arrows and while they ate their breakfast he told them what he wanted.

"same like last evening"He said "Diccon, you go left, Jon you go right and the dog and I go front on.I'll light an arrow and shoot it into the roof.and another and one into the barn, once its burning they'll come out of there like rats in a barrel, and then you shoots em down. Got it ?"The other two grinned and nodded.By now the light of day was slowly enabling them to see and they set off for the farm.About two hundred yards out they split up and Diccon crouching low made his way left towards the farm whilst Jon did the same to the right. Thomas used the same technique as he had the evening before to approach the farmhouse. All was quiet. The horses were still in the yard but from the hovel not a sound came. No smoke issued from the chimney, and Thomas knew that an evening of heavy drinking had helped the inhabitants to get a good nights sleep.

Crouching down he pulled his three fire arrows from his quiver and placed them on the ground beside him. He checked that they were still intact and taking his tinderbox he struck a spark onto the charred linen within and blew on it until a tiny flame leapt up. Touching each fire arrow with the burning linen he ignited them. The goose greese around the shafts started to burn and notching each arrow in turn he let fly towards the turf roof of the farm. With a satisfiying thunk the first arrow buried itself deep into the thatch of the hovel, and the next someway along theroof. The third arrow he directed at the barn. By now a thin spiral of grey smoke was starting to rise up from the turf roof in two places and then from the barn. Within minutes the roofs were ablaze. Suddenly the door to the farmhouse shot open and a figure dressed only in grey hose came running out. "FIRE,fire" he screamed. They were his last words as a bodkin tipped arrow shot by Jon took him in the throat. More men some naked but most half dressed came running out of the farm house. Thomas stood and let fly his aim more intuitive than aimed and three men fell pierced through the body by his arrows. Diccon and Jon were wreaking as much hovoc with their bows until a cry could be heard from within.

"We yield for God's sweet mercy we yield"

"Bring out the box and throw your weapons down"Thomas shouted.From within there was the sound of shouting and then some swords and a bow staff or two were thrown out and three men emerged. One was Father Ignatus still in his cistercian's robe. The other two were villainous looking men with scars on their faces and arms. They were carrying the box between them

"Drop the box and lie down on your bellies" shouted Thomas. The two men did as they were told. The monk was less willing to abase himself.

"And you, you traitorious scum" Thomas lunged forward with his bow and tripped the monk who crashed to the ground the air coming out of him like a split bladder.

"Make sure these three don't move Jon while I see what is in the box."

"No my son, you cannot open God's holy trunk. It is blasphemy.A sin against God and you will burn in Hell fire for all erernity."

"I think not priest, give me the key now before I break it open" "You would not dare!" "You think not?" so saying

Thomas looked around until his eye alighted on a fist size rock lying on the ground. He hefted it in his hand and brought it crashing down on to the metal casket.The monk gave a cry of horror, "No, no. Here it is "from a pocket in his habit he pulled an ornate iron key and reluctantly handed it over to Thomas. It was the work of a moment to insert it and open the padlock. He lifted the lid and peered in.

The interior of the casket was lined entirely in a deep plush red velvet and three jewelled boxes lay on a fitted tray within it. Thomas lifted the tray out and placed it on the grass beside him. In the space under the tray neatly stacked were piles of gold coins. Thomas gasped"so this is what the lives of three men are worth is it Priest?"

The monk shook his head "No those are holy relics of The mother Church, only priests and those ordained of God may touch them should anyone else do so they shall be cut off from God's grace and cast into outer darkness"

Thomas laughed cynically. "But you killed for them, is that permitted I vow you are on your way to outer darkness already even if by my hand."

"You cannot kill a priest.That is an unforgivable sin and you would not dare!" The monk glared up at Thomas defiantly.

"I can do what so ever I like " Thomas spat angrily. He lifted the lid of the first jewelled box.Inside lay two tiny yellow finger bones a pieceof parchment with illuminated writing on it proclaimed. "The finger bonesof St. Thomas called "Doubting".Thomas crossed himself reverently. He open the second box, within was a piece of withered brown wood about two inches long. The parchment proclaimed "a piece of the true cross given in Jeruselem by Joseph of Arimitheia"

By now Thomas was sweating, he knew that what he was doing was something best left to priests and the ordained, but he saw no good reason not to find out for himself.The third and final box was slightly larger and more ornate than the others and when he opened the lid what was within made him recoil in horror and awe. Nestling in the formed velvet interior of the jewelled case was a perfectly preserved female human ear, even down to some downy hairs within the opening. He grabbed theparchment within and read from it. "The ear of Mary Magdelain obtained from the Sultain Ben Ali at the Siege of Acre". Making the sign of the cross once more Thomas shut the box and replaced it and the lid back into the interior of the casket. He shut the padlock and attached the key to his hose. He felt very shaken by what he had seen, and the thought that he might have commited a serious sin kept coming into his mind. The monk sneered up at him

"You are doomed now my son, you and you friends, there is no chance you can ever be forgiven for such sacrilage!"

"Quiet priest"Shouted Thomas."Diccon,Jon, strip these men of their clothes and bind them tightly. Each one place in a separate building and make sure they cannot get free. I have had enough of killing for one day. We shall leave them to God's mercy. A night with no clothes in this cold will be enough. " He started to strip the monk of his habit. The man was surprisingly strong and writhed and fought but a sharp rap with a dagger handle to the head subdued him with time enough for Thomas to strip him of his clothes and leave him shivering in a thin linen shift. Tying the monk by hand and feet they pulled him into the first barn and bound him in a sitting position against a wooden manger.

They treated the two others in similar fashion but each of these was tied,one within th burnt out farmhouse, the other within the smaller cowshed.

"No food no water " called Thomas. He mounted his horse and taking up the leading reins of three packhorses, his companions doing the same, the long line of horses and riders set off in a westerly direction.

Chapter Four

By the time the watery sun had started to set and the bitter cold of another sub zero night was setting in the trio were riding down thesteep single cobbled street of Bishop's Castle,their srtring of ponies behind them and Orrid sniffing the road edge beside them.

"We'll find a tavern get food and a bed for the night,and in the morning try to sell these horses. I know there's a big sheep and livestock market here, I brought some ewes up from Lingen Years ago" "Aye,you're right my friend,I done the same thing myself. The Ring 'O Bells is the best drinking hole round these parts" They walked their horses down the hill until the gradient finally eased and there before them was the welcoming inn sign they were looking for. Stabling the horses in the yard at the rear they walked into the warm fug of the alehouse. A large smokey room with an enourmous fireplace liberally filled with huge burning logs which gave off a warmth and smell which instantly made them all feel at home.

A stout greasy looking man in a worn and stained leather apron came over to them. "What can I get you maisters " he rubbed his hands together.

"Ale, food and a room for the night"

"Yes,my fine sirs,rabbit pie or venison salamagundy is what we offers tonight.a penny a plate and as much ale as you can drink. A fine spacious oak bed to settle three like you, two pence the night, and you clears your own night soil. " "Done " said Thomas the other two grinning over his shoulder. They settled down at a well scrubbed refectory tablewhile a comely wench brought steaming wooden platters of food for them. They all opted for the rabbit pie being country boys at heart and the smell of the hot food had the saliva almost dribbling from their mouths.After ten minutes of serious eating Jon wiped the back of his hand across his mouth and sighed."Oh, God's mercy but that was well wanted, now I can start the serious drinking of the night"

"No, no getting drunk, we 've got a fair distance to go tomorrow to get south of here and we've got those horses to sell tomorrow. A clear head if you please. " Jon's face fell but he nodded in acceptance of Thomas' order. "Whatever you say Thomas, you are in charge " Thomas called the tavern keeper over. " Have you heard any talk or rumours of an army of Welshmen hereabouts landlord?"

"Nay Sir, no such talk has come my way. Quiet as the grave the town has been this last sennight. Only the market to liven things a little. Tis on again in the morning. I see you have a string of horses out back, are they for sale."

"Why, yes, we would like to sell those on, they come from good farms up on the Mynd." "You shouldn't have much difficulty getting rid of them, there's a geat demand for strong ponies round here." The land lord rubbed his hands together obsequesiously and turned to poke at the roaring fire. The three friends finished their food and after another pot of ale made their way to their room. Before they left they checked the horses and carried in the heavy bound casket with the relics.

Setting it in full sight on the floor Thomas called the dog. "Orrid you guard that boy"he said sternly. The dog gave a single beat of his tail to the floor an settled down next to the box.

The bed was big and comfortable for the three of them, but the straw filled paliasse that doubled up as a mattress was infested with fleas and bedbugs making them scratch and itch throughout the night..Diccon seemed oblivious and a heavy snore came from his mouth as he slept the sleep of the righteous.Jon and Thomas on the other hand had great difficulty in falling asleep but finally fatigue overcame them both and they too succumbed to the little death of sleep.

By dawn next day all three were awake and making their way downstairs to the ale house they breakfasted on bread and ale and then carried the box out to the yard where they strapped it to the back of one of the pack horses.Making their way out to the market place they were soon engulfed in the smells and sounds of the town.Even though it was but an hour from full darkness the town was humming. Peasants and their women were carrying baskets of goods to their pitches. Gaudy stalls selling sweetmeats and sugared treats were already doing a brisk trade and further along the market in the section reserved for livestock sheep were penned and cattle steamed and lowed. A hundred geese all with their feet tarred to keep them from wearing out on the long journey to market were milling about and squawking pitifully as their young goose herd penned them up safely for sale. A smell of animal dung and human excrement hung over the livestock section and already prosperous peasant farmers and reeves acting on behalf of their lords were swaggering round the market examining beasts and making disparaging remarks about the animals on sale.One or two poorly dressed villains were trying to strike barter bargains whilst in the area reserved for horse trading the more prosperous farmers were striking bargains involving silver and gold coins.

Thomas led his string of horses over to this part of the market and tethered them.As soon as they arrived three or four farmers and a pair of well dressed men descended on the three. "What beasts be these cully ?" said one of the farmers"They aint from around these parts by God's blood,they be spavined.How much?"

Thomas laughed " You beef witted bladder, that you can't tell a top riding horse from a hole in the ground. These are best riding horses and worth the top coin of the realm. "

One of thebetter dressed gentlemen broke into the conversation.

"How much are these beasts, just the riding horses, I'm not interested in the pack animals"

Thomas thought for a moment, "This quality, I reckon Ten pounds each."

The man laughed outright." Ten pounds, why they look more like Four pound each beasts to me"He shook his head and stepped away. "Why you saucy rump fed varlet" shouted Diccon clenching his fists and starting forward. Thomas put out his hand and pulled him back. "'Tis all part of the trade Diccon, never you fear"

The man stepped forward again "I shall give you six a piece and another crown for each one delivered to Hay on Wye where my master resides. I am the Reeve of my Lord of Pembroke and we have great need of horses at the moment"

Thomas gasped, he knew that the Earl of Pembroke was one of the sworn enemies of the Earl of March and was one of the leaders of the welsh army he was trying to locate. Maybe this would be his way to infiltrate that army and find out its disposition and numbers so he could report back to his master.

"Eight pounds each delivered "he replied to the reeve.

"Tis too much, seven pounds each, half now and half upon delivery. "

Thomas looked at his companions. They each nodded in turn. Thomas grinned and spat on his hand.

"Aye my lord you have a deal. Six riding horses at seven pounds each. Forty two pounds in total. Half now and half upon delivery to Hay. Where abouts in Hay?"

"Oh, you find them well enough, camped up on Hay Bluff".

"How will I get the rest of my money?

"I shall write you a note to give to my master's steward and he will reimburse you."

So saying he counted out twenty one gold coins into Thomas' hand and proceeded to scrawl a letter upon a piece of parchment his servant held for him on a portable desk he was carrying.

"I doubt you can read"He sneered",but this says to pay the bearer twenty one gold pounds upon the delivery of the horses."

Thomas said nothing but cast his eye over the letter and saw it was as the reeve had said.

"Thank you, my lord, we shall leave as soon as ever." He knuckled his head.

"One moment" said the Reeve, "how do I know you will deliver as said and that I'll not be the loser of twenty one pounds."

"Easy done my lord. Brand the horses with your mark and send your servant with us.He will see us to Hay".

The Reeve nodded.It was the matter of moments to heat an iron and brand each horse with the mark of the Earl of Pembroke.The Reeve called his servant over.

"Cedric,go with these men to Hay Bluff and deliver these horses to my lord "

"I shall my lord" said Cedric and gathering his few belongings he mounted one of the horses.

The party, now with four mounted riders and the same number of horses set off from the market in a southerly direction.

After a days uneventful travel the party came in sight of Knighton, Diccon's home town and although his mother and father had long passed on to a better place, he was well known in the town and before long an offer of a place to stay had been warmly accepted. The Reeve's servant was none to pleased to have to stay in the stable yard whilst the others repaired to the nearest ale house, but Orrid was set to guard the strong box and when the trio returned filled with good Marcher ale they found the servant and the dog asleep together the one with his head upon the box the other with his head upon the leg of the servant.

"What a saucy puttock he be " laughed Diccon."Milk livered varlet, that dog do love 'ee methinks."

"No harm in at any way " said Thomas."We're rid of him as soon as we reach Hay"

"What about the box and the Priory, Llananthony is a good few miles over the hill from Hay"

"Aye, that had crossed my mind, and I reckon you and Jon could take it down to the Prior, get the reward, and I see you back in Hay in two or three days. "What do you think?" "A good thought my coxcomb, and I promise not to drink the reward on the way back"Diccon laughed."

"By Christ's holy bollocks you better not or I'll hold back your share of the horse money, and that's more than you've seen in a little lamb's year. "Diccon looked slightly crestfallen but his sunny nature soon reassertred itself and the trio bedded down in the barn behind the farmhouse. By morning the weather had changed from the bitter cold of previous days to a misty drizzle that soaked through their sheepskin coats and caused the horses to hang their heads in equine misery

"On our way boys, mayhap this shite weather will dry up later.".Thomas mounted up and a rather dejected party set off into the rolling Radnorshire hills.

The prediction of better weather was never fulfilled but only got worse so by the time they passed the high country by Brilley above Hay on Wye they were soaked through to the skin.

As the party slowly made its way down the steep hillside towards the river meadows that run beside the Wye into Hay one of the pack animal stumbled on a muddy slide on the track. With a terrific crack the animal fell over onto its side and continued to slide down the hill side only coming to a halt when it fell up against a tree growing beside the trackway. Whinnying and snorting it was obviously in some distress. Thomas jumped from his horse as did the others and ran over to the beast. It was obvious that the front offside fetlock was broken for a white gleam of bone was visible through the mud and blood of its fetlock.

Thomas pulled his dagger from its scabbard and deftly plunged it up to the hilt into the eyesocket of the injured horse. The beast gave a great spasm and was still.

"Best way,my Babba" said Diccon. "best get all this stuff unloaded." There was a trail of bow staves, arrows and other weaponry scattered half way down the hill where the contents of the horse pack had come adrift.

They were picking their belongings together when Orrid gave a warning bark and looked hard over into the wet impenetrable woodland that edged the steep track.An inhuman cackle almost as eyrie as a night time foxes cry came drifting over towards them.

"Bollicking Christ and Jesus' bladder, what the fuck was that ?"said Diccon.

Again the laughing cackle came out of the woods. The four men had drawn their daggers and the dog had its hackles up.Out of the mist stepped an ethereal figure. Thin and tall above six feet though her feet were shod in wooden pattens dressed in green with green ivy leaves and feathery conifer twigs woven into her hair. A strikingly beautiful woman of middle age holding an armful of greenery.

"My handsome boys be not afeared, I am Daphne of the woods and my house is near.There is pottage and ale and a fire to warm ye if you would follow" so saying she turned and moved off uphill in the direction they had come from. The friends and their string of horses followed until they came to a turf roofed hovel set against the hill side. A welcoming spiral of smoke wafted upward from the sigle chimney at the end of the house.

"Tie your animals beneath this shelter and come into my house where the rain can no longer harm ye "Daphne disappeared into the interior and after seeing to the horses the men and the dog filed into the house.It was spacious with flagstones on the floor and an inlenook fire place with a large pottage pot hanging from a tripod.In the corner another striking middle aged woman more conventionally dressed with blond hair and a pleasant open face was kneading bread dough. "This be Jo of Brilley my very good friend and neighbour.Sit ye down one and all and we'll have some soup"

The four men sat around a large refectory table that took up most of the kitchen and whilst their clothes steamed in the heat Daphne and Jo set bowls of the most delicious pottage in front of them.trenchers of homemade bread beside the bowls completed the meal.

"Why mistress, you have saved our lives We have been on the road since dawn and it ain't a nice dayto travel as you can see" Thomas shook his head."What brings a woman such as yourself to these parts?" "Oh 'tis a long story, for many years I travelled in the far parts of Araby and India learning the healing ways of herbs and spices, then found myself in Hay with no hope and no money, and my good friend Jo here,"She stopped and smiled at the other woman", brought me home to her house in Brilley.Later I was able to get this house and now we sell eggs and herbal medicines on Hay market")Once more she smiled at Jo who returned the grin.

"Why it is a miracle " said Jon"and the best pottage I've tasted in many a long day."

Daphne looked at the travellers."And what brings you folks to these parts?" "We have to deliver some horses to the steward of the Earl of Pembroke"

Daphne shook her head."Those Welsh beserkers and foreign soldiers camped up by Hay Bluff ? They'm nothing but trouble in Hay, always getting drunk and singing and there's more than enough of them." "How many do you think?" "Thousands, There's a few hundred Irish and Brittany men in amongst, and some crossbow men from Italy. I've seen them thronging into the ale houses on Market day. They've been camped up there for a sennight at least and it looks like they could be here for longer."

Thomas looked at Daphne. "Can I speak a few words to you in private mistress" Daphne nodded and led him through the back of the kitchen into a small snug that lead out into the garden. "Well what have you to say Thomas that can't be spoken in front of your friends" "In front of Cedric only, for he is a servant who owes aliegance to my foes." In a few words Thomas reviled the true nature of his mission and watched Daphne's face closely to see what her reaction might be to being dragged into a potentially dangerous situation. He needn't have worried for she smiled and said "Tis good that at last someone will fight these red rose bullies,they are plunderers and rapists and they lay waste to all they touch. Whatever I may do to help I am only too happy to do."

Thomas looked her in the eye"There is one thing you can do for me, give me a tonsure" "A what?" "Tonsure my hair, for I want to pass as a monk while I try to find out about what numbers make up the army."

Daphne laughed out loud. "For sure father, sit you down and I shall bring my razor."

With a pair of sheep shears and a steel razor honed to a niceness on a leather strop she proceeded to remove the hair from the back of his skull until after some minutes his bald pate shone through in the correct ecclesiastical manner.

"There you are father," she joked"You'd best wear your leather sallet or Cedric is bound to notice".

He put the leather cap on his head and went back into the main room where the others were just finishing their meal.

"Cedric, go and attend to your masters horses. "Ceric knuckled his forelock and went out into the yard. Thomas looked at Jon and Diccon."On the morrow when the women go to market, we'll go with them. You two take the box up to the Priory and make your way back here once you've safely delivered it. Keep out of the way of the army. I don't want you ending up fighting for the likes of Jasper Tudor,and be careful.I myself am going up to the army to count the numbers and glean what I can to help my lord Edward."

"How"said Jon, "Like you are, they'll know you for an archer as soon as look at you"

Thomas smiled." Nay like this,"He pulled off his leather cap to reveal his new tonsure. Diccon gasped"Oh as a priest, I get it now with that robe from the monk and your little baldy patch you'd pass as a holy man any day" "Well that's what I hope. And I shall meet you back here in two or three days."He put his leather cap on again, as Cedric came back into the room.

Chapter Five

B y dawn the next day the weather had moderated and although the boughs of the trees were heavy with the rain of the previous day it was at least dry. The party set out from Daphne's house. The two women leading a pack horse with their market goods in panniers upon its back. Thomas leading the string of riding horses for the army and the other two leading the pack animal with the strong box on its back. Cedric brought up the rear and the dog Orrid bounded back and forth occasionally giving a yip of pleasure. Down past the site of the disaster with the fallen horse and onto the level trackway that ran beside the river. They crossed the little wooden toll bridge and headed on towards the town. As they got closer they began to see other market traders and peasant farmers on their way to market. Jo and Daphne called out greetings to their friends and neighbours and wished them luck in their trading. Within an hour they were setting up their stall on the market. Diccon and Jon trotted out of town in the direction of the Priory and Thomas and Cedric prepared to head off towards the open area of land below Hay bluff where the army was camped. Thomas held out his hands towards the two women."I thank you good souls for all you have done for us and I give you this pack horse to say thank you and to remind you of what you did for us" "My word, Thomas that is a generous gift indeed and we thank you, it will surely make life easier for us" "Onward Cedric, lead us to your master" Thomas dug his heels in and walked the horses away from the market in the direction of the army.

They soon left the town behind and started to climb up towards the towering steep sided hillside in front of them. The thickly wooded countryside on either side of the track gave way to a more open sheep eaten common ground and the vista in front of them opened out into a green area covering several acres. This ground was thickly covered with tents and pavilions of all sorts some flying gaudy banners whilst others doubled as sutler tents and smithys. Throngs of men at arms milled about amongst the tents and destriers with armoured knights upon their backs proudly walked back and forth amongst the throng. Cedric pointed to an area towards the rear of the tents where a tempory enclosure had been set up"That's where your money is to be found, Shall we ride over to them?" Thomas nodded and the pair of them started to pick their way through the crowds of humanity that made up the Welsh army.

Right in front of them was a crowd of perhaps fifty to a hundred men, all with long hair, some tied back but most just like the hedgerows that these men looked as if they had risen from. Many were tattooed about the face and arms with strange celtic symbols and their legs were wrapped in sheepskin leggings. Mostly barefoot they lounged about on the damp greensward and laughed and joked amongst themselves in a language Thomas had not heard before. They seemed only to be armed with long knives,there was no evidence of any swords, bow staves or other weapons of war.

"Irish" said Cedric,"there's well on a thousand of them, but no one understands a word they say, but they're mad in a fight "

Thomas nodded.They worked there way past the Irish. On either side cooking fires were being attended by camp follower women whose children ran back and forth playing and stumbling over each other and the debris of the camp. Some welsh archers, the most deadly accurate of all fighting archers were practising at some butts set up on the edge of the field. Thomas cast a professional eye over them, and his heart sank, for they were good.Virtually every arrow loosed hit the bulls eye of the target and each time a great shout went up from the assembled men.

Further down the field on a small promentary several gaudy pvillon type tents had been erected. hung around with flags and bunting and with portable wooden seats and tables outside. This looked like the headquarters of the Welsh army.Behind and to one side a team of servants was cleaning and scouring armour.A never ending task as field conditions always rusted the armour as quickly as it could be cleaned.The harness as it was known, was a knight's most expensive and valualed possession his servants and his squire were perpetually scouring an polishing.As Thomas watched and took careful note of all he saw three men dressed in ermine trimmed cloaks and wearing expensive curl toed leather shoes came out of one of the tents and sat down on the chairs at the front. Cedric whispered " Owen and Jasper Tudor and my lord Pembroke." One of the men shouted over towards Thomas"Come by 'ere Bach your lord wants a word"

Thomas and Cedric dismounted and walked over to the group. It was apparent that these men were hugely powerful they wore jewelled brigandines and the daggers stuck in their belts were of a stunning quality. Thomas bowed.

"What battle areyou with "Asked the eldest of the three, you're an archer from the look of you are you with my lord Owen's troop."

"No My Lord, I am no soldier with this army, I merely deliver horses bought by your lordships Reeve in a market further north"Thomas said. Cedric held out the parchment written bill of sale towards the man. He took it and casting an eye over it turned to the others and said.

"God's blood your Reeve is buying expensive horses now,how many times have I told him the money is not in endless supply, not unless we sack a rich Yorkist town,"He chuckled to himself. The other two men in the group grinned in unison.

"Go to my Steward, Percy and he will pay you, and after you shall join Owen's troop of archer's Six pence a day an as many leeks as you can eat." He laughed hugely and slapped his thigh with a bejewelled hand.Waving dismissal with his other hand he went back into the tent and his companions followed.

Thomas and Cedric made their way to the huge tempory corral that housed several hundred horses and eventually found the Steward. Reluctantly he paid Thomas for his horses and he and Cedric parted company.Thomas rode back to the edge of the woodland that surrouned the camped army and making sure he was undetected he tethered his horse an tied Orrid to a tree nearby. Looking around to see that horse and dog could not be seen from any angle, it was the work of a moment to strip off his leather sallet and put on the Cistercian monk's robe. Looking every bit the serious religious,he clasped his hands together and walked back towards the camp.

In front of him was a long tented structure,perhaps ten yards long with two or three entrances to it. There was no one outside.. Thomas looked around and strolled inside.before his eyes on three or four trestle tables laid out on unbleached linen cloths were upwards of thirty, three foot long cast iron cylinders, each strengthened by bands of wrought iron.Hand guns! Thomas had heard of these. They were a new weapon in the pantheon of killing tools but he had never seen them before. He went over to the table and picked up one of the guns. It was hugely heavy weighing twenty ponds or more. In the top was a touch holeand underneath on the casting a device for fixing the barrel to a stand.He looked around the tent and sure enough against one wall was stacked a number of wooden stands.Beside them barrels of small rounded stones each more or less the same diameter and further off against another wall two or three barrels of gunpowder both fine mealed and the coarser stuff used by the gunners to give the guns their charge.Wooden boxes containing cloth wadding lay open in front of him. With his mind in a whirl he looked at all this. He knew that Earl Edward had nothing like this for his army, and although he had heard that guns were notoriously unreliable and blew up more often than not and only really managed to frighten the horses, the psychological damage done to the men at arms was huge.He had seen the huge siege gun at Shrewsbury and although the concept of these weapons made him fearful, he realised that this was the coming face of warfare. As he contemplated all this a foreign sounding voice called from behind him.

"What are you doing Father" he turned to see a smallish squat yet powerful looking figure with a swarthy skin, dressed in multi coloured hose, with matching brigandine and a matching stripy turban. "Why my son, I have come to bless the hackbutts"

"But they've already been blessed. Father Ignatious did them this morning" "Father Ignatious" gasped Thomas.

"Yes, surely you know him he is a member of your own order" "Yes of course I know him, but he said nothing about blessing these weapons.Oh well, two blessings are better than one in God's eyes, and I don't expect he did the gunpowder and shot and other bits and pieces." "No Father, he was here only a short time." "Good, I also need to talk to the Seneshal about numbers of troops here in the battles so we can make sure enough masses are said."

"I am the Seneshal, Guisippe of Milano at your service"He gave an extravagant bow", I can help with that Father, for I have accounts of all the men at arms in my Lord Pembrokes army" So saying the small Italian went over to an inlaid wooden box and extracted a piece of parchment which he proceeded to unroll.

"Piedmontese hackbut gunners 300. Crossbow men with pavaise. 250. Irish levys from Cork. 500 Irish levys from Connemara 500. Welshmen at arms 1500. Archers 500.Francais 400 Bretonaise 500..Carts and wagons 250. Draught horses 350. oxen.200." Guisippe looked up, " this does not enclude any noblemen or gentlemen who have provided their own horse and harness."

Thomas made a quick mental calculation. Approximately 5500 men with their accoutrements. A fair sized army.Thanking the Italian he turned to the barells and gun stands and other items ranged along the edge of the tent and proceeded to make a series of spurious blessing signs and to mumble words half under his breath. Guisippe did not seem to notice any thing wrong and after a few moments left the tent to Thomas alone. Once he had gone Thomas moved over to the doorway and looked out. Over in the distance perhaps two hundred yards away he could see a group of brightly dressed noblemen and their squires kneeling on the greensward whilst a priest in a light coloured habit blessed them. Something about the man's stance and the attitude of body convinced Thomas that this was indeed Father Ignatious.

Sidling out of the tent he made his way back into the thick woodland where he had tethered his horse and Orrid. He had hardly removed his habit and put on the tonsure hiding sallet when a loud welsh voice boomed out.

"Well I never,boyo, Thomas of Lingen as I live and breathe.Don't tell me you're part of this god forsaken shite hawk army."

Thomas looked up in disbelief. Before him leaning on the neck of his horse was an old friend from his days as a travelling archer moving round the Marches and taking part in contests for prize money."Llewellyn ap griffiths " He grinned and lent forward to grasp the welshmans forearm.

"So you are an archer with this lot are you?" "Indeed,I'm with the battle of Jasper Tudor. Come on over to our camp. My woman will make you some pottage and we can drink a pot or two of ale"

"Cannot by God's bollocks.I have an errand to run for my Lord down in the town. But when I get back I'll find you and then we can talk."Thomas vaulted onto his horse and dug his heels in. The animal gave a snort and ambled off in the direction of the town. He grinned and waved goodbye but inside his head a silent scream was begging him not to loose control of this moment. Llewellyn wryly shook his head.

"God's truth, you're as rude as any Englishman ever was. See you later." He spurred his horse in the opposite direction. Thomas heaved a silent sigh. By now he was several hundred yards from the encampment and the most pressing danger was past.. On the track back down to the town he passed endless returning men at arms who had been to the market. The occasional cart squeaking and easing its way up the rutted track. Once he had to pull into the side to let a haughty brightly caparisoned rider pass him.This individual never deigned to acknowledge that Thomas had stopped for him but pushed past with his pointed nose in the air and with a look of arrogant disdain on his face.After half an hour or so Thomas was trotting through the main street of Hay and out over the bridge that spanned the Wye.Within an other hour he was climbing the steep hill that led up to Daphne's house at Brilley. Orrid ran on ahead and gave a couple of sharp barks, and from the yard at the back of the house Jon's friendly face looked out. "Ah, Thomas. You 're back. All's well with you ?"

"It is and with you?. Were you able to see the Prior?." "A blessed man and close to God, when he heard our tale and had had a chance to look in the box he gave us six of the gold coins within. as a reward and a blessing to see us on our way" "And what's become of Diccon is he well?." "Oh ar, sleeping it off right now, had a bellyful in a tavern on the way here and is not fit to be seen by man nor beast"

Thomas shook is head. As much as he loved Diccon, his drinking habits had got the pair of them in trouble a few times over the years."When he wakes tell him we need a council of war and that right soon." He dismounted, tied his horse under the shelter of the lean to roof of the stable and made his way indoors to the inviting warmth and smells of Daphne's kitchen.

The two women were hard at work preparing a meal of mutton Swedes and leeks and the smells that were coming from the cauldron was enough to set the saliva running in Thomas's mouth. It was having the same effect on Orrid for he was sitting staring at Daphne with his tongue lolling out and if Thomas hadn't known better a look of extreme ecxtacy and love on his dog like face.

"Seems like the dog's in love " he grinned

"Well met Thomas, safely home I see."Daphne looked over at him and threw another piece of steaming mutton in the direction of the dog.Orrid gulped it down and wagged his tail with a satisfied thump.

"We have to be moving on from here Daphne, I've got all the information I need and I must get back to the Earl Edward with it.Tis only forty or so miles across country to Shrewsbury, we can be there in a day and a bit I reckon"

"You be careful up around Clun and Lientwardine, I 've heard tell of a gang of outlaws that have been terrorising them parts for years now.Welsh Shauny and his pals, absolutetly ruthless.They take hostages. Wait for the ransom then kill the hostages."

"They sound like a nice bunch of citizens,thanks for the warning we'll look out for them"

Just then a bleary eyed Diccon came into the kitchen scratching under his Jak and rubbing his fist over his stubbled chin.

"Ready to go then Diccon my lovely lad?"

"Go? God's farts I've only just woke up and you want's to go"He shook his head in horror.

"Only joking, though we must be on our way today. Get some food down you and then saddle up the horses.I'd like to be half way to Shrewsbury by nightfall"

Diccon helped himself to a bowl of stew as did the other two and after a substantial meal and having saddled the horses and transferred the weapons and other eqipment equally between the three. Thomas and his companions took their farewell of a tearful Jo and Daphne and rode off in a northerly direction towards the heavily wooded uplands that lead in the direction of Shrewsbury.

Chapter Six

Alternately cantering and trotting to conserve the strength of the horses the trio had made good time by twilight and as they came over the brow of a hill leading down to the small village of Clun Jon called out. "Men ahead, blocking the road, Six or so all on horseback". The three of them pulled up. In the half light it was just possible to see that the road had been blocked by brushwood leaving a narrow pathway which was guarded by a huge brute of a fellow dressed in sheepskin breeches and with a black brigandine on his upper body. He sat astride a black stallion and in his meaty paw he held a double edged broad sword. Behind him and to one side a collection of villainous looking individuals circled their horses and waited for the travellers to approach.

"Nock your bows boys, we'll have to take these bastards down" Thomas quickly strung his bow as did the other two and each selecting a target they let fly with their bodkin points. Diccon's arrow took one of the outlaws through the neck severing the jugular vien and causing a huge gout of blood to cover his companion who knew nothing of it as his left eye was pierced through from on of Jon's arrows. Thomas had deliberately aimed at the thigh of the giant hoping to disable him rather than kill him in order to gain information. The arrow pierced the man's leg and the momentum drove the point through and deep into the side of the horse causing it to rear and whinny in pain. The giant rider shouted in agony but he was fixed as soldidly as if he had been nailed to the horse. The bodkin point must have hit a vital part of the horse for it gave another pitiful cry and a shudder and fell over onto its side trapping the rider under it. The remaining outlaws had fled and by the time Thomas and his friends had come up with the brushwood barrier there was only one outlaw still alive.Thomas dismounted and looked down at the giant sheepskin clad figure, the horse had fallen onto him crushing his leg and although he was still alive he looked close to death, a dribble of blood came from his mouth and a grimace of pain crossed his face.

"Who are you cully ?" Asked Thomas.

"Help me" a pitiful cry. "Who are you and why do you try to stop us?"

The man gave a shudder,and in a feeble voice said "Welsh Shauny they call me I'm the power round these parts.If you help me Iwill give you gold, get this horse off me"

"Can't do that Cully"said Thomas squatting down beside the dead animal." Horse is jammed up against that rock and no man may move him"

"Are you going to leave me to die ? for pities sake help me" He coughed and a great gout of blood ran down his chin.

"Where's your lair, where are the rest of your men, maybe I can summon them to come and help remove the horse"

A look of hope sprang into his eyes and thedying giant whispered "A good plan, there are eight of us and we have a camp........" His voice tailed off and his head slumped to one side.A glazed look came over his eyes.

"Dead by God,oh well, saves having to look for his camp"said Jon

"Let's away from here, Clun is just over the hill, we can stay the night there and make the rest of the journey in the morn."

The three of them edged round the dead man and his horse and made their way back onto the road towards the village. By now night had fallen and a few twinkling candle lights from the rude hovels that made up the village was all the light that allowed them to see their way.Ahead a gaudy but faded sign with a picture of a black swan swung to and fro in the night time breese.The trio dismounted and entered the tavern.The noise of talking stilled as the three occupants looked over towards them. The room they had entered had a beaten earth floor and a meagre fire burnt in an inglenook at one end, the dirt of years lay uncleared upon the beams and fittings and piles of odure and filth swept into heaps against the tavern walls.A slatternly looking woman with a dirty grey dress that matched her dirty grey hair came forward and cracked a smile that revealed blackened teeth."Ho maisters, what can Cluny Meg do for you" " A meal and a bed for the night, Mistress"Said Thomas. "No beds here, though you can sleep in the stable for a penny.Food only the best here mind"and she cackled. The trio sat at a dirty table whilst the interupped conversation of the locals started up again. Cluny Meg brought over three bowls of a foul smelling thin broth that even Orrid turned his nose up at and three leather tankards of ale. Diccon sniffed at his and smiled. "Better than some I've had in nicer ale houses than this and he took a deep swallow. The ale was the best thing about the alehouse and the three friends and the dog made the best of a bad job and then removed to the stables where they passed a flea bitten night. By early dawn they were galloping north towards Bishops Castle. The miles flew by and by early afternoon their sweat lathered horses were within sight of Shrewsbury town walls. A long line of wagons, horses and foot soldiers were slowly moving from the town southwards. An entourage of brightly caparisoned destriers with brightly dressed nobles upon their backs was making its way southwards. An open wagon with a fringed roof was full of laughing women. Whilst alongside capered motley clad fools with jingle sticks clacking against the side of the wagon.

Thomas leant on the neck of his horse and gazed over at this spectacle. It was more like a procession to a revel than the serious movement of the Earl of Marches 'army. Putting heels to his horsehe spurred down to the throng. "Where can I find my lord Edward?" He asked one of the nobles riding past with his nose held high and his sallet strapped to his pommel.

"Still in the town and what does the like of you want with him?"

"Imformation of an important kind"

"Give it to me and I shall see its delivered " "Nay My lord tis for The Earl from my hand only." Thomas Diccon and Jon forced their way against the tide of moving men and equipment and finally gained entry to the town.Within the walls the chaos was even worse, discarded broken equipment and a damaged cart with its wheel off partially blocked the road, whilst a team of workmen and soldiers was trying their best to clear the way whilst all around like a river of slowly moving ants the army of the Earl marched south.

In the bright lit solar of the castle where Thomas had had his instructions from the Earl of March several men were gathered, among them wereEdward Plantagenet Earl of March Sir Walter Devereux Henry ap Griffiths, Lord FitzWater, Sir John Lynell and severall other important leaders of the Yorkist's army.

"My lord,since learning of the sad death of your father we have all been waiting to see what you would do. A lesser man would have immeadiately moved to apprehend the villains that had done this but you have chosen to wait and fight the army of Welshmen that come at us from the west."
" Thank you my lord Devereux for those kind words. Better to move slowly and upon fine consideration and by god's will success will follow " Even though the speaker of these words was still only eighteen years old his words were imbued with a gravitas that belied his years and older more grizzled members of the group looked on with approval.

"The army is moving but slowly. With luck we shall find ground that suits us for the coming conflict. I wish we had better intelligence concerning the Earl of Pembrokes army." "No sign of the spy you sent out some days ago my lord. "None I'm afraid he must have been apprehended by ourenemies."

At that moment a servant came into the room and whispered something to one of the nobles.

"Maybe all is not lost my Lord. An archer calling himself Thomas of Lingen is outside and craves an audience." Edward's eyes lit up. "Bring him in and right quick"

Thomas was ushered forward into the room, he bowed to the Earl. "Well Thomas, what have you to say to us."

Thomas looked about the beautifully dressed throng of nobles and was acutely aware of his own filthy condition. Travelled stained and with the blood of Welsh Shauny still upon him.He stammered a greeting and proceeded to tell the Earl and his entourage of all that had passed since his breifing in that very room.When he got to the story of his blessing of the hand guns there was complete silence as these men hung on his every word. A clerk was writing down the numbers as he revealed them and the Earl of March was smiling and nodding his head. Eventually Thomas finished his tale and stood exhausted before his lord.

" you have done well Thomas of Lingen and for that I am truly grateful.I am promoting you to Sergent, this gives you more money each day and the command of up to ten archers. You and your companions shall also receive a grant of money. My Seneshall will write the details down. "Thomas bowed and withdrew from the room.There was a buzz of excited voices behind him as the nobles digested his information.

With his head in a whirl and a great feeling of relief coming over him in waves, he couldn't help but grin as he strode through the upper hall away from the solar and down towards the grand straircase that led to the ground floor of the Keep.

"You look plesesed with yourself Thomas of Lingen" a mellifluous female voice sounded from a doorway to his left.Thomas stopped and looked over.

"My Lady" he stammered"You are well ?

Elenor Countess of Hambye smiled"Aye,Thomas,and much better for seeing you. Tell me what of your adventures since last we met. Step into this room and tell me"She moved aside and Thomas came into a sumptuous small room with tapestries on the walls and a small round oak drop leaf table and two high backed chairs.

"Sit Thomas and tell all."Thomas blushed but did as she asked. Being a bit judicious in his tale he told her most of what had transpired leaving out the goriest parts that he thought would horrify her, but she was made of sterner stuff than he knew and with a conbination of questions and logical thought managed to get nearly the whole thruth from him. When he got to the part where Earl Edward had promoted him to sergent she could contain herself no longer and coming round to his side of the table she lent over and placed a warm and loving kiss on his cheek Before he knew it he was retuning that kiss and for some moments they were locked in the bliss of it. Finally she pulled away and placing a hand on his cheek she said. "Ever since you saved me back at Christmastide I have longed to do that" "My lady, myself likewise" He grinned and lent forward." "Nay Thomas, another time my love. I must prepare to move with the army. Earl Edward wants his household away from Shrewsbury today at he latest."

"Yes, we saw them moving out of the city. How shall I find you amongst so many.?" "I am travelling with the Earl's household, so where you see his banner, I shall not be far away.Now go and let me prepare. I'm sure you have plenty to do yourself Sergent Thomas Lingen!" Laughing she shooed him out of the room and shut the door.

Thomas was in a complete daze,he didn't know what to make of the last ten minutes, only that they were very significant in his life. He set off tolook for his companions.

Back at the tithe barn there was a feeling of excitement and anticipation as the occupants packed their weapons and armour onto a series of large wagons that stood in line before the barn. The oxen snorting and pawing the ground. The teamsters with their ox whips ready to start the beasts into lumbering motion whenever they were told. Thomas came into the yard and immeadiately saw Diccon and Jon packing sheaves of arrows and bow staves onto the wagons.Orrid gave a yelp of pleasure and came bounding over jumping up and licking Thomas's hand "Good dog, good boy"said Thomas patting the dog on the head.

"Hey my fine fellows,how goes it with you.?The Earl has given you both a grant of money, how much we know not but nice to be rewarded for our efforts." Diccon rubbed his huge meaty paws together. "Maybe I can get pissed tonight then, maybe we all can" and a grin started to spread across his friendly ruddy face.

At that moment a beautifully dressed herald carrying a long trumpet and with a trailing satin sleeves to his jaket that were in danger of getting muddy from the mess in the yard placed the instrument to his lips and blew a series of notes. Work stopped as the soldiers and women in the yard waited to hear what the herald had to say.

"By the hand of the Earl Edward of March the following edicts are proclaimed. Firstly the archer known as Thomas of Lingen is promoted to Sergeant in the battle of my Lord Edward with immeadiate effect. Second the archer known as Diccon of Knighton and the archer known as Jon Appleyard and Thomas of Lingen shall all receive an annual stipend of four ducats of silver. Be it so enacted"

The three men looked stunned and grinned at one another. Spontaneous clapping and cheering broke out in the yard and congratulations and back slapping ensued. Thomas and his companions were popular amonst the soldiers of the army.The herald pulled his sleeves out of the mud and lowering his horn he strode off in the direction of the castle. "Well I never, you gorbellied onion eyed miscreant. A sergeant.... I don't suppose you'll ever forget that and we'll have to call Orrid sir." Hooted Diccon. Jon clapped Thomas on the shoulder"Tis as much as you deserve dear friend"

Thomas looked at his friends"time enough for all that,now we need to load these wagons,and while we're about it think on seven or eight good men you can trust to join our ranks."

They set too with a will and within the hour the first of the wagons was lumbering out of the yard behind the rest of the army. It took several hours for the vanguard of the army to clear the environs of the town. The hard frosted road edges soon became a quagmire of deep ruts wherein unfortuneate men at arms who had slipped and fallen often had to hauled to their feet as the weight of their harness in the glutinous mud was too much for them to climb out of alone. As the army moved further and further south more discarded equipment was left by disgruntled footsoldiers. Most of the troops were on horseback but a number had to walk or hitch a ride on the already overloaded wagons.By the time night fell the main bulk of the Earl's troops and wagons had covered a mere five miles and the rearguard was only just crossing the Severn at the town bridge.It was another bright frosty night and the temperature had plunged to well below freezing. Groups of men huddled together for warmth and others had erected tempory shelters from branches covered with sheepskins and blankets. The nobles and their entourages were faring little better but at least they had the shelter of their tents and pavilions. Camp fires sparkled all along the roadside and at one such Thomas and his companions were gathered to talk of the day's business and wonder what the morning would bring.

"Aye, and for sure the Earl has a good eye for country. Why when he was a lad he lived not far off and they'd hunt all around the forests here"Said Thomas.

"God's bleeding bollocks,I've got a good eye for country and all. I leaves it outside"Diccon shivered and moved closer to the fire." I hope this weather improves its freezing my fucking bollocks off. " "And mine" said Jon"You know you saw all them hackbutts, well I was wondering what could be done to stop them."

"Don't really know apart from contaminating their powder, I suppose you could always piss into the top of the barrel, that'd put paid to it. 'Specially Diccon's piddle its like sour treacle. Fancy it Dic? You go off and find the gunner's gunpowder and pee into it" Thomas laughed. "Is that an order Sergeant dear?" inquired the huge man sitting opposite. "Well it might be, depends on how I feels and what we gets. up to tomorrow.Now, what thinks you of these men to join us. Little Dick Hughes from Presteigne. Olwen Lewis fom Crosshands. And Peter Long breeches."

"All good men "said Diccon"Mind, that Peter can't keep his dick in his longbreeches" "Must get it from you then "laughed Thomas. "So in the morning will you tell them they're to join our band?"

The next day dawned frosty and bright. Men woke and stamped their feet and shook themselves to gain some warmth. Fires were poked back into life and bread and pottage eaten.Thomas felt refreshed for Orrid had curled up right beside him and the dog and man had shared each other's warmth enabling each to get a good night's rest.

The three new comers to the troop were standing eating their breakfasts an eyeing the others.From the north a horse and rider made their way slowly through the crowded encampment. The rider calling out"Sergeant Thomas Lingen, Thomas of Lingen," Thomas stepped forward. "Aye 'tis me you're after" "I have a message from the earl. You are to take six men and ride south.. You must see how the land lies for the placement of our battles but more important find out where is the Welsh army. The last news was they had quit Hay on Wye and were fast approaching us "Thomas nodded.He turned to Diccon."Saddle up the horses and find three more for Peter,Olwen and Dick. I'm going to get more arrows."He turned away and moved over to a sutlers cart that was piled high with bundles of shafts. He picked up armfuls and distributed them to his men. Whilst this activity was going on around them a young page boy appeared with a servant in tow. The servant had a large cloth wrapped package in his hands. The page piped up "Which of you is my lord Thomas"

Thomas spun round laughing"Not so much the my lord youngster but I am Thomas." "Ah, sir, I have a message from my lady and a gift. "He beckoned the servant forward who placed the package on the ground. "My mistress says to say"Wear it well and come back safe" The page looked relieved to have discharged his duties.He nodded to the group of soldiers and he and the servant disappeared in the direction they had come.Thomas knelt down and undid the parcel. Inside gleaming as if it had just been polished lay the most expensive chain mail shirt Thomas had ever seen. Made of riveted rings of shining steel it was hip length with half length sleeves and a standing collar of smaller rings.A leather strap and buckle crossed the front opening.

"My god, what a gift" he breathed

"Aye, you're well in there my son" said Diccon in awe as he lent down to examine the chain mail." That'd keep out a bodkin point I reckon, certainly a sword slash.My my you lucky dizzy eyed coxcomb.What's her name again ?"

Thomas looked slightly sheepish."Elenor Countess of Hambye "

"Oh, quality then Sergeant. Not too far above ye I do hope ?" Diccon carried on loading his horse whilst laughing to himself.

"Enough now, we must away on the Earl's business. "Thomas stuffed another sheaf of arrows into the horses pack and mounted up. "All ready" He cried. The six men trotted their horses onto the hard cobbles of the turnpike road and headed south.

Alternatley cantering and galloping they covered many miles before they stopped for some food at a tavern just south of Wigmore.

Asking in the ale house for any news of a welsh army on the move they drew a blank both from the locals and the land lord and after a satisfying lunch of bread ale and pottage they set off towards Mortimers Cross.

Thomas looked at his companions. "We will split into three teams and go south, west and towards Hereford and meet back here tonight with any news.If you should find the welsh, keep out of their way,on no account get involved in any fighting. This is just a scouting job for us. Do you understand?"

The others nodded, and where the old roman road crossed the turnpike they split up and headed in different directions.

Thomas and Dick Huhges and the dog set off in a southwesterly direction towards Weobley and Eardisley. By the time they'd got as far as the first village and found and heard nothing it was becoming obvious to Thomas that the Welsh army was further off tha n he had thought.As they trotted into the outskirts of the main street of Eardisley,the dog gave a warning growl and Dick said softly."Riders up ahead Sargeant, could be scurriers from the welsh." "You're right Dick, lets get out of sight and see what they are. "He pulled his horse over behind a building and dismounted. Peering through the slatted wooden walls of the building he was able to look right up the main street and see a group of six or seven horsemen dressed in the livery of the Earl of Pembroke clattering down the cobbles with their bows slung on their backs. Orrid gave a low growl."Shsh, dog" whispered Thomas.The dog subsided.

The mounted men came past their hiding place exchanging jokes and laughing in Welsh. Thomas had a smattering of that language having been brought up on the borderlands of Wales and England and he was able to understand that the Welsh were talking about their army. It seemed as if it was a good days march away, having only quit Hay with difficulty.There were at least five languages spoken amongst the different merceary troops and orders were often confused or misunderstood.From what Thomas overheard the army was somewhere between Hay and Eardisley. Once the scurriers of the welsh army had left the village He and Dick mountd up and taking a circular route around the back of the houses they trotted quietly back in the direction of Mortimers Cross.

By evening tide the six scouts had regathered in the tavern. Thomas and Dick the only ones to have made contact,the other four slightly disgruntled not to have any news to impart. "So my brave fellows, its back to the earl's army as swift as ever we may ride,he will want the intelligence as soon as we can get it back to him."Downing the last of their ale they set off northerly towards the Earl's army and by midnight Thomas was standing in the plush pavilion of the Earl of March an reporting to his lord what he had discovered. "Well done Thomas" said the earl and on your route south did you see any likely ground we could use to array our battles?" Thomas felt honoured that the commander in chief of the whole army would ask his advice and nodded. "Yes Sir, there is good ground just by the cross roads at Mortimers Cross. On the right side there is rising ground with woodland on top, ideal for the archers to rain down their shafts.

On the left the River Lugg runs its course and in front, flat meadow land where you could place your battles and be assured that you had the best battle ground around. " "Aye, I know Mortimers Cross. When I was a lad we would hunt all over that land, yes, it is good ground,"The Earl mused" I think that is where we will set our battles and wait on the Welsh."He called a scribe over to him and started to dictate orders.The Herbert brothers and Walter Deveraux came into the pavilion. They acknowledged Thomas who bowed to them.

"Well my lords, it looks as if we shall bring those villainous sheep biting scuts the Welsh to battle at Mortimers Cross. I am just making the dispossessions now. Three battles. Archers before the first. Archers on the high ground.A troop of horse hidden up by The Buzzards that may fall upon the foe when ready. I shall command one battle. You my lord Deveraux the next and you William Herbert shall have the vanguard. "Thank you My lord we shall not let you down"."Now my lords to your beds for we have much to do on the morrow. The speed at which this army is moving it will be the third day of Febuary before we can bring that traitor Pembroke to battle." So saying he dismissed the nobles and Thomas, who made his way back to the camp where his men were still talking around a campfire.

Chapter Seven

The last day of January 1461 gave way to the first of Febuary. The weather was still bitterly cold as the army of the Earl of March came down the old roman road through Wigmore and started to take up their positions at the cross roads known as Mortimer's Cross. The lie of the land was such that to the right a gentle rising slope gave an effective platform for Edwards archers and most of them were deployed there in order to shoot down on the enemy who would be gathered in the water meadows below. To the left the meandering course of the river Lugg slid its silvery way through the countryside. At the cottage known as Blue Mantle Edward set up his headquarters and disposed his troops in three battle lines. Archers were deployed in front of the vanguard battle whilst to the left in a hidden defile not visible from the watermeadows Edward had hidden a troop of horse ready to fall on the foe if needs be.

For the whole of that first day of Febuary nothing much came to pass. The soldiers made campfires and cooked their pottage. The various harnessed nobles rode back and forth on busy and important errands and of the Welsh there was no sign.

By the time the watery sun was starting to set and the temperature was s plunging towards zero the soldiers in the Earl's army were complaining as any soldier will about the lack of food and shelter. many had nothing better to sleep on than the frozen ground. The morethoughtful had sheepskins and blankets brought from their homes and villages,but it was still a bitter cold night and some of the weaker men in the army were not expected to survive.

Suddenly across the watermeadows and about a mile or so away lights could be seen.Scurriers and scouts from the Welsh army were arriving on the battlefield.By midnight the whole of the welsh army was arrayed before Edward's troops in three battle lines approximately two to three hundred yards away. One battle commanded by The Earl of Wiltshire and two by the Earl of Pembroke.

About a mile back from the lines, the Lancastrians had established a wagon park where their camp followers and wagons and carts were drawn up in a defensive circular position.Slowly the buzzing noise of the armies subsided as the night drew on and the soldiers attempted to get what rest they could before the killing of the morrow.

Thomas was sitting with his men just below the tree line on the smallish rise where Edwards archers were deployed. They were warming themselves at the fire as they put the final sharpening touches to their daggers and swords.

"Well my friends, by this time tomorrow we'll know the outcome"

"I've never fought in a battle before Sarge" said Peter Long breeches with a fearful tone to his voice"What if I fears for my life and I can't fight" "Oh you'll be fine,just stay close and I'll look after you. Do what you're told and right quick and keep your bloody eyes open."

Diccon snorted "Tis only a bunch of clapper clawed Welsh and a few Irish tossers covered in ink that we've got to worry about,and lookee here those irish only seem to have daggers for weapons, nothing like bows or battle axes and that. We should be able to see them off allright."

"Aye, I think that's right "said Thomas"Now boys get some rest for tomorrow you'll need all your strength.

As the dawn gave way to the rising sun on a bitterly cold morning a strange phenomonen arose over the battlefield site. As one sun came up into the sky,on either side and many hundreds of yards apart another sun was visible and yet another so that where there should have been one only there were now three suns in the sky.

The soldiers and men at arms were stricken with terror a great moaning sound could be heard all over the field. Men were falling to their knees and exhorting God not to strike them. Edward Earl of March came out of his pavillion and took one look at the three suns. He raised his hands high and turning to his men said. "Be of good comfort and dread nought, this is a good sign for those three suns are the father the son and the holy ghost and therefore have a good heart and in the name of Almighty God we go against our foe."This speech seemed to calm the men and where as before they were terrified and asking God's forgiveness now they turned to their companions smiling and laughing at their foolishness.Edward called his herald over." "Blue Mantle, go down to the battle lines and speak with my Lord Pembroke. Ask if battle and bloodshed can be avoided and if so will he now withdraw from the field. I shall wait your return. "The herald swept a deep bow and mounting a palfrey held for him by a servant trotted down towards the Welsh army.he came level with the first of Edwards battle lines and moved into the field towards the Welsh army. He was a mere hundred yards away and reaching for his heraldic horn ready to make the announcement expected when a bodkin point loosed from the welsh side took him in the neck. A great gout of crimsom shot out of his neck and with a scream of pure terror Blue Mantle expired upon the battle field,the first casualty of the day. A long and angry sigh came from the ranks of Edwards army.Edward was watching with horror and turning to his nobles said."No quarter to be given to these dogs today. Archers loose your shafts."Up on the ridge Thomas heard the familiar orders.

"Archers, Notch, draw, loose. "An arrow storm with a sound like a thousand starlings sighing through the air fell upon the Welsh and Irish. Good English ash shafts with bodkin points slashed their way down onto the defenceless troops below.The irish were bellowing and prancing forward shouting unintellagable war cries and brandishing their daggers, but the leathal storm of arrows was decimating the host. Men with arrows through their legs nd chests through their eyes and sticking from thir skulls reeled out of the line. The Irish contingent of the Earl of Wiltshire's battle was driven sideways towards the River lugg. The great mass of men hampered each other and caused a panic to ensue which in turn affected the welsh and mercenaries. Edward gave his orders. "The vanguard battle, force these dogs back to the river and drown them" The troops gave a howl and running forward fell on the Welsh and Irish and drove them back towards the Lugg. Battle hammers and pike staffs rose and fell in an orgy of blood letting and men in harness drowned by the hundred in the lugg. Too heavy to avoid the mud and water of the river bank. The silvery sluggish wend of the river slowly turned red as it was fed with the blood of Earl Pembroke's men.

Up on the ridgeThomas and his men watched as the poorly equipped Irish were beaten and stabbed into submission.

"Lets get down there Thomas or all hope of plunder's long gone"

"Aye, you're right Diccon, "Thomas yelled"To horse, to horse for Edward and the Marches."H swung himself into the saddle and closely followed by his troop of archers stormed down the slope on to the water meadow. Instantly the feel of the battle changed, whereas before they had been watching safely from a distance now they were in the thick of it.A riderless horse bellowing in pain with four arrows embedded deep in its flanks and spitting blood and froth galloped past. A Breton mercenary wound the crank of his crossbow and was about to loose as Thomas crashed into him and dispatched him with a massive downward blow of his sword. All around the screams and cries of men and animals rose up to the skies mixed with dust and smells of fresh blood and human excrement.Ahead of Thomas and closer to the river a group of nobles were slashing at each other with their swords,A grand melee the outcome of which it would be hard to tell. Thomas parried a massive blow from a berserk looking noble with a bleeding arm whose armour was dented and covered in blood.The man had removed his sallet the better to see his enemies and to gain some much needed air, so Thomas struck upwards and through his eye with his dagger. The man fell amongst the others littering the floor.An irish man covered in black and green swirls across his face and bare chest was laughing as he swung a battle hammer with uncontrolled ferocity at anyone who came within three feet of him. Suddenly the man went down,a rondel quivering in his neck, his jugular severed and his life blood spilling out on to the battleground.Thomas looked to see that it had been young Peter Longbreeches who had thrown the knife. He acknowledged him with a smile and upraised hand.The Welsh host were slowly being driven backwards towards the river as the Earl's men gained the upper hand. In defensive terror the Welsh turned with their backs to the Lugg but the sheer weight of their own numbers and the ferocious press of Edwards army drove them into the water. Once down the river bank it was only a matter of time before they drowned or were slashed to death by Edward's men.All along the bank for nearly amile the litter of equipement and drowned bodies f illed the stream causing it to overflow onto the water meadows.Thomas and his men chased a group of Welshmen further down towards the wagon park where a great noise and grey smoke rose into the air. A futile last stand was taking place with some fifty Piedmontese crossbowmen holed up behind the barricade of some wagons encircled in a defensive position. The wagons were on fire so thepiedmontese had to loose their bolts through the smoke and burning slats of the carts. They were killing some of the earl's men. Behind them and well to the cente of the circle some twenty camp follower women and children screaming in terror huddled together under the banner of Pembroke. Some nobles had gathered by the banner determined to sell their lives dearly on this dreadful day. Around them the detritus of war littered the field. Loose helmets broken swords and unidentifiable broken things some covered in blood others just lying as if waiting to be found.

Thomas pulled back on his reins.No point in forcing his way over the barrier of the burning wagons. As he waited more of the earl's men started to gather.Some archers still with their bows, appeared and started to loose bodkin points into the groups of soldiers within the wagon park. And against the crossbowmen.It took a crossbow man twice as long to crank and loose his bolt as it did for an archer to notch and loose.Bodkin points slashed forward against the mercenaries.Again and again the quickness of the archer's draw won out over the slowness of the hand cranked crossbow, until finally hardly a crossbowman was still alive within the ring of burning wagons.The Earl's men at arms surged forward across the makeshift barricade and descended upon the group of nobles in the centre. A hard hand to hand fight started with the Welsh nobles overwhealmd within minutes and a group of the still living thowing down their weapons and calling for mercy. They were herded into a corner and left under guard whilst the victorious Earl's men charged on down the turnpike chasing the fleeing Welsh in the direction of Hereford.

Thomas and his men joined the chase. A sort of blood lust had come over them and their only desire was to ride down and slaughter the terrified Welsh and other mercenaries.Some welsh tried to hide in a building next to the road. It was surrounded by chanting screaming English soldiers and set on fire. Rather than come out and be slaughtered the Welshmen opted to be burnt to death and the smell of burning bodies not unlike the smell of roasting pork filled the air.one man braver than the rest of his companions turned in the road ahead and waited with his sword held high. Thomas and Diccon charged him down and at the last moment swerved their mounts either side of him. As they passed they each slashed at the soldier. The force of their blows severed his head from his body and his arm from his shoulder and with a scream the man fell to the ground.

On and on they galloped killing in a demented frenzy. Driven forward by an unstoppable bloodlust and a joyous feeling of relief that it was them delivering the coup de grace and not their victims.After a chase of nearly five miles and the welsh soldiers were becoming thin on the ground Thomas called a halt. "I say we've killed enough. Let's go back to Mortimer's cross and see how things fared with the Earl."Turning their horses Thomas and Diccon trotted back along the road past a scene of devestation the like of which neither of them had seen before. Some of the braver inhabitants of the hamlets and villages they passed had come out to loot the dead and like ugly crows village women dressed in black and aided by their children were rifling through the garments of the dead and removing any rings or valuables they could find.Bodies lay in profusion on the road and in the hedgerows. Thomas stopped and picked up a particularily fine steel sallet. "This will do me "He said, " go well with the chain mail I got from the countess".Many of the Earl's soldiers were re equipping themselves with bits and pieces of armour and weapons looted from their dead enemies. One Englishman was prancing up and down the road laughing and shouting, drunk as a lord whilst on his head he was wearing a bright coloured striped turban not dissimilar from the one Guisippe had been wearing in the camp back at Hay. Thomas suddenly thought about his friend Llewellyn and hoped he had fared alright that day. But so many of the Welsh had been slaughtered that his heart sank at the thought that his earstwhile friend might have suffered the same fate as the rest of his companions.Down the road a group of disconsolate Welsh nobles their armour and weapons stripped from them and dressed only in their linen undershirts and hose and heavily guarded by the

Earl's men at arms were walking with their heads down. "Whoa cully, where are you taking these poppycocks?" Shouted Thomas at one of the guards.

"Poppy bleeding cunts more like " came back the reply," They're on their way to Hereford to get their just desserts"He made a gesture as if cutting off his own head and grinned at Thomas though rotton teeth." Taken to the High Cross and heads chopped off, that's for certain." On hearing this one of the nobles a lad of no more than seventeen sobbed out loud. "Aye,choose the wrong side today my lord. Best have stayed in Pembroke" mocked the guard as he drove his captives forward.Thomas and Diccon spurred on,as they got closer to the main battlefield it became apparent that the Earl had sustained a total victory over his enemies. Many hundreds of bodies were lying where they had fallen and amongst them the victorious soldiers of the earl's forces moved through the devastation selecting armour and bits of weaponry. Occasionally a cry was stifled as a badly wounded soldier was put out of his misery by a swift strike through the eye with a dagger.The earl of March was standing outside his tent talking to his commanders and occasionally giving orders. One by one important prisoners were brought forward to be shown to him and his voice rang out mainly in sorrow as he recognised old friends and advesaries.Some of the nobles were moved to an area behind the pavilions whilst other lesser known men were herded together under guard and stripped of their harness and left to shiver in the cold of day in their undershirts and hose.

The Earl turned to one of his advisors and said."There are many traitors not accounted for here, have they escaped the field ?"

"Yes,my lord, we have made a list of known traitors w ho have vanished. James Butler. Earl of Wiltshire.Owen ap Griffiths. Philip Mansel.Sir Thomas Perot.Hopkin ap Rees of Gower.Sir John Skydmore and Jasper Tudor." "I want these men tracked own and brought to me in Hereford. Send out battle groups into Wales and find them" "Yes my lord" The steward turned away and gave orders that the earl's wishes should be carried out.The Earl of March turned and cast his eye up over the field at the ridge from which his archers had done so much damage. Just walking down with the dog Orrid on a lead beside him came Thomas.The earl beckoned a servant. "Go and fetch Sergent Thomas of Lingen to me, I would fain hear what his fight was like.The servant hurried off and within minutes Thomas and his dog were standing outside the pavilion. "Be seated Thomas, and tell me how fared the day with you?"Thomas sat on a wooden stool."All went well my lord. We chased some welsh as far as Slaughterford covert and killed them, but by that time most had gone to ground, some must have got free, but not many. I feel it has been a right God given victory for you. " "You are in the truth of it there my loyal friend. It is a God given victory and to show my love for him I shall change my livery to show three suns. The sun in splendour. "He grinned," so this is your killer hound." He lent forward and patted Orrid's head. The dog looked slightly askance and then gave a slight bark. " "Aye, my lord, as loyal a subject as I am " The Earl laughed.

"Thomas, you can help me. I wish to move our army towards Hereford, and there to carry out some trials and executions of traitors, but I need a good and trusty man to go before and smooth the way with the burghers and mayor of the city. Will you do it ?"

"Yes my lord I should be honoured. " "Good, I shall write your orders. Steward"he called. The overworked scribe came forward with his quill and ink pot and took down the Earls dictation.Thomas waited to receive the written orders then bowed to the Earl and he and Orrid went in search of his men.

He found them sitting around a campfire. Upon an upturned breast plate on the embers three or four horsemeat steaks sizzled and the succulent smells of the cooking meat made him realise nothing had passed his lips since the night before."Have ye enough of that meat for the likes of me? " he asked."Sit yourself down and feast on this, there's plenty more where that came from. "Diccon pointed with his dagger at the body of a destrier that had had several steaks carved out of it flanks. "Good meat this, not so much fat on it. What's afoot now this battle's won.?" "The Earl has asked me to go to Hereford to ease the way for the trial and execution of the traitors taken in the battle and I shall need all you men to come with me. Peter, Olwen and Dick you are in charge of getting packhorses. Diccon and Jon. arrows, bow staves and any harness you can find that's half way decent. I should like to be on the turnpike before nightfall.The others nodded and set too to finish their meal.Thomas threw Orrid a chunk of horse meat which the dog wolfed down with appreciative thumps of its tail.

As the sun started to sink over the river Lugg Thomas and his men set off through the rubbish and muck of the battlefield down the turnpike towards Hereford. Thomas had the intention of putting some miles between him and the horrors of the day and he knew his companions felt the same. Before they left the field of battle Thomas had spoken with Sir John Baskerville who was the sheriff of Hereford and gained his permission to requesition any buildings goals or other necessary items to set up the trials and execution of the captured Welsh nobles.With a signed piece of parchment giving him virtual powers of life and death over the people of Hereford he felt in a strong position to carry out his duties for the Earl.

By the time it was full dark Thomas and his men were clattering into the streets of Leominster. They found a tavern that seved food as well as rooms for the night and

Gratefully eased their tired and weary bones at the roaring fire in the alehouse.room.

The landlord. A fat jolly little man with a bald head and a greasy leather apron was only too pleased to take their money and wanted to know all about the battle that had just been fought. "They've been coming through the town like rats today, Irish, Bretons, Welsh never heard a word of English till gone lunchtime, and then the Earl's men chasing them, not one stopped for food or ale. Do you know you're the only ones have stopped all day. "He wrung his hands together sorrowfully.

"Well,landlord bring us your best meat and your finest ale so that we can toast the famous victory of Mortimer's Cross."

"Oh Mortimer's Cross.Is that where the fight was?" "Aye and what a fight.,maybe some thousands Welsh and Irish destroyed and a total victory for my lord."The landlord bustled off to fulfil Thomas's order and he looked at his companions and grinned. "Well my boys, you all did well today. Not one wounded or killed. God be praised a lucky day.Peter, you were brave today I saw you throw that dagger. Takes a cool head to do that in the heat of battle" Peter smiled and hung his head bashfully.

"As for you others, don't know when I've had better men with me. Drink up and feast on this meat and tomorrow we'll be in Hereford.

By mid day Thomas and his companions were crossing the bridge over the moat that surrounded Hereford Castle. This was one of only four exsisting pre Norman castles in the country and was reputed to be lovlier than Windsor. Thomas couldn't tell never having been further south than Hereford before. However he was quite in awe of what he saw. A moat surrounding a stone built keep with an inner keep and apartments for royalty or important guests. The crennallated walls pierced with arrow slits and with a stone parapit that surrounded the entire upper section of the walls made the place easy to defend.

Several men at arms stood guard over the castle gates. They were dressed in the livery of Sir James Baskerville. Thomas showed the most senior his written orders and he and his companions were shown through into the inner keep where they tethered the horses.Sir James' steward came bustling over to find out who this stranger was and what he wanted. Upon reading his master's words his manner changed abrubtly and Thomas and his men where given every help they needed.

"Is there a secure goal capable of holding at least ten Welsh prisioners of the first distintion?"He asked.

"Yes Sir, we have two goals here one is more comfortable than the other being above ground. But both are escape proof.

"What about apartments for my lord Edward and his entourage?

The steward looked quite hurt"Why Sir we have had kings and queens stay here since time began, I trust the Earl of March shall be very comfortable"

"Good. Please prepare the apartments for my lord's arrival. He may be here within a day or two his entourage consists of numerous nobles and some ladies."His mind instantly flew to a memory of Elenor's kiss and a warm feeling suffused his face.

"Also prepare the goal for the prisoners and I shall want a scaffold and execution block set up in the market place.Please organise that "

Thomas took his leave of the steward and he and his men set off to view the market place which was some distance from the castle near the High Cross close to the Cathederal.

When they arrived they found the market in full swing. Many brightly caparisoned stalls selling ever thing from hot pies through to silks and bolts of cloth. Geese and lambs tethered in stalls. Jugglers and musicians wandering through the throng playing airs upon their instuments. One stall was selling spices from the orient. Piles of peppercorns, cloves and that most exotic of spices nutmeg. The smell permeated that section of the market. Close by a large fire burnt, around which many of Herford's citizens had gathered to listen to a story teller relate the latest information available to him of the battle just past.

Dressed from head to toe in an all enveloping brown cloak with a large hood the story teller looked more like a monk than a teller of tales, but once he opened his mouth and the sonerous words issued forth his mesmerising delivery had his audience captivated. Thomas decided to wait a while and see what truth was encapsulated within the tale of the battle.

"And behold my brethren three suns were seen in the sky

This strengthened the Earl and made the others fly.

Irish and Welsh were killed in a great host Give

Praise unto the Holy Ghost.

And all about the muddy Lugg

Were lying the dead and dying

. Four thousand souls departed hence

And Welsh nobles captured and brought to Hereford Town

Where their heads are struck off and their bodies put down

.Give praise to the Lord for a victory entire

.May the living rejoice and the dead lie in the mire."

The story teller bowed politely amidst a smattering of applause. Thomas and his men continued to look around the market place. The high Cross stood at one end of the market with several steps up to it.This would make an ideal spot for an execution spot.Thomas marked it down in his mind. "Back to the castle lads,we shall find a place to stay and upon the morrow when the prisoners get here we shall have some work to do."

Chapter Eight

A s a bright cold dawn broke over the town walls of Hereford a long line of soldiers on hoseback and on foot, wagons,carts and other types of ox and horse drawn vehicle came slowly down the road towards the main town gate. This was Edward's victorious army finally making its way to Hereford. In the middle of the throng being driven on by chain mailed guards was a bedraggled and disconsolate group of Welsh nobles. Many barefoot all dressed only in torn hose and stained and dirty linen undershirts. With dirty hair and bloodstained faces their look of utter dejection and apprehension permeated the group to such an extent that even the citizens of Hereford who had stopped to watch fell silent.

Only one man held his head high. Owen Tudor. Amongst the rest he stood out like a beacon.Although there was a nasty red scar running down across his face from his left ear to his chin he still managed to disdainfully look past his captors to the crowds of towns folk.

"I shall be released. I shall not have my head struck from my body. I am Owen Tudor I am the Earl of Pembroke"

Some wag in the crowd shouted "Too bad you flap mouthed bastard. You'll still get your head chopped off" His friends laughed and slapped each other's backs.

Tudor glared at the man. "I am Owen Tudor and I demand respect."

"You are a traitorous swine and you deserve a kicking "shouted a guard as he used his pikestaff handle to herd the prisoners back into line.

Eventually the prisoners arrived at the portcullis entrance to the castle where they were handed over to a strong guard of castle troops.Thomas was waiting with a clerk to take down the names and allocate suitable prison cells for the Welsh.Any high ranking nobles such as Sir John Throckmorton. Sir Henry Scudamore,Morgan ap Rhydderch and Owen Tudor were immeadiately placed in the above ground goal where they were given some water to drink and a handful of yesterday's stale trencher bread. The rest were herded underground into a dank cellar goal beneath the bailey where they were chained to the walls in the gloom.

"What of the rank and file soldiery. Those men who are not noble but who also fought against my lord."asked Thomas.

"Why sir, the Earl made a declaration on the field. All common soldiers to be relaeased if they swore their oath not to fight against him again. But any of gentle or noble birth to be brought here for trial."

As Thomas was supervising the prisoners a clatter of metal rimmed wheels could be heard entering the castle keep. An ornate covered wagon with a red canvas top and yellow leather traces entered the courtyard. From the back several women dressed exquisely in velvet and brocade and with high wimples on their heads stepped down. Thomas gave a deep bow. He had seen in the group the unmistakeable figure of the Countess of Hambye, and he was determined to thank her for her generous gift of the chain mail.Before he had a chance to approach her however the castle steward had bustled up and ushered the group of women into the royal apartments. However amongst the laughing and smiling women Thomas has made eye contact with the Countess who smiled gently at him and mouthed his name.They disappeared inside and Thomas returned to his prosaic duties with the prisoners.

Edward Plantagenet TheEarl of March and his half dozen top adisors clattered over the wooden bridge that spanned the moat to Hereford Castle.

"I want all the traitorous Welsh nobles who fought against me here in front of the castle within the hour to hear their fate." He shouted to his steward as he dismounted from his charger. A squire held the head of the horse as Edward hurried up the steps of the keep into the royal apartments.

Within the hour and in front of the keep upon some hard cobbles the Welsh were made to kneel with their hands tied behind their backs.There were twelve of them, and they knelt there shivering in their thin garments as the winter chill blew around them.

Hopkin Davey of Carmarthen,Thomas Fitzharry, Rheinallt Gwynedd of Harlech Davud Lloyd,Lewis Powys Morgan ap Rhydderch, Lewis ap Rees of Carmarthen, Harry,James and William Skydmore,Sir john Throckmorton and Owen Tudor.

"Stand up, you traitorous dogs,and hear the punishment that you so justly deserve"

Earl Edward dressed in an ermine edged black wool cloak with a matching round hat on his head.stood tall before them, a stern and implacable look to his eye as he proclaimed." For daring to bear arms against me and for the crime of traitorous assembly you shall be taken to the market place here in the fair town of Hereford, and there your heads shall be struck from your bodies.Your heads shall be placed on spikes along the town walls as a warning to others and your bodies shall be buried in an unmarked grave so your kith and kin may never know what became of you."So saying he threw out his hand in a gesture of dismissal."Take them hence" he shouted.

Men at arms prodded the twelve into line and the procession set off for the High Cross at the market place. It took but five minutes to reach the spot but already a large crowd had gathered as word of the executions swept through the town.Lewd and ribald shouts split the air as the townsfolk roared their hate and derision at the prisoners.

A wooden platform with a beheading block stood at the foot of the high cross. Two huge black clad executioners with hooded masks through which only their eyes showed stood with their double handled swords at the rest.The first welsh man was led forward.Forcing him down onto his knees and making him bend his neck the executioneer wasted no time in delivering the fatal blow and with a gasp from the crowd the traitor's head was struck from his body. It flew off into the crowd and a gout of arterial blood spewed up into the air. Pulling the first body to one side the second executioner grabbed the next prisoner in line who was Lewis ap Rhys of Carmarthen.He struggled and tried to say something, but he too was forced to his knees and the death blow was administered. And so it went on, one after another the Welsh nobles were executed. The block and platform ran scarlet with their blood and the executioners were covered in the gore. The front row of spectators fared no better having to dance back out of the way of sprays of blood each time one of the heads was severed. Eventually, the prize prisoner remained,Owen Tudor.Even as he watched his companions being slaughtered he had been saying "They will not kill me, I am Owen Tudor, they cannot kill me," right up until the time the executioner tore the collar from off his doublet he still believed he would escape his fate. Then when he realised that he would be beheaded he said to the crowd."The head that was wont to lie on Queen Katherines lap must now lie on this rough pillow" and he meekly knelt down to his death. The heads of all the traitors with the exception of Owen Tudor were hung and spiked along the town walls. Owen's head was collected by a mad woman, washed carefully and with its hair combed it was left on the top step of the High Cross surrounded by one hundred candles.

Thomas had been watching the executions from the distance of the town wall and he felt a certain sympathy for the executed nobles. Shaking off the feeling of dread and despair that the beheadings had left him with he determined to try and find the Countess in the Castle and get back to some normality. Calling Orrid to his side he walked back towards the castle. By the time he crossed the drawbridge his head had cleared and he felt better able to face her.He walked through to the inner keep and in past the huge oak studded door that stood open at the foot of the stairs leading to the royal apartments.

On the first floor he could hear the sound of laughter and women's voices coming from the solar at the back of the keep.He walked towards the door.It opened and a sevant in the livery of Sir john Baskerville came out carrying a wooden tray on which was piled several goblets and an empty wine bottle.

"Can I help you at all" said the servant.

"I wish to speak with the Countess of Hambye if she is available." "One moment sir and I will find out,and you are

?" "Sergeant Thomas of Lingen" The servant disappeared through the door and moments later ushered Thomas in. He was confronted by a light open room with a large stone mullioned window at one end with a semi circular window seat beneath it.Colourful silk and wool cushions lay scattered on the seat and three noble ladies sat there in the noonday sun.One of them was the Countess with two ladies in waiting beside her.

Thomas bowed. "My lady, I came to give you thanks for the exemplary gift of a chain mail shirt which you were so good as to give me before the battle." "Ah, Thomas,I hope it was useful and protected you well."She smiled up at him.

"I must protect my protector as well as I am able and that seemed but a small thing." "That's as maybe my lady. But that was the most expensiveItalian,Milanese, I would guess chain mail vest I ever saw. I thank you. "Thomas bowed again.

Elenor smiled"Dost know what the Earl has in store for you Thomas? Has he another adventure to send you on.I feel he trusts you to do what he asks of you." "Aye my lady, he can trust me. But on this instance he has said nothing to me.I am but a soldier in his army." "So you are free from orders at the moment?" "Yes my lady." "Good, in that case you can walk with me in the lower garden here in the castle. It is nearly spring an I would fain breath some fresh air."

"Thomas inclined his head and offering his arm to the Countess the pair of them left the solar and the two ladies in waiting. Once they were on their own The countess moved closer to Thomas and gently caressed his arm. "Oh Thomas, I have missed you, and I was anxious during the battle, but I prayed you would be spared and my prayers were answered."She smiled radiantly up at him and he was once again struck by the exquisite beauty of her flawless skin. He noticed that her hair had a very faint red tinge to it and that and her pale blue eyes set off her complexion to perfection.

They passed through the gate to the lower garden and proceeded to stroll past the parterres and neatly raked gravel paths that made up these formal gardens.Eventually they went through a door in a red brick wall and into a kitchen garden. Here there was a hive of activity with kitchen servants and gardeners picking and tending to vegetables of the season.One had a large wicker basket that was filled with leeks and turnips. Another had a small handful of lamb's lettuce.

"Not such a bounty from God this time of year"commented Thomas on the scarcity of lamb's lettuce in the kitchen man's hands.

They passed on and up a gravel path towards the aivery. This was a brick built low single storied structure with metal open cages in front of a nesting area and divided up into three or four separate areas each inhabited by different hunting birds. In one a sullen looking falcon sat on a stump and glared out at the world. At his feet the remains of something furry on which he had just dined. In another cage two or three hen harriers side stepped along a branch as they tried to gain ascendancy over one another.In the third cage, several, up to a dozen, brightly coloured yellow and blue canary birds tweeted and stirred in the sharp air.Eloner clapped her hands in delight. "Oh, how I love canary birds. When I lived in France we a lways had some to entertain us with their songs.I know not what became of them."Her eyes filled with tears.

"Do not be sad my lady, for I am here to protect and look after you, and that I would do with the utmost of my strength and skill."So saying he pulled her into a close embrace and kissed her on the mouth. He felt her lips part beneath his and a tiny warm tongue snake out and twine itself in his. His breath came faster as did hers and a feeling of warmth and contentment spread between them. Eventually they pulled away from one another and grinning like naughty children caught with their fingers in the honey jar continued on their walk through the gardens.As they walked up through a more wooded area ahead they could see a group of persons in conversation. They drew level and realised that it was The Earl himself and his closest advisors

The Earl looked at them. "Well met Countess and Thomas of Lingen, one of God's better days don't you think?"He laughed."My advisor's tell me That the Queen and her army of northern pillagers are rampaging through the land killing, maiming, torturing and stealing all they can lay their hands on.This I must put a stop to.I have today ordered Warwick to raise the western shires and to fortify the town of St Alban's and there to confront this army of Scots and other plunderers.I have trust in him and he has several days to prepare. I and the army shall march on London.In God's name we shall gather forces as we go."He clapped Thomas on the shoulder. "I have another task for you ere long Thomas.Please attend on my steward later in the day for my orders." Thomas bowed and the Earl strode off down the path followed by his advisors. "More adventures my love!.Pray God to keep you safe."Elenor held his arm.

"I shall be safe, in the full knowledge of my love for you.Nothing can protect me more. Not even Orrid,"and he bent down and ruffled the head of his faithful hound. Later that day when he had taken his farewell of Elenor and after he had gone to seek out his companions and tell them that there was a potential job waiting for them, he made his way back to the castle and asked for an audience with the Earl's steward. He was admitted to a narrow parchment strewn room with a long table and three clerks with their heads down hard at work copying orders and writing details of the everyday running of the army.

"Do you have orders from my lord for Thomas of Lingen?" He inquired of one of the clerks.

"Yes, sir, I have just finished writing them this instant."The clerk handed him a small parchment on which were some close written words. Thomas moved to the window better to see in the light that filtered in through the mullion.He read.'To our beloved Thomas of Lingen, greetings.Take six men with horses and ride to find The Earl of Warwick, either safe in St Albans or somewhere upon the road at Burford or Oxford. Ascertain from him the state of his forces and when he shall meet with us.Plunderers and Scottish villains are laying waste the countryside as they march to London, ascertain what damage has been done and by whom. Report back to me as soon as you have found the information I require. Signed Edward Plantagenet Earl of March.

Thomas folded the parchment into his leather pouch and left to find his men.In the castle courtyard Diccon and Jon and the others were gathered round a small fire sharpening their swords and daggers.

"We have our orders from the Earl, to find The Earl of Warwick, someway away one hundred or more miles, as far as St Albans. "

"St Albans?, never been anywhere near there before, what road do we take ?"

To Burford and Oxford and on to St Albans. On our way we have to discover just what horrors and damage the Scots army has wrought in its pillaging through the land. We leave as soon as the pack animals are loaded."Instantly there was a bustle of anticipation amongst the six men as they hurried to load any weapons and armour they might need.Before an hour was out they were trotting over the cobbles and out in the direction of Burford. They put some distance under their hooves along the good paved road that led in the direction of Oxford and when they stopped for the night they had covered twenty miles. The next day and the day after were similar with the miles being eaten up as they rode eastwards. Burford passed and the outskirts of Oxford hove into view before they heard anything of the scots army. Then it was just hearsay, The landlord of the alehouse they rested at come lunchtime had heard a rumour that the scots were torturing men and women to get them to reveal the whereabouts of their stashes of coins and precious goods.

"Aye, I heard they roasted a woman over a fire whilst her man had to watch. He soon told 'em what they wanted to know that's for sure."

"And you know this for a fact?"asked Thomas.

"Oh ar, I had it on good authority from Oswald the Farrier who had it from the Seneshall of Whitney castle." The landlord rubbed his hands together and shook his head in mock horror."They be devils, they murdered them monks up at the Abbey and they killed all the lepers, and I heard" here his voice took on a solem schocked tone"They eat the plumpest monks" Diccon gwaffawed with laughter."Oh a likely tale, all monks are plump any way, so they'd make a good meal. "

"No maisters 'tis all true"the landlord shuffled off to get some more ale for the group.

"Well that's the first rumour we've heard. Where there's one there will be others I shall write all this down for The Earl to peruse"

"And another thing maisters.Those scotch devils stole all the plate and relics from the Abbey and what they didn't carry away they just threw away" The landlord looked defiantly.disgusted at what he was saying. Thomas just nodded and continued to write in his little leather bound notebook.

Next morning on a bright early spring day Thomas and his group set off in the direction of St Albans. They had not gone but five miles when the sound of galloping hooves could be heard approaching from the distance. They dismounted and took up positions in the hedgerows on either side of the road. They notched their bows and waited. Around the corner a wild eyed horseman galloped. His clothes were torn and he was bereft of any weaponry. The look of terror in his eyes was hard to avoid. Thomas stepped out into the road when he was still one hundred paces away. He levelled his bow and shouted. "Stop in the name of the Earl." The rider pulled up on his reins and the lathered pony slithered to a stop.The man on its back slumped to the ground and gasped"Defeat, they massacred us.! St Albans a terrible defeat!." "What are you saying man? What defeat, I thought Warwick had weeks to prepare the town. There couldn't be a defeat." "There has been. The Lancastrians outflanked us and fought through the town killing us as they went. Warwick split his forces and that made it worse. Hundreds, nay thousands dead and now Queen Margaret rides on London."

What of Warwick and the army. ?"

Thay were still fighting when I fled"The man held his head low."there'll be more of us along this road soon, mark my words."

As if to signal agreement with this statement the sound of horses approaching could be heard and within minutes a further group of defeated fugitives were giving Thomas their version of the battle.It appeared that The Queen, Somerset and Northumberland had outwitted Warwick and that a decisive victory had been achieved by the Lancastrians. Even now Warwick was retreating westward with the remnants of his army.

Conferring with his men Thomas made the decision to return as soon as he could to Hereford to bring the terrible news to the Earl. Taking Diccon and Jon with him and leaving the pack animals with the others, they turned and spurred their horses westward.

In two days and nights of hard riding, dirty, thirsty and dishevelled they came in sight again of Hereford town walls.They were admitted to the solar where the Earl of March was poring over a parchment map.

"Thomas of Lingen"He said in a surprised voice "I did not expect to see you hence for some days" "Aye sir, I have to report some grave news. The Earl of Warwick has suffered a bad defeat at the town of St Albans and even now the Scots army and the queen are marching on London"

"Holy bleeding Christ on his cross, can that man do nothing right"The earl jumped up and paced back and forth angrily waving his arms in the air."I told him to fortify the town, put calthrops down and other fiendish devices to stop the scots.What happened Thomas. ?" "I understand Earl Warwick divided up his forces My lord and then he was outflanked and when they tried to fight off the scots they were too strong and clever in the streets of the town,and they killed many of his men." "An what now,where is the fool.?" I believe he comes westwards towards Hereford to meet you my lord."

"All to the good, not a moment to be lost, we shall march to join him and on to London.With the two armies and what men we can garner on the way we shall take on the Queen and defeat her "Shouting out orders and galvanising his staff and advisors the Earl sent the whole administration of the army into a flat spin as the movement of so many men was put in train with the minimum amount of time lost.The Marcher men amounting to some two thousand souls were eager and willing to follow Edward now they had vanquished Jasper Tudor and many of them were happy to follow at their own expense.The army kept gathering more and more men as it snaked its way eastwards towards a rendezvous with Earl Warwick. No matter how well behaved the army might be, the sheer number of men and materials, the horses, oxen,wagons and carts churned up the roads and emptied the countryside of food and forage.many soldiers went hungary,especially if they were in the rear of the column,for the early arrivals had the best of the foraging leaving empty barns and pigsties for the rest to stare at hungrily. Thomas rode out into the forest that fringed the road to Burford.He was determined to get some meat for his men even if it was only a few conies. He took Diccon and Jon with him. They rode north for three or four miles until they were well away from any sight or sound of the silver grey river of men that slowly moved across the English countryside.

They broke out of the trees above a glade overlooking some heathland and stopped. "A good enough place for a hart I think" said Thomas. "Lets split up and circle this open land and see what's to be had" He dismounted as did the other two and they tethered their horses and made their way quietly in different directions into the open heathland.Thomas had not crept more than two hundred yards when up ahead he heard a rustle in the long grass. Freezing he slowly raised his notched bow and there ahead of him stood a beautiful speciman of a fallow deer. A male stag with three to four years growth of antler.It was just cropping the grass unaware that its nemesis was creeping up on it.Thomas drew back his bow string. He deer lifted its head and looked warily in his direction.Thomas loosed. The arrow sped true and fast and embedded itself deep in the body of the beast behind its front shoulder. A killing shot through the heart. The animal gave a snort and blood ran from its nostrils. It shuddered and fell. Thomas ran over ready to give it the coup de grace with his dagger, but the animal was already dea.d.With a shout to his companions he proceeded to gut the beast and by the time the other two had run up the deer was trussed and ready to be taken back to camp. "He's a beauty right enough"said Diccon."But this must be Lord Oxford's land and what you done is out and out poaching. If they ever finds out you're for the noose. " Thomas laughed. "Bugger that,we're fighting a war here and we have to eat don't we.Tell you what, we'll butcher it here and take smaller bits back in our saddlebags. That way no one will know what we're carrying. " "Now that's a good idea worthy of a sergeant"laughed Diccon, and the three men proceeded to cut up the carcass into manageable bits which they stuffed bloody into their saddlebags.

Dusk was falling as they rode slowly back towards the Oxford road. The army was setting up camp where it could. Some tents and pavilions had been erected on river meadows whilst most of the men had improvised shelters from branches and bracken and anything else that came to hand. Lines of campfires sparkled along the edge of the roadside where improvised kitchens had been set up. Pottage and hedgerow stew and loaves of flat bread on offer. The smoke and smell of the cooking filled the air.

Thomas and his men withdrew slightly off the road into a small dell which seemed dry and set up a shelter. They found kindling and had a fire going before long. They slung a haunch of deer meat off a tripod and it twisted and turned and dripped its fat into the fire below,whilst the saliva inducing aroma filled their nostrils. Peter Longbreeches produced an earthenware crock of strong cider and presently they were as happy as men could reasonably be.

Chapter Nine

The army of the Earl of March and the remnants of that of the Earl of Warwick met at Burford and joined together. Swelled in number by levies and arrayed men from the countryside, the cumbersome snake of men and equipment slowly made its way in the direction of London. Edward Plantaganet knew only to well that the key to his success would lie in the fond embrace of the citizens and aldermen of that great city,and as the news of his victory at Mortimer's Cross proceeded him more and more of the inhabitants of the towns and villages on route came out to cheer him and some to join him.

Queen Margaret and her army of rampaging scots had in the meantime shown what the other side of the bitter coin of warfare could do to a reputation.Dissatisfied with their lot in the effete southern lands,her army of Scotsmen encumbered with their loot and still unwilling to cease from yet more pillaging was starting to leach away as more and more of them turned their faces back towards their harsh northern homelands.Plundering as they went.

Their repution for rape and pillage proceeded them and rumour and counter rumour flashed through the land causing the good burgers of towns thoughout southern England to shut their town gates to the Scots army.

So it was that when Margaret finally came in sight of London the terrible reputation of her army had caused the aldermen there to bar every single gate around the walled city and no amount of coershion or pleading would allow a single soldier entry into the city,and there was no food forthcoming.

Angry and frustrated she turned and marched northward taking her unruly hordes with her and the good citizens of London breathed a sigh of relief.

Edward Earl of March and the Earl of Warwick on the other hand were welcomed as conquering heroes, and where Margaret and the plundering Scots had been denied acess, they were welcomed with open arms and the joy of a victorious army.

Thomas and Dicon stopped their horses on a slight rise and looked down on the smokey haze beneath them. "By the Good Lord's bollocks, this looks like sin and wickardness" said Dicon."Look how big it is,must be all of forty thousand souls within those walls."

"Aye, you wouldn't want to get lost in amongst that lot that's for sure"said Thomas.

"Lets ride down and see what London has to offer"He put heels to his horse and trotted down the hill towards the city and the wall that surrounded it. The road was crammed with carts and wagons all trying for entry into the city before curfew came on them and the solid stream of pedestrians making their way towards the gate ahead of them. All along the city wall houses and lean to shelters had been built to take advantage of the solid walls and the mire and muck that the constant movement of people generated was thrown up onto the walls and the wagons and the clothes of the citizens.

They approached the gate through the walls, being funnelled forward with the constant tide of other citizens some on horseback but most on foot. The occasional cart slowed thing to such a degree that the slow moving onward thrust of the people was often halted by the cumbersome wooden sides of a cart squealing up against the stone walls of the archway through into the city.As Thomas passed the bored looking guard who was watching the onward procession he asked "What gate is this cully?"

"Don't you country cousins know nuffin"came back the reply"Why this be NewGate, this leads through to the most important building in town," "Oh yes, and what's that? " asked Dicon.

Why,the prison. You don't want to find yerself in there not no way. Cos you'll never get out"The guard cackled"perhaps only on Tyburn tree"

"Where is the prison?" "Oh don't you bear no mind to it cully,cos you'll smell it bye and bye" and he gave another unpleasant laugh.

As they moved inexorably forward past the gate and onto a cobbled street with an open gutter running down each side they could see and smell their first sights of London. The gutters were filled with a noxious semi liquid made up from dead small animals such as dogs cats and rats floating in the miasmic stench of human and animal urine. Pieces of discarded linen, bits of bone and other things too difficult to identify, passed slowly down the gutters only to be joined by yet more liquid of a horrid nature as householders emptied pots of piss out of upper windows with only the occasional shout of "gardez loo" to warn the passers by.Each time more effluent and waste hit the street below the smell given off was reinforced so much so that many of the citizens were holding linen cloths or pomanders stuffed with healing herbs to their noses and mouths. The carts and wagons passing one another in both directions only made matters worse and very soon the fetlocks of the horses were covered in the noxious mess that made up their first experience of the city.

Thomas had already lifted Orrid up onto his cupper to keep the hound safe and clean and the dog looked out with increasing interest as they moved deeper and deeper in to the streets of the town.

A raucous voice shouted out at them."hey fly bitten malt worm, can't your dog walk, aint he got no legs"The voice came from a fat florid young man holding a flagon of ale whilst he swigged from it.Each time he brought it to his lips his eyes crossed and then he seemed to have difficulty in focussing again.

Dicon lent across to Orrid. "See that bastard...., bite him!" Orrid gave a great snarl and bared his fangs. He balanced on Thomas 's saddle cupper and lunged in the direction of the youth. Taken completely by surprise the drunk fell backwards into the gutter where his fat body splashed the laughing onlookers with filth. The pair rode on.After some time they came to the end of Watling Street where it joined Billingsgate and ahead of them they could see what they took to be some thin houses rising into the sky as if they were suspended in mid air. Drawing closer they realised that enterprising Londoners utilising any space available to them had built houses on the bridge. Extending out by means of wooden frames over the water in order to make as much space as possible for their structures. These higgledy piggaldy dwellings lent this way and that some leaning so precariously that they looked ready to fall at any moment.Indeed as Thomas and Dicon started to cross the bridge there came a rending crack from ahead and tons of dust and debris was thrown into the air as one of the wooden houses started to collapse.Screams and shouts of horror came from the bridge and many people started to run back past Thomas and Dicon to escape the destruction.. "We must help" shouted Thomas and dismounting, tethering the horse and the dog he plunged into the melee ahead. It was seconds later that Dicon joined him.

They looked out onto a scene of utter devastation.A three story wooden house roofed in clay tiles had collapsed onto the bridge itself, whilst the wooden raft that supported the side of the house and pushed out across the river had completely disappeared into the turgid waters below leaving only a few timbers to float away.

Screams and shouts for help were coming from the ruins. A dishevelled man dressed in the most high quality velvet doublet and hose but covered from head to foot in a grey dust and with rivulets of blood flowing from a head wound staggered to wards Thomas. "my daughter is inside, prithee sir, help me." He croaked. Suddenly he collapsed and sitting on the roadway of the bridge started to sob uncontrollably. Thomas turned and ran forward to a pile of wreckage. The front door of the house had come to rest across some timbers and by a supreme effort of strength he and Dicon were able to pull it away from the other debris leaving a way into the house.They both tentatively edged forward. Creaks and groans were coming from the collapsed building and it seemed as if the rest of it might slide into the Thames at any moment.They walked through the hall past luxurious tapestries now sadly torn and damaged by the collapse An oak coffer with its lid torn off and two broken chairs were all the furniture that remained in this room.Ahead of them another door askance as one hinge remained keeping it upright.Thomas pushed his way through.Ahead of them they could see amongst theswirling dust the river Thames, for the whole side of the house had been sheered off and had disappeared into the water. Hanging from her arms with the loose material of her dress caught up on a splintered beam was a young girl of no more than ten summers. She was shocked into silence by her predicament. Hanging there over the open water and slowly twirling as the material of her robe started to tear.

"Hold on youngster, we'll have you out of there in a minute"Thomas lent across and holding on to Dicon's outstretched hand he was able to reach the child and lift her to safety.She burst into tears. "Is there anyone else in the house?" Thomas asked."Only my father, Mary had just gone out for milk when this happened, is he safe?" she looked round in terror.

"Aye he's safe, lets get you to him now," and scooping the young girl into his arms he walked gingerly back towards the bridge being careful not to disturb the collapsed building.

Back on the roadway a group of onlookers had gathered next to the wreckage.Some were comforting thegirl's father whilst others were pulling at the wreckage trying to clear a path across the bridge.

"This was a disaster waiting to happen" called a voice."Why only a sennight ago some men belonging to the Earl of Warwick came off their horses on account of the bad road here and tumbled down and were crushed to death"

Someone else chimed in "Aye,Alderman DeVeere banned metal wheeled carts from the bridge starting soon."He pointed down at the ruts in the roadway crossing the bridge. "Look at this road,its got more ruts in it than any road should rightly have,and building houses on the bridge should never be allowed" A chorous of approving sounds and nods camefrom the gaping onlookers. Thomas strode forward with the girl clinging to his neck.

"Sir, I have your daughter safe!"The merchant looked up through tear rimed eyes and his face lit up in relief as he saw that she was indeed safe.

"Tis a God given miracle"he stammered "Oh bless you in the name of the giving Lord.Isabella, are you hurt at all.?"

"Nay father, but my dress is torn, "she started to snivel. Laughter broke out at this which only made the girl cry louder.Aservant woman dressed in sombre black and white carrying a milk jug ran over to comfort her. "Hush my darling, you're safe now thanks to these good men. Stop your crying".Eventually she calmed the youngster and gave her over to the care of her father.He looked up at Thomas and Dicon.

"You are my saviours and I shall reward you. Have you a placeto stay in London?" "No Sir"

"Well you shall stay with us" "Not here I hope "smiled Thomas casting his hand at the wreckage.The man laughed "No indeed, this is just one of many houses I own in the town. I am Alderman Sir Richard Lee, and also mayor of London."He smiled and wiped some dust from his face."and this is my light and my love,my daughter Isabella. Come we shall repair to Bishopgate where I have a house that you can stay in."

Hailing a carriage for hire the alderman and his daughter and servant climbed in and set off for Bishopsgate closely followed on horseback by Thomas and Dicon. After crossing most of London they arrived at an area just this side of the Bishopsgate entrance to the city where substantial stone properties lined the street.At one of these the alderman and his party entered through a stout oaken door that was opened by a liveried servant and Thomas and Dicon were ushered into the splendour within. A large hallway panelled in old dark oak gleamed and shone from years of daily waxing. Likewise the flagged floor that had a polish on it in which you could see your face.On the walls bright tapestries depicting biblical stories and also a painting of the Alderman himself.Past this room and through another panelled oak door into a splendid airy room all of thirty feet long with two mullioned stone windows with small diagonal glass panes which overlooked a formal garden in which two men were hard at work cutting small privet hedges in the parterre.A gleaming refectory table with eight upright chairs placed around it held pride of place in this room. "Sit yourselves down and have some wine, I must go and clean up. My steward will see to your needs.Anything at all you want, just ask. We shall be back with you in minutes. "Sir Richard Lee bowed and he and his daughter left the room.A small thin man dressed in the alderman's livery came into the room."What can I get you sirs. ?we have Rhenish wine, the best in London, Gascon wine like wise. Good ale or any such. As my master bids so shall I bring what you require. "He bowed.

"Good ale for me " said Dicon rubbing his hands"And I'll havea goblet of Rhenish wine"said Thomas.

"A good choice" The alderman's voice said from the doorway "Bring me the same John and some sweetmeats and frangipani tarts."The servant bowed and left the room.The alderman had washed the dust from his face and hands and had changed into a beautiful ermine lined doublet with multicoloured hose and curly toed Italian shoes of such fashion that the curls were at least eighteen inches long and had to be kept supported from the floor by scarlet laces.

"Tell me my saviours. Who are you, where are you from and what brings you to our fair city"

Thomas started to tell the alderman their immmeadiate story, that they were soldiers of the Earl and they were following the army as it made its way to London.As soon as the name of the Earl of March was mentioned a huge smile came across the face of their host. "Why Edward Plantaganet,he and I have known one another since we were small boys.Although I am ten years his senior we played together with wood swords and hobby horses. It will be a great pleasure to meet him again and be able to tell him what a valuable service you have rendered me. Now Thomas and Dicon, I want you to treat this house as if it were your own. Any food you wish any drink you require you have only to ask,and I have sent for a draper and a mercer to completely recloth you, for I have every intention to show you about as my bounden saviours." He smiled and nodded."We shall meet again ere the curfew bell rings for supper.Until then, I have taken the liberty of preparing a bath for you so you may wash away the dust of your travels."

Thomas looked ruefully at Dicon, he himself had not had a bath since before Christmas tide, and he was not sure if Dicon had ever had one."My lord, what of my dog. He is very partial to me and I to him,dost know where he is ?" "Aye he is in the stables. Isabella has given him some meat, she has taken a shine to him I think"

"He is an easy hound to like,may he have a bath too?"Sir Richard laughed. "Of course he may and a silken collar for his neck" and chuckling to himself he left the two of them in the dining room.

"Bloody hell Thomas what's a bath ?" Thomas grinned"Oh you'll find out soon enough, and from your smell Its best you have one soon." "I don't smell, well not too much!"

"Like a rancid ox with overtones of the gutter, you do"Thomas took a swallow from his goblet and wiped the back of his hand across his mouth. "By God that's some good wine " he said appreciateivly. Just then into the room came two comely serving maids each one carrying a long handled scrubbing brush and with some lye soap in their other hand. They each gave a bob and the prettiest one said"your bath awaits sirs. Please follow us" and she proceeded to lead them through another door into a much smaller room in which were two wooden hip baths filled to the brim with steaming hot water

"If you'd take your clothes off sirs we can set about washing you. "She giggled."What?" exclaimed Dicon. Take my clothes off, why I don't take nothing off not even when I goes to bed. " "Come on you great Knighton Lummox, you're in the capital now, and must do as you're told." Thomas ordered him. He himself quickly disrobed and slipped into the wonderful scented water of the bathtub. Reluctantly Dicon followed suit and his white pallid muscled body was soon immersed in the water. Instantly a grey scum floated to the surface and as the serving girl scrubbed at his back with the long handled brush liberally covered in lye soap the water turned greyer and greyer.

"Oh,Lord"sighed Dicon, so this is a bath, I could get to like this once a year or so."Thomas laughed. "Don't make you feel too weak then" "No, lovely, and its warm" He tried to grab the comley wench who was scrubbing him but she laughed and deftly moved out of his way.

Thomas said to the girl washing him. "Fetch my dog in from the stables, he's due for a bath as well, can't be living in this luxury and smelling like a butcher's pit "

She disappeared and moments later came in leading a worried looking Orrid who was slowly wagging his tail. "Well, boy, tis time for a bath, "the dog cocked its head quizzically to one side and gave a plaintiff whine."Come on, in you get " and Thomas clicked his fingers.The dog put its paws up on the edge of the tub and reluctantly sniffed the steam."Come on now, tis not like the river I saved you from and think how nice you'll smell after, all the bitches round here will love you".He grabbed the dogs neck and pulled him into the tub. There was a splashing and a growling and a moment of general unease, but then Orrid realised he wasn't going to suffer the ignomy of being drowned out of hand and he submitted t.o a thorough scrubbing from the soap and brush.When both dog and master had finally rinsed the soap from themselves and the wenches had gone leaving coarse wool towels behind, the two men and the dog emerged from their tubs and dried and dressed in fresh linen undershirt s and hose, they looked around the room. On a table against the wall was a selection of new clothing.Some yellow and black hose, and a matching doublet trimmed with scarlet caught Thomas' eye, and upon pulling it on he realised that this was the very clothing that would make him stand out as a man about town. Some fine cordova leather slipper boots with excessively long points completed the ensemble.Dicon chose a more sombre blue and black stripped hose but the doublet he chose in a light green with orange tassels and a matching stand up collar did him no favours in the sartorial elegance stakes. However he paraded himself in front of a long cheval mirror that stood against one wall mincing back and forth with his hand on his hip like the latest arrived macaroni at court until Thomas could stand it no longer and broke down in gales of laughter

"Why, what's wrong,I thinks I looks like a young lamb's year, especially the coat, its beautiful." "More like a mutton chop dressed like a lamb's ear" laughed Thomas.

"well sod you, you'm like a bee or a wasp in that pair of tights.I should think any woman would flee in terror of getting stung." The two of them looked slightly sheepish as they caught sight of one another in the mirror.

"I think we'lll see if we can get some good straight forward livery sometime soon."

Meanwhile Orrid's fur had dried and a tuft upon his head was standing up like a tusk, giving him the appearance of some sort of fierce attack hound. The rest of his fur was soft and nicely curled and he skipped and barked like a cross between a puppy and a lamb.

"Ah, dog's happy then !" said Dicon laughing.

At that moment the door to the wash room opened and the alderman's steward came in. "My lord would see you in the solar when you are dressed."he bowed.

They followed him out of the room and up an elegant staircase to the first floor. Dark oak panelling lined the hallway off which several doors led. At the end of the hall way was a panelled oak door on which the steward knocked. "Enter" came the voice of the alderman. The three of them went in.

Thomas nearly fell over in shock, there in front of him sitting on a long cushioned bench under the mullioned window sat Elenor Countess of Hambye with her hands crossed demurely in her lap and a huge smile of welcome

on her beautiful face."Why Thomas, welcome, I did not
hope to see you so soon. "she smiled.

"My lady" Thomas stammered," nor I neither, how is
it you know Sir Richard.?"

"My late husband was a friend and Sir Richard was
his banker, we have been friends for a long time,and when
he told me of your heroics saving Isabella from what was
otherwise certain death,I could not stop myself from seeing
you.Anyway, when I visit London Sir Richard kindly lets
me stay in this house." "So you are staying here?" asked
Thomas.

"I am, and it shall be my base. For I can no longer
follow the army,for the Earl has told me he intends to
follow Queen Margaret northwards and finally put paid
to her."

"I'm glad you will be safe my lady, for my duty lies with
the Earl and I must follow him north."

Elenor looked at Dicon and Orrid. "Ho, who is this
gorgeously caparisoned coxcomb,? The dog I know tis
Orrid,but this....." she rolled her eyes in mock horror.

"Allow me to present my good friend and companion
Dicon of Knighton."

Dicon stepped forward and gave a clumsy bow.He
blushed, "My lady"

"Your doublet is a fine piece of work and the orange
tassels do set off your eyes so well" she giggled. Dicon
blushed a deeper red. He was totally enraptured by the
beauty of the countess and stood in front of her tongue
tied.

Sir Richard came forward. " I am told the Earl will
declare himself King, ere long maybe as soon as tomorrow,
he has called all aldermen to a meeting in Baynard's
Castleand I think he is going to ask for money to pursue

the war.We must do what we can to help him. The old order must never prevail again.If we lend him money to take the army north maybe a final battle can end this terrible war where one family fights another and no quarter is given on either side."

"Where is Baynard's Castle,sir? " asked Thomas.

"Further along the river and south of St Pauls. Edward has made his headquarters there.I feel we should go there and see what's a foot.I have to anyway as I am summoned for the meeting of aldermen.I have a boat moored at the London Bridge steps which can take us hence and it will save us much time, for the streets are full with citizens making their way there for they know momentous times are upon us."

The party consisting of seven or more persons including the Countess of Hambye, three servants, and a maid, and the alderman Thomas and Dicon set off in the direction of the river.They were mounted on sturdy ponies from the alderman's stables. Eloner and the maid riding side saddle. It took them some time to force their way through the crowded streets of the town,although they were heading south and most of the crowd was making its way westwards towards Baynard's Castle.At last they arrived at the steps leading down to the river close by the bridge. Many small boats,wherries and pleasure craft were tied up at these steps. The classic cry of "wagge wagge go we hence" rang out in the cold air. The regular fare was a penny to cross the river on a fine day in an open boat, but two pence to cross in foul weather in a tilt.The boat men where doing a fine trade rowing citizens west up river towards Baynard's Castle.Sir Richard's steward and two servants soon had his pleasure boat brought up to the landing stage. It was a fifteen to twenty foot long low slung craft painted in a dark blue with a canvas canopy to protect passengers from the weather. Thickly padded velvet covered seats in three rows filled the interior. The boat was equipped with a pair of oars on either side.Four boat men standing idle on the bank were hired to row and they climbed aboard.

There was almost a party atmosphere in the low fast boat as it set off up river. Neither Thomas or Dicon or Orrid for that matter had ever been on a small boat before and the pitching and rolling as the river waves smacked into the side of the vessel drenching them with the foul smelling river water had them grunting in disgust or laughing at the discomfort of the others.

"Sit still or we shall all be over" called Sir Richard"Then you'll have had two baths in one day.!"

Thomas grinned at Elenor"By the good lord, tis more interesting to travel this way than ever it is on horseback"she smiled back at him and wiped a smear of river water from her face. "Yes, but slightly more dangerous"She gave a cry as the boat lurched wildly as it struck a piece of river debris floating past.

Ahead of them they could see the huge square pile of stone that was Baynard's Castle.With two courts and numerous towers and with a large gateway in the middle of the side facing the river which lead to a bridge with two arches. At the foot of this bridge were several stout oak posts driven into the riverbed. Each of these posts had chains hanging off them and at least two had the bodies of drowned men hanging from them.

"Tis where,traitors and pirates are left to drown" said Sir Richard nonchalantly."They are left chained for two tides as a warning to others of their just fate." Elenor shuddered and buried her face into Thomas's doublet.By now their boat was waiting with several others to gain the shore.

Ribald remarks and shouted greetings were coming from the other boats as the occupants recognised one another. Most of the aldermen of London seemed to have chosen the boat method to arrive at their meeting.Eentually their boat tied up at the quay and they disembarked. A crowd of brightly dressed men and women excited and chattering to one another made their way across the bridge and into the crowded main hall of Baynard's Castle.

There were close on two hundred persons present in the huge hall which could hold many more, at one end on a raised dias stood a group of noblemen and important dignatries dressed in ermine trimmed robes and with their chains of office.A miasma of close packed humanity, sweat and excitement filled the room.At the other end of the hall common soldiers from the army and ordinary citizens were held back behind a line of pike staffed soldiers.The noise was huge as the crowd shouted their excitement over the already raucous clamour of the gathering.

On to the stage strodethe Earl of Warwick's brother, the chancellor George Neille.He raised both arms into the air, the noise hardly diminished. He nodded to a herald beside him who blew three notes on his horn. Slowly the sound in the great hall diminished until there was near quiet."My Lords ladies and citizens of London"a huge cheer greeted this "Who shall be the king of England and France?" There was silence for a split second, then came the hugeshout throughout the Hall. Ed...ward, Edward,Edward. Cheering rose to the hammerbeamed ceiling and the room shook with the stamping joy of the onlookers.

"Dost not ye want the King Henry?" shouted Neville with a certain misceviousness in his tone."Nay, nay. We want King Edward." The crowd screamed. Stamping and chanting his name, the levels of excitement in the hall were reaching fever pitch, when from a narrow doorway hardly visible behind the dias stepped the tall and well known figure of Edward Plantagenet,Earl of March. He raised both arms to the sky and the hall fell silent.

"You do me much honour by asking me to be your monarch, and I am proud and humbled before you to accept. "The crowd bellowed their approval "I shall endevour to be a just and pious king putting my trust in the Lord God Almighty and living in a way which shall give my subjects no cause for alarm."The hall was filled with an expectant dread as he continued. "However, any who are traitors, any who hold aliegance to the witch Margaret of Anjou or her followers shall suffer the full wrath of my anger.We shall send an army north to finish her, and to regain the plunder taken by her ravenging scots. Where it can be it shall be returned to its rightful owners."Here he looked around the hall. Some sceptical glances followed him but by and large the occupants had listened to his words and approved.

"Now, my good citizens, there is much to do. I have called a meeting of my aldermen to discuss many important matters not least where I am to get the silver to pursue the war against The Queen."His rueful smile was directed towards some of the aldermen and Genovese bankers who had gathered in one part of the hall. "Now go home and spread the good news and In two days time we shall give thanks in Westminster Abbey. "The king raised his hand in a royal benediction and after a few seconds disappeared back through the door behind the dias.

Thecrowd in the hall started to disperse and Thomas and Dicon and Elenor were left with a slightly deflated feeling of excitement.The crowd in the great hall of

Baynard's Castle started to disperse with much noise and excitement. Thomas looked across at the crowd of seething humanity and suddenly his eye fell on a familiar brown robed figure. "Father Ignatious! As I live and breath, what does that bastard want here."He turned to Dicon"Go round to the left and head him off, I'll take him from this side. Countess, stay here where you're safe."He set off at a run towards the brown robed figure who was swiftly moving through the crowd towards the door at the end of the hall.The priest had seen the two men and knew he must escape.

"Move, out of the way!, traitor!, stop that priest, he's a traitor to the king!"Shouted Thomas above the cacophony of sounds rising from the crowd.His voice only had the effect of startling the people immeadiately in front of him who gaped open mouthed at him.Thusting his way into the funnelling crowd at the doorway he finally burst through onto the bridge only to find that the priest had vanished.

"God's blood and bollocks" he swore.Then a hundred yards ahead and close to the moored boats on the river he saw the brown robes of the Cistercian.He had two companions with him and the three of them were boarding a small wherry which pushed off from the bank and made its way downstream with the tide.

Thomas ran down towards the boats and finding one with a boatman free shouted. "Double fare if you catch that wherry ahead." The boatman looked up avariciously and cast his eye out onto the river. "I dusn't think so maister, not on my own, now with Tom ere to row as well and a triple fare it might be done!"By now Dicon and Orrid had run up."The two of us and the dog and a triple fare if you catch him."

"Aye, my lord, climb in and we'll try for it. "They hardly had time to seat themselves in the stern of the boat before the powerful shoulder muscles of the boatmen were propelling the small vessel quickly through the water.Their adversaries had a good two hundred yards advantage over them, but the tide and the current were in their favour and as they swept down towards London Bridge Thomas could see that they had narrowed the gap by half.Their skiff shot through the middle arch and up ahead Thomas saw that the priest and his two companions were heading towards the north shore. "They're stopping, double your efforts for the King "He shouted. The boatment with sweat pouring down their faces and their shoulder muscles locked in a pumped up rhythmn gave their all, but by the time Thomas and Dicon and the dog got to the spot where the priest had landed there was no sight of the three men.

"Damn, damn, red hot needles up thy arse and yer bollocks cut off! They'm gone " said Dicon.

"Calm yourself, they can't have gone far. We'll try up this alleyway, it leads back towards Billingsgate I believe" and they set off towards the feotid smelling tunnel like track running with raw sewage that arrowed straight towards the city.As they entered the alley day seemed to turn to night for the overhanging buildings on either side had the effect of excluding almost all the light The earthen track with a gutter down one side was clogged with the stinking mass of odure that passed for cleanliness in this part of London. A dead dog vied with unspeakable filth as the ceaseless trickle of raw sewage flowed over their boots.They had not gone ten paces when from a dark and sinister doorway three figures launched themselves at the two men.Thomas felt a sharp pain in his ribs and the warm flow of blood across his skin as a dagger blow struck home. Dicon gave a great bellowing cry which was suddenly cut off short, as darkness claimed him and he slipped into unconciousness Thomas heard the whimpering whine of his dog in severe trouble and pain.

Chapter Ten

Thomas opened his eyes, he could see out of one, but the other was covered with a gause bandage. He was lying on a bed in a small room. He tried to move but a searing pain thrust through his ribs and he felt the warm flow of blood. He groaned. From a basket at the foot of the bed there came a whine and turning his head Thomas was able to see Orrid with his front paws bound in bandages and his fur shaved fom his neck where some rough stitches had been inserted to bind a nasty looking wound. Thomas gave another groan and tried to call out but the pitiful weak sound that was his voice barely carried across the room. The door opened and Elenor came in followed by a serving maid carrying a small table and a manservant with a cauldron of soup.

"Ah, Thomas, you are awake, I hoped you would wake this day." "Why what day is it, how long have I been here?"

"Two days now since we found you in that stinking alley" "What of Dicon? Is he well?"

Tears filled her eyes "Nay my love, Dicon will never walk again. He took such a wound to his left leg that the surgeons had to remove it and now he lies between life and death in the Hospice Infirmary. I visited him this morning but he is deep in a fever and the doctors say he has little chance of living." Thomas turned his head away as he felt the hot tears of despair flood up into his eyes.

"Did we kill Ignatious and the two other traitors? "No, I'm afraid there were only the two of you and the dog when Sir Richard's men arrived. All sign of your assailents were long gone." "How did you find us?" "Well, I could not stand and wait whilst you went off so I called Sir Richard's steward and he gathered some men together and we followed you down river. We

missed your landing place at first but then thanks to some very exhausted wherry men we were shown where you had disembarked.it was only a matter of time then before we discovered you and Dicon lying as if dead in that dreadful alley."She clasped his unbandaged hand to her face and kissed it. "Thedoctors say that your wounds are not life threatening though you will have a nasty scar upon your face where a dagger skimmed your eye."She grinned slyly at him, "it may make you even more handsome! "

"And the dog?"

"Oh, he's getting better all the time, he had a bad cut to his neck from a dagger and his paws were sorely treated but he eats well and in days he'll be recovered. "She pulled thecover from his shoulders better to see to his wound. "So,it still bleeds, you were lucky that the thrust missed every vital part.But it was deep, an inch either side and I would not be talking to you now." She dressed the wound with a fresh bandage"Now, try and eat some soup, it is the very best restorative"She ladled some into a bowl and helped him swallow the soup. It was delicious and Thomas eagerly gulped it down and had some more.The effort was as much as he could manage and he fell back across the bed with a long sigh."Now sleep and I shall visit you again this evening." He closed his eyes and fell into a deep dreamless slumber.

For two days more Thomas slept and woke and eat and slept and on the third day upon waking in the morning he realised that he was recovering. His wound hurt him especially when he coughed, but it no longer wept blood,and the cut on his face had a nice crusty scab across it. He swung his feet out of the bed and tried to stand. Everything spun around and he fell back.He was as weak as a kitten. Orrid gave a warning bark and the door to his room flew open and Elenor came in.

"Now now,my love, you cannot be getting up yet, you are not strong enough!"

"But I must, I have to visit Dicon and see how he is" "Nay,Dicon does well. His fever broke yesterday, and although he is weak he is resting and the doctors say he will recover for he is a strong man."

Thomas lay back on his bed."Tell me what has come to pass since I have lain here."

"Much has happened, The King as been proclaimed sovereign and a service of thankgiving has taken place in Westminster Abbey where it was confirmed.But the best news is that the aldermen and bankers have advanced him the huge sum of twelve thousand pounds to pursue the war against Margaret.He has already sent out Norfolk into Essex to gather forces and this Saturday 7th March the Earl of Warwick is due to start for the north. The king and his men leave later."

Thomas grinned. "So I still have time to go with him" Her face fell."I think not, you will not be well enough to go with him, you must stay here in London with me until you are better."Thomas shook his head. "Nay my lady, it is my duty to be with my king when he leaves for the north"

"We shall see!" and with an angry toss of her head she left his room. He tried to get up again and this time succeeded and he was able to walk over to the window and look out on the garden beneath. Orrid limped over to him and gave his bare feet a lick and looked up devotedly at him."Aye lad, we shall go with the king, no matter what my lady says"Orrid's tail thumped the floor and Thomas bent and ruffled the dogs head.

It was another day before Thomas was able to put on his clothes and walk to the Hospice infirmary to visit Dicon.The infirmary building was an ancient part of the London Chapter House and had served as a hospital for many years. The patients that were housed within its stone walls were the victims of accidents and mishaps that had befallen the citizens of London and they were looked after by nuns and lay people from the Chapter House. It took Thomas some time to locate Dicon for there were many unfortunates within. each lying on a pallet on the stone floor. Some of the more severly injured had small private rooms to lie in and it was in one of these that Thomas finally found his friend.

He was lying on his back on a rough pallet bed his good leg stretched out and the bloody bandaged stump of the wounded leg beside it. The leg had been amputated from just below the knee, and Thomas could see that the wound was enflamed and throbbing. Dicon had changed, his once striking dark hair now had streaks of silver in it and his formerly splendid strong body seemed diminished and shrunk.

"How are you my babba?" cried Thomas in compassion."Why tis Thomas. I do well I thank you, less a half leg. But I seen an old sailor boy once who stumped about on a wooden peg and I reckons I'll get

Roger Carpenter to make I one and then I'll be good as new! What of you though, it were a close run thing in that dark alley by all accounts. Those bastards just jumped us before we knew what hit us."

"Yes, well I have every intention of tracking them down, and when I do I'll kill that renegadepriest. I should have done it long ago, but I was afeared of killing a priest. Not now though. Now I know what he is capable of, the sooner the better for him to meet his maker."

"Aye, but you got to find 'ee first, he could be anywhere." "He's a spy for the Lancastrian faction and Queen Margaret, I should be surprised if he isn't still skulking in London somewhere.Remember it wasn't just him on his own that nearly had us, he's being helped alright.I shall keep my eyes open and I'll ask Sir Richard for his help. He owes us one." He turned back to his friend."Now my Knigton lummox you'm coming back to Sir Richard's. I'll send a cart for you. We can look after you better there than ever you'll be cared for here "He waved goodbye and set off back in the direction of Bishopsgate.

By the fall of night that day Dicon had been safely delivered back to the house in Bishopgate, and although the journey had taken it out of him and he had fallen into a deep slumber beforehe finally succumbed to sleep his joy at seeing faces he knew and especially that of the dog was obvious to all around him.Thomas felt sure that now he would recover quickly amongst friendly faces.

As the days progressed Thomas gained strength and his wounds healed.He was practising with a sword and trying his strength with his bow in the yard infront of the Alderman'shouse when a commotion of noise and the sound of hooves heralded the arrival of a messangerof some sort. A gorgeously dressed individual wearing the king's livery and wearing an extravagent orange and green turban wrapped round his head dismountd in the yard. "My man!" he called towards Thomas who was dressed only in a linen shirt and hose. "Summon sergeant Thomas Lingen at once.!"

"You're speaking to him coxcomb " The messenger's demenour changed somewhat and with a more deferential manner the man said.

"A summon's from the king, sir, he asks that you attend him as soon as you can at Baynard's Castle." "About what pray" said Thomas.

"I know not Sir, I am just a messenger"

"Go then I shall follow "The messenger bowed and mounting back up onto his horse walked away in the direction of the town.

Thomas went inside and finding his doublet and best hose and his cordova leather boots he donned them and leaving a message for Elenor and for Dicon he mounted one of the alderman's ponies and set off in the direction of the river.It took him some time to work his way westward to the castle for as usual the streets were thronged with people and upon each major thorough fare markets had been set up and traders were shouting their wares whilst their customers milled about like chickens. Eventually he came in sight of the vast stone pile that had become the king's headquarters.He crossed the defensive bridge and dismounted within the yard.There was a strong feeling of purpose in the air as liveried officials came in and out on missons for the king. Thomas strode through the entrance and into the main hall. A steward in the royal livery stepped forward and asked him his business. Upon being told his name and the nature of his business Thomas was ushered into an anteroom and told to wait.After five minutes a servant entered and beckonimg Thomas told him to follow as he led him deeper into the castle. Up a set of oaken stairs and along a dark corridor they went until the man knocked on a panelled door at the end.

"Enter" came the unmistakeable voice of the king. The servant opened the door and announced Thomas. Inside the room which was simply furnished with an oak table and four chairs stood the king and his closest military advisors.

"Ah, Thomas, how fare ye, are your wounds healing?" asked the king.

"Yes, Sire, I am much mended thank you"

"Sir Richard and the Countess have been regaling me with stories of your heroism. I thank you for your saving of my god daughter Isabella, she is a lovely girl and I would fain have any harm come to her " Thomas bowed.

The king looked at him. "You have done me much service in the past, and now I ask you to undertake another for me. Again I wish you to be a scurrier ahead of my army, gleaning information of the army of Queen Margaret, where it is, where it's going but more important I must have information of any traitorous dogs who are prepared to change sides against me. You may have to infiltrate your way into the viper's nest to find these things out. Do you think you can do it?"

Thomas nodded" Yes, Sire, I shall disguise myself as a priest as I did before "

The king smiled "Oh, Thomas, you give me great hope. Go now and prepare, for my army is starting for the north in two to three days hence and you should have a head start." Thomas bowed once more and backed out of the royal presence. He was slightly worried at the nature of his task for he didn't know who amongst the nobles and ruling elites owed aliegance to whom, but his native wit and intelligence had brought him this far and as he rode back towards Sir Richards house he mulled over in his mind several stratergies.

Back in the Bishopsgate house he gathered together the items hewould need for his subterfuge.A brown Cistercian habit and simple cord belt went into his saddlebag.along with the mail shirt Elenor had given him, 'sweet slayer' was oiled and new bow strings obtained,two sheaves of straight ash bodkin points and a roll of sheepskin and a blanket to sleep under joined them in the saddlebags.A leather roll of silver and gold coins and two rondel daggers completed the kit. He changed his clothing for something more homespun and not so fashionable and replaced his cordova leather boots with a more substantial pair suitable for the journey ahead.Then ordering Orrid to guard his equipment he went in search of Elenor and Dicon

He found them in Dicon's sick room. This was a small antechamber on the ground floor where the big man had been put when he came back from the Hospice on the understanding that he could be better cared for at ground leval than on the first floor, and so it had turned out. His natural strength and resilience had helped towards a remarkable recovery and his amputated stump had healed to such an extent that he was already getting about on a pair of crutches. Elenor would look in each day to see how he was progressing and had come to respect the huge bear of a man. Dicon for his part had fallen totally under her spell and looked forward to their daily meetings almost as a medicene to aid recovery.

"Good morning, my lady, good morning Dicon." Thomas smiled at the two people he loved most in the world."I have come to say goodbye,The king has asked me to do a task for him and I may be gone from here for some time" Elenor jumped up and ran over to him and threw her arms around his neck.

"Oh Thomas, you are hardly recovered from your wounds, and now you have to go again"tears came into her eyes."May God protect you and my love go with you."She clasped his arm and kissed him tenderly on the lips.

There was a disceet cough from Dicon."By the time you gets back, cully,I promise I'll be walking again!" "How's that them ?"

"See this?" Dicon held out a sheet of parchment upon which was a diagram drawn."The Countess has kindly drawn this for me and she has said she'll have it made by a carpenter. Tis my new leg!"

The drawing showed a single wooden stump with a cup attached to the top from which came two or three leather straps."Tis the wonder of the age " said Dicon.

"Tis Italian in design, they have been using such things for many years now"He smiled broadly."May God and the dog protect you where ever you go!"

Thomas grinned. "I'm to be a scurrier for the king, I go north maybe as far as Scotland,to gain an insight into the army and to root out traitors for his majesty."

"Please take care, my love, and keep the dog Orrid close by. I shall not worry if I know you have him with you.!"

Thomas grasped Dicon by the hand. Kissed the Countess lovingly once more and turned towards the door.

In the stable yard a strong dark pony had been readied for him and with his saddle bags slung across its back and Orrid on a lead beside him.They set off for the north.

From the house of the alderman at Bishopsgate to the open fields north of the city was a short journey once they had negotiated the thronging mass of the people entering and leaving the city via that gate. Once they were away with the smokey loom of the city behind them, Thomas untied Orrid from his lead, and the dog happily ran ahead and back to his master as Thomas sat contentedly on the broad back of his pony and let the early spring sunshine play on his face.The road surface beneath the pony's hooves was relatively sound being so close to the capital but the further north they went the more it deteriorated. By Hackney marshes the ground was so sodden that he had to lead the pony and it wasn't until the ground started to rise up towards the forest edge that he was able to mount up again. The hamlets and wayside hovels he passed looked as poor as the surrounding countryside and he had to ask directions several times. The dialect of the country folk being so hard to understand he found himself backtracking at one stage so that he passed the same villain who had directed him twice in an hour.

By the time his stomach told him it was time to eat he had covered less than ten miles in a northerly direction but more than twenty miles in useless detours and excursions.The road at this stage was cobbled and it seemed as if they would be coming onto a village of some size as some other travellers were converging on the same path.Thomas asked what village it was. Chingford came the reply and there ahead of him lay a group of low evil looking thatched hovels each with a midden beside their walls. The road passed through this uninspiring place and where it forked up ahead there stood a fingerpost and gibbet. On the fingerpost pointing north had been carved the word Cambridge. On the gibbet slowly turning in the breeze was the remains of a felon executed for crimes to terrible to mention and left to hang in decay as a warning to others.Thomas shuddered and his stomach growled in hunger.Taking the road in the direction of Cambridge the countryside became more open the forest trees were not so close to the road and soon he was trotting the pony over open heathland. Orrid ranging far ahead and then waiting as Thomas caught up.There was no sign of a tavern,so Thomas unslung his bow and decided to catch a meal for himself. Calling the dog to his side he dismounted and the two of them moved stealthily through the undergrowth of the heath. Thomas had seen a sandy well worn bank riddled with rabbit holes and he knew lunch could be had here if he was quick and quiet.Creeping downwind of the warren he could see a number of does with youngsters sunning themselves on the warm bank.

Lying on his back he drew back the bow cord and taking aim on a huge buck that was rubbing its ears in a contented manner he let fly.Fast and true the bodkin point pierced the body of the rabbit. So quietly was it done that the other coneys were not disturbed. Another buck loped forward and sniffed the warm body of its companion. A second bodkin point killed this one outright through its eye. Thomas ran forward and retrieved both rabbits and arrows and moving back to his pony he lead it off the road into a little dell where he tethered it. Searching the saddlebags for his tinder box he soon had a small fire going and having butchered the rabbits and skewered them on to twigs above the fire he settled back to wait for his dinner to cook. Orrid pounced on the offal from the rabbits and soon he too was lying with his paws crossed and his eyes barely open. The smell of cooking meat wafted up into the air.

In time the meat was cooked and man and dog made a good meal together. What was left,and it wasn't much,Thomas wrapped in a piece of linen, and stored it in the saddlebags..Calling the dog he mounted up and trotted out of the dell and back onto the roadway crossing the heath.heading northwards in the direction of Cambridge.

They had barely travelled five miles when up ahead they could see smoke rising into the still afternoon air. Billowing black and grey it looked like a major fire. Thomas spurred his pony on and they came up to the conflagration.A largish hovel turf roofed with a yard beside it was well ablaze as several women wailed and moaned and on the ground lay the bodies of two peasants.

"What has come to pass here?" he shouted.

"Scots plunderers sir" replied one of the women"May God strike them dead.They stopped to ask for directions and the next we knew Oswald and Larrikins were killed dead, but not before they stole what little we had." She threw her shawl up over her head and fell to the ground."Oh Lord have mercy on poor sinners what shall we do.?"

"Put the fire out" shouted Thomas and he tried to organise a bucket chain to douse the flames, but it was too late and the roof of the earth walled hovel fell in with a crash.The woman who had spoken to him before and seemed to be the leader of the group spoke up."Tis but five leagues to Waltham Abbey, we shall go there and ask for God's charity." Thomas nodded. "Aye, gather what you need and make your way there, I shall ride ahead and see if I can find who has done this to you"

He mounted his pony and without a backward glance, for to do so would have pricked his concience so much he would have had to stay,he put his heels to the horse and cantered off.

The road led through the royal hunting grounds of Waltham Forest and directly ahead nestling in a bend in the river stood the town of Waltham overshadowed by its Abbey, an imposing stone building housing Augustine monks and an all powerful Abbot who had a voice in the parliament of the kingdom.

Thomas dismounted and tethering the pony and tying his dog to the saddle he strode forward to the huge double doors that closed off the Abbey precinct. Normally such doors were open on the understanding that the church was there to help all citizens, but for some reason those of Waltham Abbey stood ominously shut. It didn't take him long to find out the reason.He knocked on the small wicket door that was set into the left hand main door.A voice shouted.

"Begone devil's spawn.God shall curse you and your kind! You agreed to leave us alone and now you return again to haunt us. Begone in the name of Christ.!"

"Holy Father"shouted Thomas through the oak.Who do you think I am. ?"

"Black hearted Scotsmen, raping and stealing. We have given you all we have!"

"No Father. I come from the king, I too seek the Scotsmen to discover their whereabouts. Can you help me?"

A small shutter in the top of the wicket door opened and a frightened eye peered out.. "You are not a Scotsman you say ?" came a querellous timid voice. "Nay Father, I come with news and for information."

"One moment my son" Thomas heard the sound of metal bolts being pushed back and the little gate opened. He stepped through. In the courtyard beyond several monks, maybe as many as twenty were gathered all looking schocked and worried.

Thomas bowed."Fear not brothers. I come from the king God be praised" "What king?" came a sonerous voice from a chair on a raised dias that he hadn't noticed at first "King Henry?"

"No my Lord Abbot, your rightful king and sovereign King Edward. Proclaimed as such days ago in Westminster Abbey!"

The Abbot rose from his chair. He lifted both arms into the air and said."Holy God be praised sing Hosannas to the angels in the heights. We have a new King. A good man, a man who can stop this senseless killing."He turned to one of his monks."Prepare a special f.east for all who can come.In honour of the new king. I must talk privately with his young man. "He beckoned Thomas over and the two of them went into a small anteroom just off the main cloister of the Abbey. The Abbot called for wine, when it arrived he motioned Thomas to sit and asked him to tell his story from the beginning.

Thomas started by talking about the women burnt out by the scots who were making their way to the Abbey. The Abbot interrupted to explain that it must have been these same plunderers who had tried to rob the Abbey only hours before.Four or five heavily armoured men at arms with full harness and accoutrements and with a pack horse across whose back was lying the body of a half dressed man with slashes and burns on his body. They had approached the Abbey, ridden in through the open gates and demanded food and shelter. Their dialect was so hard to understand and their demands so outrageous that it wasn't until one of the novices who came from Scotland was called to translate did the Abbot finally understand just what he was confronted with.The Abbot told them through his interpreter that men of war and especially men armoured and with their weapons drawn were not welcome and they should leave at once. The leader of the gang a truly insensitive black bearded giant laughed and lifting the front of his mail shirt he urinated on the Abbots shoes causing great humiliation and shame to come over the Abbot. The Scotsmen had stolen food and two holy relics from the Abbey. One was a piece of the true cross kept in a monstrance by the main door for pilgrims to kiss as they came in and the other was the knuckle bone of Harold Godwinson the founder of the Abbey and a much revered relic which the Abbot was devastated to have lost.

Thomas listened in silence to all this then asked. "How long ago did this take place."

"Sometime earlier today between matins and vespers" replied the Abbot.

"And how long had they been gone before I arrived.?"

"Just minutes, my son. We had but bolted the gates when we heard your banging. We assumed it was the scots returning." "So they cannot have gone far. With your permission My Lord abbot I shall go and find them." "What one man on his own?" the Abbot looked sceptical, even with God's blessing that's a strong task to undertake" "Nay my lord I have my dog Orrid, worth three men and 'sweet slayer'. I shall return for the feast, once I have put paid to these Scotsmen. " "Go in peace then my son, " the Abbot smiled wryly at Thomas as he blessed him.

Thomas ran out of the Abbey and putting heels to his horse galloped north.His instinct told him the scots would head north plundering as they went. Three miles from the Abbey and as dusk was falling amongst the forest

trees that fringed the road Thomas smelt woodsmoke.
Carefully tethering the pony and calling Orrid to his side,
he unslung his bow and notched an arrow to the bowstring.
Pushing another four bodkin points into a quiver across
his breast he silently infiltrated the woods in the direction
of the smell of the smoke.The new spring growth on the
trees and bushes hid his advance from a sentry who was
drinking from a flagon with his sallet off to aid the process.
The first bodkin point took the man in the eye socket and
without a sound he tumbled to the ground.Ahead in the
clearing where the other four scots had gathered a scene
from hell was being enacted.A wooden tripod cut from
forest branches had been suspended over a fire and slowly
revolving over it his bare feet only inches from the red
hot cinders a giant of a man more than a cubit taller than
Thomas who measured as tall as his bow stave. No sound
came from this giant although tears were rolling down his
burnt and slashed cheeks. Thomas notched his bow and
as swiftly as he was able fired more by instinct than aim
and four bodkin points sped towards their targets. Each
one a credit to the arrow maker sped on its way and buried
itself deep into the bodies of the unharnessed Scotsmen.
Running into the glade,he slashed through the rope that
held the tortured man up over the fire. He fell forward
onto the cinders. Thomas rolled him to one side. Then
with his rondel he turned to finish off the torturers. There
was no need.One scot was sitting on his backside with an
arrow protudin g straight through from front to back whilst
his blood pumped out onto the ground. Orrid had another
cornered and was savaging his neck, but the bodkin point
had already done for the man. Theother two Scotsmen
were lying dead within the glade each one skewered by

the straight arrow shaft.Thomas approached the living Scotsman."Well Cully, what hope for you now.?"

"Shit on you fucking Englishman.... " blood spewed out from his mouth and he slumped forward.he was still just alive. Leaving him Thomas ran over to their victim. This giant of a man, tall and as wide as an oak looked greatfully at his saviour. Thomas cut his bonds, and gave him some of the water he carried in a leather flagon.The man gulped it down then tried to speak.Suddenly Thomas realised that he had no tongue, but that this was an old injury and had healed up many years before. The man gurgled at Thomas and made writing gestures. Thomas went to his saddlebags and pulled out a pen and a small bottle of ink. With a tiny piece of parchment he had been given by the king's steward before he left London. He gave all to the man who proceeded to write.

"My name is Billie, I lost the power of speech many years hence. I was taught to read and write by monks. Now I am your servant As the musselmen say, a life saved is a life gained. I am strong. Your dog has accepted me."

Thomas looked at the man and saw that Orrid was licking the burned feet of the giant.

Calling he dog away,he said "By God's strength, I have need of a companion Billie. I welcome you. First we bind your wounds then we return to the Abbey for food and a rest. "The giant grinned and nodded.

Rifling through he saddlebags of the Scotsmen he soon found a clean linen shirt with which he was able to bind up the worst of Billies injuries and in the process discovered the stolen relics and a large quantity of gold and silver coins. Dividing the gold from the silver he repacked the saddlebags and with Billies help, for the giant had made a quick recovery, they repacked the harness of thescots for they were worth several pounds each. Choosing the strongest looking horse for the giant he helped him into the saddle and gathering the reins of the pack horses together they set off in the direction of the Abbey.Full night had fallen by the time they were able to bang upon the wicket gate in the double doors which Thomas noticed were now permanently closed.It took some time before they were admitted, but once the huge double doors swung open and the cavalcade came into the cloister yard, they were welcomed. Even more so when Thomas returned the stolen relics to the Abbot.His eyes filled with tears and he fell to his knees and gave thanks to God.

"A service of thanksgiving shall take place tomorrow to remember the wondrous thing that has taken place here, but now, the feast that I called for can commence." He clapped his hands and two novice monks appeared with basins and towels and started to wash Thomas and Billie. They subjected with a good grace and as soon as that was over they were ushered through into the Abbey refectory where the brothers were gathered at the long lines of the rectory tables. Other tables had been placed at right angles and these were filled with the local peoples of Waltham who had been summoned to the feast.Bowls of fruit were placed in front of each half dozen or so guests and when every one had taken a piece, dishes of pottage werebrought in these were consumed with relish and the level of conversation became deafening A huge fish from the abbey pond stuffed with forcemeat and capers was placed on the table, as soon as it was carved up and placed on the trenchers before each half dozen feasters,another fish appeared until each of the brothers and the common people had a portion. Thomas and Billie were ushered forward to the top table where the abbot and the prior, the sub prior the cellerer and other leading abbey officials welcomed them.

"Sit down my sons and enjoy God's bounty" the abbot smiled at them. Wine was poured into leather goblets and a never ending sieries of dishes of food was brought to the tables by a stream of sweating novices, who would eat later. Maeanwhile at a lectern set up under the refectory window, passages from the bible were read aloud to aid digestion. Thomas helped himself to a dish of coddled pigeon, pickled cabbage and mashed turnips. He noticed that Billie had piled his tr encher high with slices of beef, slices of pork and some juicy swan topped off with cabbage and turnip. Both men set too with a vengance neither having eaten a good meal for some time.Bakemeat pies and lighter tarts followed and then cheese from the district and candied fruits all washed down with Hippocras wine.

By the time the sweating novices had carried away the last remove, Thomas and Billie were in a state of extreme heat and fullness.Both of them had broken out into a sweat and their stomachs were distended with the good fare. The Abbot rose to his feet and called for silence. Eventually the hall fell quiet

"It is with great joy that I give thanks today for three things that God has seen fit to bless this holy church with. Firstly I thank him for the gift of a new king, a man so righteous that we may have utter faith in his doing the Godly thing for us sinners. Secondly, I give thanks to these two noble souls "Here he indicated Thomas and Billie" who have today retuned to the Abbey the Holy relics that were so foully snatched away. God in his holiness be praised. Thirdly I give thanks for this excellent and wonderous feast given us by God and prepared by the cellerer and his unstinting novice brothers."The Abbot smiled and sat down. The refectory erupted into cheers and the stamping of feet,the banging of table tops with the general good humour of the brothers after such a feast.

The Abbot turned to Thomas."My son, any guests who arrive for the night here are usually accommodated in the novice's dormitory. However for special guests and noble men we have some private chambers just off the cloisters, and I have ordered that two such rooms should be prepared for you and your companion."

Thomas smiled his greatful thanks. He had not relished the thought of being woken at 2 a.m when the monks arose to take part in the first service of the day.In private rooms both he and Billie could get some restorative sleep.he could see that the giant was having trouble keeping his eyes open and he himself felt stuffed full with the bounty of the meal, and all he wanted was to sleep and sleep. He thanked the Abbot and the senior monks for their hospitality and the two of them were escorted to their stone walled rooms just off the cloisters.

The ringing of the matins bell brought Thomas awake with a start and lying on the horse hair paliasse he luxuriated in the feeling of well being.There came a knock on his door. "Enter" Billie came in carrying a basin of hot water. He placed it beside the bed and taking a stylus from his pocket proceeded to write.'Good morning Thomas, I have come to shave you'

"How are your wounds Billie, are you feeling better at all.? "

'Much recovered and fit to start my new life as your servant'

"Thomas laughed. "Not my servant Billie, my companion and friend I hope."

Tears came into the big man's eyes,and he scuffed them away.

"Whence came you upon the tablet and stylus?" asked Thomas.

Billie wrote.' From the librarian. When he knew I was dumb, he gave it to me as a gift'

"Well we have much to do today, we must get you some clothing and boots also some decent weapons might not come amiss, because where we are going and what we may be called upon to do may warrant it "The big man nodded and made shaving gestures towards Thomas. So sitting on a stool in the morning sun he allowed the giant to shave his face.

They made their way to the refectory where a late breakfast of bread and pottage was still available to them and after breaking their fast they wandered through the Abbey grounds and out into the town of Waltham. Waltham had been granted a licence to hold a market in the previous century and the bustle and activity in the main square was evidence of the thriving economy that had grown up around the town.They stopped at a cobblers stall and Thomas asked for a pair of sturdy boots to fit Billies feet. The cobbler took a look at the size of the man and shook his head. "Nay, maister, nothing to fit he, mind I can make a pair by tomorrow if the gentleman wishes. Two groats, and they'll never let the water in." The deal was struck and the cobbler drew the shape of Billie's foot onto a piece of leather. "Tis all I needs, call back to this stall tomorrow and they shall be done." The two of them wandered off along the myriad stalls of the market. One in particular held their attention. Selling Hose, doublets, brigandines and all manner of garments made from sheepskin. Coats, waistcoats, leggings and other garments.

Again there was nothing ready on the stall which would have fit Billie, but Thomas insisted he was measurd up for a bright multicoloured pair of hose. A brigandine and a sheepskin waistcoat and leggings.Promising to return the next day and having left a penny as a deposit of his good will the two men repaired to the nearest tavern where Thomas ordered two tankards of best ale.

"Tell me Billie, how come you have no tounge.?"

Billie pulled the wax tablet to him smoothed the surface with his thumb and started to write.'When I was a child, I lived across the sea in Hibernia.Pirates from the south raided our village and I was captured.I was only about six summers old but big for my age and mouthy.They did not like it and the overseer cut my tounge out.'He smoothed the wax tablet again.

'Later, they sold me to the galleys and I spent some years at the oars..Eventually I escaped and found myself in the monestry at Perpignan.The monks looked after me and taught me to read and write.'

Thomas shook his head in amasement. "Well, your story is one it is hard to believe, how come you were the prisioner of those Scotsmen.?

Billie smiled ruefully and wrote.'my fault entirely. I was walking north enjoying the sunlight when the next thing I know I'm slung across the back of a pony and trussed tighter than a virgin's bodice. ' Thomas laughed" Doesn't seem to have dented your sense of humour any way!"

Billie wrote'Not now, but at the time I felt I was done for and when they started to roast me and cut me I felt the depths of despair, so it was a wonder and a miracle when you saved me. Thank you.'

"Twas nothing, you would have done the same. "

The giant smiled and nodded.

Thomas took a last swig of his ale and said. "We will look now for weapons, have you ever used a bow? Billie shook his head. "Well that can come later. I think we will pay the blacksmith a visit."He threw some copper coins on the table and they set off in the direction of the smithy. A single story open fronted building with a heaped open furnace which was kept at red heat by the action of a muscular servant to the smith on the huge bellows, whilst the craftsman himself struck the anvil with his hammers.

"Good morrow Smith" Thomas shouted above the bellows of the forge."What daggers and weaponry have you to sell?" The smith looked up. He wiped his huge ham like hands on a piece of stained linen and came over to them.

"Why,maisters, tis my stock in trade, what do you desire, I have rondels, short swords, battle hammers and axes, come into my shed and look at the goods. "He led them into a shed with a door, inside hanging from the walls were a variety of weapons as the smith had stated. Thomas's eye fell immeadiately on a 15 inch long rondel with a complicated spiral handle all made from one piece. Billie first picked up a battle hammer weighing two to three pounds with a sturdy head from which a spike protruded. Then replacing it on the wall went over to the battle axes. One in particular had caught his eye. It was a double headed axe, each blade more than a foot long with a stout ash handle that made it a good cubit in length. He hefted it in his hand and swung it against a log of wood that lay on the floor. With a satisfying clunk the log split in two.

"By God's bollocks and cock, he's a strong un!" snorted the smith. Most of em who pick that up can't hardly lift it let alone heft it. "He shook his head in amusement.Thomas called. "How much for the rondel, the battle axe and the battle hammer.?"A look of avaricious greed briefly flashed across the face of the blacksmith. "Why your honour, I could never sell the three things for less than twenty shillings." Thomas turned away in disgust. "Well I'd give you ten for the three. "Nay maister. A poor man has to make a living like. Fifteen shillings and the'm yours.

"Only if you make me a iron studded coller for my dog. Then Fifteen it is."The smith looked down at Orrid who was basking in the sun. "You'd have to provide the leather."Thomas nodded. The smith spat on his hand and held it out in the universal gesture of a commercial transaction finalised.

"Bring the leather to the forge today, and by the morrow you shall have your dog's coller.Thomas and Billie nodded and turned away back towards the market.At a stall selling leather worked goods Thomas bought for a penny a handsome piece of red leather thick enough to make a coller and had the stall owner fix a strong buckle to it for a further farthing,then with the purchase complete returned to the smithy and left the leather piece in the hands of the smith.

Billie was writing on his tablet.'How much shall I owe you for the weapons and the clothes?'

"Nothing,that's all courtesy of the Scotsmen. Think of it as payment for their torture of you.They had a bag of gold and silver with them which became ours when they departed this life.And so we'll enjoy spending it.Also you better try on a sallet and a mail shirt,see if any fit you, I doubt it but those northerners were big men. We may have to have something made, but that can be done later"

They made their way back to the Abbey precinct just in time to participate in the frugal evening meal that was being served to the monks.

Another night's restorative sleep on the horse hair mattresses invigorated them and by dawn the next day, having checked out their horses and taken their farewell of the Abbot and his monks they were heading to the market to pick up their ordered goods.At the cobblers Billie tried on his new boots and nodded delightedly. He wrote ',they feel like gloves for the feet.' Thomas smiled

"Let's hope the clothes are as good." Indeed they proved to be and by the time Billie was arrayed in his new finery and strutting about the market place with Orrid barking and prancing around him a huge crowd of interested onlookers had gathered.News of their exploits had flashed through the town and as the pair set off to the smithy a huge cheer rose up from the crowd.Both men turned and gave elaborate bows.

The smith had their new weapons oiled and polished and ready in a leather harness which Billie slung across his shoulder. Then the smith produced the new dog coller. It was a work of art. Inset into the leather but not protruding through the other side so that it might rub he had fashioned alternate iron spikes and studs.

Thomas called the dog over."Here boy, time you got beautified!" At first the dog was slightly suspicious of this new weight about his neck, but when each of the humans had complimented him on the beauty of his new neckware he seemed to relish it and his head came up and he gave a satisfied bark.

Back at the stable yard of the Abbey Thomas and Billie mounted their horses and leading the pack animals and with Orrid in his new coller they started north with the good wishes of the brothers ringing in their ears.

Chapter Eleven

An uneventful journey of two days brought them to the outskirts of Cambridge. Built around a bend in the river the town had prospered over the years being a centre for the import by water of salt and rushes and in the latter days a fair each fortnight had generated more wealth. Once some colleges had been established and a class of student from all parts of the kingom had established it as a centre of learning, the town was destined to take its place in history. The streets were peopled by many different monks from the religious orders in the town. Benadictines, Dominicans and Cisterians. The ordinary citizenswere a mixture of peasants from the surrounding countryside and market traders intersperced with students, some in the sombre clothing of the legal profession, more in the gaudy appareal that set them apart from the other citizens.

Billie pulled his tablet over and wrote on it."In Perpignon, I lived with the Benadictines maybe they can help us. " Thomas nodded."Let's find a tavern and discuss this" A black and white wood framed building with a covered entrance into a yard and with a bright painted sign 'The old Three Bells' hanging over the street was right in front of them. They rode into the yard and ostlers hurried up to take care of their mounts and packhorses.

In the welcoming main room of the tavern ensconced by the fire and with a tankard of the landlord's best ale in front of them they mulled over their next moves. Thomas said."I want to track down the renagade Cistercian Ignatous, and then kill him.Also we need to discover where the Queen and her army are.That is more important as that is our commission from the king.

Billie nodded and wrote. 'Maybe the Benadictines would know if there was a renegade Cistercian anywhere near!'Anyway they may have information concerning the army of the Queen'

"Good thinking, let us away to their Abbey and ask them." The two men finished their ale and Thomas threw a few copper coins on the table and they left. In the yard one of the ostlers was only too happy to give them directions to the Benadictine Abbey.Leaving their horses in the care of the tavern ostlers they took the dog and walked through the streets.

They had gone a few hundred yards when ahead of them two monks came down the street towards them. Each looked the worse for drink and they were conversing in latin as they came level one turned to the other and dismissively said" Two giants lead by a dwarfish dog".

Billie pulled his tablet free and wrote on it. 'These pigs have just insulted us'

Thomas stopped in his tracks. "What did you say brothers?"

The fatter of the two looked owlishly at Thomas. "Why nothing my son, I was merely commenting upon the weather. "

Billie wrote.'They said, two giants lead by a dwarfish dog.!'

Thomas grinned and forced his arm up around the throat of the fat monk. "I don't mind you calling me and my friend giants, for that is what we are. But how dare you insult my dog!I have two things to say to you. First. Manet semper merda modo variat altitudo(the shit remains the same only the depth differs). And secondly, prefer et obdura dolor hic tibi proderit olim. "(be patient and tough some day this pain will be useful to you)

He pulled his fist back and struck the stomach of the fattest monk who doubled up on the road with a sound like a deflating balloon.

Billie was wheezing with laughter and his huge shoulder shook he wrote.'Didn't know you had any latin!'

"Yes, when the monks taught me to read and write it was in latin, So I can get by, " The two monks had scurried off one helping the other with out a backward look.

The two of them set off to look for a Benadictine monk in order to get information as to where the nearest monastry might be. Eventually they came across one standing. on a bridge contemplating the rushing waters below.

Thomas approached him"Good day Brother, can you help us?"

"If I can, with God's help."

We wish to know where is the nearest Benadictine house to this town for we need certain information and also to ask the abbot some questions. "

The monk looked askance at them. "Why should two obvious soldiers and giants come to that with an attack dog be interested in our order. ?"Billie wrote on his tablet and passed it over to the monk. ' I lived for some years with the Benidictines in Abbye de St Martin Du Canigou. And I wish to rewew acquaintances. "

150

The monk nodded "I know that abbey well. What single thing sets it apart from other Benidictine abbeys?"Thomas looked at the monk."Do you doubt us Brother? you sound suspicious?"

"Nay it is but a natural curiosity to see if you know the Abbey."

Billie wrote. 'There is an extremely long and arduous walk up to the abbey as it is perched on the top of some rocks in the Pyrenees."

The monk smiled "Yes my son, many times have I blessed the lord for that walk!"Billie wrote' me too father !' He then scribbled on the tablet and handed it over.Is the Abbee Jonathan de la Tour still in charge?'

"No my son, he passed to sit on God's right hand last year.Now the new Abbee is Father Jean Paul Souterne who was the cellerer. "

Billie wrote 'I know Father Jean Paul well, it was he who taught me all I know about cooking. But tell me Father Jonathan must have been aged, for when I was there he was in his eighties. ' The monk smiled" Yes, God be praised we think Father Jonathan was ninety four years old when he passed away."

Thomas said. " mayhap Father you can help us with our questions. We work for King Edward and he asks that any one who can help in his Godly mission to free the country of war should do so" The monk nodded." I shall help to the best of my knowledge. You asked where was the nearest Benidictine House to here, and it is some way away Denny Abbey in Essex. More than a day's ride., so what else do you need to know." Thomas looked the monk square in the eye. First, have you seen or heard of any renegade Cistercian monk going by the name of Father Ignatious. He is about my height wiry and strong and with a scar running the length of his face, he may be with two companions. Rough looking soldier types."

The monk shook his head "

"No one of that description my son"

Thomas looked at him again "Secondly, have you any information as to the whereabouts of the army of Queen Margaret and the Scots.?"

"I can be more helpful there I believe. A supplicant came to see me yesterday. He lives twenty leagues to the north and his farm was attacked by Scots on Friday, three days ago. They stole his cattle, burnt his home and foully raped his wife and two small daughters.I hear stories like this all the ime. I surmise that the army is moving back north from whence it came and the soldiers are making the best of their journey through foreign territory.One such tale was of a woman suspended above a fire whilst her feet roasted, her husband looking on until he revealed where their pitiful horde of silver coins was hidden. "Billie shuddered. "Then the two of them put to the sword. "He shook his head sadly. " Man's iniquities to his fellows!"

"And you say this was twenty leagues hence and due north only three days ago. Good, we are catching up with them. Thank you Father, we will go now and try and find more to tell the king.I thank you from the bottom of my heart.It will not be long before the righteous wrath of the Lord strikes these brigands from the north, for the army of the king is due through here before long." Thomas waved goodbye and the two of them returned to their horses and mounted up.Within half an hour of their conversation with the monk they were clattering over the bridge that spanned the Cam.

The further north they rode the more evidence of the plundering of the scots army came to light. First it was the occasional wayside hovel burnt to the ground and with the pitiful remains of the inhabitants lying beside their homes. The nearer they got to Peterborough the more and greater the devestation. Whole village and hamlets had been raised to the ground and the few inhabitants left alive were wandering the roads in a shocked condition reminding Thomas of scenes he had witnessed during the plague years. No matter how hard they rode the next atrocity was perpetuated before they could come upon it,As they traversed the road between Peterborough and Stamford they came on a small village Wansford where a narrow wooden bridge crossed the River Wan. As they rode up the road towards it they could see a crowd of people standing just on the outskirts of the village. Smoke grey and black was billowing into the air above one of the houses. Thomas pulled up. Calling his dog he dismounted and approached the group. "What happens here maisters?"He inquired."Those bastard Scots are burning our village and demanding a shilling to cross the Wan out of harm's way on a bridge that was never a toll bridge." "How many of them" demanded Thomas.

""Close on twenty we think. Too many to take on, and they are harnessed" The man who spoke looked like a farrier with strong muscles and a leather apron into which were stuffed the tools of his trade. "Dost thee have any weapons?"Thomas asked. "Nay, only our tools, hammers,scythes and a bill'ook or two. ""They'll do,we need to surprise them, and as they are cowards we can attack them and have every chance of seeing them off. "The villagers looked dubious."I shall creep up to them and loose my bow at the ones holding the bridge and Billie here will come at them from downwind of the bridge, you villagers walk towards them as if you would pay the toll, act subservient, pretend you want to pay and are frightened of them. When you are level with them bring out your hammers and your bill hooks and beat them down. Fight firewith fire, tis the omly way! Now are we ready.?"The villagers nodded dubiously looking sacredly one to the other.Thomas set off in the direction of the village and the bridge.The main street of thevillage looked as if it had been looted haphazardly by vandals. Bolts of cloth,dead dogs, items of food and furniture lay scattered along its length. Suddenly a piercing female scream lashed the air. Thomas started to run in the direction of the sound. He was aware of Billies' huge shape lithly loping along beside him. The giant had pulled his battle axe out of its sling and he hefted it in one hand whilst in the other he held the wicked battle hammer with the three inch steel spike on top of it. He was grinning with the excitement of battle in his eye. Orrid loped along side. His fangs bared and a continuous growl issuing from his throat.

Thomas unslung his bow and notched a string. Placing an arrow he slowed slightly as he took in the scene ahead of him.Lying on her back on the ground and surrouned by Scots lay a village girl she had been stripped of her clothes and she turned this way and that trying to protect her honour and her virginity. A continuous high pitched scream came from her mouth.The Scots soldiers were laughing and making lewd suggestions in their outrageous accents. Thomas drew back his bow and let fly.he took another arrow and did the same. By the time he had shoot three of the Scots they were only just waking to the fact that they were being attacked, but by now Billie was amongst them. Towering over them and swinging his weapons in a dance of death he cut off the head of one, slashed through the arm of another and split a third from neck to crotch with the fearsome battle axe. All this done in relative silence. It was not for the want of a war cry, just that the mechanism was missing. Six scots killed and the rest running as if the hounds of hell were after them. At the bridge a huge man in a steel suit of armour was standing with his sword resting with its point downwards as if to take on all comers. However he had removed his sallet the better to see and gain some air. Thomas loosed an arrow that spun through the air and into the throat of the Scotsman. A gout of arterial blood came pumping out of his neck as he sank to the floor with a stangled gurgle. His mate at the other end of the bridge turned and ran, and a bodkin point buried itself hard through his brigandine. By now the howling mass of the villagers brandishing their working tools had run up onto the bridge and emboldened by Thomas's and Billies example they set too with a will slashing and hammering down their opponents until there only remained one surviour who begged for mercy from the enraged crew. Thomas pulled the man free and tried to interrogate him. He was bloodied on the head and arms and a look of terror in his eyes had caused him to piss his hose.

"Get up you bastard" Thomas shouted at him "How many innocent women and children have you murdered.?"

The man looked terrified. He was only a youngster perhaps sixteen or seventeen and snot smeared his bloodied face as he snivelled in fear.

"I dinna dae nuthin' He shivered and trembled before Thomas.

"Pull yourself together man, we're not going to kill you" Some one in the background muttered 'not yet'.

The man wiped his sleeve across his face and tried to square his shoulders. With a certain degree of bravado he said "I am Ewan of the Black Iles' son. Robert the Long.I can be held for ransom. My father would willingly pay." "So how come you are with this bunch of heathen bastards?" said Thomas.

"My father thought I would get more experience riding with them than with him. He is with the Queen. In Pontefract."

Thomas nodded."If you swear your solemn oath on this holy book not to try and escape,and give me your parole you shall accompany us until I can get a message to your father setting your ransome. What think you is your worth?"

Robert looked relieved and tried to grin, but the severe visages of the villagers surrounding him deterred him somewhat.

"I shall swear my oath and my father would pay 700 ducats of silver for me I believe."

"Hmm, " mused Thomas. Billie passed him his tablet upon which he had written.'This is the son of one of the top ten families in Scotland. His father is an Earl. Ask for one thousand ducats.'

Thomas looked at Robert, "One thousand ducats I think." Robert nodded.

Thomas held out a copy of the prayer of St Antony that the Abbot of Waltham Abbey had given him and said to the lad." Repeat after me.

I, Robert the Long, son of Ewan of the Black Iles do solemny swear upon pain of death and everlasting damnation to neither escape or run from my captors or to bear weapons against them, and this is my parole before God in his heaven."

The boy repeated the words and started to take of his armour and to divest himself of his dagger.

The villagers looked on with anger one said. "We should kill ee now, look what they done to Lucy!" There was a murmer of agreement from the others but Thomas raised his hand. "No friends, enough killing for one day, He has made a promise and now he rides with us."

One villager picked up a rock and threw it hard at Robert.It struck him a glancing blow on the shoulder. "Enough" shouted Thomas."If it wasn't for Billie and I coming on you like this, you'd still be timidly waiting at the edge of the village while yet more of your women would have been raped and killed. Is that not so.?" The villagers looked sheepish and the rock thrower hung his head.

"Now we leave. You have your village back and your lives, God go with you". He and Billie with Robert between then turned and made their way back to the horses.On route they retrievd Robert's horse, a stunning looking black stallion with silver bit and silver embossed reins. "By Christ I think your ransom should be ten thousand ducats, not one!" Robert shook his head. "Nay Sir, my brother was held by Northumberland for six years because my father judged the ransom too high.Eventually Northumberland refused to keep him any longer and killed him. "Thomas looked shocked."How could a father do such a thing to his son?"

"My father could, he is a ruthless man. But now I am his only son and heir to the Black Isle. Have no fear he will pay. "He better" muttered Thomas as they mounted up and set off in the direction of Pontefract.

Billie was writing something. He passed his tablet over to Thomas. 'When we pass through a town I would like to buy some supplies to make Greek Fire.'

Thomas looked at him. "Greek fire!, I thought the secret of that had been lost for hundreds of years!"

'You're right' wrote Billie' but I know a recipe for liquid flames that stick to flesh. I got it from the Turkomen of Aleppo.They had been experimenting for years to find the right mixture and eventually they got it nearly right'

"What do you mean nearly right "said Thomas dubiously.

Billie smiled dangerously and wrote'It tends to set itself off spontaneously for no reason whatsoever. Specially if it is shaken too much'

"Oh, that'sgood, you want us to carry this dangerous stuff around the north of England.!

'No, not at all,we keep the ingredients separate until we need to mix it up. They are all quite inert.' Thomas shook his head. "so what do you need.?"

Billie wrote a list on his tablet.. 'Pitch, sulpher, quick lime, bitumen, saltpetre,naptha and some glass or pottery containers to put it in. We make what the Italians call 'grenados'. Mix it in the right strengths and you have a formidable weapon.'

"How do you set it off?"

Billielooked him in the eye and wrote,' there is a wax wick that pokes into the grenado held there by a stopper. You light it and throw it and when the container breaks, the fire spills out and it is impossible to put it out.Water wont serve and beating with cloths only makes it worse. It sticks to any surface it falls on.Wood, stone, flesh. All is consumed.' He put his tablet away and digging in his heels trotted his horse level with that of Robert. Thomas came up beside him and the three of them went forward together..

Thomas looked at the young Scotsman."Tell meRobert the Long, why is it you fight for the Lancastrian cause? Robert thought for a moment then said. "Why, I believe I

fight for the true king. King Henry and his wife Margaret."
"But what of my true king Edward?"

"He is not ordained by God, he is an upstart and a traitor!"

"Better that than a weak and vacillating monarch run by his foreign wife. And I believe King Edward is ordained by God, he has a direct inheritance to the throne through his family tree."

"Yes, but we are Scots and a proud race.and we fight for whosoever asks us." Billie waved his tablet at them. Thomas read out.' For whosoever pays the most!'

Robert looked sheepish. "Aye, that too, well, a bodies got to make a living."

Billie wrote some more.'

That's so typical of you northern races, not satisfied with raiding across the border as reivers and killing the good English citizens of the north country and stealing their cattle you have to come down in an army and fight us for money!'Thomas broke into the conversation. "So, if King Edward offered you more you'd switch sides and fight for him. ?"

Robert nodded. "Like enough, we only owe alliegance to our own clans. If someone offers more gold and plunder we'll go along with that. " "So that's why you were mixed up in that disgusting display at the village the other day is it ?"

Robert hung his head in shame. "No.I was one against many, I had tried to make them stop their torture, but they were too strong for me and ridiculed me and threatened me and they all want plunder. They are sick of this England and want to get back home. It is March now and if they haven't started planting by May, they will have lost the harvest for this year. So most of them are making their way north into Scotland, stealing what they can.They feel that the plunder is a legitimate perk for the trouble of coming south".Thomas broke in"Why do they bother then if its so much trouble to come over the border into England woulln't it be better if they stayed their side of the border.

Billie scribbled furiously on his tablet and passed it over to Thomas who read it aloud.' Have you seen Scotland?, it's a god forsaken place where it rains every day and when it stops you can't see anything for the mist. On the rare sunny days you get eaten alive by midges and all the inhabitants have to eat is porridge. I'd give it a miss if I was you. Its so poor up there the people can't afford trousers and the men go round in skirtles.No wonder they come steaming over the border any chance they get.' He laughed. Robert looked absolutely incensed and his face coloured up a nasty crimson.

"That's a damn lie, and if you weren't twice my size I'd challenge you to a combat." 'Any time my little Scottish lordling' wrote Billie laughing.

Thomas held his hand up. "Enough now, we have ground to cover if we're to find the Queen's army."He put spurs to his horses flanks and the three of them cantered northwards.

Chapter Twelve

One hundred miles south in the comfort and warmth of the Alderman's house in Bishopsgate Diccon was taking his first tentative step on the new wooden leg that a local carpenter had fashioned for him. It was a solid piece of ash shaped like a human leg with a calf muscle and a hinged ankle piece and a foot. The top of the limb had a smooth cup shaped top and three straps led off the topOne that went round his shoulder and two that tied the limb securely in place to his existing leg. The countess had helpd him put the wood limb on the first two times he had worn it and so determined was he to master walking again that he spent too long with the thing in place and his stump became inflamed and raw. Once that had settled down he was able to wear the limb for shorter period and soon started to overcome the difficulty of the wooden leg. The articulated ankle, although a wonder of its kind and a work of art in its own right proved to be impossible to use safely and comfortably and soon Diccon had removed it in favour of a plain brass ferrule which enabled him to stump around the hall across the flagstones. The Countess laughed and said that he'd never be able to creep up on any one again. Diccon blessed God that he could creep at all, and as March progressed his mastery of the leg went with it.

King Edward had sent The Earl of Norfolk into East Anglia to raise forces from the landed gentry and nobles of that district and early in March the Earl of Warwick set off north with a large body of men to raise levies from his own lands.

The king's footmen largely made up of soldiers and followers from the Marches and Kent and containing many men whom Diccon and Thomas knew left the capital some 10000 strong under the leadership of Lord Fauconberg. The King himself led his own troops out of the city through Bishopsgate on the 13th March having admonished his troops under pain of death that there was to be no rape or pillage of any sort by his troops and that any sacrilage was prohibited. The king had managed to aquire large loans of money from the aldermen and bankers of London and was able to pay for fodder and lodgings on his march north and as importantly to pay the troops. The king marched north to St Albans gaining more soldiers as he went. Meanwhile the Earl of Warwick was recruiting in Coventry where he managed to capture the Bastard of Exeter who had been responsible for the execution of his father after the battle of Wakefield. Exeter received short shrift and was beheaded. In response to this event Covertry offered 80 militia and the promise of a further 40. Warwick then marched on Lichfield and then towards Doncaster hoping to meet with The king and Fauconberg.

However the king had headed instead for Nottingham where he had been told King Henry was staying. His army reached the outskirts of the town on the 22nd March only to find that the enemy had gone north and crossed the Aire into Yorkshire.

Thomas,Billie and their earstwhile scots captive Robert rode throug h the main town gates into the thriving town of Nottingham.Cobbled streets wended backward throughThe part known as the shambles where animals were slaughtered for the meat trade. The streets were slick with animal blood and offal lay in profusion against the walls of the houses that lined this part of the town.Thomas was in desperate need of some information concerning the Queen's army and as they rode deeper into the town the castle started to assume larger and larger proportions ahead of them. Some soldiers supposedly guarding the entrance to the castle but in fact playing dice before the raised portcullis caught his eye.

"Good day to you,where is your sergeant?"

"Who wants to know?" the belligerant voice of a poorly dressed soldier the worse for wear with a flagon of cider in his hand came back at him.

"An officer of the King" this was said with such authority that the glazed eye of the soldier focused on Thomas's face and the man hurriedly got to his feet.

"Err,the serjeant Sir,? Why I do believe he is in the inner gatehouse." "Show me!"

Yes Sir, " thoroughly cowed the man put down his flagon and led the trio through the portcullis gates and into the inner court yard of the castle. To the left past the murder hole above in the workings of the portcullis ratchets was a small stone built room which was a part of the castle walls.

"in 'ere I think he be sir" the soldier knuckled his forelock and scuttled back to his companions.

The sound of female laughter came from the room and as Thomas pushed open the door a roar of disaproval came out at him.

"By Christ's holy bollocks,how many times must I tell you to knock before coming in!"

In the room itself a man was sitting on a chair in a state of undress his female companion of the lower sort, a penny a trick harlot from the sordid side of town was sitting on his lap,lying on his lap would be more accurate and engaging in an act of sexual depravity. The man was drunk and he caressed the back of the woman's head as he groaned in excitement.He saw Thomas and jerked upright as if an arrow had srtuck him.

Thomas shouted at him. " Is this the way you guard the King's castle?. Get rid of her and make yourself decent! I need information from you and right quick."

The man sobered up and throwing off the woman he adjusted his clothing nd some seconds later was standing to attention in front of Thomas. "So, you are the sergeant here are you?" The man nodded miserably.

"Well if you don't want me to make sure you'rebroken down to a common foot soldier again,you better give me as much information as I require."The man nodded.

"First what news of Queen Margaret and the scots"

The man shook his head as he thought. "Why Sir, they left from Nottingham days ago heading north I believe.I hear tell they crossed into Yorkshire by way of the bridge over the Aire.

"How many days hence.?"

The man scratched his chin. "Must be three days now. Tis Friday today and they was gone on St Margarets feast day which was Tuesday of this week." "How many?"

Why I can't say Sir, there was an aweful lot of em,they camped below the city walls and madea right mess. Could have been ten thousand of 'em.

"And any news of the King's army."

"I did hear from my coz who has a farm out on theGrantham road that the Kings army was a good league or two away from Grantham, but that was again three days ago." By now the sergeant had quite sobered up and he was happy to do his duty and report correctly all he knew.He didn't seem too worried as to who it was asking the questions just that he wasn't demoted. "Thank you sergeant, we'll say no more about what we saw earlier, but if the King's army does arrive here in the next days, there'll be a reckoning with you and your men unless you sharpen them up!"

The Sergeant pulled at his forelock and hurried off to see to the slack castle guard.

Thomas turned to his companions."We'll find a tavern and stay here till the king arrives, I feel it will be tomorrow or the next day, and we can report to him then." They mounted up and rode further into the town. At a large brick built tavern with the sign of the White Swan hanging from its yard entrance they stopped and gave their horses and pack animals into the care of the tavern ostlers.

Stepping intothe warmth and shelter of the alehouse they were immediately overcome by the welcome and friendly atmosphere of this old inn.

"Why this is better" said Thomas. A pleasant rotund bald man in a leather apron bustled up. "How can I help Sirs" he said.

."We would like a room for three and the dog, for two nights maybe more"

The land lord cast his eye over the size of Billie and then down to Orrid who was gently wagging his tail on the floor.

"Oh lord, that's no problem. Our very best room you shall have, there be two beds in it, the giant here can have the one and you other two gentlemen can share the other. Dog can sleep on the floor. Two groats for two nights and you removes your own night soil. " Thomas stuck out his hand. The landlord spat on his and they slappd the bargain down together.

"Now Sirs what of food,we have Nottinham pie or a nice piece of venison or mutton chops I believe."

Thomas cast his eye over to his friends."well I'll try the Nottiham pie. What's in that." "Oh 'tis loverly,Sir it's a raised pie with goose, rabbit, swan and pigeon in an ale sauce with roast parsnips and braised swede." Thomas felt the saliva run in his mouth. The other two nodded ferociously.

"So three Nottinham pies it is?"The land lord rubbed his hands together. " and ale to drink?" They nodded. Thomas said. " can you find a nice bone for the dog to chew on?" "Oh yes sir, I expect I can" and he bustled off into his kitchen. The three of them choose a table next to the fire and sat down.Billie sighed with relief. He pulled his tablet out and wrote on it.

'I would like to find an apothacaries to get my supplies after we have eaten, I need a speaker to come with me.' Thomas nodded. "We'll all go, there may be some weight to carry back."

A serving wench carrying three tankards of ale approached and placed them on the table. She bobbed prettily and said in a broad accent." Nottinham pie will be a minute or two sirs.But the dog's bone is ready.!"

"Bring it on lass " said Thomas," I expect he's as hungry as we are. "She returned minutes latter with a huge ham hock bone from which shreds of meat still adheared and placed it on the floor in front of Orrid. The dog looked round in a slightly surprised way as I all his birthdays had come at once and then gave a small warning growl and set too, his tail thumping the ground as he eat.

The Nottinham pies were next to arrive and for some time there was no other sound than the contented munching of meat pies and the slurping of ale. At last replete, their appetites assauged by the good food the three of them lent back against the bench back and took stock.

Robert was the first to speak. "I dinna know if there was a meal to beat that!"

"What, not in the whole of Scotland!?" Thomas mocked him.

"Not in the whole of the world I don't suppose" said the scotsman good humoredly.Billie smiled and nodded and rubbed his belly.

Thomas looked at Orrid. The dog was possesively guarding his bone which had shrunk in size with his eyes half open and his front paws crossed over the remnants.

"Right my jolly lads, lets away to the apothacary.Billie write down what you need and the weights and we'll take a stroll into the town. " He asked directions from the landlord who told them there was an apothacary and barber surgeon in an alley way just of the main market place in There and Back again Lane. They made their way through the crowded streets being jostled by the inhabitants and stepping carefully to avoid the odure and filth underfoot. At last they saw the entrance to the alley way and left the main market square for the darker envirions of the side street. About fifty yards in there was a bowed glass window front, filthy with grime fronting a small premises with a solid oak door. The door stood open. To one side a skeleton of a human hung from a stand to the other a stuffed aligator. The three of them squeezed into the shop. The smell inside was a combination of exotic spices rotting meat and human sweat. Every inch of space was taken up with jars on shelves strange things hung from hooks in the ceiling,and from behind a counter only just visible under piles of parchment a thin and wispey voice rose up into the air.A pair of bright gimlet eyes peered out from under a black felt hat.

"What do you need kind sirs, I got everything. For the lovelorn, for the sick or the blind the halt and the lame. I pulls teeth and I cuts hair I ma kes spells and I writes letters, you name it I does it Isiah the apothacary at your service.

Thomas looked at Billie's list. "We need the following. Shulpher one pound in weight.,pitch.two pounds in weight. nitre and saltpetre half a pound each in weight,quick lime naptha and resin half a pound of each. Can you supply us. ?The apothacary cackled "Oh you're making Black Fire, of course I can.Sit yourselves down and I'll get what you need. "He shouted into the back "Simon, Simon,get your lazy bones out here and see to these customers." A hulking youth in a linen apron and with a white skull cap came through from the depths of the shop.He nodded respectfully at the trio and noted their order."This is all in stock bar the saltpetre. Since theQueen's army was here all stocks of saltpetre are gone, all used up in gunpowder making. Don't know where or when there'll be more." Billie was writing on his tablet,he passed it over to Thomas. 'We can get saltpetre fom the walls of old stables, it grows on the bricks, we don't need to get it here from him!'Thomas nodded his thanks. " please get the rest of the items we want and tell me how much is all comes to.Also we will need a dozen of glass or earthenware jars no bigger than a pint in sizewiith stoppers and some wax candles. " Simon knuckled his head and lumbered off to fill the order. An hour later Simon and an apprentice apothacary set off for theWhite Swan with the purchases and upon the exchange of some silver the trio were walking back to their lodgings when up ahead Thomas saw the brown hood of a familiar habit. "Ignateous"he breathed" see that monk in the brown, I want a word with him, split up and try and head him off. He is dangerous so watch yourselves. " "Dangerous!" scoffed Robert"How dangerous can a monk be for God's sake!"

"Well this one is and a killer to boot so be careful."The three men circled round the crowd of market goers and each approached the monk from a different direction.The cisterian was unaware that he was being followed and he stopped occasionally at various stalls in the market once to buy a pasty the next time to peruse some silk cloth.Robert was the first to get close. He put out his hand and touched the monk on the shoulder. "Father, my master has need of a few words with you." The monk swung round furiously, his scarred face grimacing horribly. "Who dares touch a holy man of God?" he cried.Then he saw Thomas and Billie and the dog coming for him and grabbing Robert by his shirt snapped a dagger under the young scotsman's throat."He dies Lingen, one step nearer and he dies.!"

Thomas and Billie backed off and the monk hustled the frightened scotsman away into the crowd and they were lost from sight.

"Shit and blood of Christ " shouted Thomas. Billie urgently pulled his sleeve and pointed upward onto the ramparts of the castle where a brown robe was disapearing through a small door. They ran towards the walls and climbing some steps came out onto the fighting platform that ran around the top of the castle battlements. Every ten paces or so doors led off into the interior of the walls enabling troops and defenders to come and go as they pleased. Thomas Knew these doors led into a maze of different passageways and that their quarry would be hard to trace. He plunged through the one he had seen Ignatious enter and just inside the door lying against the wall and pale as pale lay Robert, a crimson stain colouring the front of his shirt. "You were right "He gasped'he's dangerous, the holy bastard just stabbed me" and his eyes rolled upwards and his head fell to one side. Billie knelt down and put his finger against his pulse. Seconds later he shook his head. Thomas felt tears start in his eyes. Although Robert was the enemy over the short time they had known him they had come to like him and value him as one of their own, now he was gone, stabbed to death by a renegade priest who kept getting the better of them.

"By the Holy Christ I shall have that priest " he breathed. This is the third time he's bested me. I should have put paid to him all those weeks ago when first we met."

Billie urgently wrote on his tablet. 'We know he's here in the city and that means he has accomplacs, we must be vigilant.' Thomas nodded.More writing. Let's away to the tavern where we can talk it over, work out what's best to be done. '

They returned to the White Swan in a sombre mood each feeling the loss of the young scotsman. Once there they found that the apothacary and his apprentice had delivered their purchases which had been neatly stowed in a small stable next to the ostlers room.They went into the ale house and sat at a table.The pretty young serving wench came over. "What maisters only the pair of you, what's happened to the tall one?" She looked into their eyes and immeaiately understood what had happened. Clutching her apron to her mouth she ran from the room sobbing.

"Well Robert affected her anyway" said Thomas. Billie wrote.' He affected us all, I liked the lad even though he was a Scot'. Thomas nodded.

"Now what are we to do about this priest. He's a danger. First to us as he knows us but mainly to the king, for he is a spy in the pay of the Queen and as such we must stop him "

'But how, one man dressed as a monk in a large town like this we'll only find him by chance'Billie scrawled on his tablet.

" Could we set a trap?"

'Yes but how'"One where I was the bait"

'What have you in mind?' wrote the giant.

"Well, we find out where the Cistercians have their house, chances are he'll be nearby and then I approach asking for him.You stay hidden, when he comes out for me, as he will, for he would love to finish me, you fall on him and kill him."

Billie looked dubious.'A simple plan, often the best, but I'm loath to kill a priest!'

"Why such scruples,you've never been so particular in the past." 'For certain, brother, but then I've never entertained killing a priest before.'

"Well think of this one as an out and out fake. He's a killer and a torturer and his only claim to priesthood is his brown habit, and that he could have got anywhere."Bilie smiled and wrote. 'You've convinced me, when do you want to do this. ' "Tonight, late when all are abed." Thomas asked the land lord if he knew where the Cistercian friary was and he was given directions to a stone building and chapel nestling up against the city wall. It was some distance from the White Swan more than a mile and so they waited for the curfew bell and for night to fall before they set off through the streets.Although the curfew bell was tolled with evening regularity each night, only the most law abiding citizens paid it much heed. That is not to say that the streets teemed with people rather that the few who were out and about avoided the foot patrols who would pillory any one they caught out on the streets. Thomas and Billie slipped quietly through the filthy streets of the town trying to avoid the rubbish and human and animal dung that covered the cobbles. Difficult in the dark and before long their boots were covered in odure.At last they came to that part of the city walls that the landlord had directed them to and ahead they could see a sturdy oak door with a small sliding grill in it. Thomas whispered to Billie. " hide back here in the shadows, and no one shall see you with God's help, I'll try and intice him out. Once we have him alone, no qualms straight in with the daggers and put paid to him!" Billie nodded. Thomas approached the grill and knocked on it with the handle boss of his dagger.No reply. He rapped again, this time the grill slid to one side and a benign white bearded face framed in a hood of brown peered out. "Yes my son, what can I do for you"

"I have a message for Father Ignatious, Father. Most important that he recieves it from my hand " "Wait there, I shall see if he is in the Priory" the grill was pulled shut and silence descended.After a few moments back went the grill and this time there was a different monk on the other side."Who wants the Father and what is your business with him."

Thomas looked round furtively. "A message from the Queen to be given into the hand of the Father. Most important, we have come far to see him and there is no time to lose."

The grill slammed shut and there was the sound of a heavy key being turned in a lock and bolts being thrown back. Thomas losened his dagger from its sheath and held it behind his back. The heavy studded oak door swung back and three monks stepped out.Two of them Thomas did not know but the third was without doubt Father Ignateous. Thomas sprang forward and stabbed upward with his dagger, he felt it slip off the steel of a mail shirt but penetrateinstead the upper arm of the priest. He gave a frightened bellow and in turn pulled a battle hammer from under his robe swinging it with ferocious skill at the head of his assailant. Billie leapt from the shadows flailing his twin headed battle axe and cleaving the head off one of the monks who was now wielding a double handed sword pulled from under his robe.The melee rolled up and down the road outside the priory. Ignateous stabbing down with his dagger just caught Thomas on the forearm leaving a long bleeding gash. In return Thomas was able to parry the thrust and plunge his dagger into the thigh of the priest. Billie was coverd in blood, not his own as he finished off the second monk who fell back reveiling under his habit a mail shirt with the emblem of the Queen on it.

From the precint outside Thomas heard the sound of running mailed feet. A street patrol alerted by the sounds of the fight.He shouted at Billie.

"Leave it now, street patrol. Run!" The two off them turned and sprinted into the darkness of an alley way splashing their way through the filth beneath them they ran full tilt back in the direction of the tavern. Some twenty minutes latter panting and filthy with blood and shit,they came out onto the street of the White Swan.Entering the ale house they tried o avoid any contact with the landlord as they made it up the stairs to their room. Once inside Thomas slumped in a chair whilst Billie tended to the dagger gash on his forearm.The giant was covered in blood, his brigandine dripping and his hose ruined with it. But he was grinning. He pulled his tablet out and wrote. ' A good little fight'. Thomas said " Shame we didn't kill that bastard though.I got in two good blows, one to his am and one through the leg. With luck they'll go poisionous and the bastard 'll die in the agony he deserves."

Orrid who had been left behind to guard their possessions whined fitfully as he smelt the blood dripping from Thomas and Billie.The two men changed their clothes and did their best to remove some of the evidence of their fight and then turned in for the night.

The dawn came up over Nottingham in that odious way of an late winter revenge on the people. Thin grey clouds laced with a cutting freezing rain and the occasional gust of a notherly that blew the leaves and muck across the market square. The stall holders setting up their stalls for the day's market were huddled in their sheepskin jackets against the cold and with reluctance were starting the days trading. Some enterprising trader had set up a brazier selling roast chestnuts and beside it some mulled wine was bubbling away.This was the most thriving part of the market and the gossip going the rounds centred heavily on the terrible events of the night before.

"And God forbid, two priests killed and another so badly wounded he's not expected to live."

"What devils could do that?"

"Aye devil's right, one was a giant, taller than Nottinham steeple and 'tother only had one eye, right in the centre of his head" The market trader who had given this opinion shuddered and crossed himself. Another trader took up the tale. "I heard tell from the sergeant of the patrol what found the priests that those devils were scotch and they wanted in to the piory to steal the gold and the holy relics" He crossed himself. "Tis this terrible war! When will it ever end?"

Another man dressed more finely than the rest with a coney fur coller and multi coloured hose said. "Well thewar's done us all some good. Think of the trade brought to the town by the armies. First Queen Margaret's, yes I know most of that trade was thieving from her soldiers, but now I hear King Edward is but a league away, and he has made a solemn declaration that all goods are to be paid for and there's to be no looting."

Another man laughed. "Oh aye, I'll believe it when I sees it." "Why Seth, who'd loot your stinking tanning pits any way? There was general laughter around the group.

In the White Swan Thomas and Billie had broken their fast with fresh baked bread and pottage and they were discussing the previous night's excitement.

Billie wrote on his tablet ' I hope none of those soldiers got a look at us, for none will believe those so called monks were soldiers in disguise.'

"You're right my friend, I think we should lay low today until the heat is off and maybe on the morrow the King will have arrived."

Billie nodded. He wrote.'I shall wash our bloody clothes and prepare the weapons and other such household chores'. Thomas laughed. "What house has chores like that ?" Billie laughed in turn,' Why the house of war, and I fear there are some battles ahead. The Queen cannot retreat forever into Scotland. She has to face us eventually.'

From the yard outside the tavern a loud noise of jingling harness and the shouts of male voices drifted up and through the open window of their room. Orrid gave a warning bark. Thomas quieted him and went to look at the disturbance. Below were several mounted and harnessed men in the livery of King Edward.milling about amongst the ostlers and giving orders.He called down.

"Hey cully art thou with the King.?" One of the riders looked up and lifting the lid of his sallet he shouted in delight.

"Why Thomas of Lingen, so this is where you've found a billet?".

Thomas could hardly believe his eyes, for before him and apparelled in the finest armour sitting on a strong looking bay mare was his earstwhile friend Dicon whom he had left behind in London recovering from an amputated leg.

"Dicon.....!" He cried in amazement. "What are you doing here.?"

"I am a scurrier for the king" Dicon announced proudly. "And what's more I hold the same rank as yourself now. Sergeant Dicon of Knighton so I don't need to bend the head or knuckle my forelock to you any more." Thomas laughed outright."Well you never did anyway you old toad. Tell me how has all this come about.?

Dicon shifted in his saddle and Thomas saw the fine ash stump that had replaced his leg. "Well, your lady The Countess helped me with a new wood leg and saw me through the pain of learning to use it, and one day whilst I was stumping around the garden at the alderman's house, who should arrive but the King himself.He remembered me, and was impressed by my progress with the leg and offered me a scurrier post and promotion to sergeant."He held his hands wide in supplication. "What could I do but accept?"

Thomas asked"So where is the King now,? I have vital information for him."

Dicon thought for a moment. " He should be here by sundown. He believes King Henry is staying in these parts somewhere and he seeks him out to give battle." "Nay Dicon, the Queen and King Henry are long gone from here they flee in the direction of Scotland with their army. It may be possible to bring them to battle, but not near here, further north I think. "

Dicon noddd. "Come down and share some ale with me. I have a letter for you from the countess" He dismounted being careful not to put too much weight onto his stump and went into the main room of the tavern.

Thomas Billie and Orrid were only minutes behind. The dog saw Dicon and whined and barked and pawed the ground and generally behaved like a puppy that had just found its milk mother.Dicon ruffled the dog's head. "Well I see all's well with the dog then?"

"Oh aye, good as gold he is. Dicon, may I present my good friend and companion Billie" he gave Dicon a quick resume of their adventures since they had first met. Dicon listened in silence then held out his hand and clasped that of the giant.

"Thank you for looking after this lummox Billie. I was main afeared that anything could have befallen him without me by his side.Now the three of us can cut a swathe through the king's enemies." He raised his tankard and took a long swig. Thomas did the same. "To the three of us " he exclaimed with a huge grin crossing his face. Orrid barked delightedly. Billie grinned

"You say you have a letter for me Dicon?" "Aye Thomas, from your lady, she was most insistant that I put it into your hand as soon as I saw you."

"Hand it over then" Dicon pulled an oblong packet tied with a ribbon from the depths of his brigandine and handed it to his friend. Thomas took the letter and undid the ribbon. Nestling inside between the folds of the parchment lay a silver chain with a beautifully wrought silver pendant hanging from it. The pendant was made up of the two letters E and T entwined together.Thomas felt a welling up of love for Eloner and pulled the parchment towards him and read it..

To my much beloved Thomas. I hope in God's mercy you are well, and that you sometimes think of me. I spend my time wishing I was a soldier so that I might be with you. I have helped your friend Dicon with his new leg and also with his harness, although he did insist on paying for most of the latter.! I am well and still living at the Alderman's house. I await your return in good health and by God's grace I hope we may be united again soon.Please accept this small token of my love for you and wear it always. Eloner.

Thomas folded the letter and put it in his bigandine. He placed the chain over his neck and it fell in place as if it had always lived there.Looking up with tears in his eyes he saw his companions were looking at him.

"She is well and sends me a gift."He sniffed. Orrid whined and pawed the ground.

Thomas said." Now we await the arrival of the king."

By sundown that day the first vanguard of the King's army started to arrive beneath the walls of Nottingham.All through that night they came, archers, foot soldiers, men at arms with their destriers and the carts and wagons that accompany any army. The flat land beneath the city walls was soon covered with the tents an d shelters of the troops whilst campfires glowed in the dark like fire flies. The camp followers women and children soon made themselves busy and Edward once again reiterated his edict that everything was to be paid for on pain of death.The merchants and market traders of the town smiled and rubbed their hands togrther at this trading bonanza.To one side of the makeshift camp a huge wagon park was established and just south of that a slaughter area where butchers both from the town and from the army were killing beef cattle and oxen to feed the men. By the morning of the first day some ten thousnd souls had arrived to swell the population of the city. An atmosphere of exciement akin to a major fair or festival pervaded the air as Thomas and his companions made their way towards the gates of the castle in order to gain an audience with the King.

An offical looking steward dressed in the King's livery was vetting the many supplicants that were streaming through the portcullis gate hoping to see the king and to be granted his favours. His eye fell on Thomas and slid away defensively. "You are ?" his arrogant manner bridled with the March man.

"Sergeant Thomas of Lingen to see the king on urgent business"The man instantly straightened up and his whole attitude changed.

"Yes sir, this way if you please" and he ushered Thomas and his friends through an oak studded door ino the castle keep. Inside another official looked at the first Steward. "This is the man the king specifically told me to watch out for, and to immediately admit him no matter what time he arrived,"

The second steward bowed. "Please follow me Sir" and he led the trio through the gloomy passage way into an inner living area where many nobles were gathered in a large meeting room with a high hammer beam ceiling painted with noble crests and gargoyle heads carved into it.At the far end bathed in the weak spring sunlight falling through the windows and raised upon a dias sat the King. he was surrouned by his top military advisors and the generals who would lead his army into battle.

The king looked worn and tired. He was gesticulating at a piece of parchment that was unrolled on the table in front of him.

"Well my Lord Warwick. Where is he, I was led to believe that Henry and his queen were staying here in Nottingham!"

Warwick shrugged "I know not Sire. Our last good information had their army here in Nottingham."

Thomas stepped through the throng and up to the dias. He bowed.

"Sire, if I may" The king looked up in surprise and a smile played across his face.

"Ah, the loyal Thomas of Lingen. Welcome Thomas, what news have you. ?"

Sire, The army of the Queen with King Henry was here, but some days ago maybe four or five. They have fled north trying to reach Scotland where they would fain disperse and we would have lost them for good.My best information is that they are near Pontefract.Also I believe that a fair proportion of the Scots would change sid esfor money. "

The king bellowed with laughter " By the holy blood of Christ. Some decent information for once. Thank you Thomas, you always were a good man. Those heathen scots "He shook his head in mock disbelief" Change sides for money will they,thank Christ then the good burghers of London loaned me so much to keep this war going. "My lords tomorrow we march on Pontefract He stood up, the lines in his face seemed to have eased and now the decision to move had been taken a lightness filled the room and an excitement filled the air.

Chapter Thirteen

Slowly the huge yorkist army started to unwind itself on the way north to Pontefract..The merchants and traders of Nottingham were loath to see this golden pot of money disapearing up the road. But some of the citizens breathed a sigh of relief at the depature of the hoard.There would always be a few die hards who hate change and ten thousand men camped under your walls portend change.

Scurriers and scouts had set off ahead of the main army some ten to twelve hours previously and now the main baggage train with the camp followers and the endless procession of oxen and beef cattle whipped on by their minders churned the road up until it was virtually impossible to walk on it.The high stepping destriers of the nobles beautifully caparisoned in bright colours and with their bits and reins a jingle gave an almost carnival air to the march.Most of the archers in the army were mounted on sturdy winter coated ponies but the common soldiers had to trudge muddily onwards with their few possesions and maybe a sleeping blanket thrown across their shoulders. Hour after hour the marching army passed the outer limits of the town of Nottingham and at times it seemed as if the procession would never cease.

Thomas, Dicon and Billie mounted upon their strongest horses and with Orrid riding on the crupper of Dicon's horse had been ordered north the night before to scout out the road to Pontefract.Now they rested by a small copse of trees just outside Pontefract.They had ridden through the night and most of the next day. They were hungry thirsty and tired and their scouting had reveiled very little in terms of any armies opposing the King's advance.Some monks leading a line of lepers with their wooden clacker boards wending thir way back to the leper house had shouted the message that the Queen was in York. This made sense as there was a large Lancastrian faction of lords and lands around that town. But sight of any soldiers they had not had.

Resting his arms on the leather saddle boss Thomas looked at his companions. They all looked worn out. Dust and grime from the journey caked their faces. Dicon was stroking Orrid's ears and Billie was writing furiously on his tablet. He passed it over to Thomas.'One of us should head back to the king and let him know there is no army oppposing him here that we can find.'

Thomas read it aloud and said."Yes, we'll draw straws and the other two can carry on. If indeed the Queen is at York we will surely come across some of her troops sooner or later." He took three pieces of dried grass and made one short and the other two the same length then holding them in his closed fist he offered them first to Billie and then to Dicon and took the last himself. A big grin came over Billie's face. He pointed to his chest and quickly wrote. 'tis me with the short straw. All to the good I can make up my greek fire grenado's when I get back to the king.'

Thomas said. "Billie, I shall write a quick report for the king, then you return the way we've come. You should meet the army north of Nottingham, I have heard that Warwick is hoping to meet with the king at Doncaster, I think that's where you'll find him. "

Billie nodded.He wrote 'I shall see you both in due course with God's luck and look after the dog!'He ruffled Orrid's head and the dog looked up at him and whined. Thomas finished writing his quick report on a piece of parchment and handed it to the mute giant. "God's speed dear friend, and we will meet again before long." Dicon held out his hand which Billie clasped and with a wave he turned his horse's head south and cantered away in search of the King.

"We'd best find a place to stay, there must be an inn on this road!"They walked their horses out from the shelter of the trees.Suddenly they heard the wicked snickering sound of arrows, one hit Dicon, the other passed by Thomas's head leaving a graze on his cheek which spurted blood. They spurred their horses to a gallop and fled up the road.

"Areyou hit?" called Thomas to his friend."Aye," Dicon laughed"But in my wooden leg. What chance of that ?" They had galloped fast for a quarter mile when they came upon a ruined hovel fronting the road. Its mud walls offered some shelter and they pulled their horses in behind the low walls and strung their bows and waited for their persuers.

Up the road in hot chase came four horsemen. Each dressed in the distinctive livery of Lord Clifford with a wyvern badge on their smock fronts.Thomas loosed his first arrow, it sped true and through the raised vizor of the leading horseman's sallet. He tumbled from his horse which kept galloping. Dicon took the next soldier in the chest with one of his bodkin points which were specifically designed to penatrate plate armour.he too tumbled from his saddle. The other two emeny soldiers drew their swords and rushed the low walls of the ruin.Thomas fired again and his arrow pierced the neck of his advesary between the sallet and the top of his mail shirt. A great jet of blood shot out and the man fell with a gurgle. The fourth soldier seeing he was the only one left tried to surrender, but Dicon limping forward on his wood leg with the arrow still in it. Swiftly despatched him with a blow from his sword."Try and damage my lovely leg will you you bastard. Take that," and he skewered him again.

Thomas staunched the flow of blood from his head wound with a piece of linen. Dicon smiled and said."Another battle scar to impress your lovely lady!"

"Well God's blood I never saw those bastards, they must have crept up whilst we were saying goodbye to Billie.I hope he got away all right. "

"Oh yes, I saw him some way off before we came out of the wood. Still better be more aware next time.These boys are the very ones we're looking for !"Dicon broke off the arrow that was protuding from his wooden leg and threw it down on the ground. "What luck was that, an inch either way and the horse would have taken the point. An inch or so higher up and I would have had to make a longer leg for myself." He bellowed out his huge laugh which in turn set the dog off and for a moment the sounds of barking and laughter filled th air.Leaving the bodies of their assailants having rifled through their pockets for any coins or valuables, they mounted up and trotted northward until they came upon a inn nestled in a grove of trees just off the Pontefract to Ferrybridge road. The sign of a wild boar with curly tusks glared down at them as they dismounted and left their horses with the ostler in the yard. Inside the inn a log fire blazed and they discovered they were the only customers. A room was rented and two bowls of pottage and bread was brought to their table by the cheery slattern who passed as the landlady.

⟨Chapter Fourteen⟩

A bitterly cold night, the wooden bridge that spanned the Aire at Ferrybridge encrusted with hoar frost and the sluggish waters of the river below almost but not quite frozen at the margins. Five hundred Lancastrian troops descended on the bridge and started to slight it. Removing the roadway and trying to destroy the heavy oak timber structure that made up the old bridge. Their tools were not up to the job and after having diminished the road bed to one single plank they turned and rode off in the direction of Towton.

Some time later a detachment of Yorkist troops arrived. Seeing the damage they started to repair the road bed as best they could. They finally managed to make a repair enough to enable troops to pass over in single file. Then seeing that all was quiet settled down for what rest they could get on that bitter cold night.

In the early hours when all good or evil men slept, when the human spirit is at its lowest ebb and woodland creatures escape the silent wings of hunting owls, Lord Clifford, 'The Butcher', leading 500 mounted men returned to the bridge. The sentries, such as they were, had succumed to the arms of sleep and lay wrapped in their blankets and sheepskins, when the vengeful hordes of Lancastrians descended upon them.Resistance was weak and limited and Lord Fitzwalter was killed when he heard a commotion and believing it to be amongst his own men came out of his tent unharnessed and with only a pole axe for a weapon. He was soon finished off along with Warwick's brother The Bastard of Salisbury. The slaughter was completed and once all resistance had ceased the victorious Lancastrians again had dominion over the crossing of the river.

However a fleeing Yorkist soldier pelting back hell for leather was able to warn Edward of what had happened and the young king in his descisive manner gathered a large group of men together and set off for the bridge,ordering the main army to come after him.

In the bedroom of the Wild Boar, Thomas and Dicon had been sleeping the sleep of the just. Orrid whined a bit as his dreams included the never ending chase of some rabbits which he couldn't quite catch.Outside on the cold road a sudden commotion woke the two men and peering out from their window they saw a troop of horsemen cantering past.

"By the Holy Christ they look like king's men to me. Best we try and join them.!"Hurridly they put on their mail shirts and riding boots gathered their gauntlets and their sallets and with their weapons to hand clattered down the stairs and into the yard. Their horses wild eyed at the excitement pawed the ground of their stable.Mounting up they cantered out of the yard and joined the tail end of the troop."Where are we going boys ?" Demanded Dicon.

"To the bridge across the Aire, the enemy have taken it and slaughtered all who were there.Fitz Walter is dead we must wrest it back as it is the only crossing north."The speaker raised his bevor to gain some air and Thomas realised it was the King.!"

My lord! " He stammered, forgive me I knew not it would be you riding beside me."

"Well met Sergeants Thomas and Dicon, it does my heart good to have such loyal men beside me."He tipped his gauntleted hand to the side of his vizor and spurring his destrier forward joined some nobles in the ranks.The mounted troops canterered through the frosty night. Their breath and that of their mounts mingling together as a counterpoint to the jangle of their horses harness.

The head of the column had reached the bridge and the clash of sword on sword and the high shouts of excitement and the wail of wounded men reached back to Thomas and Dicon. Most of the king's troops had dismounted, for the way across the Aire was only one plank wide and no horse could pass. A ferocious hand fight was going on as the Yorkist faction tried again and again to wrest control of the bridge. The Lancastrians were just to strong or just too determined and men were falling in numbers into the river as battle hammers and axes wreaked their frightful work. The clash of the harnessed soldiers upon the bridge was in stalemate.First one side gained the ascendant and then the other forced the troopers back. Once a man was wounded or tipped into the icy cold of the sluggish red tinted Aire his timewas up, for no heavily accoutreted human could hope to surive in that cold water and many were drowned. The young King fighting with a fury that set him apart from is troops paused for breath. It is true to say that even the fittest and youngest soldier in full steel harness could only fight full on for about ten minutes before thirst and exhaustion forced him to withdraw. Thomas was fighting alongside the king. His broad sword bloodied up to the hilt and his brigandine covered in blood from soldiers he had killed.

The King gasped " Back Thomas, we must regroup and try again!" Thomas nodded and stabbed down with his sword through the vizor of a Lancastrian who had somehow managed to gain a foothold on the bridge.

Edging backwards the group surrounding the king gave way to another fresher set of men who shouting and screaming the litany of battle took on the fight across the Aire.

"Sire, there is a ford three miles north of here at Castleford. If you send men to cross there and attack your enemies in the flank from the north bank I believe you shall win the day."Thomas was able to shout this message at the King above the swelling sounds of the clash of steel on steel.

The King looked pircingly at him."How know you this Thomas?"

"I was at this ford only two days ago on my scurrier mission for you.Sire."

"Good man" The king smiled wearily at him.He turned to one of his squires." Bring me Lord Fauconberg and Sir William Blount just as soon as they can be found" he ordered. The man pulled his horses head round and galloped rearwards. Within minutes whilst the battle for the bridge raged with even fiercer intensity the two noble lords appeared beside the King.

"My Lords, Thomas here assures me there is a ford across the river at Castleford some three miles north of here,Take a good part of the army with you and cross there and come down on the enemy from the north bank. Thomas will show you the ford. Go, and go quick for Lord Clifford is not going to concede the crossing of the river here I fear." The two nobles saluted and led by Thomas with a good part of the army galloping behind them headed north to the ford at Castleford.

By some oversight on the part of the Lancastrians this ford was completely undefended and the Yorkist army splashed and clattered its way through and onto the north bank of the Aire. Stopping there to regroup and give instructions to the soldiers Fauconberg then lead an unstoppable charge back towards the fighting still raging around the bridge across the Aire.His men fell on the Lancastrians from the north bank and Clifford seeing he was outmanouvered called upon his troops to retreat.The slaughter was imense,as the Yorkist troops rode pell mell into the fleeing Lancastians as they desperately tried to escape northwards up the road towards Sherbourne in Elnet. Back at the bridgethe few remaining Lancastrians tried to surrender, but the King showed little mercy and they were cut down. The whooping hollering Yorkists crossed the bridge and chased northward to catch Fauconberg and take part in the plunder.

Fauconberg chas ed the enemy as far north as Dinting Dale and fell upon them in a slight valley two an a half miles short of the village of Towton.The slaughter was terrible as the victorious Yorkists cut down their enemies. Lord Clifford exhausted from the fray removed his metal gorget to gain much needed fresh air and by an unlucky chance a headless arrow, no more than an ash shaft struck him in the neck. Through the jugular and out the other side leaving the main artery severed. Within minutes his life's blood had pumped out of him and he sank to the ground never to recover. Still the slaughter continued,at Dinting Dale and Ferrybridge. The heralds counted three thousand slain.By now the short winter'sday was coming to an end and the temperature was starting to drop even further than it had during the day.The king decided to camp his army just south of Towton.

Thomas and Dicon pulled their horses off the road and into the thickening undergrowth that grew alongside. Chopping some branches from a small sapling they fashioned a basic shelter which they covered with turf and vegetation scavanged from the surrounding country. Within miutes they had a campfire going and were boilingup some porridge into which they cut onions and carrots and shaved off some of the precious dried beef they had carried all the way from Nottingham.All along the roadside and far into the forest on either side similar campfires sparkled and flickered as the king's army settled. Some were less fortunate,having only a meagre ration of hard bread to supliment their diets.Meanwhile out in the freezing cold and all the way back to Ferrybridge the wounded and the schocked the traumatised and the near death soldiers moaned and called out for their mothers and loved ones. Local peasants crept along the road stealing and robbing the wounded and the dead and a swift dagger through the eye soon put paid to the harrowing calls of the suffering.

By midnight and soon after the noise of the dying had started to diminish and a strange expectant hush had started to settle over the encamped army.In their shelter huddled together for warmth and with the dog adding his to the mix the two men slept the sleep of the just. Worn out from the battle at Ferrybridge and with their bellies full of the pottage they had cooked,the oblivion of sleep recharged their energy for the next day Palm Sunday.

Dawn broke on Palm Sunday 1461 with a swirl of bitter cold snow blowing northerly up the hundred foot slight slope that defined one part of the battlefield.To the west the deep and deceptively sluggish Cock Brook flowed past steep and difficult to climb banks. In a bend of the river north west of Saxton lay the piece of open ground which was to become the notorious and horrific 'Bloody Meadow' The battlefield was bound on the east by marshy ground and on the west by the steep and slippery slopes running down to the Cock Brook.The Lancastrians secure in the knowledge that their choice of battleground had led them to this flank secure battlefield. All they had to do now was wait the onslaught of the enemy who were

arrayed in lesser numbers and cold and hungry from a night in the open.Surely a recipe for success.!

As the dawn gave way to the grey bitter snowy weather that was to epitomise that battle day the two armies started to wake and like some gigantic monster to shake off the lethargy of the night and gird its limbs against what was to come.Priests moved amongst the men blessing them and giving absolution. The nobles and men at arms lucky enough to have passed the night in the shelter of a tent fortified their courage with wine.Some ale was drunk by the common foot soldiers but their courage was mainly left to the almighty for help. Portable grindstones whirred and spat as a killing edge was put upon swords and bill hooks, battle axes and hallberds.The contingents of archers amongst whom Thomas and Dicon now stood where collecting ash shafts. Two dozen each, mainly bodkin points but some steel coated with wicked barbs for use agai nst plate armour.

Thomas stashed his shafts in a waterproof quiver that slung across his back. His bow strings, three of them which he had been slavishly protecting from the worsening weather he had kept wound around his hair under his leather sallet cap. Diccon had done the same.Suddenly

Orrid started barking. Thomas had him tied on a line but the dog was in a state of excitement and was barking and jumping. "Whoa boy what's amiss?"Thomas called to him.Dicon said." Ah, he's only espied Billie coming over." Sure enough in the distance and towering over the other soldiers by a good cubit the giant was making his way towards the archers position. He had a wicker creel across his back from which the tops of many terracotta an glass bottles poked out..Finally he arrived and placing his burden down he hugged both Thomas and Dicon and ruffled the dog's head. He pulled out the ubiquitous tablet and scribbled a message. ' I come with greek fire grenados of my own making.Let me at these scots and other devils. Dicon and Thomas grinned."Well met good friend. It's a pleasure to see you here upon the battlfield. " Billie gazed round taking in the colourful sight of beautifully caparisoned destriers being pranced up and down by their noble owners in a ritual high stepping dance that brought some colour to the grey and bitter day.

"Archers form company, notch your bows" a bellow from the sergeants rang out across the field.The Kings archers formed into line and taking their precious dry bowlines from whereever they had kept them they notched up their killing bows.The next orders came almost at once. 'Advance ten paces.' Through the slush of the newly falling snow and with the bitter wind at their backs the King's archers moved forward.'Notch,draw, fire,' the three orders most beloved of the English archer pealed out across the lowering battlefield.Two hundred paces off at the top of the slope the Lancastrian army peered down through the thickening weather.T he silver hiss of a thous nd arrows fleeing on target towards the ememy filled the air. Helped on by the strong wind they flew further than they would have on a windless day and they spun with brutal force into the chests and limbs of the Lancastrian foe.

The Queen's army gave the same orders and a dark shower like a flock of descending starlings rose from the Lancastrian side and beat its way towards the Yorkists. Falling short in front of their archers by as much as forty feet. Fauconberg seeing this in his expierience gave the order to the archers to return the spent arrows of the foe and the next volley from the Yorkist ranks was the return of spent Lancastrian shafts. But a once fired arrow has the same killing tendancy to a one shot one and with the wind assistance King Edward's archers caused much devestation amongst the ranks of their opponents.

Unable to sustain the sheer killing power of the Yorkist archers Lord Northumberland gave the order for the advance of the Lancastrian horde.With a great shout and a milling forward of horsemen and foot soldiers the killing began. The two armies clashed in a bitter hand to hand brawl where only the strongest and the luckiest survived. Above the sickening sound of metal on metal rose the cries of the wounded and the smell of blood and excrement filled the air. Horses with three four or five shafts sticking out of them bellowed in pain as they crashed uncaring into the foot soldiers. Blood gouted everywhere, underfoot the ground already unstable from the falling snow became more treacherous as blood mingled with mud in a slippery mess that no one was able to avoid.

Thomas watched as one lancastrian foot soldier swung his sword forward against a harnessed Yorkist coming for him. The man's feet slipped on the sodden ground and before he knew it he was spawled on his back and a yorkist archer had slipped a rondel into his eye through his vizor.Billie was crouched down next to his creel with a tinder box from which smouldering linen was helping to ignite the grenados which he was firing into the advancing Lancastrians by means of a hand held capapult. The grenados were catching fire as they fell and shattered over the enemy. Some were trying to beat out the flames but with little success. In a frenzy of killing lust the huge giant fired and threw more and more of the deadly fire weapons into the hordes opposing him. One lancastrian noble was a mass of flames as he ran squealing and crying for mercy from God only to collapse in a charred mess of pork smelling meat. A riderless horse with an arrow through its chest was hit directly on the head by one of Billie's grenados and with its head aflame like some beast from the depths of hell it ran across thefront of the armies and disapeared down the banks of the Cock river to plunge into the cold waters, where even then the flames kept burning.

The slaughter on the field was awful to behold. Banks of men fell in rows one upon the other. The wounded groaning and twisting in their agony But still the armies fought.

Thomas found himself fighing alongside Dicon who was in that beserker frame of mind where the next slash of the sword heralded another blood lust victory leading on to yet another death. on the other side of him a man in a bloodied but valuable suit of harness was wielding a huge broadsword as he slashed at his enemies, shouting out meaningless oaths and challanges. Suddenly this man slipped in the mire and tumbled backwards. A Lancastrian footsoldier lunged forward for the coup de grace with his battle axe. Thomas straddled the man and pierced through with his sword taking the lancastrian's head off at his shoulders. He bent down to help up the noble who pushed up his vizor.

"By God you blessed man Thomas you've saved my life. I thank you"For the noble was the King. "Tis nowt Sire, you'd do the samefor me I warrant!" The king grinned through the grime. "How goes the day?"Thomas shook his head "Many dead sire and they have the numbers of us" The king looked thoughtful. "Aye Thomas,I fear the day is going against us, I have few reserves to throw into the battle. I am still awaiting Norfolk's arrival, with his fresh men we could turn the day." He snapped his vizor shut and lurched forward into the melee. Thomas and Dicon one on either side of the king killing in a frenzy of blood lust that no man could stop. The ground before them was littered with the bodies of nobles and commoners. Ahead around a battle standard a group of nobles and men at arms were slashing and driving swords and battle axes into each others flesh. The snow that was falling was melting instantly as it hit the heated bodies of the soldiers a steaming mist laced with a pinkness of blood rose over the field.

From the west of the field of horror a sudden incursion of two hundred or so Lancastrian horse thundered into the battle.Lord Somerset had hidden these troops in Castle Hill Woods with the specific intention of ambushing the Yorkists. Screaming their war cries they thundered down onto the wing of the Yorkist army causing it to turn and fall back towardsthe ridge line above Saxton village.

Fresh troops from the Lancastrian side were being pushed forward into the front line where inexorably the exhausted Yorkists were slowly being forced backward to the ridge. Lines of dead and dying men and horses lay behind the line of the advancing Lancastrians. With a touch more force Somerset could push the Yorkists over the ridge. Their line would break and they would run. The crisis of the battle had been reached.

King Edward surrounded by his most faithful troops was everywhere, where ever a weak link in the line showed itself the small group of soldiers were there harrying the enemy and encouraging their own side. Fighting beneath a banner with the black bull of Clarence proudly streaming above them this group put new heart into the faltering steps and muscles of the Yorkists.At the fiercest parts of the battle Thomas and Dicon pierced forward with their swords. Thomas had taken a slash across the top of his sallet which had peeled it back like an open tin can missing the top of his scalp by millimetres and leaving him with an unending ringing in his ears.The fresh air that flowed in went some way to revive him.His arms and legs were cut and stabbed in several places, but the fever of battle had made these wounds of little significance and he hardly felt them.Dicon was limping badly, for the bottom two inches of his wooden stump had been cut through by a Lancastrian halberd. He was helmetless having thrown away his sallet long since, and the blood was pouring down his face from several cuts. Still he thrust and swiped the enemy in a inexhaustable and angry manner.The dog Orrid had somehow managed to stay close to Thomas through out the fighting. From the start Thomas had turned him loose but the loyalty of the creature would not allow him to leave his master's side.One lancastrian archer had had his throat ripped out by the dog as he drew his bow to loose an arrow at Thomas.Gathering its haunches Orrid launched himself upward at the archer falling on his neck with his fangs barred and the schock of the attack demorolised the man so much he hardly was able to fight back.The dog bit through the jugular and the man fell senseless to the ground.Slowly the Kings troops were giving way to the fresher more numerous Lancastrians as they poured down from the ridge onto the battlefield proper.Line upon line of inert bodies littered the ground. Thomas glanced up at the sky, but the day was so murky that no sun was visible. It could have been two hours into the fighting or ten he knew not.Again and again the steel clash and sparks from the weapons filled the air alongside the pitiful calls of the wounded. A young nobleman and his squire lay huddled together both eviscerted, their blue grey guts spilling out onto the ground.The squire was still alive and he looked up with pleading at Thomas who stood over him."Finish me Sir for God's sweet mercy" he murmered. Out of pity Thomas lent down and swiftly thrust his dagger into the neck of the boy killing him instantly.He looked back towards the Ferrybridge road, tears pricking his eyes, a movement on the road caught his eye.Troops were moving up it towards the battlefield.At first he could not tell under whose banner they marched. Could this be yet more Lancastrian troops fresh and sprung from who knew where. If so all was lost. The exhausted army of the king would be cut to pieces by fresh troops. Then the snow moderated for a moment and the battle standards streamed out in the freshening wind. There for all to see was the King's banner of the sun in splendour and the standard of the Earl of Norfolk.. Thomas gave a great sigh of relief and turning he ran towards the melee where the King was still fighting. Above the din and the screams he was able to shout to the King. "Sire,Sire, Norfolk comes!"He pointed back down the ferrybridge road. The king looked bemused for a moment then a grin split his features and he bellowed" Norfolk comes, the day is ours," and with renewed energy threw himself once again into the fray.Thomas followed and felt new energy flow into his limbs. Slashing and piercing he fought alongside his monarch till a ring of dead and dying foemen lay akimbo at their feet.

The Earl of Norfolk ordered his horse forward against the left flank of the lancastrian horde. With a crash that could be heard over the whole battlefield the heavy horse of the Yorkists mowed into the exhausted foot soldiers. Cutting them down in their hundreds.Lancastrian troops from the rear of the lines seeing the debacle broke and ran. The Duke of Somerset seeing his troops break called for his horse and galloped from the field his battle flagsstreaming behind him. His other troops watched their commander fly, lost heart and they in turn ran. Fleeing down Towton Dale towards the river hoping to cross there at a ford if such existed. Noned id.! Chased by Yorkist horse they fell before the onslaught, most crushed through the head by the vicious swinging battle hammers with the hooked head. When some soldiers made it to the banks of the brook they realised that the snow had made them treacherous and slippery and many harnessed men slid to their deaths by drowning into the deep waters of the icy brook. Meanwhile the Yorkist horse rode along the banks of the river despatching anyone who still lived.More lancastrians fled northwards looking for a way across the river. At any shallow point they died in their hundreds chopped down by the milling victorious horsemen of the king.Some made it up the Tadcaster road but were killed crossing the River Wharfe, while others safe in the knowledge they had gained thesanctury of Tadcaster where sought out and butchered in the streets.The bloodletting continued late into the night. All along the road between Towton and Tadcaster the bodies of the fleeing Lancastrians littered the way,In the river Cock the bodies lay so thick that at one place where a ford had existed now a 'Bridge of Bodies 'took its place where men so panicked had trampled one another and the fallen had formed a causeway over which others had in turn been slaughtered.

On the battlefield dispirited groups of Lancastrian soldiers threw down their weapons and tried to surrender but some vengeful Yorkists slaughtered them there and then, The king rode through the field his heralds calling loudly "spare the commons, kill the nobles." The battle commanders tried to organise the remaining Yorkist troops into companies to attack should the Lancastrians try to fight again, but after nearly eight hours of non stop savagry there were no takers.Groups of archers and foot soldiers were robbing the dead and dying.Moving silently amongst the corpses slitting open brigandines pulling harness to one side to rob the dead of their few coins and valuables.Slicing a finger here and pulling gold rings from an ear lobe there. If a wounded man cried out at the desecration of his ring finger a sharp blow to the eye socket with the rondel silenced him.Across the field of Towton as far as the eye could see lay piles upon piles of dead men. In places they lay four bodies thick where they had been pulled by the living to make way for the continuing dance of death. Through this macabre wilderness wandered the few shocked survivours, some looking for a friend, some seeking a lord or master.Overall hung a miasma of blood and shit and in the air a low moaning sound and the occasional scream as one more poor sufferer met his maker.

Thomas and Dicon were looking for Billie.They had not seen their friend since the incident with the grenados and Thomas was beginning to worry. He had given Orrid a piece of Billie's clothing. The dog sniffed it and now was questing with his nose down through the battlefield.

Back and forth he ran in a ceaseless hunt for the giant. About a hundred paces from where they stood there was a mound of bodies mostly liveried soldiers with thewyvern crest upon their coats but also some with that of Somerset and three prehaps four mail harnessed nobles. They lay in a pile. Blood dripped from the mound. All around broken swords and discarded sallets. Battle hammers and halberds littered the ground. Orrid was sitting on his haunches with his head back to the sky and an eirie moaning wail was coming from his mouth.Thomas with Dicon limping behind him approached the dog. "What's up boy, have you found him?" the dog kept moaning.Thomas started to pull the heap of bodies away from one another. Even though this pile had suffered death some hours before there was still warmth within and the smell of human shit and putrid blood welled up out of the pile. Eventually he got to the bottom and there with a beatific smile on his face lay their giant friend. His body had been pierced with sword blades so manytimes that his brigandine that Thomas had had made for him was a shredded mess.Thomas lent forward and placed a finger on the giants pulse. Nothing. Their friend was dead, he had sold his life dearly in the service of the king. Dicon counted the bodies surrounding him and made it twenty five.Orrid came forward and gently licked the face of the mute.

"We shall take him for burial.He was a man amongst men" They pulled his body free from the mass of dead men and with one at each end they started across the battlefield with their sad loa.d.

They arrived eventually at Lead church a small chapel giving solace to two of Towton's landed families and there in the grave yard they interred their friend. Thomas said a few words over the grave and then in sombre mood they turned back to the battlef.ield.

Niether of them had words to say, each was thinking of the giant and how in the short time they had known him he had come to affect them so profoundly.Dicon looked over at Thomas to see that through the grime of battle on his face two runnel where tears had fallen streaked his cheeks.

"Fear not brother, he died a death any man could be proud of and now he sits with God."Thomas tried to shake off his melancholy."Aye Dicon you are right,But I did love that man!" He scrubbed a filthy hand across his face smearing away his tears."Come, lets find something to eat, for I am as famished as a man can get."

They settled own in a part of the field that was relatively free from bodies and built a small fire, then using a piece of breast plate armour from a fallen noble as a fry pan and having cut two huge horsemeat steaks from the flank of a fallen destrier they proceeded to cook the meat over their improvised fire. Orrid looked on, saliva dripping from his jaws. Thomas cut him another piece from the same horse and threw it to him. The dog wagged his tail and set too with a vengance.

The smell of the meat as it cooked seemed to settle the two men and they had just started to cut into their meal when a commanding voice carried across the field towards them. On a black stallion surrounded by heralds and grinning nobles the young victorious king was making his way through the carnage towards them.Thomas and Dicon stumbled to their feet and waited in some trepidation. Bowing to the party as it stopped beside them.

The king rode up to them and throwing his riens to a page dismounted." "Kneel down the pair of you" he commanded.!

They both did so. The king turned to his herald and held out his hand.The man placed a gleaming ceremonial sword into it The king lent forward and placed the blade first on the right shoulder and then on the left. "Arise Sir Thomas of Lingen. I dub thee knight For loyal service to me and not least for saving my life." Thomas looked up in surprise as he was lifted up by two grinning noblemen.The king continued"All new knights may have a squire and so I name Dicon of Knighton your squire. Long may the two of you loyally serve me."A polite s ound of clapping came from the group on horseback. "I see you have already eaten but tonight in York There will be a celebration and I command the presence of all my Knights" He pulled the head of his black stallion around and the heraldic group cantered away.

Thomas looked at Dicon in shocked surprise then he threw back his head and a bellow of unbelieving laughter issued from his throat. "Sir Thomas of Lingen and his loyal squire Dicon.! Well am I dreaming?"

"Nay Sir Thomas" said Dicon, "It couldn't have happened to a more deserving person, and think how that will impress the countess."

⟡ Chapter Fifteen ⟡

D ressed in their best apparel with their horses caparisoned in cloth of gold and damask, taken from the field of battle. In immaculate jaks and hose with ermine collared cloaks and the grime of battle wiped from their faces,the two friends rode sedately side by side through the portcullised gate of York Castle. Above them on spikes newly arrayed were the heads of various traitors beheaded that day by order of the King. The older more putrifying skulls, some of the plantaganet family, including Edward's father and brother had been removed with all due reverance and consigned to vaults and graves with in the cathederal precints. These new grinning skulls including that of the Earl of Devon,a sick man, who was left behind in York as Queen Margaret and thefrightened king Henry fled like scared rabbits north to Scotland. These freshly impaled heads dripped blood as the scavaging crows pecked at the eyes and other soft parts.

It was under this macabre backdrop that Thomas and Dicon dismounted from their horses and consigning them and Orrid to a servant stepped through the bright panopaly that surrounded the door into the great hall of York Castle.

A huge noise of laughter and talk greeted them. The warmth and smell of hundreds of unwashed bodies eddied over them. At one end of the great room underneath a stone mullioned window upon a raised platform the king was sitting. He was dressed in black with the occasional spash of silver at his coller and cuffs. Upon his head he wore the crown of Edward the Confessor sent from London under armed guard and on either side of him the victorious battle commanders,Fuconberg. Warwick,The Duke of Norfolk,looking sick and wan and to all intents a dead man already. Slightly to one side the two rear guard commanders Sir John Wenlock and Sir John Denhim. They were laughing and drinking and shouting and belching and each in his way enjoying the fruits of this victory celebration.

The King had already created his young brother Duke of Clarence his uncle Earl of Essex. Fuconberg was made Earl of Kent and several knights became emboldened. From the field of battle eighteen men whom previously had been mere commoners were raised up to the status of Knight or squire, amogst whom were both Thomas and Dicon.

They made there way slowly through the throng greeting friends and aquaintances, bowing elegantly before the slim women of the court who had followed the army up north and who now were harvesting the fruits of their loyal labours.

Dicon turned to Thomas and said. "I thank Christ in his manger that I got that smith to lenghten my leg."He tapped the metal extension that had been put on by a blacksmith that afternoon.Thomas grinned.

Then suddenly they were standing before the raised platform upon which their leige and master was sitting.

They both bowed.The king looked at them and breaking into a delighted grin he summoned them forward up onto the dias.

"My good and loyal Sir Thomas and his squire, welcome"The King raised his hands for silence and when eventually the great hall had succumbed to a gentle murmer he stood and addressed the room.

"My people,my lords my ladies my friends. Before you here you see two of my beloved soldiers without whom I could never have completed this victory. Sir Thomas of Lingen will always be in my debt, for it was he who saved my life upon the bloody field of Towton, and his loyal squire Dicon of Knighton. Now these two men I have raised to the nobility because they derserve such. But niether of them have any land. So under the act of attainder from the Battle of Mortimer's Cross the land belonging to the traitor Gruffydd Tudor which runs from Radnor west to the township of Presteigne now becomes the rightful desmesne of Sir Thomas. I am sure he can find a suitable house somewhere upon that tract for himself and his squire. "The King grinned. And sat down. A huge stamping and clapping broke out in the hall.The king beckoned a shell schocked Thomas towards him. "Sit Thomas, I wish to ask you something. " Thomas collapsed into a x framed glastonbury chair and leant forward to listen to the king." Now, you have served me well in the past gleaning information and intelligence and generally acting as my eyes in difficult situations, and I want you to go on doing so. What say you.?"

"It would be a great honour Sire, and I thank you for the gift of land." "'Tis nothing, whatever is in my power to give. Is there aught else you would like?"

Thomas's brain was in a whirl but he was still able to blurt out "Sire, if you would give me your permission to marry your ward the Countess of Hambye,I should be the happiest man in England."

The King looked askance at Thomas."So that's the way the land lies is it? Would she have you?" "Aye Sire I believe she would"

"Then so be it,and I shall attend the wedding !" Thomas bowed and in a state of extreme excitement and wonder he backed away from the dias and went to find Dicon who was already being feted by other squires and minor nobility.His rough hewen humour and his huge hands not to say his very unusual wood leg making him a cause celebre amongst the crowds in the hall.

They sat down to a feast that had been preparing for twenty four hours when the victory of the battle had become known. Awhole ox was slowly revolving on a spit before an open hot wood fire and it juices dripped and spluttered into the ash giving off the most delicious smell. Servants cut huge slices and carried them on trenchers to each guest as and when required. Venison, swan, chicken and pigeon, rabbit and hare adorned the groaning refectory tables.Whole salmon and eel, trout and mussels upon huge platters were interspersed with vegatables and fruit. Small bowls of precious peppercorns stood upon the board and dried tyme and parsley and rare ground nutmeg worth more per pound than gold itself waited the pleasure of the diners.Before long the area behind the diners was awash with discarded bones and pieces of gristle and bits of meat difficult to eat. The revellers looked greasy and red in the face after such a feast, but it didn't stop them. The best Rhenish wine was served and ale fresh brewed,and still the noise rose up to the ceiling.Some of the nobility had come equiped with the new fangled eating forks, but most including Thomas and Dicon made do with their daggers. Eating a slice of beef from a dagger point when drunk was a skilled occupation,and several of the worst for wear had cut lips and stabbed chins.

Thomas pushed his half eaten trencher away and slumped down against the table edge. He belched and looked across at his companions. One was fast asleep whith his head cradled in a half finished bowl of trifle, another was being violently sick. Vomiting up all the goodness he had just consumed. Thouhtfully he had turned away from the table and was vomiting in that area where the castle dogs were scavaging their supper. Thoms did a double take,for there with the other castle dogs was Orrid. He had laid claim to a huge rib bone from the roasted ox and he was seeing off all comers with a snarling and a bearing of teeth.Thomas shook his head in wonder and he turned to Dicon whose eyes were rapidly glazing over. "Look at yonder dog! How the hell did he get in here?" "Oh, leave him be Thomas, he's got the right to enjoy hisself as much as us" So saying he slumped forward and started snoring. Thomas threw back his head and roared with laughter. In to his mind came images of the extraordinary few days that had just passed. The horrors of the battlefield and the bloody aftermarth. The knighting by the King and now the promise of marriage to his beloved Eloner and not least the grant of a subsantial piece of border countryside that would make him one of the most powerful men in that area.Cradling his head in his arms he lent forward and fell into a deep restorative sleep.

By dawn the next day most of the revellers had departed the hall including Thomas and Dicon and the dog. Gathering their cloaks and weaponry from the stewards at the castle keep they mounted their horses and rode sedately away. Each thump of the hooves sending blinding flashes of pain through Thomas's head and his companion looked green about the gills.

For some miles there was no talk between them but as the weak spring sunlight started to warm the day so their spirits lifted and they were able to communicate.

"We ride south now my squire!" stated Thomas"There is much to be done.I have an inkling to see my lands and to find a suitable house for my bride. " "Oh all's well with the young lord then?" laughed Dicon "Inkling to see your lands!.house for the bride!. Don't run afore ye can walk my son!"

Thomas laughed in turn"Nay,Dicon, you have the truth of it. Tis far to easy to think like a lord and act as if the world is yours to do with what you like. I must be more humble". Dicon looked at him and raised his eyebrows. "Well, Sir Thomas, what plan haveyou in mind.?"

"I thought an easy ride south to Shrewsbury and then skirt westwards to Llandielo and back towards Presteigne. That way we can take in the whole of the land I have been given. "

"That may take some time "

"Aye but we have it "

By now the road had widened as it approached the town of Pontefract carts and oxen being driven in by their owners to market slowed the traffic, and the citiens on foot and those on horseback skirted round the cobbled road widening the road with new ruts and hoof marks. Calling Orrid to heel Thomas slipped a lead on the dog and they clattered through the gate in the town wall. He saw a soldier ahead and asked him directions to the guild hall of merchants. He had it in mind to ask for the best route south to Shrewsbury and who would know that better than a merchant who traded with far flung parts of the kingdom. Eventually they came to a timber framed building beautifully ornate with carved corbels and intrically painted infills to the framing.Dismounting they tied their horses and Orrid and entered through the heavy oak door.Within in the long room stretching back to a stone mullioned window all was silence. Then from a side entrance a small rotund man dressed in an expensive fur trimmed robe with soft cordova leather boots on his feet came into the hall. He swept a bow. "How may I help good sirs.?"

Thomas smiled. "We desire to know the best route from this town to Shrewsbury."

"Why, that would be first to go to Chester and then southerly to Shrewsbury. For Chester the road takes you over the moors and is not recommended for persons on their own. Far too many bandits and outlaws are living in the hills and they do prey on single travellers. 'Tis best to go with others. Stength in numbers " He smiled ingratiatingly.

Thomas asked "When is the next party due to depart to Chester?"

"Oh, not before a sennight, one left yesterday, you might catch up with it if you hurry.They spend the first night on the road at Wakefield in the best tavern there and then on over the Saddleworth Moor. That's the danger don't you know, The Saddleworth. Miles and miles of nothing and the wind and snow blow so hard up there....."he trailed off shaking his head.

Thomas thanked the man and they left the Guildhall.

Francis Lecane

"I think we should try and catch this group,they can't be too far ahead of us."

Dicon nodded and shouted out to a gawping peasant who was admiring the horses and dog tethered before him. "Oi Cully, which way to the Wakefield road. " The man knuckled his forehead and pointed ahead of him. He mumbled something but his dialect was such that niether Thomas or Dicon understood him.They mounted up and leavingOrrid to run free cantered off in the direction the man had indicated.They made good time along the paved road and before the curfew bell was sounded in Wakefield they were ensconsed in the warm log fired main room of the Duck and Dragon. The party they were chasing had stayed the night but that morning had set off for the high ground of the moor having told the landlord in the Duck that they would sleep the night at Holmfirth before tackling the moor itself the next day. According to the landlord a slightly supercilious individual with a greasy demenour and a lazy eye that slid away from contact, Holmfirth was a tiny place only fit for swine and no one in their right mind would entertain staying in such a place.For a groat Thomas and Dicon and the dog were fed, the horses were stabled and the flea ridden bed in the main chamber was readied for them.They slept well that night and by dawn they had broken their fast and were cantering away from Wakefield. An uneventful day of hard riding brought them to Holmfirth and the only tavern The Saracen's Head. This was the most substantial building in the place,having two stories, one jutting out over the other and a substantial yard behind double gates.The rest of the dwellings in the town consisted of mean single storied hovels with turf roofs and middens piled high along the street.There was a lot of activity in the yard as Thomas and Dicon rode up.Six or seven packhorses and a similar number of palfreys and hacks were being attended to by ostlers.

"What happens here cully?" shouted Dicon to the oldest one.

"Ah, maister, this be a party on'tway to Chester, but one have fallen ill,s o they'm staying another night."He knuckled his head and continued"I dusn't expect there be any room in the inn, but I'll ask for 'ee " he hurried off indoors.He was back again in moments."landlord says there's the attic room you'm welcome too sixpence a night and all found. "Thomas looked at Dicon."Well my squire if this is all that's to be had, we better take it. " Throwing the reins of their animals to the ostlers they walked into the tavern.The main room was full of people.Three or four prosperous looking merchants in fur trimmed cloaks a woman and her maid with high white coifs upon their heads and two small children both standing with their thumbs in their grimy mouths.

"Well met my masters and ladies, we would fain join you in your road over the moor

The oldest of the merchants looked up at Thomas"And who are you sir pray.?"

Thomas bowed and introduced himself. "Sir Thomas of Lingen and this is my squire Dicon of Knighton." There was a decided warming of relations in the room at these revalations and the merchants swept bows and the two women bobbed curtsies.

Thomas continued." I hear tell that one of your party has fallen ill?"

"Nothing to fear Sir Thomas, a bad lamphrey in the fish pie last night, but he would insist on eating it.Now he suffers on the privy, six times today already.He will be fit to travel tomorrow."The merchant shook his head in an authoritive way and at that moment a thin and very pale young man emerged from the yard.His hands were stained black from the oak gall ink he made and used and Thomas surmised that he was a clerk and most likely the clerk of the merchants travelling together.The young man had hardly entered the room when a spasm of pain crossed his face and he rushed out again."Seven times today" said the second merchant with a grin.

It transpired that two of the merchants were waiting for a courier to arrive with a consignment of Blue John felspar which was mined across the moors in one place only near Castleton a tiny village where only the mineral miners lived. They were beginning to feel anxious as the courier was over twelve hours late and they feared he had been robbed,for many outlaws and branded thieves lived up on these god forsaken moorlands.Once bought, the valuable mineral was taken to Chester where it was transformed by craftsmen into exquisite objects which commanded a premium price. No coin had changed hands as yet so the merchants hadn't lost anything,but the muttering and murmering between them about it very soon caused Thomas to rise from his seat at the table and go out into the yard to see to the horses. It was but seconds before Dicon joined him. "By Christ's bollocks they're a boring crew whining on over their precious Blue John which none of them have got as yet" "Tis only merchant's cant, best they whine amongst themselves than join us in to the discussion."

"Let's hope the road travelled on the morrow may be somewhat more interesting !"

Chapter Sixteen

The next day looked set fair to being one of those early spring days where the old crone of winter has finally given way to the young and vibrant maid of spring. The sun streamed across the open moorland as the merchant's party with their pack horses and riding hacks slowly wound its way upwards onto the top of Saddleworth moor. Thomas and Dicon with Orrid running beside them were in the van walking their mounts at a sedate pace partially to conserve their energy but mainly so the party should not get strung out and so leave it vulnerable to attack from outlaws. On either side of the road small wind blown hawthorn trees were just coming into bloom and short sheep cropped grass underlaid the trees. A mild breese was blowing on the top of the moor and the two friends could see for miles in the clear air, picking out the way the road looped and turned as it crossed this high country. About a mile or so ahead where the road seemed to drop into a defile amongst an outcrop of rocks Thomas saw a glint of light reflecting from something metal. He turned to Dicon.

"I fear someone is lying in wait for us up ahead."
"Aye, I saw it too. shall we take a look." They put spurs to their mounts and splitting up each galloped away in a circular move that would bring them up to the outcrop

from either side.Thomas unslung his bow and saw that Dicon had done the same. As he got closer to the rocks he slowed his pace and dismounted about a hundred paces from them. There was no sign of activity and he crawled quietly forward towards the outcrop.Reaching the top he looked over.Where the road passed between the rocks, it narrowed to such an extent that it had been an easy matter for someone to block it with trees and branches. Aligned on either side of the rocks behind chest high barricades of stone stood half a dozen thin and evil looking men each with a bow and drawn sword.Their leader equally scrawny and dressed in dirty green hose and brigandine and with an enormously long beard was haranging them. His voice hardly reached to Thomas's hiding place,but his dialect was so strong that had Thomas heard it he would not have understood. Taking a bodkin point from his sheaf he notched it to his bow and fired it down at the leader taking him in the chest.The point pierced the metal plated brigandine and the force of the arrow bowled the man backwards till he slumped against the rocks. From the other side of the defile Dicon had selected his target and shot down onto the gathered outlaws. The surprise was complete.Thomas chose another and shot him.The remaining brigands looking wildly around but unable to see from whence came their nemisis threw down their weapons and called out their surrender.Thomas shouted to them to lie on the ground which they did and he climbed down to the road.Dicon followed.They tied the arms of the outlaws with strips of cloth torn from their clothing and awaited the arrival of the rest of their party.

Two of the merchants cantered forward into the defile and pulled their horses up in astonishment.

"Why, Sir Thomas, what has passed here" said one of them.

"We stopped a ambush upon our party.Luckily we saw light glinting from metal and Dicon and I came to find out what it was. "The other merchant was looking at the corpseof the outlaw leader.

"By the sweet Lord in his mercy, you have killed Black Jack of Howarth. Such a name for terror on the moor has never been heard in many a long year.There is a bounty on his head, fifty shillings, to whomsoever can prove they have killed him. Constable in Chester will pay. Black Jack has been terrorising these parts for years now.

I trow his men know what has happened to my Blue John." He walked over to the bound prisioers and aimed a vicious kick at one of them."Well, varlet,you'll swing at Chester assises 'ere long. Dost know aught of any Blue John.Hast thou robbed any these past days.?"The man shook his head and received another kick for his troubles. The other prisioner tried to speak, but he had a old facial wound that had cut away part of his cheek and jawbone. Long healed now which only allowed him to grunt and gurgle."What's he say?" demanded the merchant. Sullenly the other prisioner said "Look in the baggage."Thomas and Dicon and the merchants walked back along the narrow path to where a pair of pack animals had been tethered. It was the work of moments to pull the goods stolen by the outlaws from the panniers that straddled the two animals. There in amongst bolts of silk cloth, damask from Araby and many silver coins was the Blue John that the merchants so craved. "Thank the Lord in his mercy " crowed one of the merchants.

Thomas spoke up." Now my masters we must clear the road and make our way onwards to C hester."

They untied the prisioners and forced them at sword point to pull all the obstructions out of the path,when that was done they made them carry the body of Black Jack and sling it across the back of one of the pack animals. Thomas had every intention of collecting the fifty shilling bounty on the man's head once they arrived in Chester.Tying the prisioners securely with hempen rope they securely tied that in turn to the pack animal and the prisioners had to stumble along behind the party.

There was an air of excitement and a carnival feel as the enlarged group set off across the moor.

The general consensus amongst the merchants was that Thomas and Diccon should be due the silver coins and the silk and damask as a reward for their prompt action against the outlaws, and anyway they were well pleased to get their Blue John without the expenditure of a single groat.For who knew, only God in his heaven, what had become of the rightful owner.

By nightfall the party was off the moor and wending their way into the tiny hamlet of Mottram in Longendale. There was a monastry here and the monks made them welcome putting them up in a communal dormitary. Many travellers passed this route over the moors and the monks were used to catering for large and not so large parties.Once it was known that a knight and his squire accompanied the party the Abbot called the cellerer to him and a feast was laid on. The Abbot was anxious to know how the war was going,for though his monastry was out of theway and had not been affected by any fighting he was an erudite and learned man and any information from the greater world outside Longendale was greatly appreciated.

Thomas had to regale the Abbot and his monks with a slightly sanitised version of events from the Battle of

Mortimer's Cross through to Towton.Upon revealing the numbers killed at Towton a gasp of horror rose up in the refectory hall and many monks crossed themslves. The Abbot owed aliegance to the Yorkist faction though there were some amongst the brothers who favoured the Lancastrian side.Thomas could see that a genuine difference of opinion was evident amonst some of them as they argued for one side or the other.He raised his hands for silence and when the hall had fallen quiet he said. "Brothers in God, the fighting is now over.The Queen and her erstwhile king have fled deep into Scotland and my Liege lord and your King, Edward, is the rightful king in this country."The monks nodded and the Abbot smiled benignly as he called the cellerer over to dispense some more of the excellent Rhenish wine that lay in the Monastry cellers.The monks settled down to their feast whilst a novice read enlightening texts from the hand illuminated bible that lay open upon the lectern at one end of the hall. The story of Nebucanezar and the burning firey furnace had everyone gasping in amazement and after that the tumbling of the walls of Jerico had a similar effect.

Thomas and Dicon left the refectory hall and made their way to the dormitory where several of their party had already taken to the thin pallets that were their beds f.or the night. Thomas said. "I'm just going to check that the dog's alright and see where they've put the prisoners. "He left the sleeping room and hurried through the cloisters into the cobbled yard that lay on three sides of the Abbey. In the stables along one wall the pack animals had been unloaded and fed and watered. In a small secure room with a thick oak door the two prisioners were lying on some filthy straw.Of Orrid there was no sign. Thomas called him several times but the dog did not reappear. Thomas shrugged and made his way back to the dormitory.

By morning after a simple breakfast of fresh baked bread and ale the party was preparing to depart. Amidst the bustle and noise of the reloading of the pack horses and the excitement of the leaving, into the yard came a very self satisfied looking Orrid, closely followed by a long haired yellow coated bitch. Thomas grinned. "So that,s your game is it? You dirty dog. I hope she was worth it" Orrid gave a sharp bark and looked at his doggy friend.

Dicon shouted to the party. "We have many miles to go today and tomorrow before we get to the city of Chester. Mount up and let's go. "He swung himself into the saddle and settled his wooden leg comfortably into a leather cup that had been adapted by him to take the end of his stump.

The merchant's party wended it's way slowly out of the confines of the abbey whilst the Abbot and his top officials looked on. The two prisioners bound again behind the last pack animal were pulled along stumbling in the rough ruts of the road.

The day was one of those beautiful spring days where the early hawthorn perfumed the breeze and the sound of blackbirds and song thrushes filled the air. At the head of the party Thomas and Dicon rode together in companionable silence whilst at their feet running forward and back in a joyous state of playful exuburance Orrid and his lady companion passed back and forth sniffing the ground and occasionally looking back expectantly towards the riders.

"Oh my Lord in his heaven we seem to have got another dog!"

"Well I quite like her looks" "So does Orrid by all accounts,what are we to do with it. ?"

Dicon shrugged. "Nothing, I'll take her on, if a knight can have a dog so can a squire" Thomas laughed heartily, "and you'll deal with the pups will you.?"

"Well if they're half as quick and intelligent as Orrid there wont be a problem. Anyway people love puppies. Lady Eloner could have one "He grinned mischeviously. Thomas just shook his head in a resigned way.

As night fell the party had had an unevntful day and nearly half the distance to Chester had been covered. The two prisioners were exhausted as they had had to walk the distance and when they were locked into a stone holding cell by a constable in the small village of Knutsford they both slumped to the ground and were asleep before their meal of bread an water was brought to them.

The rest of the party were able to find rooms in the White Swan and although the rabbit pie they eat had a slightly rancid taste to it they passed a quiet night and were saddled up and ready to go by early sunup the next day.

With approximately forty miles of hard riding left before they saw the black and white buildings of the north's most important town the party was anticipating a pleasant ride through the Cheshire plain. However the weather had a different plan for them for by eight o clock that morning a downpour so heavy and strong was slashing out of the sky. Making the rough roads almost inpassable as they turned to streams and rivers. Sheets of rain fell from above, lashed horizontal in places by a high wind that had sprung up in the wake of the storm.

The merchants party battled forward against the elements with their clothes soaked and their horses half drowned.With their heads down they were hardly able to see ahead of them and the strong wind was blowing bits of bush and small twigs in a stinging attack that cut faces an d whipped the flanks of the horses.The darkly lowering sky all grey with black shot through it glittered as lightening flashes lit it from within.

At last Thomas called a halt, and the party moved off the road and into the trees that edged it.There was some respite here,but only in as much as the strength of the wind was cut by half amongst the leafy branches.He shouted above the roar of the storm. "Well masters, we best sit this out, for there is little sense in going further." One of the women was crying copiously and trying to cover her head with a corner of her shawl. The wind had completely blown off her coif, and thewig under it, leaving her bald pate as a humiliation for her.Both dogs were looking bedraggled and wet with their fur plastered hard against their bodies whilst the walking prisioners were a complete mess being plastered head to toe in a thick clinging mud that had been thrown up by the hooves of the pack animal they were walking behind.

Still the rain hammered down but at least the wind was starting to moderate.After sheltering for nearly two hours the wind had dropped to the occasional sharp cold blast that caught everyone unawares. Thomas finally gave the orders for the party to continue and so into the relentless rain they struggled. The going was easier but the rain hampered everything.The road wound its way past several small hamlets which for all intents and purposes might have been completely devoid of life so few inhabitants showed their faces to the rain. A forlorn and crooked fingerpost stood at a cross roads. Upon the sign was carved Northwich, the road was well used here and had been cobbled at some time so Thomas decided to take that direction. The party swung left and proceeded along the road. Some sandstone rounded low cliffs came into view and the road led them down hill towards thevillage.Ahead a group of twenty men and women were frantically clawing at the mud and debris that had slid down the slope and engulfed a pair of timber framed houses. Thomas rode up to them and dismounted. It was obvious what had happened.The hillside behind the houses was unstable and the fierce storm had loosened the earth and stones causing a land slidethat had knoocked over one house, and completely engulfed the other.

"Tis the priest's house and he was within teaching some of the village lads how to read. " "How many folk inside?

"We think seven or so" this said by a burly individual with strong looking arm muscles and a leather apron."I am the village blacksmith and my son Jess is with them".

Thomas quickly organised two parties. One to pull out stones and large timbers from the debris the other with wooden shovels to scoop away the brown and glutonous slime that had come down with the land slip.They struggled like maniacs to remove thesludge that covered everything and the rain fell in a relentless sheets that soaked everthing. One of the timber framed houses had been knocked off its stone retaining wall and pushed over. The lathe and plaster infill panels between the timber framing weregaping wideleaving holes through which the interior of the dwelling could be glimpsed. One of the villagers climbed in to the house through one of these holes and the others could hear him moving around inside.His face appeared at the hole.

"Old Megan's in 'ere" he called."She'm covered in shite but she'm not hurt. Just shocked.Help I out with her. "He pushed the old woman out through the infill hole and the others realised that his comment was told in truth and not an exagerated expression for indeed the old lady was covered in excrement having had the contents of the privy fall on her when the house was pushed over.Thankful that she was safe and grinning at her predicament the other villagers wrapped her in a blanket and continued with their rescue.Theother house was in a much worse situation having been almost totoally covered by earth and stones from the land slip. They worked their way into the mountainous pile of rubble and debris that covered the priest's house. Eventually they came upon the front door,a stout oaken affair that had hardly suffered from the land slip. Try as they might they could not pull it open until Diccon had the idea of harnessing one of the pack animals to it and using the horses superior strength to pull the door open..In moments they had fixd a rope around the door handle and whippin up the horse pulled the door open. Inside dust swirled. Silence greeted them and they could see that debris eath and stones had infiltrated the interior. Scrabbling with their hands they removed the detirus as quickly as they could and as they worked their way into the house they came upon the leg of a child sticking up through the pile of debris.Gently they removed the earth from the body and pulled the small still figure from the rubble. One of the female villagers gave a sudden heart rending wail as she glimpsed the face of the dead child. Grim faced the rescuers passed the little figure back to its mother who took it in her arms and sitting on the ground in the pouring relentless rain swayed back and forth in her unconsolable grief.

Another body was pulled from the rubble, this time a female. It was the priest's housekeeper. The rescuers kept digging. Suddenly the rain stopped. The last few drops pattering on the heads of the villagers and a flash of wintery sun illuminated the doorway to the priest house.Thomas heard something.He put his hand up for silence and the work stopped. There it came again a weak tapping fom within the house. With renewed vigour the rescuers clawed their way through the debris.Removing piles of earth and stones they came upon a sieries of large timbers that they took to be the partition between rooms in the house. Some had fallen forward and onto the top of a stout oak refectory table making a cave into which the priest and five children had crawled. Covered in dust and filth and shocked to their souls by their narrow escape the survivours were brought out of the house to much rejoycing by the village smith and others whose children had escaped.

Making sure there were no others still inside Thomas and Diccon rounded up the villagers and they slowly and sadly made their way back to the main street of the village. Northwich was a centre of the wool trade and although there was no licenced market there there was a guildhall and a wool exchange, both substantial timber framed buildings built up on stone plinths in the centre of the village. The villagers ushered Thomas and his friends inside and the seneshall of the local lord Sir Edwin Makepiece came forward to thank them.

"On behalf of our town I thank you and your companions for the help you gave us this day.As a mark of our respect a meal is being prepared and should you wish, rooms will be made available to you to stay the night."

Thomas con ferred with the merchants and the rest of the travellers and given the state of their soaking garments and that it was now coming late into the afternoon they opted to stay in the village.A substantial meal of mutton in a caper sauce with huge trenchers of bread filled their hunger and rooms in various houses around accomodated them. The weary travellers were soon sleeping off the excesses of that relentless rainy day.

Next morningt it was as if the rain had never occurred A bright spring day greeted them, the air was clear and clean, any dust in the sky having been washed out by the rain.The hawthorn blossom gleamed in the morning sun and Orrid gave a joyful bark as he and his lady friend capered about around the horses feet as they were being saddled up.It was a day's travel to Chester and The merchants were chafing at the bit in anticipation of their arrival. Eventually after much hand shaking and expression of undying friendship from the villagers, the merchants party was able to leave the town and as it wended its way over the hill in the direction of Chester Thomas looked back. Behind him he saw six riding horses without counting himself and Diccon and another six packhorses. The two bedraggled prisioners, at least they were dry being pulled along by their bonds and two not very well behaved dogs. He grinned to himself thinking back over his adventures since he had teamed up with these merchants.

The day's travel was completetly different from what had harried them the day before, for now a begnign nature showered them in a balmy spring day a breeze as soft as a silken scarf caressed their cheeks and from the hedgerows the smell of may blossom filled their noses.

Contentedly the party travelled ever closer to Chester until by early afternoon the first of the outlying houses and waydside taverns came into view. Chester was a major town one of the most important in the north having road links with all parts of the kingdom and extensive wharfage which allowed quite substantial vessels to tie up, bringing goods from the near continent and from theisland of Ireland. Some smaller luggers and polacres traded up and down the coast of Wales calling into towns such as Barmouth and Tenby and Whitehaven and Maryport on the Cumbrian coast.

In fact Thomas had toyed with the idea of sailing to London, it would take four days down past the wicked sea currents off the Pembrokeshire coast and then rounding the rough and often fog enshrouded cliffs of Lands end before tacking up channel into the reaches of the Thames. He dismissed the idea as he wanted Diccon and himself to assess the new lands he had been granted.He did not know what sort of reception he might find amongst the loyalist supporters of Thomas Gruffydd and so he wasdetermined to hire half a dozen out of work archers from the garrison at Shrewsbury in order to back his authority should it come to it and any unpleaantness ensued.

Therefore it was with a light heart that he saw the black and white pantiled buildings in the centre of town. He handed over to the constables the two outlaws they had captured up on the moor and spoke with the official who dealt with the payment of reward money. After much discussion amongst this worthy with several of his officials it was accepted that this corpse stinking now of purtefaction was indeed that of Black Jake and the fifty shillings bounty was paid over into his hand.Turning away from the smell of the constables holding cells he and Diccon and the dogs made their way to one of the many inns that filled the narrow streets of Chester. For two groats they were able to secure accomadation for themselves and their animals and they spent a pleasant quiet night upon the flea filled straw palliases that passed for beds.Unfortuneately, excitement in the night between Orrid and Booful,for that was what Diccon had decided to name his dog, resulted in the near full chamber pot being upturned and the banishment of both dogs to the stable below. There was a deal of whining but eventually all settled and Thomas and Diccon were able to get back to sleep.

ᴄChapter Seventeenᴐ

By morning and another beautifulday had sprung up bathing the stable yard in a dust mote speckled fresh air that uplifted the heart. Thomas and Diccon came down to the yard to saddle the horses to find the ostler and the dogs in a mutual frenzy of goodwill and tail wagging. The ostler knuckled his forehead

"Why Maisters thy dogs have done me a favour the like of which I'd give my arm for. They'm killed Big Bad Billie"

"Who's Big Bad Billie?

"Why sir he be this 'uge big and ugly rat what I'e been trying to catch for a six month. He eats all the horse oats and he fathers more little uns than what I'd like to say. " The ostler pointed to a truly enormous rat body that lay on the stable floor. From tail to head it was a cubit long and wide and sleek with a fat tail the size of a man's finger. It's jaws sagged open to reveal curled yellow teeth covered in a horrid saliva. The dogs stood proudly by wagging their tails.

Thomas lent down and patted Orrid on the head. "Well, you're forgiven for knocking over the piss pot. Good dog !"

They saddled their horses and the two pack animals that now held all the other plunder and goods they had aquired through their months of travel and left the city through the southern gate over the River Dee in the direction of Wrexham.This road was a well travelled thoroughfare and as they trotted on they passed a myriad colourful stream of other travellers. A dray loaded down with oak barrels and driven by a fat monk in a brown habit,.A gaudily dressed jester playing on a lute to entertain the passers by and with a leather plate out in font of him to catch any offerings. Haughty ladies and their maids disdainfully holding their dresses out of the mud whilst slyly casting glances at Thomas and his companion.Up ahead a huge crowd had gathered by the road mainly good humoured but with the occasional snide remark being bandied about. They were all watching an impromptu performance of a huge and hairy black bear from the Russian Caucauses.Its minder was a man six foot or so tall swarthy skinned in true gypsy fashion with a wide brimmed feathered hat and a curled whip in his hand. The bear was towering above the crowd its tiny feet incongerous against its huge body as it swayed and moved in time to the music of a flute played by a small gypsy girl whose neck and ears were covered in silver filigree jewellry.The bear was wearing a spiked metal collar to which a substantial chain ran back to its owner's other fist, and Thomas noticed that the skin around its neck was fur free and suppturating with pus from sores where the collar and chain had cut it.

They edged past this spectacle, even the dogs seemed lothe to look at or even sniff this huge captive wild beast. The crowd around the bear meant that the road ahead was quite free of traffic and putting spurs to their animals thay cantered away leaving the crowds behind them. For some miles they made good time on the road and by lunchtime they were entering the border township of Wrexham. The law stated that no Welshman could enter the towns of Chester or Wrexham upon pain of death, they were not allowed to carry weapons except for a knife to eat with and in the case of Chester no Welshman was allowed within the town precints from sunset to sunrise.They were forbidden to gather together and also forbidden to own or keep a tavern.Naturally these draconian rules had gone a long way to fuelling the hatred the welsh felt for their neighbours.

"Good job we were born the English side of the Lugg" sniffed Diccon," or we'd be banned from here." Thomas was looking around him at the poor state of the houses and hovels that made up he main street."Don't think I'd mind if I was banned from here. What a hole. Look at that place"He ponted to a timber framed building that was canted over on one side so severely that the gable end was resting on the ground. Still people were coming in and out of the door way and then he realised it was an ale house.

"My God in his heaven these folks don't give a damn, as long as they can keep on drinking!"He sniffed"Come on Diccon lets get out of here. He brushed past an importuning hand held out by a huddled figure, a woman with a dirty shawl wrapped around her bone thin shoulders and holding a toothless baby to her flaccid breast.

"Help me kind sirs I beg of you. I ain't eaten in three days, my babes dying of hunger. "Her imploring eyes sparked some sympathy in Thomas and he lent down towards her. "How is it you find your self in a state like this mistriss?Cannot the local Abbey help out or the town poorhouse?"

The woman swallowed and tears started heavily from the corners of her eyes."Twas a time when I never thought I'd fall this low, I come from Brecon way and did live on a farm up in the hills. We had a good life Edmund and me then come the soldiers,Thomas Gruffydd the Welsh devil, the owner of the farm, said we was to go. Giving the farm and the land to his men. Edmund fought them and they killed him. Me they turned out onto the road six months gone and they speared m y little ones to death. "She sobbed inconsolably.

Thomas squatted down beside her. "Listen goodwife. Tis I who am now the rightful owner to all Gruffydd's land, so that makes me owner to your farmand your landlord.. Take this groat, feed yourself and the babe and meet me here in one hours time an we shall ride to your farm and take back possesion of it for you."The woman looked first at the coin then at Thomas. "Tis a miracle, Lord it is a miracle"She took the groat and stumbled off in the direction of the market where food stalls were doing a desoltory trade in rabbit pies and pottage.

Diccon said. "God's bollocks and cock, you'd pick up any lame duck that looked at you.!" "Not in this instance my squire, she is one of my tenants and I owe her a duty of care, and anyway I'd like to see her farm"

They in turn bought food in the market and after satisfying their hunger they helped the woman whose name was Megan up onto the back of the packhorse and set off once again.

Night was falling as they came within sight of Shrewsbury Castle and made their way straight to the Three Tuns where the land lord remembered them from Yule tide but was truly amazed at the change of fortune that had happened to then in the six months since.They were given the best room in the place as befitted their new status and Megan and the baby were ensconced in a garret room. They all eat a hearty meal and were snoring off the effects of the travel within an hour.

Next morning as they broke their fast with fresh baked bread and ale sitting companionably around a strong oak table in the main room of the Three Tuns.Thomas spoke up."We need to find six likely archers to come with us into the wild country round where Megan's farm is.Thomas Gruffydd's men are very unlikely to want to give up their power and what they see as their land. We may have a bit of a fight on our hands" "Do you think six is enough?" "Aye, for now, all must be excellent shots, take 'em down the butts and five out of six hits on the bull and they are in. Pay will be a shilling a day and all found. Each man to bring his own weapons and horse, I'll supply the shafts.." Diccon nodded. "I'll get on that straight away"He jumped up from the table and calling the dogs to heel set off in the direction of the castle. He knew that a number of unemployed soldiers usually hung around the keep in the hope that a bit of freelance work would come their way. It often did for in these lawless times many disputes were best solved with the expression of a bit of muscle. Sometimes legitimate soldering oppurtunities presented themselves, other times it was merely a frightening exercise taking place. After Mortimer's Cross many of the survivours had ridden on to London with the king in a fit of euphoria and plunder lust but many more had returned home to be with their families.

Diccon crossed the drawbridge into the keep the dogs by his side. Ahead of him squatting by a small fire half a dozen mail clad soldiers were dicing and laughing together.

"Any amongst you archers ?" He asked.They shook their heads"Nay Maister,all archers are down the butts today 'tis the 'Golden Arrow shoot out"Diccon tipped his hat and turned away, he walked briskly across the river and down to the water meadows were he knew the practice butts were set up and sure enough a crowd of young men were milling about flexing their bow shafts and their fingers joshing one another or inspecting a variety of arrow shatfts laid out on a rack some hundred paces from the butts. The targets themselves had been modified from the usual, making the central boss much smaller, so it would be even harder to hit the bull accurately time after time.Some tables had been set up under an awning, on these were a number of leather purses of various sizes and in pride of place a golden arrowupon a wooden rest.. Cast entire in the precious metal right down to the bodkin point. It must have been worth a small fortune, at least a years salary for an archer. It was the most coveted prize and had been provided by the Honourable Company of Bow makers one of the most important guilds in the town.

A trumpet rang out over the field and the hubbub of voices died away until a virtual silence had descended.A thin faced man with silver hair blowing from beneath his feathered cap stepped up to the dias.

"My Lords ladies and bowmen. You all know why we are here today and what are the prizes, but for those of you too deaf to have heard or to drunk to have noticed I shall run through them and the rules once more. "There was a collective sigh of resignation. The man continued "First the prizes. Fourth prize a purse of ten shillings. Third prize a purse of twenty shillings,second prize a purse of fifty shillings. And finally the Golden arrow itself and the knowledge that the winner is the best archer in Shrewsbury and that shall be proclaimed around the town."There was a smattering of applause.The man held his hands up for silence. "Each participant shall fire three arrows of his choice at the targets.Closest to the bull wins. Judged independantly by the Sherrif of Shrewsbury. "He pulled off his hat and bowed deeply in the direction of a gorgeously dressed individual wearing the chain of office that designated him Sherrif.This worthy nodded back.

"Let the games begin"The trumpet bellowed out once more and those men taking part shuffled forward into a line of some sort just behind a marker on the grass. Diccon looked over at the butts. They were at least one hundred paces away and the central bulls were tiny in comparison to normal.

An archer stepped up to the mark. Dressed in green kersemere with a jaunty feather stuffed into his skull cap he grinned round at his mates.Giving his name as Jed Long Trousers he notched his bow and taking careful aim let fly his first shaft..There was a collective sigh of dissapointment as the arrow quivered to a stop in the outer ring of the target. The other two shafts faired no better and hanging his head in shame the man went to collect his arrows from the target.The next archer up and the next were no better and Diccon was beginning to despair that there were any accurate bowsmen there when a strikingly good looking youth of no more that eighteen stepped up to the mark. His bulging shoulder muscles rippled under his cut off linen shirt and the muscles in his neck were like cords as he effortlessly hauled back on his bow."Peterkin of Petersham" he announced himself, and letting fly his arrows one after another with hardly a second's thought between each, the shafts spun true and fast towards the butts. Again a collective sigh went up amongst the crowd,but this time in admiration, for each shaft had struck home within the tiny area of the bull.The young man grinned and stepped away from the mark.Another took his place. This one not so accurate but still with one sure hit to the bull.Then up to the mark came a huge muscular looking man scarred across the face with an ugly countanance and his head shaved both sides to leave a cocomb effect of bright red hair. "Red Roger" he called to the clerk who was writing down the details. "And I be from Stoney Stretton."This was a village a few miles to the west of Shrewsbury.As he stepped up to the line it became obvious to the crowd that this man was covered in intricate black tattoos across his upper chest and arms and the whole effect was one of a frightening and mysterious stranger in their midst. Red Roger loosed his shafts. Again they fell within the bull's centre. He bowed mockingly towards the crowd and stepped away from the line.A thin idividual no more that five and a half feet tall was next up to the butts.Cedric Stevens was his name, and although his slight size and generally undernourished look had the audience catcalling and shouting derogatory remarks at him,his accuracy was of the highest. Three arrows again on target, but this time so close together that the Sherriff had difficulty seperating them. And so it went on. Many hopefuls stepping up many hopefuls dissapointed.By thetime thirty bowmen had competed Diccon had a list of six men he wanted to ask about. Finally the last competitor stepped up to the mark.A striking young man again with the bulging shoulder muscles of the archer, but this time the look of expirience on his face led Diccon to think that here was a time served soldier. Dressed in Lincoln green jak and hose and with a sturdy pair of leather boots upon his feet the young man turned to the clerk.In a broad Devonian accent hard for northern

Shrewsbury folk to follow he said." I be Bittersweet John of Oakhampton" there was a laugh from the crowd. "Oh ar, what sort o names that then, Bittersweet, babies name innit.?"The crowd laughed, Bittersweet John ignored them and stepped up to the mark. Pulling three arrows from a quiver on his back he stuck them in the ground before him then taking the first he examined it for flaws and finding none he notched it to his bow string and loosed it at the target. It spin close and true and hit the butt plumb centre. He examined the next arrow in the same way and loosed. There was a sigh of disapointment from the crowd for they could not see where the shaft had gone, but then the Sherriff raised his hand and shouted "He has slit the first arrow with his second. "The sigh changed to applause as the crowd woke to the fact that here was a true champion. The next shaft left Bittersweet's bow and plunged straight through the goose feather flight of the last splitting the arrow as cleanly as a bill hook might have done.A huge cry of astonishment went up from the crowd. To split an arrow once was not unheard of but to do it twice, this could be devil's work or at the very least supreme accuracy.The Sherriff shouted up the field. "A winner, Bittersweet John wins the Golden Arrow "

The young winner bowed left and right and a huge grin crossed his comely features.He stepped up to the dias to receive his prize from the Sherriff.The other three prize winners followed suite and with varying degrees of humility accepted their winnings.As soon as the ceremony was over and the crowds in the Butts field had started to disperse Diccon approached the winners who had gathered beside the dias to talk about the contest.

"I salute you worthy winners "He said" and I have a proposition for you. My master Sir Thomas of Lingen has need of some accurate archers to ride with him into the Forests of Radnor and south towards the town of Presteigne to check his land for marauders and outlaws.It may be dangerous work but the pay is good, a shilling a day and all you can eat and drink. Warm dry lodgings where practicable. All arrows supplied by us, the only part which is your responsibility is that you must have a horse and to bring your own weapons. What say you?"

Red Roger and Peterkin instantly agreed. Cedric Stevens declined on account of having to look to his aged mother who was in a poor state of health in their hovel home on the outskirts of town.

Bittersweet John turned down the offer flat.

'No way maister do I want to be fighting for some lordling. Not when I have just won a gold arrow worth a years wages. "He shrugged dismissively and walked away back towards the town.

Diccon called after him'Should you change you're mind we're staying at the Three Tuns, ask for Diccon.' Bittersweet John raised his hand but did not turn his face back.

Red Roger and Peterkin followed Diccon back to the tavern where he introduced them to Thomas and the dogs and set them down with a trencher of good beef stew and a pot of ale.

He turned to Thomas and said. "Could only find these two, but they're the best, Roger here has got a real good eye for an accurate shot, and so has Peterkin.'

Thomas eyed Red Roger. He saw before him a well set up beefy individual with the overdeveloped muscles in his upper body that always denote a well practised archer. This man was covered in black tattoo swirls that ran across his chest from armpit to armpit giving him a slightly repellant appearance.That combined with the fact that his head was shaved up to the crown with only a three inch strip of bright red hair like a comb on a cockerell and the three silver hoops that adorned his left ear lobe all combined to give him the appearance of a thug. Prehaps this is what he wanted for many young men a frightening appearance was enough to deter most bullies and thieves.

'So Roger, where do you hail from' asked. Thomas. Roger grinned and in a suprrising melodious voice he said.' I'm from Stoney Stretton, tis a village just north of Shrewsbury, Just three hovels and a leper hospital. Before I took to archery I helped with the lepers, you know, cleaning their rooms and changing bedding. ' Thomas felt an involuntary desire to move away from the red head, but steeled himself against his feelings, for he knew that a leperosy was not as frightening or contagious as many other illnesses or disease that ran rife through these times.' Roger noticed his body language and smiled. ' Ah I see you'm not afeared of the rotting contagion.Not like some, who wouldn't let me into the alehouse for fear of summat, I know not what.That's what set me on the archer's route. Reckoned I ought to be able to stand up for myself. ! Diccon broke into the conversation.'Have you had any expirience of soldering?

" none at all sir,but I am keen to learn." "Good, well you'll learn well with our team. Welcome.Now tether your horse along side ours and have another pot of ale. "He smiled at the man and turned his attention to Peterkin of Petersham. "Now what about you, cully, where be you from." "Petersham, Kent, once a levied soldier in Calais, invalided out when I got an arrow through the leg.He pulled his hose down to reveal a nasty puckered but long healed arrow score across the calf. >"Took a good half year to heal, that did, but none the worse now. "He nodded at Diccon, "didn't have to have the leg off thank the good Christ " Diccon smiled. "Welcome Peterkin. Same applies, tether your animal and get a pot of ale.

There was suddenly a flurry of activity around the entrance to the tavern yard with the ostlers trying hard to stop a pair of scrawny looking but almost identical young men from getting into the yard. Both were wearing rusty and holed chain mail vests, both carried well cared for yew long bows and both had a shock of bright blond hair and an identical fetching wide smile. "In unison they cried out. "We are the twins, we can shoot an arrow straight, you can't tell one from 'tother but your're getting the best of the two. I be better than 'ee and he be better than me."Thay gave mocking bows and waited expectantly.

Thomas laughed outright. "Well boys, you've raised my spirits stright away, welcome. Have you got mounts?" "No Sir, tis the one let down to our plan to join you. I told 'ee "Here he pointed his thumb at his twin"We ain't got a chance without a pony and 'ee said."Only a Pony,Tony that's balony, let's go in for it, we shan't be lonely !"Thomas laughed again. "Well well, rhyming twins. You boys could bring us luck. Have you been soldering before?" "Oh yes Sir, in a fight not in the night. It were dross at Mortimer's Cross. But only but only for they Welsh. " "Ah, we fought at the Cross. A good swift battle.And after?, you didn't want to stay with the King and fight more?"

".Plenty 'o plunder, we knocked 'em asunder, they drowned in the river, but we had to go home to see to the little 'uns dying from fever." Thomas shook his head in sympathy. "Well boys, welcome to our band. Have some pottage and a tankard of ale and we'll find you mounts after. "He turned to Diccon. "What think you Diccon?"

"Seems alright to me, the dogs like 'em any road up.!"He pointed at Orrid and Booful who were siting on the ground with expressions of great interest on their faces as they watched the two identical twins in front of them.Once all the new recruits were fed and watered Thomas and Diccon went about getting hold of some riding horses for those that didn't possess any.They were able to buy two palfreys which suited the twins and two more packhorses, for what with the extra kit they would need to carry, such as arrows, shelter material and cooking equipment the original pack animals were too laden down to take anything else.So now their convoy consisted of seven humans less the baby, and four packhorses with two dogs running free. They set off from Shrewsbury the next morning striking west in the direction of Bishop's Castle.This was dangerous outlaw country on the borders of England and Wales and maraurdering Welsh men were known to make raids across the hills, steal cattle from the prosperous English farms,and dissapear back into the depths of The Radnor Forest which covered the hills for as far as the eye could see.There were not many roads of any type leading towards the west and what tracks there were often made by sheep or cattle and petered out before they began.Thomas and Diccon rode ahead of their party leaving the others to protect themselves a.nd the woman. In fact Megan had been a bit vague as to where exactly her farm had been situated saying only that she'd recognise it when she got close.. The other side of Bishop's Castle was the best she could come up with.

By late afternoon they were clattering down the steep mainstreet of the market town of Bishop's Castle making their way towards the Ring 'o Bells where they had stayed before.The landlord welcomed them as long lost customers but his prices had risen and by the time Thomas had negotiated a price for the whole party and the stabling of the horses he was a shilling worse off. They were sitting in the ale houses' main room with tankards of ale before them. The baby suckling contentedly at the breast and the convivial conversation running happily between them all when suddenly the door to the outside crashed open and three heavily armed soldiers strode in. They were dressed in chain mail vests and each carried a sallet. Their weapons were sheathed, but their attitude proclaimed that they weren't to be trifled with. Thomas felt Megan tense up and look with horror at the tallest of the trio. She lent across the table and whispered. "That be 'ee, the tall one, the one that killed my man and threw me off my farm" Thomas whispered back"Quiet for now, we'll find out more, but let things lie for now. He motioned to the others who had fallen quiet at the entry of these strangers.

"Ale, landlord and be quick about it!" the leader shouted as he threw himself down onto an oak chair that groaned under his weight. The other two glared around the room. They too sat beside their companion..As soon as their ale arrived they set too as if no drink had passed their lips for months and drained their tankards, calling for more. When they were satiated with the drink one of them produced a pair of bone dice which he idly tossed up into the air."Anyone wanting a bet on the dice?" he asked. This was said in such a way that they all knew it was an invitation to be fleeced. "No takers then, what's wrong with you, you lily livered or what?"

Red Roger looked across at him and said mildly"I'll play ye, but only with my own dice. "He produced a worn pair of yellowed ivory dice that had seen many a session and tossed them onto the table.

"You must be joking cully, dost think I come up the brook ?Why take on a pair of dice I don't know, I don't think so "and he shook his mop of dirty grey hair."

"well Cully! Same applies!" said Red Roger dismissively.

"You sayin' I'm a cheat?" The soldier half rose from the table and looked beligerantly at Roger.

"No mate, but what's good for the goose is good for the gander." The soldier subsided with much muttering and evil glances in the direction of Thomas's party.

"Who are you, anyway and where you going.? We look after the district around here and we don't like cocky bastards with red hair and their mates."

Thomas looked up "Who is it then that looks after this district.?" The tallest and meanest looking of the trio tapped his chest. "Tis I, Morgan ap Griffiths who run things here on behalf of my liege lord.. Thomas Gruffydd"

"When was the last time you saw your Lord?"Asked Diccon.

What's that to you you wooden stumped freak"The soldier sneered."I might not see him for a month or two but he'll be back you mark my words." Thomas produced a piece of parchment from his satchel and held it out to the man "read that!"

"Can't read "

"I shall read it for you. 'By the power invested in me as rightful monarch of all of England and Wales I hereby attainder all lands previously owned by the traitor Thomas Gruffydd who fought against me at Mortimer's Cross and I give them to my beloved and well trusted servant Sir Thomas of Lingen. Signed with the great seal of Edward. King of England."

The three mailed soldiers looked shocked. One of them had his mouth hanging open in amazement."You can't do this, this is our land this is Gruffydd's land." "Not any more" said Thomas. You'd do well to clear out from the district as soon as possible before you are arrested as traitors and put on trial. " "You wouldn't dare" shouted the leader.He reached for his sword, but before he or his companions had time to draw all Thomas's men had drawn their daggers and menaced the trio. Realizing they were seriously outnumbered the three soldiers sheathed their swords and gathering their bits of armour left the Ale house. Thomas breathed a sigh of relief. "Thank the Good Lord for that. I didn't want bloodshed in the Ring 'o Bells," He called the landlord. "Where do those men live and how far from here.?" "Up in the hills Sir about three miles, they took over Ty Twt farm and they have fortified it with a wood pallisade.They are dangerous men and best avoided." "We'll see about that!, more ale,and then we depart to our beds for we have a nest of vipers to clear out on the morrow ".

In the yard of the Ring o' Bells Thomas's warparty was getting a last minute breifing from both Thomas and Diccon.

"Ty Twt Farm is about three miles from here in the direction of the hamlet of Mainstone, it's right on the edge of the Clun Forest. We'll ride there and surround the farm. Each archer will be given a postion to cover and I want you to faithfully stay in that position. They have fortified the farm by making a palisaide in front of it. So it may be a hard nut to crack.We think there are only three of them, but there may be more living there than we expect I shall give them every chance to leave peacefully, but I expect a fight. Now each of you take two dozen shafts and a spare couple of bowstrings. Tis must be a shooting fight and not a sword fight. Do you understand." The twins looked dubious and for once didn't rhymthe their words.

"Sir Thomas, what if our arrows fall short, what if we don't hit anyone?" "Oh, you'll be alright" Thomas reassured them"Just count it as good shooting practice."The twins nodded in unison and went to collect their allocation of arrows. Once the party was fully armed and accoutred Thomas gave the signal and they trotted out of the yard. Megan had opted to stay behind with the babe being apprehensive that things could go wrong.

They trotted out of Bishop's Castle on an overgrown track that led them in the direction of the forest After some time the hills around had taken on a lovely rounded shape and although they were clad all over with thick forest trees it was still possible to make out the stunning beauty of the land scape. Ahead of them in a commanding position and within a cleared area giving a field of fire over the whole hill side stood Ty Twt Farm.A single story stone building thatched in reed with small windows and a large chimney.A spiral of smoke issued from the chimney

"Someone's home then "muttered Diccon.

Thomas raised his hand to halt his party some hundreds of yards short of the farm.They dismounted and hobbled the horses.They were below the sight line of the farm as the house itself had been built on a small mound to give a better view of the area. A wooden palisade three trunks high ran all the way round the front of the farm.Cut from forest pine trees and pulled into line by heavy horses this was a formidable defensive object that had Thomas puzzling over the best way to approch it. He fanned his men out around the farm leaving the twins to the front between himself and Diccon and putting Red

Roger and Peterkin at the back of the building to stop any escape from there.

Cupping his hands together he shouted out "Ty Twt Farm, come out where we can see you !" There was no reply. "I 'm giving you one chance to leave. If you go now we shall not molest you. This is your last chance to leave peacefully." Suddenly there came the sound of an arrow's flight and a crossbow bolt struck the ground in front of Thomas. He ran back into the cover of the trees. Things went quiet, then from one end of the farm where a stable or byre was adjoined the double doors flew back and with a thundering bellow of a war cry and a smashing of hooves the three men they had seen the night before charged out on horseback their swords unsheathed and their horses wild eyed.

"Shoot them down boys. "Cried Thomas as he notched and let fly.Accurate arrows from all in front of the house spun towards the soldiers. Three shafts buried themselves in the chest of the leader's destrier and another two arrows hit the brigandine of one of the soldiers. He tumbled from his horse and lay still. The third man had escaped the arrow storm and was riding off as if the hounds of hell were after him.The leader fell forward trying to extricate himself from the weight of his mortally wounded horse as it collapsed on the ground and lay there quivering. Another three arrows slashed into him, two in the chest and one through the slit in his vizor.He fell back all life gone from him.Thomas shouted "Stop firing.We'.ve done for them. Twins, take a look in the farm, but careful there may be more hiding out!.The twins ran forward across the palisade and into the house within minutes they were out again shaking their heads

"Nothing in the house, quiet as dust and like a mouse. Nothing in 'ere but a kitchen maid tied to a chair and very afraid. "On hearing this Thomas and Diccon ran forward and into the farm. In the one long main room with a large fireplace at one end where hung the kitchen utensils beside the inglenook, a young woman was strapped to a chair. Tears streaked her face and the bodice of her gown was torn so that her breasts were exposed. She had been branded and burnt upon her chest and nasty deep wounds covered her body. "You're in no danger now, mistress "Said Diccon sympatheticallyWe have killed your tormentors and they'll never hurt you again."

The young woman burst into tears and Thomas undid her shackles and covered her modesty with a table cloth. Once she had composed herself enough to tell her story it transpired that the three soldiers were in the habit of raiding nearby farmsteads and houses and carrying off the female inhabitants for their own unspeakable pleasure and she was just the latest in a long list. The men Thomas's party had killed had been terrorising the district ever since they had arrived six months before.Thomas explained to her that he was the new owner of all this land and that all the farms here about were now under his jurisdiction and protection and that he intended to set up a court of common pleas to address the concerns of his tenants and right any wrongs that had gone on under the jurisdiction of Thomas Gruffydd.

The young woman whose name was Jane of Mainstone and whose farm was run by her brother and elderly father was a mile over the hill deeper into the forest.She was weak and sore from her brutal treatment, but she was determined to return to her father and brother, so Thomas ordered Peterkin to accompany her back home and the two of them set off into the depths of the forest.

He sent the rhyhming twins back into Bishop's Castle to gather Megan and the babe and sufficient supplies to keep her from falling into starvation until the farm was functoining again, and the remaining men settled down to cook a meal and see what state the farm had been left in by its last tenants.

Later that day the sound of horses hooves was heard coming up the track towards the farm.Thomas deposed his men but it was the return of the twins and Megan and the baby. She had a huge smile on her face as she gazed round the farm that was once her home and was now restored to her.

"Thank you, thank you, my lord," she stammered in gratitude.

"Why 'tis nothing, Megan, yours is the right to this farm and so I return it to you.To live here in peace and harmony for as long as you want. I am your landlord, so any problems or worries send me a message and I shall do my best to put them right." "There is one thing,lord. " "What'sthat?" "I am a weak woman on my own with a babe, and although I am happy to be here, I do not know if I shall have the strength to carry out all the duties of a farmer."

Thomas rubbed his chin in thought. "Aye, I see what you mean,"He raised his voice and addressed his men. "Megan here has need of help and protection for a time until she is re established on the farm. Is there any amongst you who would give her that help.?"There was silence for a moment then the twins stepped forward.

"On this farm where Megan lives,a better life for us it gives.

We'll stay and help her each long day until she sends us on our way." They looked around and gave idential extravagent bows.Thomas clapped his hands."Good lads. I shall continue to pay you a shilling a day until you finish here."The twins grinned and nodded.

"Now,we shall dismantle some of this palisade and make the farm less of a fortress and more of a farm. To work!"

The rest of the archers set too with a will and removed the defensive palisade remodelling it into two post and rail enclosures into which sheep or goats could be kept. This instantly transformed the look of the farm and a benign feeling started to overcome the place. By the time the evening meal had been cooked and served the old atmosphere of dread that had surrounded the place had been exorcised.

Thomas and Diccon stood together in the gloaming looking out over the forest ahead of them.

"Well, this is a good place to be I think." "Plenty of work ahead for them all though, and there's not much silver to start them off. " "Don't fret on that score my fine squire. I intend to loan her some ducats to buy stock. She can pay me back as and when."Diccon nodded.

Thomas continued. "On the morrow the rest of us can depart. We'll make for Knighton and after Presteignne. We'll post notices declaring the new land ownership and information about the courts we'll hold. I think Presteigne could be a good place for that,don't you?"

"Yes,Thomas, Presteigne would be prime. First court of common pleas in a month's time. What say you?"They clasped hands and grinned at one another.

Thomas said"I still need to find a suitable manor house for my bride. " "If she'll have you!"

"And a hovel for my squire !" Diccon laughed outright. The dogs both barked at his exubrance."The two friends turned and moved inside the farm out of the chill night breeze that blew up across thehillside.

The morning of the next day dawned bright and fair.The mellow spring breeze that wafted up the valley towards thefarm Ty Twt brough twith it the inticing scent of hawthorn and bluebells. The song birds were in fullthroated glory as they praised the start of another beautiful spring day.Thomas had been up before dawn checking that all was well with the farm and the packhorses. From a leather bag he had extracted twenty ducats in silver coin which he was now counting out onto the table in the farm kitchen. Megan and the twins looked on in awe.

"Now Megan. This money is only a loan from me to you so you can buy stock. A cow. Some goats and sheep to get this farm up on its feet again. Once things are running smoothly and you've made some profit on your animals you can start paying me back. Do you understand?"

Megan nodded dumbly. "Aye, lord. I thank you from the bottom of my heart. We shall go to Bishop's Castle this next market day and buy some animals."Tears came into her eyes and she clasped Thomas's hand." You are my saviour and the best landlord I have ever had. Bless you"

Thomas shook her off. "'Tis only a loan mind. I expect it back next time I call by here."He turned to the twins. "You two make sure Megan is not cheated in the market place,for a woman alone is very vunerable!"They nodded.

"Here are your wages for the time you've been with me" and he passed over seven shillings each to the twins. They accepted with alacrity and stuffed the money away into their filthy brigandines.

Thomas called the others over. "We leave now for Knighton.This is wild country and dangerous.. You have only to look at my squire to see that, he is from these parts. But I thank God in his heaven that I have Diccon with me. He knows many people hereabouts and more to the point he can tell a n outlaw from a hundred paces off." He bowed in the directon of his squire who laughed.

The party consisting of Red Roger, Peterkin, Thomas and Diccon set off in the direction of Clun.The hills here abouts were thickly forested with mature oak ash and elm and the undergrowth was riddled with coney paths and small animal tracks.The silence was complete as the horses hooves padded down silently on years of leaf mould that had covered the way. For not many people passed this way and those that did were fleet of foot and did not wish to stay to long in the forest.Eventually the forest gave way to a cleared area of land that had had stone walls enclosing it. With in sheep with black faces and ears that stuck out comically from the sides of their heads were penned. These were ewes gathered together to give birth under the eye of the farmer and to be protected from predators such as wolves and eagles.

The owner of these animals was checking them against blow fly and maggots whilst his trained sheepdod lay panting at his feet his tongue lolling out between his teeth.

"Good Day. Are you the owner of these sheep. ?"The farmer looked up as if unwilling to exchange a word with these strangers.Then he gabbled a few words in Welsh and went back to his examination of the sheep's arses.Diccon replied in the same language and the farmer instantly relaxed and pulled at his forelock in a subserviant manner. He then reverted to English but with such a strong welsh lilt to it no one could make out what he was saying. The gist of his speech was that he thought the party was part of Grufydd's rent collection, and he was complaining that he had only just finished paying the last quarteres rent and he had no money anyway till after the lambs were born and why didn't people leave folk be to get on with their jobs.

Thomas explained that from now on he was the legitimate landlord and that a quarters rent was a gift from him and for the farmer to tell his friends and neighbours this news and that there would be a court conveyned in Presteigne for the righting of wrongs from the Gruffydd era.

Upon hearing this a delighted grin spread across the face of the old man and he almost capered with delight. Knuckling his forehead and grinning he stood by the side of the track as Thomas and his party cantered away.

And so their progression towards Knighton continued. At every farm and hovel thay came too the same message was passed. A quarter's free rent and a court to right their wrongs. By the time they rode into the hillside town of Knighton. The streets were lined with cheering citizens who had somehow heard the news as it had passed from one to another quicker than fire. Thomas rode into the yard of the Guildhall and dismounted. An official dressed in an ermine trimmed cloak and with a silver chain of office about his neck came bustling up.

"Sir Thomas? " he enquired. Thomas nodded. Diccon leaned across and whispered into Thomas's ear"This be Charlie Mortimer, right tosser. Thinks he's better than all of us put together.!"

"I am alderman Charles Mortimer, mayor of the township of Knighton and I welcome you. "He bowed. Thomas returned the bow and pulled the parchment with his royal warrant from its pouch and handed it to the Alderman. He blushed and passed the document on to a dark clad priest who was standing beside him. "I never have learnt to read" The monk heredoes it for me." The priest took the parchment and looked it over. His eyebrows shot up in astonishment and he proceeded to read out the warrant. By the time he had reached the end the Alderman was almost wetting himself with excitement. For here in front of him stood potentially the most powerful individual in this part of the Marches. Not a man to cross in fact one to be deferred to in all things.

Thomas said "Two things I shall ask of you Alderman. First I need a team of clerks with clear writing to make me some notices to be put up in the villages and townships around. I shall need at least one dozen of these." The alderman looked a bit shocked at the severity of the order, but he passed it on to the priest who bustled off to fulfill it amongst the novices in the Abbey that was but a stone's throw from the centre of town.

"Secondly, I want a list of all empty manor houses in the district down as far as Presteigne. Especially those used or occupied by Thomas Gruffydd." Again the Alderman looked a bit worried but after some thought he said, "Stapleton Castle outside Presteigne, a league from the town. A fortified manor house on top of a hill. Owned by Grffydd, but empty since the battle at the Cross. That may do you Sir Thomas" Thomas nodded. "I shall look at it on the morrow. But now a place to stay and some food."

The best room in the White Swan was prepared for the new land lord's party and the packhorses were stabled alongside the riding horses in the ample yard that filled almost the whole of the bottom part of the town. Whilst they gathered in the main room of the ale house awaiting the pigeon pie and leeks the land lord had promised them a constant stream of supplicants passed before them. Some with stories so horrowing about treatment by Thomas Gruffydd's soldiers that they were instantly referred to the court conveined in Presteigne later that month.Other less important problems were dealt with there and then. Usually amounting to nothing more than neighbour disputes or rumours of thefts or adultery commited by bored housewifes with their neighbours or worse their servants. One story concerned two peasants who had trapped a swan in a net in the local river and each was claiming jurisdiction over the bird.One was holding it by the neck and the other was gamely holding its feet as the creature struggled to escape them both. The peasant at the head had several nasty cuts and bruises about his face where the bird had tried to peck him and gain its release.Thomas's judjment was as follows."Neither shall have the swan.We shall cook the bird and distribute the meat evenly between them,less some meat for our table. "The two peasants accepted this verdict equitably and then stupidly let go of their victim. With a sieries of squarks the swan flapped around the room and disapeared though the open door to the ale house and freedom,leaving the peasants with slack jawed disapointment writ large on their country faces. Diccon and Thomas roared with laughter as did the others in the party.

"Well that's one problem solved "Thomas chuckled. The two peasants with disconsolate faces and still arguing the toss left the Guildhall.

The young priest who had been given the task of making several notices to nail up around the villages came into the room. He approached Thomas and said "Sir Thomas. The novices are gainfully employed on the task you set them and by vespers I should think they will all be copied out. I have here a finished example for you to look at and approve." "Thank you Father."Thomas took the proffered parchment sheet an looked it over.Within some curlicues and other swirly edging the following message had been skillfully executed.

'Take note. All citizens who hereto for owed alliegance to The TRAITOR Thomas Gruffydd who was KILLED at the battle of MORTIMER'S CROSS. Now shall owe their aliegance to SIR THOMAS OF LINGEN who is their new liege lord and to whom all rents and dues are to be paid.

The said SIR THOMAS will be conducting a court of COMMON PLEAS in the township of PRESTEIGNE on MIDSUMMER DAY 1461.

To right wrongs and settle disputes arising from the rule of The TRAITOR GRUFFYDD.

"Yes, that will do very well. Thank you father for the efficient way you've done this for us."The priest nodded and said "Should you have need of any spiritual matters that I can help you with or if you are in need of a personal priest for your household I would be available, my name is Cedric."Thomas nodded in return.Father Cedric turned and left the room carrying the parchment notice. "Well, he seems a likeable priest, nothing too devious in his eyes."

Diccon looked dubious. "Well you could do worse I suppose.Give him a trial as your household priest and see how he goes. You can always dismiss him if he seems to arrogant." "Or too Godly !" The two friends laughed. Thomas summoned Peterkin and Red Roger over to the table."A task for you two if you wish it.? Take these notices and ride throughout my holdings. Nail one up in each village or town you come to. Talk to as many folk as you can about the court on midsummer's day. Explain about the rent amnesty for one quarter.That should bring you a lot of friends! And ride back here once you are done. Diccon and I are going to inspect some demenses that Gruffydd owned. But we shall return to this alehouse.Any questions?" "Aye, Sir Thomas. We shall need some silver to pay our way no doubt." "Indeed Roger, and you shall have it. Your wages for the time you have been with me and another five shillings each to ease your passage through these lawless regions.I don't need to tell you not to drink it all away Do I ?"Never fear Sir Thomas.We shall make a note of all expenses" "Good man, now go and find Father Cedric and see when his notices will be ready."

The two men turned and left the alehouse. Diccon and Thomas finished their ale and saddled up their horses. Calling the dogs to their side they trotted out of the stable yard and up the hill in the direction of Presteigne and Offa's Dyke.

The road rose steeply for about two miles. Heavy forest glowered down upon them with the occasional field cleared by farmers for their sheep. The rounded flowing hills of Radnorshire stetched away into the distance.

As they gained height so the forest started to thin and the sheep enclosures became more common. Eventually the road levelled out and then ahead of them they saw the ancient earthwork that King Offa had built a thousand years before to separate the warring English from the Welsh.Although long fallen in to disrepair the substantial ditch and bank was still a formidable obstacle on the face of the counrtryside.Thomas pulled his horse up and lent on the saddle bow and contemplated the scar on the ground ahead of him.

"Some work needed to make this I think"He mused. "Why it must have been twenty feet deep, and the bank another ten feet above that. No warrior would have survived long against such an odds"He shook his head in amazement as he gazed out into the distance to follow the line of the Dyke as it stretched away into the blue haze of the spring day.

"Diccon nodded "Aye, a devil of a ditch, and they say it runs from here north all the way to the sea and south again right down to Chepstow way,at least it kept those bastard Welsh out!"

Orrid and Booful had flushed a rabbit and there was frantic barking and tearing about. But the wild coney was too swift for the dogs and now its fur tail bobbed out of sight down its burrow leaving the dogs panting and unable to get at their prey.A deal of scrabbling and whining and scratching at the entrance to the rabbit hole left the dogs none the wiser and the rabbit free to breed again on the uplands of Offa's Dyke.

Calling the dogs to heel the two friends slowly made their way across the high land and started the descent into the township of Presteigne.Once again the forest encroached upon the track they were travelling, but both men knew their way in this district having been born and bred in the area.Maybe a league from the settlement of Presteigne and about the same size and importance was the village of Stapleton. For years Thomas had known about Stapleton Castle a fortified manor house standing with some prominance upon a single hill that rose from the floodplain of the river Lugg as it meandered through the lush green river meadows that provided so much wealth to the area.The house itself was a stone and timber structure built upon an earlier motte and bailey castle that had fallen to the depradations of the welsh and been slighted by them.However in later centuries other owners had fortified the new dwelling with a deep defensive ditch and a wood drawbridge which had put off any other attackers and for some hundreds of years each time Stapleton Castle had been the subject of attack, the attackers had taken the course of least resistance and avoided attacking this stronghold on the Marches.

Thomas and Diccon rode slowly towards the castle.

"God only knows why they call it a castle"Said Diccon deriseively,"Why 'tis nothing more than an alderman's house on a tump" "Some tump!" mused Thomas looking up the steep approach to the house.A hard cobbled trackway led up, passing a steep sided quarry,from which the stone for the building had been taken. Ahead of them a deep earthen ditch fifteen feet deep and thirty wide ran round the periphery of the building channeling anyone approaching towards the timber drawbridge.This had huge chains that drew it back towards the entrance to the keep effectively denying entry to any attacker. Behind the bridge the keep was cobbled and a yard big enough for several horses gave way to a charming half timbered and stone manor house with mullioned windows that looked out over a stunning vista to the valley of the Lugg and beyond.

Suddenly a shout rang out across the spring morning.

"No further. Villains. Dismount and come on, on foot, on pain of death"

Diccon cupped his hands together and shouted back. "Who dares call the Lord of Stapleton villain. Show yourself.!"

There was a flurry of activity beyond the bridge and into sight stepped Two old men flanked on either side by two callow youths of no more than ten years, each with a drawn broadsword bigger than they were tall.

"Lord of Stapleton,you say.? Why there has been no lord here since Thomas Gruffydd departed to the war!"

"Well there is now and bow before him, Sir Thomas of Lingen, your rightful lord and master."Diccon put spurs to his horse and cantered over the drawbridge.The old men and the boys could only watch and stare in wonder as these two powerful young men came forward. "And who are you in God's holy name?" The elder of the two bowed. "I am the Seneshall of Stapleton and this my brother. My name is Henry Mortimer. These, "pointing to the two boys "are my grandsons Arthur and Edric." Thomas dismounted and swept a bow."So, before you you see your new lord Sir Thomas of Lingen, made such by the king after The battle of Towton and my squire Diccon of Knighton.Read this if you will." He passed the dog eared piece of parchment forward. It being the royal warrant. The seneshall in turn passed it to the thinner of the two boys who read out what was written on it.Instantly a change of attitude came over the two old men. They bowed obsequesiously and smiled ingatiatingly.

"Enter your castle Sir Thomas. We shall prepare food"Leading the way the seneshall moved into the yard and then through a strong iron nail studded door that was the entrance to the house.Clapping his hands and calling out orders to a team of servants who had been hiding within the house."Bring food for your new lord and his squire. Make haste!" A comly wench dressed in a low cut drindl blouse with a patchwork skirt below hurried forward with a jug of ale. She took one look at Diccon and dropped the jug."Why Alice you always was unable to hold your ale. "Diccon laughed uproariously.

"Dic, is it really you?" she asked as she gazed up at him. "Aye, tis me, and now a squire made up by the King of blessed memory. So hurry off and bring more ale girl, I have a proper Knighton thirst upon me!" Alice ran off. The dogs fell too, licking up the spilled ale. Thomas gazed round at his new hall and felt content

ᴄ⸺Chapter Eighteen⸻

Thomas felt weary and travel stained as indeed he was, for the last eight days he had been riding towards London. Hewas alone, having left Diccon and the dogs behind at Stapleton Castle. His mind was filled with the thought of seeing Elenor again and it was that that wasdriving him ever onward towards the capital.He had invested Diccon with the authority to carry out any works necessary at the castle to ready it for the triumphant return of himelf and his bride to be. Should she have him.,Came his squires jocular farewell. Thomas grinned to himself as he galloped over the downs leading towards Windsor Castle and the smokey haze of London Town.He was still a good seven leagues from the centre of town but already the haze on the horizon was obscuring the brilliant late spring day and a smokey coal scented smell of animal dung and humankind filled the air.

It was nearly six months since he had last seen the woman he loved and doubts and worries filled his mind as his liveried palfrey gathered its feet for another burst of speed. He had been exchanging horses at each tavern he stopped at for the night, and this last was courtesy of the White Swan, Guildford. She was a game little palfrey, more suited for a ladies riding horse than for a sustained

gallop across the roads of south England. He could feel
that she was flagging, so he eased back on his pace and
started to look for a likely tavern on the road.

He passed through the fields and market gardens of
Richmond the houses and dwellings started to become
more substantial and hesaw ahead of him the sign of the
Crooked Wheel..He was soon seated at a table with a
jug of ale and the landlord of the Crooked Wheel before
him to serve his every wish. A fresh black gelding,the best
in the livery stable, or so the landlord said,was on hold
waiting for him to continue his journey.Prices for the
rent of riding horses had increased with his proximity to
London, and to hire the black gelding was costing him
three shillings and sixpence and the palfrey left behind to
be returned to Guildford at the landlord's convienience.
Thomas willingly paid this sum, he had a purse in his
saddlebag that was more than half filled with silver ducats
and crowns obtained on his travels. Money was no object.
He finished his ale and threw a groat down onto the table.
He lifted his weary travel stained frame and climbed into
the saddle. Kicking on his fresh mount he wheeled out of
the stable yard and into the ever increasing traffic that was
flowing along the road into the city.His breakneck speed
of previous days was now severely restricted as more and
more pedestrians, carts, huge hay wains and much other
road traffic hindered the route, slowing everything to not
much better that a slow walk.

Another hours travel brought him within sight of the
walls of the city.He had been riding along Watling Street
from the direction of Richmond, but the pace of travel had
slowed to such an extent that he would have been better off
walking. When Newgate hove into view and the foot traffic
ground to a halt owing to an upturned hay cart right in

the entrance between the two stone towers that designated the way into the city, Thomas knew it was time to take another route.Turning left off the main street he entered a warren of tiny alleyways and tracks that ran around the city walls passing close to and sometimes through the very dwellings that had been thrown up by chance builders against the walls of the city. This slum of hovels stretched back away from the walls for several hundred yards and was being added to everyday by the enterprising citizens of London.A cachophony of shouts and hammering,the smell of excrement and newly sawn timber. The bellowing of cattle and the overall hum of humanity filled the air. Thomas dismounted and led his black gelding. He made better progress and soon had passed the bottlenecks of Cripplegate and Moorgate, two of the other entrances to the humming city.Keeping the towering walls to his right at all times he eventually found himself directly in front of The Bishopsgate.With a sense of relief he joined the snaking and good humoured queque that was slowly being admitted into the overcrowded interior of the city walls.

He passed through the twin towers under the eyes of two bored looking soldiers in the livery of the king. His gelding's hooves ringing on the cobbles that paved the way.Instantly the crowds started to thin as they dispersed into and around the city. Thomas made his way towards the alderman's house. He was feeling more nervous at seeing Eloner again than he had done at any of the battles he had fought. He tried smoothing his hair, but it still stuck up. He looked at his hands, they were calloused and dirty from the journey. Filth engrimed under the nails and the backs of them scarred from the many fights and encounters. He cupped his hands before his face and tried to sniff his breath, but the myriad other smells that assailed him prohibited any knowledge of good or sour breath.Straightening his back he approched the door to the Alderman's house and swung the heavy iron knocker that was there ensconced.

A hollow ringing thud upon the door had no effect, so once again he hammered.

A small iron barred window beside the main door came open and the alderman's servant looked out.

"No one home 'till this evening Sir" this was delivered with a slightly dererential air." "I have come to see the Countess of Hambye" cried Thomas.

"She ain't here Sir, gone to France this last two sennights. Who shall I say called." Thomas felt stunned. After having ridden pellmell across half England always with the thought of Eloner upmost in his mind only to find she was not here quite threw him.

"Give the Alderman my duty and say Sir Thomas of Lingen was asking after him and the Countess.I shall return at eventide, and I hope to see him. "The servant nodded and swung the barred window shut.

With a heavy heart Thomas entered the first substantial tavern he saw and calling for ale and a meal he tried to come to terms with this new knowledge.The food and ale revived him and he ordered a hot bath to be filled in his room. His next set of instructions included a suit of fresh clothing.By the time the servants had toiled up the stairs with the hot water and filled the hip bath to the brim. Thomas had selected and paid for a new set of fetching hose in yellow and black and an equally smart velvet jak which just covered his waist and hips in the new style that was becoming popular.The haberdasher tried hard to sell him a gaudy round hat that made him look quite ridiculous,but succeded in passing off a soft pair of morrocan leather slippers with excessively long points and pretty embroidered edges that he fell in love with straight away. With his purse lighter by seven shillings and threepence, Thomas slid into the hot bath and lay back luxuriating in the soapy water.There came a knock at the door. "Come in "

"More hot water,lord?" The servant girl came forward with a huge steaming jug and proceeded to top up the bath. "Can you shave a man ?" asked Thomas. "Aye Sir, I shaves my father and brothers when they want."

"Then you shall shave me!" He lent back in the bath as she stropped the razor and proceeded to take off the two weeks growth of breard that adorned his face.He felt younger and fitter and more worried about Eloner as he called for towels to dry himself. A great feeling of lassitude overcame him and giving instructions that he was to be woken by sundown he crawled over to the bed and within seconds was deep in a dreamless sleep.

A knocking at his door drew him from the bottomless pit, and with a groan he called 'enter' the servant girl who had seen to his bath stood in the doorway. "Tis just getting dusk Sir Thomas, you asked to be waked then!" "Aye, so I did and thank you." He swung his legs out of the bed and started tp dress in his new finary. By the time he had pulled on the new leather slippers of which he was so proud he was fully awake with thoughts and schemes rushing through his head.His first move he thought was to call on the Alderman and try to find out just where and when Eloner had left for France.He bounded down the stairs and out into the noisy streets of the city. Dusk had not improved either the state nor the smell of the roads and picking his way delicately through the filth so as not to ruin the good new leather of his shoes he made his way back towards Bishopsgate and the house of his friend and mentor Alderman Sir Richard Lee.

It was moments later that he stood before the iron studded door hammering on it with his fist.The small side window opened and the suspicious face of the alderman's servant peered out.

""Oos that knocking?"

"Sir Thomas Lingen to see Alderman Sir Richard Lee."

"Yes sir, one moment sir. "The door swung open and Thomas stepped through. In the yard the servant bowed and ushered him in to the interior of the house. He made him wait in the great entrance hall and bustled off to annonuce him. Suddenly there was a great roar of welcome and approval and Sir Richard came bounding out of the solar running over and embracing Thomas.Holding him at arms length and examining him as if it were the first time he had seen him. Then with an extravagent bow he exclaimed " SIR Thomas, welcome, welcome indeed Sir Thomas of Lingen and a huge grin filled his face. Thomas grinned back and soon was regaling the alderman with the tale of his adventures from the time they had last seen one another.

Sitting at the table in the solar overlooking the pretty garden in which Eloner had walked so often Thomas asked Sir Richard.

"What of the countess, have you any news of her whereabouts." Sir Richard looked worried. "I must say Thomas It is a good thing you are here at last,for I am beginning to worry slightly as to what may have befallen her. She left my home two weeks ago to board one of my carvels bound for France,for a message had come from there to say her mother in law was gravely ill and not like to survive. Eloner assured me she would send a message back with a servant when she knew more, but all is silence. Nothing have I heard since she left."

Thomas looked shocked. "I must go to her, I feel she is in danger Can you help me find passage to France?"

"Of course. I have vessels trading all the time with our near neighbour. In fact The Saint Mary and Saint Martin is due for northern France tomorrow. Pack your saddlebags, we'll have a meal together and I will ride with you to the dock and speak with the captain. As I recall Eloner was Heading for Normandy and this vessel of mine docks in Honfleur. You can buy horses over there. "Thomas nodded in gratitude. He was relieved that now not a moment was to be lost for he had a nasty suspision that Eloner was in some kind of trouble and all he wanted to do was get after her and protect her.

The two men shared a simple supper and by the time Thomas had returned to his inn to pick up his belongings Sir Richard had organised two riding horses and they were trotting through the restless streets of the city on their way to the Pool of London where Sir Richard's vessels tied up.

The rancid river smells interlaced with rotting fish wafted over them as an early evening breeze found its way up from the river. Ahead of them in a natural bow in the river were many craft tied up against a departure sooner or later. Large Caravels with two masts vied for space with the more common cog, the workhorse of the river. These vessels were single masted often with a raised platform in the stern and bow These were the more numerous, in places they formed a floating bridge, o.ver which sailors and tradesmen carried their goods. Sir Richard hailed a wherry and had them row him and Thomas out to one of the largest vessels in the port.Proudly Sir Richard said. "This is my boat The Saint Mary and Saint Martin." Thomas was duly impressed as its carvel sides towered over the tiny wherry below.The boatman hailed the vessel"St Mary and Martin, gents coming aboard"A weatherbaten face with a gold earring under blond curls peered down at the wherry."Sorry Maisters, Capn. Says to say no more passengers. Cabins be full and we sail with the tide." "You tell Capn Fordyke he better find room for this passenger or he's out of a job and he won't be sailing on this tide nor any other." Another equally weatherbeaten face appeared at the rail. This time however after a short perusal of the wherry the face broke into a delighted grin and a rope ladder was thrown done the side. Both men climbed up and Sir Richard explained The problem of Thomas's sudden departure for France.Captain Fordyke was all subservience, and bowing to Thomas he ushered him into his own cabin and stowed his saddlebags. Thomas and Richard clasped arms together and wished each other luck and then Sir Richard clinbed back down the rope ladder and before the wherry was half way back to land a sieries of orders had been shouted that raised the anchor and the lug sail and had the elegant caravel heeling to the slight offshore breese and tacking out between the other vessels in the Pool of London. Thomas stood by the rail and watched as the river bank slowly passed by and then as way was gathered and more open water reached the vessel started to hiss through the water as if it had a mind of its own.The sailors seemed to know their business for with a minimum of orders the main sail was raised and sheeted in, lanterns were lit on stern and at mast heads and the Saint Mary and Saint Martin stood fair for France.

The estuary of the Thames widened and widened until as the sun sank and extinguised the daylight The shore on either side diminished into the darkness. Thomas retired to the Captain's cabin to find that he had been allocated the wooden cot that was the captain's whilst that worthy had had a common hammock slung between the deck beams.

"The owner thinks highly of you Sir Thomas, " "As I do of him.".

"What brings you so quick to France?"Thomas explained his mission and Capn Fordyce listened with some sympathy."We'll be off the Goodwin Sands by midnight, we'll drop anchor there and ride out the night, for'tis too dangerous to go through the sands at night. Many a good ship have foundered on they shallows.By tomorrow eve we should be off the coast of France and all being well with God in his heaven and the weather we dock in Honfleur on the morn."

"What cargo are you carrying?"Thomas asked.

"Mixed. candles. Iron ingots. Timber, rum and good English calico cloth. The Frenchies do like our cloth.There is a ready market for it all in Normandy.On the return we bring wine and spices, onions and hides and anything we can turn a profit on."Thomas nodded, he felt a great tiredness come over him, engendered not least by the neat rum he and the captain had been drinking."I'm for my bed Captain. Fordyce with your permission." "Aye Sir Thomas, sleep well I have a course to plot and after must check the smooth sailing of the vessel till we gets to Goodwin. " Thomas tumbled into his cot and was instantly asleep. He didn't hear rhe rumble of the anchor hawser as it was dropped in the water and he was oblivious to the rising wind that started to howl over theshallow seas around the Goodwin Sands.

Dawn broke on a grey and choppy sea. Visibility obscured by low scudding clouds that wisped across the anchorage. About twelve vessels of different types rode at anchor whilst small cobs and wherries plied their trade from Deal beach with late coming passengers and cargo. Theweather was cold and Thomas had to hold a blanket round his shoulders as he watched with interest the various comings and goings of England's maritime trade.Captain. Fordyce stepped over. "Good morrow to thee Sir Thomas, I trust you slept well?" "Oh like a babe thank you. "Thomas smiled back at him.

"We up anchor shortly and head for France. The tide is on the turn, and that will give us plenty of keel space under us.See those masts?"He pointed his hand out in the direction of the sands and Thomas was suddenly aware of a myriad forest of masts some upright some canted over that stood ahead of them. "Those be ships unlucky enough to fall foul of the sands.There are many more you can't see."Thomas shivered.Suddenly a small figure dressed in striped pantaloons and carrying a fiddle had jumped up on top of the capstan. He struck up a jaunty air and sailors ran to put their weight behind the capstan bars. The anchor came free of the ocean bed and the Mary and Martin swung free.The mainsail was hauled in and the caravel heeled to the quickening breeze soon leaving the other anchored vessels behind.Before one glass had run through they were on a deserted ocean with the chop of thesea throwing spray up and over the decks. The capn. Set a southerly course and beckoned Thomas up to the half deck that contained the ships wheel. Two dubious looking sailors both scarred and with gold earings had solid hold of the spokes of the wheel. They were grinning through blackened teeth.

"They do like it when there's a bit of a blow, makes em believe we'll be in France sooner. More chance to see those dark eyed girls in the taverns of Honfleur." Thomas smiled."Tell me about Honfleur, I believe it was an English posseseion up until a few years back?"

"Yes, we controlled it up until 1450 then the French got it back, those buggers use it as a raiding port to cross the channel and attack places like Sandwich" "Why don't we put a stop to that?" "Too much trade involved both ways, better to let a few marauders have their fun than stop all commerce between the countries.Anyway, they treat us with some respect.Mind you we have been calling in here for the last twenty years, even the stupid Honfleurais must know us by now"He gave a cynical laugh."We'll be off the coast 'ere long and then we tack down to the estuary of the Seine and Honfleur is at the start of the river.You might like to see a chart of the peninsular to find your way."Thomas nodded. "That would be most useful,for I have never been to Normandy."The two men went below into the captain's cabin and he pulled out a rolled parchment chart which showed both side of the Contentin Peninsular. Being a navel chart it was light on detail on land but had every rock and fathom marked at sea. "What are these islands?"Thomas pointed to some well marked islands due west from the coast of France and approximately five to eight miles away." "Oh those, they are the Isles de Manche, Channel Islands.Bad rough waters around those and the weather changes quick. Best avoided if at all possible. There's a good trade between England and the islands however From St Peter's Port.English owned and has been for many years." Thomas was looking at the chart."I see there's a road that runs from Honfleur across the peninsular to Avranches, I think that would be my best route. I have to make for Hambye" "Oh yes, I 've been to Hambye. There's a very well established Abbey there. Yes you could get to Hambye within a couple of days on that route."So saying he rolled the chart up and stashed it back in its drawer.As they climbed the companion way up onto the deck a hail camefrom the crow's nest "Land ahoy, Land on the starbord bow, bout ten leagues off " The captain cupped his hands and shouted up to the look out. "What part Simeon?"

"Could be Cap Gris Nez Capn, could be further dowwn't coast.Find out as we get closer"The captain nodded.The caravel edged over the grey and choppy sea until eventually the whole of the coast of France was revealed about five or so miles off. A low lying grey mass of land hidden for the most part under a low cloud of grey fog that swirled around obscuring one moment and revealing the next..

"Oh I know where we are, see those towers?"He pointed at a sieries of squat Martello type towers that marched down the coast at roughly five mile intervals. "They are the French equivaleant of our towers along the south coast. Mind you,everytime we attack them, the soldiers run off,sothey can't be that good as defences. Another five hours and we'll be off Honfleur."

Thomas nodded and said"Is there a barber or someone able on board, for I have to practice a deception on the French if ever I am to gain the freedom of my beloved. " "Aye, Martin can shave and cut hair. "He cupped his hands and bellowed "Martin, come aft and bring your shaving razor." A sallow thin cheeked man appeared in due course,in his hand he held a canvas roll that he proceeded to unwrap and laid out on the deck several razors and a pair of ornate chased handled scissors.Thomas explained what he wanted and before long he was once again tonsured as he had been all those months before when he had infiltrated the camp of Owen Tudor.Once the hair was removed to his satisfaction Thomas pulled on a leather sallet liner which hid the tonsure and made him look as like a soldier as ever he had been. His thoughts had been running on the best way to gain acess to Eloner and his plan was to pose as her English confessor and gain entry to where she was being held and from there spirit her away as best he could.

The weather started to moderate as the St.Mary and Martin ran down the coast towards Honfleur and by the late afternoon when the estuary of the Siene came into view and the Caravel hove to to take on a local pilot.The sun was streaming down with such force that the pitch in theplanking on deck was starting to melt. "Tis best if we get into port today, with this weather we'll melt soonest if we hove to off Honfleur."Captain. Fordyce was looking over the side of his command as he watched a swarthy fat heavily pespiring frenchman as he tried to climb the rope ladder that dangled over the side.

"Bonjour Jacques! No thinner I see" he shouted good humouredly.The pilot looked up and raised a hand in greeting. Finally his fat thighs and buttocks emerged over the side and with an imense sigh of satisfaction he farted."Mon Dieu Capitain, I have eat too much"He waddled off towards the stern and glancing up at the wind burgoo he gave his orders to the two helmsmen.The St. Mary and Martin got underway and slowly threaded her way through the treacherous and ever changing sand banks off the port of Honfleur.Thomas watched as the town took on shape before him. A long wharf with boats of many sizes tied up against it whilst running back up a gentle hill the houses and warehouses of the traders and merchants of Honfleur. The town was dominated by two structures,the first was the fortified keep a bold four square tower that overlooked the harbour.It bristled with cannon that commanded the whole of the harbour.The other building was the hugeChuch of Notre Dame with its twin towers that almost obscured any view further inland.The wharf bustled with business as sailors loaded and unloaded cargo. A stink of old fish and packed humanity wafted off the land towards the St.Mary and Martin. Overall the raucous cries of herring gulls filled the air above the port. Their vessel nudged up against the wharf and with a minimum of fuss the crew tied her up and furled the great main sail. Capn Fordyce dismissed the pilot with a handful of silver and turning to Thomas said. "Mostly they speak English here, and there is an honest horse broker in St Pierre Eglise Street. Goes by the name of Luc. Tell him I sent you. Now I have much to do and I'll wish you farewell and good luck in your quest."He bowed towards Thomas who returned the gesture and thanked him once again for all his help. Gathering up his saddle bags he left the ship down the gangplank that now joined land and vessel together.Pushing through the crowds of sailors, hangers on and whores who gathered all along the wharf he made his way towards the centre of town. Asking directions for St.Pierre Eglise St.he eventually found an alleyway that led down to a yard with a sign dangling over the gates. Luc Bruisson,Maitre de Chevalier. The sign was newly painted and swung in the breeze with a fiendly creek. Thomas pushed through the gates.Inside a hive of activity greeted him. Several horses, riding and pack animals, were tethered against a post and rail fence whilst ostlers and servants moved amongst them inspecting their hocks and withers and lifting their hooves to examine their shoes.

A tall well set up Frenchman with a black beard and twinkling eyes approached. "Bonour Monsieur, Je suis le patron Luc Bruisson."

Thomas replied in English."Yes, I was sent by Captain. Fordyce. I want to buy two riding horses, on for my self and one for a lady which could also double as a pack animal. "Luc scratched his chin. "I have just the animals for you sir. Please come this way,"he led him to an enclosed stable wherein stood three or four well fed and muscled horses. A pretty looking alert palfrey and a black gelding caught his eye straight away and he asked Luc the price. The stable owner beckoned a servant and ordered him to pull out Thomas' chioce.He walked them up and down and Thomas inspected their teeth. Each animal looked in the prime of health.

"These animals are six english pounds each. "Thomas nodded"How much for bridles reins and saddles for them both?" "Another english pound."

"So thirteen pounds in total. ?" "Oui Monsieur"

Thomas nodded again and said. " you have a sale Luc."He spat on his hand and Luc did the same and they sealed the deal with a hand shake.

Thomas counted money out of his purse and Luc's servant saddled both horses.Fixing the saddlebags across the back of the palfrey.

"I now need to buy clothing and some weapons. Where is an honst trader for those in this town Luc?"

Luc beckoned another minion over. "Lucien, show the English milord to the shops of Fabricant the armourer and Deliel the tailor.You may leave your aimals here until you have completed your business. " Thomas thanked him and

followed Lucien out into the street. The young servant set
a good pace as he walked quickly back towards the town.
They were soon engulfed in the bustle of the market that
went on each day in the cobbled market square. Lucien led
Thomas to another alleyway and pointed down it "Fabricant
la!" Thomas saw a sign with a sword and a dagger painted
on it Lucien turned and pointed to another doorway that
stood framed by gaudy pieces of cloth and several pairs of
hose." Deliel pour les vetements." He smiled. Thomas gave
him a few copper coins and the youth quickly disapeared
back into the crowds.Thomas entered Deliel's shop.A thin
woman of more than middle age with a plethora of hairs
upon her chin came over.

"Do you speak english?" She shrugged" what do you
require?" "Two monks habits,in black, though brown will
do".

"One moment. "She turned into the dark depths of
her shop and a moment later came back clasping a bundle
of wool habits. She unrolled two black one. Each had seen
better days having been stored unwashed and with traces
of food upon then so that they stank of old sweat and
damp. "Four sous each and the girdles another two sous.
"Thomas paid the money and bundling up his purchases
left the sh.op.

Next to Fabricants which was a completely different
expirience. The sign over the alleyway led him into
a spacious yard where the sound of hammer on metal
filled the air as busy smiths made and fulfilled orders.
All around the eaves swords pikes daggers and pole axes
hung in gleaming rows waiting for clients.Thomas strode
into the yard.

"Monsieur?" a smiling blacksmith with overdeveloped sinews and arm muscles dressed in a leather jerkin with his chest bare came forward.

"I wish to buy a short stabbing sword and an english archer's bow. Can you help me?" "Certainly Sir, the bows we keep in this room". The owner ushered Thomas into a high ceilinged square room which had lines running across it from which hung long bows, hunting bows and cross bows.Thomas could see at once that the quality of the weapons was second to none and they were kept in the best of condition. He walked along the rows and selected three bows. A regular archer's bow of yew heart wood, a smaller ladies bow and a small hunting bow. "May I try these?"The owner nodded. "We have butts at the back of the building. But first allow me to show you my stabbing swords." Heclapped his hands and a young lad appeared. A stream of fast French had the lad running out of the room to return moments later with a long box containing half a dozen beautifully wrought short stabbing swords. Thomas selected one that had a nicely tapering blade and a handle delicately made from cow horn and steel entwined. He hefted it and the weight was exactly right. He held it to his waist and the point end only just reached his knee. "Perfect, "He breathed"I shall also require a scabbard for this. Now let us try the bows. " The propriator led him through the yard and out into an alleyway, about two hundred paces long, at the end of which a straw target had been set up.Thomas strung up the yew archer's bow and taking a shaft from the stack that lay on a table in front of himhe flexed the bow. Pulling right back to his ear he let fly. With a whirring sound the shaft buried itself in the centre of the bull."Bravo" cried the owner. Thomas proceeded to shoot both of the other bows and choose the smaller hunting bow over the ladies bow. He ordered two dozen bodkin points and six bow strings and left the armourers thirty shillings lighter by purse but immesurably stronger in weaponry.

The road to Hambye led across the whole of lower Normandy passing through Caen and St Lo and eventually d own the heavily wooded valley to the Abbey itself.This was a two day jouney and after fortifing himself with an eel pie bought in Honfleur market he set off in the direction of Caen.

An uneventful ride brought him past Caen and half way to St Lo before the light went and he was forced to look for accommadation.He found it in a wayside tavern Le Coc D'Or where the food was hot and the bed was infested. But he slept well, and next morning after a wash in the horse trough and some fortifing onion pottage he continued his journey.

He had no proof at all that Eloner was being held in the Abbey, but his instinct told him this was likely. He rode into St Lo, a small market town with some big chuches. A bright day enabled him to look across the heights towards the wonderful abbey at Mont san Michel. He had heard that the sea rushed in from low to high tide at such a rate it could outpace a galloping horse.There was a causeway linking the Abbey to the mainland, but twice a day this was covered by the sea. Many monks and villagers lived on this island to cater for the thousands of pilgrims who visited every year.The stone houses and single storey hovels that clung to the base of the rock, above which the abbey towered, all looked quite substantial to Thomas as he rode down the road until the Abbey was out of sight.The countryside started to take on the heavily wooded bocage aspect that was so typical of Normandy. Small enclosed fields divided by sunken lanes down which the inhabitants of the villages came and went.It was a lush rich landscape with many tall trees.Small hamlets and villages of cob built hovels and farms often inhabited by members of the same extended family covered the land. Peasants working in the fields wished him good day as he sedately walked his two horses ever closer to Hambye. When he saw the long slate roof of the monk's chapter house emerging from the surrounding woodland and he could discern the towers of the stone built abbey, he pulled off the narrow track he was on and swung into a bocaged sunken lane. Stopping his horse he dismounted and proceeded to pull the dirty black monk's habit over his own clothes.Making sure his short stabbing sword was under his robe and out of sight. Checking that nothing suspicious was evident on either his horse or the palfrey he mounted up and walked towards the Abbey.He came out of the bocage into a pleasant open area with cropped grass kept so by several well fed sheep. A cobbled way ran straight to the gates of the Abbey which stood open before him. Several monks in brown habits were working in the grounds that surrounded the abbey. He walked forward until he was level with and then through the double gates. No one challenged him.Through the gates the interior of the Abbey yard was extensively cobbled., with grass growing up to the elegant gothic arched cloisters that ran around three sides of the main stone built church. Monks came and went. Thomas dismouted and tied his horses to a metal ring convientaly placed at waist hight in the wall opposite. He had just finished and was about to turn when a voice said in Latin.

"Welcome, Brother,and who art thou?"

Thomas turned and saw that the man before him was a tall thin monk with a scarred face and a benign smile on his face that was framed by a well cut and razored white beard that ran thinly from ear to ear by way of his chin.The monk raised a quizzical eyebrow."Not from these parts I'll warrant.?" Thomas answered in the same language, "God's blessings upon you Brother. I am from England. Brother Thomas of Lingen. Personal confessor to the Countess of Hambye." "What brings you here Brother.The Countess is in retreat while she waits for her impending nuptials.We have many confessors here and have no need of another."

"For that very reason, Brother.The Countess is an English woman and therefore has a right to an English confessor. She has known me many years and trusts me and a full and honest confession before her marriage could only benefit her and the greater glory of God."

"That is very trueFather. I shall see if she will admit you.. There has been some difficulty with the Countess.,for she has not wanted to see her bethrothed for some days now."He smiled consipitorarily"I fear it is nerves. For after all Phillippe de Peynil is her brother in.law "

Thomas nodded"Why of course, The count's younger brother. I remember him from the time of the previous marriage." "He must have been a mere child!"

"He was"Thomas shut his mouth. knowing that to fabricate any more knowledge he didn't have about the family of Eloner's dead husband would lead him down paths that could lead to terrible danger. The tall monk turned on his heel and dissapeared into the cloisters leaving Thomas in the pleasant warm sunshine.Within ten minutes he had reappeared a warm smile on his face.He beckoned Thomas over and in heavily accented English said"Come Brother, The Countess has graciously agreed to see you.I have never seen her so animated. It must be the thought of talking to another English."He ushered Thomas in to the cloisters and over the well worn sandstone pathway until they came to a gothic arched doorway that led by some stairs to the first storey of the Abbey building.On that level were several large contemplation rooms set with simple tables and chairs and a lectern at the end of each room.An imposing wood staircase led upward to the third storey which contained more rooms. Mostly cell like in monkish terms but several were larger and grander,some with fireplaces. The tall monk led Thomas to one of these and knocked on the door."Entrez." That one word uttered in Eloner's voice was enough to send a frisson of love and excitement through his heart.The door was pushed open and the tall monk went in.

"Countess I bring your English confessor. Father Thomas of Lingen"He bowed and backed away leaving Thomas to gaze upon the woman he loved and thewoman he had come to save.Two steady blue eyes framed by fair curly hair gazed back at Thomas.No recognition passed through the eyes and Thomas realised that the tall monk was waiting for a reaction.

"My Lady, it is by God's good grace that we meet again."He bowed.

She bobbed a small curtsey"Thank you father Thomas, it does my soul good that I can speak with an Englishman again."The tall monk rubbed his hands together"I shall leave you now Father. After you have taken the Countesses' confession would you join us in the refectory for an evening meal." "I should be delighted Father and I look forward to it."The tall monk turned on his heel and left pulling the door too behind him. As soon as the door had clicked shut Eloner was in his arms.Tears streaming from her eyes and a huge smile wreathing her face.."Oh my love. I never gave up hope of seeing you again,and now you are here. Nothing matters any more !"

"Have you been ill treated in any way?"

"No, my love. Only decieved by that swine of a brother in law Phillipe.His pretence that his mother was ill and like to die was what brought me to France in the first place. Then he forced me to agree to think about marrying him, and now he has fixed thedate for midsummer."

"Not if I can help it my love. For I am marrying you at midsummer if you'll have me as your husband!" "Of course. You do me much honour. But I fear the King will withold his consent. I am his ward."

"He has granted his consent. When he knighted me upon the field of Towton I asked a special favour of him, and it was to have his permission to marry you. He gladly gave it."

"Knighted! Sir Thomas.!" Her shining eyes took in the scruffy habit and tonsured head of the man she loved.She stepped forward and into his open arms.

Their kiss was long and sweet and contained many months of seperation.At last they broke free from one another and Thomas said. "I have a plan to get us away from here. How long can you deny them access to this room?" "All night if needs be. I have a sign to hang upon the door, but better that that I have the key."She felt in the pocket of her kirtle and produced a small chatelaine upon which hung an iron key."They have trusted me with this from the first day I was here. They do not think I am a prisoner. 'tis only I who think that."She grinned up at him. "well Sir Thomas what of your plan.?" "'Tis this."He reached up under his habit and from around his waist proceeded to pull out the other habit he had bought in Honfleur. "You must don this ill smelling thing and passyourself off as a monk. With God's grace and a good dash of luck we shall be gone from here in minutes."

Elenor took hold of the habit and pulled it over her dress. Her bulky kirtle forcedthe material out and it looked as if she was a woman wearing a monks habit. She pulled it off again and removing the kirtle and any other garment that bulked out the habit she slid the wool robe over her shoulders. "A much better effect"Said Thomas, though Your hair is somewhat of a dissadvanage"He snapped his fingers"I have the very solution>From within his robe he produced the leather sallet liner he had worn to disguise his tonsure. "Try this"> She bundled her thick and luxuriant hair up on top of her head and placed the leather cap on it.It filled the cap an she was able topull it down over all her hair giving the impression of a young novice wearing a skull cap.The robe was too long but they hitched it up and with the girdle they fixed it so that the hem just trailed the floor.

Eloner laughed out right "So I'm. Father Eloner now. My word but this habit stinks. "I'm so sorry my love, but monks are not the cleanest cratures in Christondom!

"Wait I have an idea!"She bundled all her excess clothing together and making the shape of a sleeping figure in the truckle bed she pulled a blanket over the deception. "Now should they come in it will look like I am asleep. She turned to Thomas, "I am ready"He pulled her hood over her head in such a way as to almost obscure her face. He left his tonsured head bare and clasping their hands together in monkish attitudes the pair of them left the room. Eloner hung the parchment sign upon the door and used the key to lock it then they descended the stair past the first floor and out onto the cloisters.

Some monks were tending to the garden there but none noticed them. Thomas led Eloner over to the horses tethered against the wall where he had left them. Helping her up onto the back of the palfrey he mounted his gelding and they walke sedately out of the Yard. of The Abbaye D'Hambye.

Chapter Nineteen

They were five leagues or so from the gates of the Abbey trotting their horses gently down a wide thoroughfare. Cobbled with grass verges. One of the better roads Thomas had encountered in France. They had been passing peasant farmers and villains about their business for their road lay in the direction of St Lo and the Mont san Michel. Ahead of them a commotion on the road. Dust was flying up from the hooves of horses. Thomas could see some brightly coloured streamers and what looked like a veraflamme. Trumpet and clarrion calls split the air and any pedestrians hurried to get off the road. "We best get into the side, this copse of trees will do." He pulled Eloner's palfrey into the shelter of an overhanging branch of a walnut tree that spead its leaves across the dappled shade of the little glade. He followed her into shelter. A stream of outriders made up of armoured soldiers with bright polished helmets flashed past. Then a group of Knights at arms on destriers with their bright caparisoned horse cloths and glittering head harness. Eloner breathed fearfully. "It's Phillipe. He must be on his way to the abbey. He said he would return for my final answer today" She looked wildly around.

"Don't be frightened my love. I shall protect you." Phillippe's entourage swept past and off into the distance. They had not been noticed by the group. Thomas knew however it was only a matter of time before the disapearance of the countess was discovered and once that happened the hue and cry would be raised,and the whole country would be against them.

"We must go, ride as fast as we can, put as much distance as possible between us and Phillipe. We'll make for the coast. Maybe we'll get a boat or steal one"He smile grimly. She smiled back. "Let's go Sir Thomas" and clapping heels to her palfry she galloped off in the opposite direction from Phillipe's party.

Eloner was a consummate horsewoman having learnt to ride as a small child in Wales and she was strong with imense stamina. For ten minutes at a time they galloped then rested their horses in a canter then a trot, then once again a gallop this way they covered the maximum amount of ground and the horses retained some of their strength. By the time the afternoon was wearing into the evening they had covered many leagues and they were riding with the sea to thei r

right. At this place on the coast however the cliffs were fully wooded and steep and ran straight down to the crashing rocks below. Thomas saw that ahead the landscape started to level out. He hoped to find a boatman who would take them across the tide race to the Channel Islands.

They came off the high ground and the nature of the landscape started o change. Long sand dunes now rolled away infront of them interspersed with pine trees. Marshland, cropped grass, covered twice a day by the in rushing sea that gave the sheep that grazed there their distinctive salty tang rolled into the distance where the shimmering grey waters of the ocean met the shimmering grey of the sky.

A thin wisp of smoke rose from the beach. Thomas headed his mount in that direction. They came out on to the strand that stretched away for miles in either direction.A group of fisher women and chidren were gathered around a fire of driftwood that was blazing on the beach. A couldron of sea water was steaming away. One woman larger than the rest with arms strong from pulling on ropes was ladling fresh mussels into the pot. Another was boiling some samphire. The raggedy children barefoot and with their clothes torn stood and watched as the horses came over.

"Bonjour Madame" The woman bobbed her head. Eloner said in French "Do you know of a boatman who would take us to the Ilse de Manche.!" The woman shook her grey curls." Non mon pere.c'est pas possible. Tous les hommes sont mort." It transpired that in that village at least all the men had been called to fight and not one had returned whole.Therefore it was down to the women to fend for themselves and their children as it always had been.However, the next village was bigger and they might find someone there.Declining a bowl of mussels Thomas and Eloner took their leave of the women and cantered off in the direction of the next village.The strand stretched out ahead of them and a chill wind started to blow in from seaward. A bank of glossy black clouds rolled up from nowhere and sat lowering over the horizon. The sun shone off the underside of the clouds imparting a frightening feel to the late afternoon. Ahead of them they could just make out a small fishing village with sereral hovels grouped around a stone wharf,whilst drawn up on the beach were half a dozen at least of small fishing boats and cobs. A group of men were mending nets. They looked up as the two monks cantred towards them. The leader rose and putting his awl on the ground. wished them good day.

"Good day my son and God's blessings be with you all. Is there any man here who would take us to the Isle des Manche.?"The leader shook his head. "No father, there is not, it is too far for us and too dangerous. The currants and the tide race are fiendish devil's work and many a genuine good fisherman has perished in them"He crossed himself.

"In that case would any one here sell us a boat to get to the islands.?" "Sell you a boat? But you are priests not fishermen. " "Jesus our lord was a fisherman. We have to get to the islands as soon as possible. We are offering these two horses and their harness in exchange for a boat that is seaworthy enough to get us across."

One of the fishermen's eyes had lit up with the greed of avarice.

"I might sell you mine!but there would have to be some silver involved in the deal for these boats are hard to come by and this is my living." Thomas looked at the man. He stood and beckoned them over to the line of cobs lying on the sand. "This be mine Father, and a stronger nimbler boat you'll not find this side of St Lo."He pointed down towards the carvel built cob that lay on its keel. He boat looked sound although most of its paint had long worn off. It was about ten feet long with a thwart amidships through which a sail could be stepped. The mast and sail lay inboard along side a pair of oars. There was a small three plank deck that gave some shelter from the weather at the fore peak and which was being used as a store for fishing nets and two or three creels.The rudder lay out of its pintles against the side of the boat.

"She seems sound enough.So with a barrel of water and some food what will you settle for?"

The fisherman scratched his head, then his backside as he thought about selling. Greed momentarily flashed through his eyes as he stared first at the monks and then at the boat.

"Why 'tis my lively hood. I shall have to get or make another. The two horses then plus ten ducats of silver."He flashed them a take it or leave it look. Thomas laughed in his face "Ten Ducats? Why you thief. I shall give you eight and you're lucky to get that. You're trying to rob men of the cloth. That's a mortal sin you know. "The fisherman hung his head and then with a grin spat on his palm and held it out to Thomas. Thomas did the same and the deal was concluded..Thomas and Eloner transferred their belongings such as they were into the cuddy of the boat once it was clear of fishing gear. The fisherman provided a barrel of water and a cask of salted mackeral. He also threw in a baling bowl and a rudimentary magnetic north south compass."You keeps that needle pointing to the top yo'm going north. Any other direction you works out for yoursel." "What direction for the Isles Des Manche.?"" North through Les Minquiers. Then you'll see the islands. Due west after. This journey will take you the better part of tonight and tomorrow." He cast a weatherly eye at the clouds building over the horizon. "Looks like bad weather. You'd do best to start on the morrow." "We need to get going straight away"Thomas was also looking at the blackness of the horizon and weighing up the likely hood of being trapped on the beach by Phillippe's men or drowning in a fearsome storm at sea.He turned to Eloner. "What do you think?"

"Same as you, my love, I want to go now,but I'.m frightened. Neither of us has any knowledge of boats and how to sail them. Maybe we would do better to start in the morning when we are rested,"Thomas nodded thoughtfully. "Yes I think you're right. We'll find a place for the night and start on the morrow." A look of relief came over Eloner's face."Let's stay with the boat. We can sleep in it. We have food and water and by the morn we'll be ready to go."Thus they agreed and making themselves comfortablein the cuddy they opened the mackeral barrel and made an oily but very satisfactory supper before falling asleep in one another's arms.

Before dawn, and dawn comes early in June be it France or England.Thomas came awake. Sounds of searchers further up the beach had disturbed him. Peering through sleep matted eyes he could see the light of several rush torches burning in the distance and the eerie disembodied calls of searching soldiers.He shook Eloner awake.

"Soldiers looking for us.We must defend ourselves"He pulled the bows from their covers and handed her the hunting bow."Have you ever used one of these before.?"

"Yes Thomas, many times in Wales, and also later, I always liked to keep my eye in."He smiled back at her."You are a true strong woman and I love you. Take cover behind the boats and when the soldiers get here give no quarter. For they won't give us any.!.Here, take a dozen bodkins and good luck. Hide down behind that cob over there, and keep your head down."She threw her arms round him and kissed him desperately on the lips. "I love you my Thomas".Keeping her head bent she ran over to the boat that was about ten yards further away from their boat and crouched down behind the gunwale. Laying her arrow shafts out beside her, shestrung up her bow and waited.

Thomas stuck his bodkin points in the sand in front of him and notched his bow string. The light from the torches was coming closer and the sounds of the searchers getting louder. Thomas saw that they were led by a knight in harness who carried a broad sword with which he stabbed the undergrowth and beat anything remotely like a hiding place.

The light of dawn was fast coming up giving Thomas a better view of his opponents. He notched an arrow to his bow and when the searchers were a hundred paces off he suddenly stood and loosed. His first arrow took the knight between his breastplate and his gorget. Causing him to be thrown backwards on the sand in a welter of blood. A cry of rage came up from the others and they unslung their crossbows. But it takes twice as long to fire a quarrel as it does a good ash arrow, and while they were fumbling with their bow mechanisms three of them fell, two with shafts sticking from their bodies one with a direct hit through the eye.

Eloner stood in the classic hunting pose her arm bent and her bow extended. Her arrows she shot true and another two soldiers fell to them. The remainder of the soldiers had taken cover behind a jumble of rocks that stuck out into the strand and were firing off their crossbows as quickly as they could. Two quarrels struck the gunwale of their boat and another two went straight through the bottom boards of one of the other cobs lying upturned. Thomas grinned to himself and thought good job we didn't buy that one!

A soldier stood up for a moment to take better aim nd fell with two shafts embedded in his chest one courtesy of Thomas the other of Eloner. Suddenly from behind the outcrop the remaining soldiers were running. There were only two and a bodkin point through the calf of the first only spurred the second on to greater speed as he legged it up the beach away from the deadly hail of arrows.

Thomas looked at Eloner who had a wide smile across her face. "Good work, my love. I never thought you would be such a shot. If ever we fall on hard times we can make a living at archery shows.Now, can you help me launch the boat, for more soldiers will arrive before long." They hurried to the cob which had two bolts sticking out of its gunwhale. Thomas took one side and Eloner the other and by a supreme effort they ran the small boat down the beach and into the water.Eloner climbed aboard and Thomas followed. He shipped the rudimentary oars in the rowlocks and after three or four pulls the boat was floating on the green depths at the edge of the beach.Looking at the sail between them they worked out how it was stepped in the midships and they erected the mast and tied off the stays that kept it upright. Thomas pulled on the rope that rose the sail up the mast and immeadiately the little boat heeled to the offshore breeze and a largeamount of water splashed over the side soaking them both. Thomas desperately swung the tiller in the other direction. This only made it worse and the boat took another wave over its side.Using less motion with his tiller hand he soon got the boat under control and headed away from the shore. Eloner set too with the baler and had the vessel empty within a few minutes.

Thomas laughed outright."She seems a strong enough boat, and I do believe with God's grace we are free !"

Eloner made her way stern wards and sat beside him on the thwart.

"Thomas of Lingen, you are my saviour and my hope for the future,with you by my side I can do anything." "Aye my lady. The same is true for me" and he lent across and kissed her lovingly upon her salty lips.

Their small cob headed nothwards towards the Minquiers for several hours. The coast of France becoming more and more indistinct behind them the further offshore they went. The day was grey with a short horizon merging into an equally grey sky so that at times it was difficult to see anything ahead at all. Thomas kept refering to the north compass that was swinging from the mast head and every so often correcting the tiller to keep the boat on its northerly course.

The lovers had been talking non stop since they had felt themselves out of immeadiate danger and Thomas had related his adventures from the time of his ride north to the field of Towton. Eloner was sad that the giant Billie had died but proud beyond belief that her man had saved the life of the King of England and been knighted on the field for his heroics.She was even more impressed with the grant of land In the Marches and when he told her of Stapleton Castle she gripped his hand in true amazement. Outright laughter issued from her mouth when he related the story of Orrid and Booful and the rat.It was as if this time they had alone on the ocean was a blessed gift from God.

Thomas peered through the sea mist that was starting to creep up around the boat. "That looks like rocks ahead "He said pointing towards some oily black looking rocks that came and went as the swell covered and uncovered them. "Yes, more over there" said Eloner. Suddenly they were surrounded on all sides by the out lying rocky outcrops of the Minquiers. "We'd best drop the sail,for our speed will make us hit anyone of these and then we're done for. "They ran the sail down into the boat and immeadiately way came off her. Taking up the oars they negotiated their way through the sullen swell, sometime missing outcrops by inches as the sea rolled over the dangerous teeth of the rocks. The sea mist deepened and the sound of the sucking of the waves coming from every quarter disorintated them. A dark mass of rocks loomed up ahead with another close by. Thomas steered a course between them. They were now in an open channel, though they could not see that, for the mist had sunk down in a clinging wet blanket that covered the sea and the little boat. Slowly they rowed ahead. The channel widened but once more a further more extensive outcrop of rock almost an island in its own right loomed out of the mist.. Thanks to the slow speed of their motion and the calmness of the sea they were able to avoid the suck and the scend of the ocean as it gripped and let itself go against the rocks of the shore. For what seemed hours they floated past these submerged and semi submerged rocks avoiding them by inches. Once a horrible grinding sound came from the keel of their boat. Thomas swung thetiller in panic and they slipped off into deeper water. Sweat was running from his brows as he battled with the tiller and the oars. At last the rocks appeared to diminish and the mist started to lift and then they were out in the open ocean again. Behind them like a malevolent beast sat the Minquiers clad in mist and grinding its teeth against honest trav llers.

"What's that over yonder?" Eloner pointed over to the right. A low lying mass of land inistinct for it was several leagues away seemed to fill the horizon. "I know not. But I'll wager 'tis the Channel Islands." "God be praised, we are safe!" They raised the sail and headed in the direction of the land. They had not gone much of a distance towards the large island ahead of them when the nature of the sea ahead srtarted to take on a very frightening aspect.

Sudden long swells rolling in from the east iterspersed with a choppy area of scum topped ocean was all around them. A small whirlpool pulled them off course and it was only by judicious use of the tiller that Thomas was able to avert disaster.A fast moving tidal race shot the little boat forward and spun it out of control.The sail slatted over first one way and then the other. Sea water rushed over the side as the race pushed the cob inexorably towards its own destruction.Eloner was screaming in fear and Thomas was shouting and wrestling with the tiller. What ever he did, the sea was his master. The currents pulled the little craft first one way and then the other.The wood sides creaked in unison and a terrible crack sounded from the fore peak. A plank of the decking spun past their heads and back into the sea behind them. Then sudenly as if they had been spewed up by the leviathan the boat was in calmer water. Floating serenely on the ocean as if nothing had happened.Thomas grabbed the baler and started to empty the boat. The water was almost up to the gunwhale and it was a wonder the barky floated at all.he looked up first at Eloner who was wiping sea water from her face and then at the island. The bulk of the land was so much closer now. So much so that they could make out stone built houses and the occasional farm house.On one promentary a stone built fortified castle stood with its grim walls shouldering away any newcomers.A silver strand, not long but enough to beach the boat was directly ahead of them and they headed into shore. The keel ground up onto the sand and the next wave shoved them further inland and towards safety. Thomas jumped out and pulled the boat further up the beach.. Grabbing Eloner in his arms he carried her high up the golden sands and flopped down upon them.

The next thing he knew or felt was a toe in the ribs and a rough country voice saying.

"Aye, aye, what have we here. Looks like two sodomite priests caught in the act." Thomas rolled over and came awake instantly.

"Nay cully,you have that very wrong!You are adressing Sir Thomas of Lingen and the Countess of Hambye lately washed up on your shores after escaping from France." The country man stepped back in amazement. "Why be you dressed in monks clothes. How come you've got a shaved head. I don't believe you. You're on devil's work"He crossed himself. Eloner shook off her leather sallet cover and her luxuriant fair hair tumbled out around her face

"Ever seen a monk with hair like this ?"She enquired."Now take us to your master for we are tired and hungry and we have need of a change of clothes."The hair had swung it for the farmer and bowing and scraping he led them off the beach and up a steep animal track onto the cliff top.Nestled in a hollow and almost invisible from the surrounding fields lay a substantial stone built farmhouse of two stories with buildings around a yard and a purposeful air about it.

"The Siegneur do live here.Sir Peter de Carteret. He'll tell us what's to do." He led them down the path and through a wooden gate into the yard.

Several men were working with hay forks lifting swathes of hay high off a large cart and storing it in a long substantial stone built barn.One of them, the tallest and burliest of his fellows lent on his fork and shouted down."Who have you found now Francis, you've got to stop binging waifes and strays home." "Found these two asleep on the beach Sir, they claims to have come from France. There was a boat beside them." The burly man jumped down and came over.He was over six foot in height and his muscles gleamed with a sheen of sweat. He was wearing rough country trews and a leather apron.

"My word, looks like a lady monk. Now there,s a thing."

Thomas bowed. "Sir, allow me to present Eloner Countess of Hambye, and I am Sir Thomas Lingen.We have been washed up on your shores and we ask you for succour until we can continue our journey."

"Sir Thomas Lingen!.Who saved the king's life at Towton! " I was there, I watched the king enoble you. Was one of those who lifted you from the mud after you were made knight. Sir Peter grinned hugely.He turned toward Eloner."And you my lady are the Countess of Hambye. My word,my word. Wait until my wife hears of this. Come,lets go up to the house.A feast is called for. " Clasping Thomas to him in a great bear hug and bowing so elegantly to Eloner he led them out of the yard and into the manor house.

Soon all was bustle and hurry as water was heated. Sir Peter's wife summoned from some distant fields and food ordered for the feast. Servants running here and there to do their master's bidding all with infectious grins on their faces as the story of the fugitives became known

At last Cecily de Carteret appeared over the hill in a dog cart clip clopping at pace to attend her lord's summonsWhen she realised who she was dealing with she instantly whisked Eloner off into the private rooms of the family where she quizzed her as to her adventures and helped her choose some more suitable garments to wear than the etremely dirty and salt stained monk's habit.

Meanwhile Thomas was being fitted out in some choice garments of the dandy variety being a yellow doublet and a pair of red and blue hose and a small round hat that disguised his tonsure.. These belonged to Sir Peter's son who was at court in England learning the trade of courtier and squire.

After an invigorating hot,hot bath steeped in country herbs both Thomas and Eloner found themselves in the grand hall waiting for their hosts and for the feast to begin. Eloner looked stunning in an ermine trimmed red velvet gown that fitted her like a glove and with her hair entwined with pearls.

Sir Peter and lady Cecily came down the stairs smiling and happy to see their guests.

"Come into the refectory and we shall see what wonders await. "He led them through a door into a long oak panelled room the centre piece of which was a huge refectory table laid for many peopleand laden down with chooice items from the farmhouse storerooms.Cold rabbit and pigeon pie, game pies of all descriptions.Mackeral pate,pate de fois grasse. Cold sausage of several varities and three or four huge cheeses,all helped to burden the table. Sir Peter clapped his hands and in from the outside came all the workers and labourers who previously had been around the farm

He turned to Thomas"any excuse for a feast I say.these are my loyal workers, and we haven't had a chance since before I was off to the wars, so its long overdue.Now bring on the main dishes. " Two kitchen boys in white aprons carried in a huge dish upon which was laying a monster eel fish."This is a speciality of our islands, conger eel. And a nicer fish 'tis hard to find.Some may say he's a muddy fish. But that depends on how he's cooked."He pointed to some dishe s beside the conger. These are ormers, again only got in the isles. A tasty treat.".Thomas looked down to see a steaming bowl of over large cockle type shells appear beside him A plate of conger eel was awaiting his pleasure and suddenly relising he hadn't eaten for nearly twenty four hours he fell too with a will.

The conger was a taste treat only expirienced by few people, but its oily flesh and deep taste went a long way to satisfy Thomas's hunger with the addition of the ormers and other side dishes he was soon feeling replete.After several glasses of a deep red Burgandy imported from their neigbour Thomas felt fit to fall asleep at the table. The joyous babble of happy voices flowed around him as the farm workers tucked into the largesse of their seigneur.

"Sir Thomas!" called Sir peter holding high his glassA toast! To all the brave men that fell at Towton" "Thomas was happy to drink to that and in return he called across the table"To you Sir Peter, for putting on this feast at such short notice and fo ryour hospitality."Th seigneur inclined his head in thanks and then said, "I should think you and Lady Eloner will want to continue your journey back to England as soon as you can. There are many boats leaving from St Helier each day and I'm sure a comfortable berth may be found on one of them."

"How long for the voyage?" asked Eloner

"Well with God's favour and a following wind. Three days to cross to the mainland.Of course it depends what part of the mainland you want.Portsmouth town is closest, but there is London or Bristol."

She turned towards Thomas. What part think you best for us Thomas. "Well, We could buy horses in Portsmouth and be back in the Marches in another week or so, if we stay on the vessel 'till Gloucester ' would be only a two day ride to the Marches.

"Let us do that then, for I'd feign rest easier on the deck of a ship than I would trot through the counrtyside." Thomas nodded,. Gloucester it is. We will look for a vessel to carry as there tomorrow If Sir Peter can show us the harbour."

Sir Peter agreed to take them into St Helier and help them obtain passage back to England.

By now the feasting was coming to a natural conclusion. Several of the guests were the worst for wear with at least three old men and ladies asleep at the table. Kithen servants started to clear away the remains and Sir Peter led Thomas and Eloner into his private quarters where he filled their glasses with rare imported cognac from Brittany and they selltled to reminisce over good and bad times.

As the sun sank into a cloudless sea and a mild onshore breeze bringing the smells of myrtle and gorse acrossthe cliff to the Seingnourie at Rozel, Thomas found himself nodding off in front of the fire in the private rooms of Sir Peter and Lady Cecily.With a great effort he took his farewells and he and Eloner climbed the stair to the sumptously appointed bed room their hosts had laid on for them.

Morning dawned as calm and sweet as the night before. Small clouds across a blue sky and the weather loked set fair for that day at least. Sir Peter had lent Thomas and Eloner a pair of riding horses and he and Cecily accompanied them to the harbour town of St Helier.This was the largest forified town on the Isle of Jersey with a stone built castle overlooking the bay and harbour.As most of the citizens of the islands made their living from the sea the harbourwas packed with vessels of all sorts ranging in size from the cobble that had brought Thomas and Eloner to these shores right through to several large caravels being loaded with theproduceof the islands. Salted fish, ormers French wines and brandy.Down on the quayside where a substantial wharf was a hum with activity, sailors in stripped jersey smocks with their swarthy sunburnt faces inevitabley finished with a gold earring. Wealth enough for a decent burial people said, although most of these hardy men kept the rings as a form of vanity,came and went carrying barrels and wheeling hand carts of more fragile goods up gangplanks onto the decks of the cargo ships.Whilst above in the clear blue sky gulls wheeled and screamed and fought over bits of discarded fish and other offal thrown into the harbour.

Thomas and his party arrived on the quay and looked at the boats. Sir Peter called out to an idler leaning on the gunwhale of one of the cargo vessels. "Any boats here bound for the port of Bristol or Gloucester?"

"Can't say your honour I'll just ask the Captain " he vanished below decks and moments later a gaudily dressed seaman in a slashed doublet with earings in both ears and an awful scar disfiguring his face appeared on the deck.

"Looking for passage to England?"enquired this speciman of manhood.

Thomas stepped forward "Aye captain,my lady and I require passage as far as Gloucester, is that your destination?"

"Yes Sir, en route we call at Weymouth, Falmouth,Ilfracombe,Bristol and finish our voyage God w illing in the port of Gloucester."

"How long doesthat take and what would be the cost?"

"Eight to ten days according to the weather, this time of year seas are usually calm and cost would be for a private cabin and all food eaten on the voyage.Twenty shillings for the two of you. "

Thomas nodded."When do you depart?"

"Just as soon as the ship is loaded and the tide is right. "He cast a knowing look up at the sun. "I'd say no later than this evening.Do you require passage or not?"

Thomas reached into his saddlebag and withdrew his leather purse. Pulling out twenty silver shillings he handed them over to the captain who called the idler and ordered him to show the passengers their accomodation. This proved to be a tiny cabin in the forepeak with two wood cots fixed to the sides of the ship, just giving enough room for one person to pass at a time.A straw paliasse was the mattress on each bunk and a grey wool blanket the covering. "I've seen and been in worse "said Eloner having inspected the cabin," at least there don't seem to be any fleas." "Ca'nt be sure of that" grinned Thomas scratching himself vigerously.Eloner laughed and slapped his chest.

They went back on deck and said their fond farewells to the De Carterets extending an invitation to the wedding. Cecily's eyes lit up at the thought of an adventure to England and a true holiday away from the parochial island life of Jersey. The invitation was accepted gladly and with much kissing and many farewells Thomas and Eloner bid goodbye to their Jersey hosts.They stashed their belongings such as they were, the saddlebags and weapons in the tiny cabin. Their money which they kept on their persons in soft leather purses was holding out suprisingly well and Thomas was sure they'd have enough to buy horses once they were back in England.Then for the rest of the afternoon they watched in idle astonishment as the crew laboured to fill the ship with goods and cargo. Sitting on the sterncastle out of the way of the bustling activity under an awning that Captain Amos had had rigged to provide some shade.

Four more passengers appeared. A merchant swathed entire in black with two small boys at his side. It was hard to tell if they were his sons or his servants. The last passenger to board was a thin and elegant man of late middle age. His clothing was of a high quality with an ermine trimmed cloak and heavy leather riding boots. A beautifully wrought venitian silver dagger swung from an ornate scabbard at his hip. He looked around at the others gathered on the quarterdeck and gave an elaborate bow.

"Messieurs et dames, good day, I am The Seignour of Le Petit Dixcart on the Isle of Sark and I travel alone to visit my son." He bowed again. The others introduced themselves and before long a convivial party was underway on the aft deck fuelled by some ale provided by Capt. Amos, who despite his fearsome appearance turned out to be an erudite and well travelled man having been on voyages as far south as the Bight of Benin and into the Atalantic as far as the Azores.

As the afternoon drew on into the evening and the off shore breeze started to freshen. The captain left the gathering and started to give orders that had the Maid of Gloucester brailed up to the wharf by a single line and the crew in place to take her out through the multitude of other vessels. At last he was satisfied and with a single shout the line was cast off the foresail was raised and the ship heeled to the breeze, gathering way as she moved majestically out of St Helier harbour and set course for England.

⟡ Chapter Twenty ⟡

A good night's sleep in the tiny bunks had restored their spirits and their appetites. Upon the open deck a brazier burnt and the appertizing smell of frying fish wafted towards them. A sailor with an apron tied around his stomach was in charge of the cooking and he soon had a plateful of sprats raedy for them. Knuckling his head he said. "I caught 'em this morning just as dawn was breaking. Enough for the whole crew to get a plateful. Eat well and enjoy." The tiny silver fish were as fresh as fresh and required no boning. They were eaten whole, heads and eyes and all. Both Thomas and Eloner joined in with relish and made a good breakfast.

The weather was set fair again and a powerful breeze was moving the Maid of Gloucester along at a fair speed. The mainsail was drawing well with a full bellied look to it and the smaller forsail was taut and pulling to its maximum.

"At this speed we'll see Weymouth afore lunchtime" Captain Amos cupped his hands over his eyes and gazed out towards the horizon. The bright day stretched away into infinity the horizon indistinct in the distance. No other boats were visible upon the ocean, it was if they were the only ones upon the shiny surface of the sea. For several hours as Thomas and Eloner took advantage of the mild sun upon their faces from a vantage point in the fore chains, the Maid of Gloucester made her steady progress. in the direction of the south coast.Just as the sun wasbegining to take its toll and a delightful feeling of drowsiness had overcome both of them so much so that with their eyes closed and in that state of semi wakefulness when confusion sets in and one thing is not known from another a huge shout from the crow's nest came ringing down on deck. "Land ho,land on the larboard bow, about fifteen leagues off."

Thomas jerked awake and stood up in the chains and looked out over the bows. He could see nothing. Indeed it was to be another hour before the land came into sight, and then it was an indistinct low lying grey mass hard to distinguish from the bank of grey low lying clouds that covered it.

"Weymouth Bay, a good landfall. We should be there by nightfall God willing.A day in port to unload and take on cargo then ownards to Falmouth."Captain Amos knuckled his forelock.With each hour that passed the land became more distinct and by even tide they were only a league away and sailing paralell to the low lying coast. A huge bay curved round and on the shore some meagre hovels of fishermen and other boatmen lined the high water markSmall cobbles were pulled up on the shore and nets laid out to dry.At the end of the bay a church spire pierced the sky and a stone wharf came into view. Two caravels were already tied up there, but there as space aplenty for the Maid to berth and before the sun had sunk below the horizon she was brailed up snug for the night.

Thomas, Eloner and the other passengers disembarked and made their way to the substantial ale house that stood back from the quay. Light poured out from the open door and a stream of good humoured invective and laughter followed it.They went in.A large room with flagstone floor and several tables at which a mixed crew of regulars sat. Serving wenches came and went with trays of ale, deftly avoiding the grasping hands of their randy customers.The noise diminished by half as Thomas and his party came in, then no threat was percieved and the level rose back to the good natured hum that had greeted them previously. They settled at a table and a serving wench appeared with a tray

"Ale and some food please mistress" "Aye Sir, we got pigeon pie and the best ale in Weymouth. " "Well then, that'll do for us all. "She nodded and turned away to wards the kitchens.

Pigeon pie for six and ale to go was soon on the table. They tucked into the food and sat back replete"Well thanks be to The Good Lord for our deliverance across the sea" said The Seigneur of Petit Dixcart.

"Why, sir, surely you are due some more sea travel. ?"The thin man smiled. "No, not at all. For tonight I leave you and continue my journey by land. " Where do you make for Sir?"

"The Abbey at Sherbourne. My son is a novice there. He knows not that I am coming so I hope to surprise him!"

"Good luck with your journey"Thomas said and turning towards the black dressed merchant he asked him the same question. "Wherefore art thou bound Sir?"

"I take my sons to the school at Winchester, where they are to be enrolled as pupils.I too shall be leaving you by the morning. It has been an honour to travel with you all as companions, and I hope your onward journey is as easy as that which has just passed."He bowed and his two sons did likewise. The party started to break up and before long Thomas and Eloner were walking back along the quay towards the Maid of Gloucester.

"Why my love, you'll just have me for company afore long. "Teased Eloner.He stopped and took her in his arms. " My love,you are the very best company a man could desire and the only one I want." "Prettily said Sir Thomas." She laughed and drew him closer to her side. Thomas continued."Are you sure you want to stay on the Maid for another week or so. Tis only another hundred miles or so to Bristol from here and we could well ride that in five days" She looked thoughtful"Well at first I wished for thesolitude of the voyage and to be with you alone, but now thinking of it the adventure is as appealing on dry land s it is on the water." "Dry land, yes, there are dangers everywhere but at least our feet remain dry shod on land. Our store of money is such that we can afford riding horses and to stay in taverns all the way back t o the Marches. And we get to see some more of this great kingdom."

"Oh Thomas, you have convinced me. Tomorrow we ride!" he kissed her and they climbed the gangplank up onto the Deck of the Maid of Gloucester.Speaking to the Captain they were able to get a refund on their passage money and well content with their lot they turned in to their tiny cabin for the last time.

Another calm bright day ahead as they walked down the gangplank for the last time with the good wishes of the captain and crew ringing in their ears. They soon found a horse broker and were able to buy a pair of riding horses and all the saddles and harness they needed and before the matins bell had finished tolling from the church spire they were walking sedately out of Weymouth and in the direction of Yeovil.

The country side had a very much more open aspect here than either of them were used to with chalk downs long cleared of forests and the road winding like a white scar across the downs.They passed few travellers and as the sun beat down upon them they were able to talk at length about their forthcoming wedding and all that that entailed.

"His majesty has pledged to be there!" said Thomas tentatively, for this was the first time the subject had been broached.

Eloner looked schocked. "Oh Thomas, that puts a new light on things. Are there enough rooms in Stapleton Castle to accommodate the King and his entourage?"

"I know not. But something shall be done and Diccon is a good steward and friend and he will help out for sure. But first I have to hold a court in Presteigne on midsummer day for my tenants to right any wrongs done to them under the rule of The Gruffyydd, and there are sure to be many.This is a perfect chance for you to get to know our tenents and for me to do the same" She nodded,for her duty instilled in her as a little girl in Wales was a major part of her character and like it or not she was about to become thewife of one of the most powerful men on the border land of Wales and England and take on some of the responsibility that that entailed.

"Midsummer day. Why that is only three weeks from now. Have we time ?" "I think so. Let us concentrate on that and think of the wedding later in the year. Maybe when the harvest is gathered in and the autumn is just around the corner. " She nodded again. "There is much to do and many people to contact."They rode on contentedly each with myriad thoughts winding round their brains. Each with different outlooks and hopes and inspirations but both with the one central idea of the joining in wedlock of them both.

By nightfall they were safely ensconced within the walls of the Black Swan on the High St. in Yeovil and a comfortable night in a flea free bed left them refreshed and invigorated for the next day's journey.

Having spent most of the previous evening talking about their coming nuptials,who to inviteand more importantly who not to, it was with some relief that Thomas was able to saddle the horses and leave the inn without any wedding talk from Eloner. In fact she was uncommonly silent and after some miles of no conversation whatever he rode up beside her and tentatively asked. "Are you well my beloved. You say little and I fear I may have offended you in some way."

"Not at all my love. I was only musing on the fact of becoming your wife and how wonderful that would be. Also what life might hold in store for us both."She smiled

"That is in God's hands, but for sure I can make it as good and as happy as I can.

See that elm tree yonder?"He pointed to a single ancient elm whose verdant green canopy shaded the road some hundreds of yards ahead just where the road crested the hill and ran straight down again. "I'll race you there!" So saying he put heels to his horse and shot off. Eloner was taken by surprise but determined not to be outdone she crouched low over her horses neck and gave him the heel. Together they raced towards the elm tree.Neck and neck they rode Eloner's slim weight and fleet pony giving her the edge.Laughing and with the light of love in her eyes she pulled ahead until with a great bellow of triumph she pulled her stead up. Thomas shamefacedly called out"You're a worthy winner. Remind me never to make a challenge like that again.Where oh where did you learn to ride like that.?"

"I told you, as a girl I was a free spirit riding every day about Carew Castle.I would always win the riding races we held as youngsters.And I'.m no slouch when it comes to jousting either>" Thomas raised his eyebrows."But the lance must be too heavy for a woman!" "Not at all, it's all in how you couch it upon the saddle.What is too heavy is broad sword play and the use of the mace. At that stage I withdraw."She gave him a confident smile which left him in no doubt that he was marrying a very determined and unusual woman.

All day they rode, until by nightfall they could see in the distance the pall of smog and smoke that overhung England's second largest city.A reknowned centre for the trade in leather and cloth the city itself was constantly expanding as more and more country folk swarmed into the ever growing town to take advantage of the work oppurtunities.

The river Avon was lined with wharfes and jetties from where trading boats sailed to the far flung parts of the known world. Explorers such as John Cabot fitted out their vessels hereand both Thomas and Eloner were struck by the similarity to London with its crowded streets and exciting hum of humanity.

The smell in the air was excruciating,a mixture of leather tanning and, wet cloth fullering,thesmell of human and animal excrement and the over riding smell of the rancid mud of the river and all the dead things and half decayed rotton detritus thrown away in the course of a day. As they trotted down past St Mary Redcliffe church towards the centre of the port area both of them covered their mouths and noses from the horrible smells that caught like acid in the backs of their throats.

"We must find a sweeter smelling part to stay this night!" said Thomas coughing into a cloth. Eloner just nodded. Across the harbour the hill side of the area known as Christmas Steps trended up steeply towards a heavily wooded hill top. Thomas led the horses in that direction and once they were above the hanging miasma of smog and shit in the low lying harbour the air became much sweeter. Ahead of them some substantial half timbered merchants houses had been built and right up against the cobbled street an open yard gate with the sign for the Crippled Swan swung in the wind. They entered the yard. Two young ostlers ran forward and held the horses bridles as they dismounted. "A room for the night for the two of us" cried Thomas. The younger of the ostlers knuckled his head. "Certainly Sir, our rooms are the best in Bristow, never been slighted and never been known to give offence has the Crippled Swan" He grinned and ushered them both into the main hall of the tavern. A large room with opulent tapestries depicting religious scenes of the life of Jesus hanging from the walls. A flagstone floor neatly swept clean with sweet smelling rushes strewn here and there upon the floor. Two or three serving maids in neat bonnets and clean aprons stood ready to take their orders.

"My word this is a clean seeming place" said Eloner approvinly. "I shall not mind staying here for one moment." The landlord bustled up to them. "A room for the night is it Sir and Madam." They nodded. "Please to follow me." He led them up the wide and highly polished staircase to the first floor where a number of doors led off into bedrooms. Arriving at the first he opened the door and ushered them in.A spacious light and airy room with a huge four poster bed and several old pieces of heavy oak furniturestood before them. Flowers in a vase sweetly scented the air and the leaded light window open a crack let in enough fresh air to make the room seem fresh and light. Eloner nodded her approval. "How much for this room Landlord?"

"This one is sixpence a night for the room, but all is done for you.In that price there is the use of a maid and man servant if you require. Any food is extra."He bowed and withdrew. Thomas sat on the bed and smiled up at Eloner. "This is the right sort of place for us. Mayhap we'll stay a couple of days before continuing. "

"It certainly has a touch of luxury about it that other places have lacked "said Eloner.

They unpacked their saddlebags and ordered some rhenish wine to be brought to their room. Toasting one another and the finish of another day on the road they decided not to eat and to retire for a good night's sleep

By morning, much refreshed and with a subsantial breakfast within them, they set out to explore the port city of Bristol. In something of a holiday mood they gathered some money and set off in the direction of Christmas Steps. At the bottom of the hill the double doors of St Mary on the Quay stood open and the sound of sombre church music, horns and symbols sounded from within. Stepping forward to see what was going on Thomas peered into the darkened depths of the church. Several priests swinging chausibles full of incense were chanting from the paslms as they progressed around the church blessing the congregation who meekly kneeled upon the flagstone floor.Thomas looked keenly at this sight and his eye fell on one priest a thin brown robed cistercian monk. Father Ignatious. Hurridly stepping back before the priest looked

311

up and saw him he grabbed Eloner by the arm and hustled her away from the church.

"God's blood" he whispered"Tis my deadly enemy Ignatious. The man I told you of who has tried to kill me on numerous occasions.What does he do here in Bristol. The last time we had dealings was before the battle of Towton.He is devil's spawn and I shall have to finish him once and for all." Eloner looked worried."'Tis a sin to kill a priest" "Not this one" replied Thomas."You go straight to heaven for dispatching this one. He is a lier and a theif and a traitor to his king. I must find out where he goes and who he sees. He may be formenting dissent and revolution with his friends. He must be stopped.!" Eloner looked dubious but said nothing.A priest came out of the chuch and started to cross their path.Thomas stopped him and asked. "Father, who is the Cistercian priest within and where does he stay.?" "That my son is the blessed Ignatious, one of the kindest most loving of all priests I have ever met. He lives at the Cistercian Abbey upon the Downs to the north of the town.He works with the poor and needy in the harbour area here and he is well loved by all."The priest made the sign of the cross in blessing and continued on his way. Thomas decided to follow Ignatious when he finished at St Mary's and he told Eloner of his plan. She was dubious but insisted on coming with him on the principle that two people were better than one in an argument or fight.. Eventually after an hour or so when the service in the church was done Ignatious emerged from the door an set off in the direction of the north of the town. Thomas and Eloner followed at a discreet distance. The renegade priest set a fast pace keeping his head down, oblivious of the fact he was being trailed. They left the edge of town and were in an area where market gardens predominated. Wending his way through the vegetable and fruit plots that covered the area Ignatious made his way towards a substantial stone built single storied farmhouse that overlooked the plots. A sieries of small glazed windows looked out onto the fields. He knocked the door and went straight in. Thomas raised his hand and he and Eloner stopped before they had to expose themselves across the market gardens. Thomas whispered. "Do you think that is the Cistercian house of which that other priest talked?" Eloner shook he head. "No I think he mearly visits.within" "I agree, we must find out what goes on in there, I shall skirt round the back and look in on him. You stay here. If trouble erupts do not tackle him for he is ruthless and has been known to kill women. "She nodded grimly, kissed him and urged him to be careful. He set off around the back of the plots and was soon hard up under the rear wall of the farmhouse. There was but one window in the rear,and he slowly raised his head above the cill and looked in. Ignatious was sitting at a long refectory table talking to two men dressed in sombre merchant's garb each with a short sword carried at the waist.The window was ajar and the sound of the priest's voice carried with clarity towards Thomas.

"Well,my Lords.The time is nigh for the House of Lancaster to take back the country from the usurper Edward and reinstate our rightful soveriegn on the throne. My recent intelligence has told me that he is still in the north country and that he has had major victories. But Queen Margaret and the King are both anxious to start the march south to London.But we need money and men. My business with you is to ascertain if I have your backing to obtain finance from the Florintine bankers and also to discover how many men would follow us against the usurper. The two sombre dressed men listened then the first a swarthy italianate looking man with a gold earing and a dark goatee beard said."Father, as you know my brother is Luigi Lombardi the richest banker in Florence, and he has assured me that almost unlimited funds are available,upon the right rates should you require them."Upon hearing this Thomas' blood ran cold, for with such an offer on the table the chance of peace in the kingdom diminished.

The other man who had the demeanour of a soldier and whose face was disfigured with a deep scar running from left to right across his eyelid and down his cheek said. "Men to fight are no problem. We have mercenary soldiers from Piedmont and The Low Countries, also from Ireland and The Scots will come south again given enough incentive.This time we shall be victorious!"Ignatious smiled a mean and wintery smile. "Yes, my Lords, this time we shall be victorious.I shall send a message to your brother and accept both offers of men and money.Now I must return to my Abbey for I shall be missed otherwise. "He stood and bowed to both men who returned the bow. The party split up and Ignatious left the farmhouse.Thomas and Eloner followed once more as Ignatious made his way up onto the thichkly wooded hills that lay to the north of the city.Thomas knew he had to stop the traitor before he was able to send any messages requesting men and money. If cold blooded murder was the order of the day then so be it, but his inate sense of fair play forbid the cold steel dagger between the ribs. So when the pathway started to pass through some thicker woodland he called out. "Hey, Priest"

Ignatious turned and a look of schocked recognition crossed his face as he saw who it was had called out. "You,like a devil's spawn always after meWell now we finish this once and for all." From under his habit he pulled a beautifully wrought slim dagger about 15 inches long with a razor sharp steel bladethat gleamed in the sunlight. Holding the dagger like a rapier he advanced on Thomas. who had drawn his short stabbing sword and stood waiting for the priest's attack. Eloner shrank back against a tree and watched with horror as the two men circled one another. Suddenly as quick as the eye could see Ignatioius ran in and stabbed at Thomas's eyes. He pulled back but felt the needle pain of a cut across his cheek.Blood flowed half blinding him and he shook his head to clear his vision. The priest laughed.Once again he stabbed forward, this time piercing Thomas in the forearm. Once again the laugh. Eloner sobbed with fear. Thomas knew he was in danger of losing this fight. Suddenly he stumbled and went down on one knee. With his good hand he scooped up a handful of road dust and gravel from the pathway and flung it with all his strength into the priest's face. Ignatious screamed in fear and recoiled. Thomas gave a cry of triumph and spang forward with his sword outstretched and felt the weapon pierce the chest of the Cistercian monk.Ignatious gave a strangled cough and dark blood welled from his mouth. He fell forward onto the path driving Thomas's sword deeper into his own body.Blood was flowing freely from Thomas as the wounds in his arm and cheek bleed profusely. Dragging Ignatious' body, which was suprisingly light in weight off the path and into the cover of the trees, They set about binding Thomas's wounds.He searched the body and under the habit in a small canvas satchel found a mass of parchments, maps and incriminating documents that proved utterly to Eloner's satisfaction that the priest had been a spy and a traitor.

"He was a dog and a traitor and was responsible for the death of many honest and good men and women and the world is well rid of him."

She clasped his good arm and kissed him tenderly on the unwounded side of his face."Back to the Crippled Swan for us and a night's rest my love. "He nodded in humble gratitude and they retraced their footsteps back towards the market gardens and finally down to the tavern where they were staying.They saw no one and were able to gain the safety of their room where Eloner attended to his wounds. Neither of which were more that scratches, although the stab in the arm pained him and caused him to call out.

Next morning the tavern was abuzz with rumour and counter rumour. A priest had been foully murdered and his body dumped. Must have been the work of the devil, for priests and monks were sacroscant and holy people and everyone knew it was a mighty sin to kill one.What made this worse was that this priest was a well known local Cistercian who was reknowned for the good works he did amongst the poor in the locality.Thomas was only just able to avoid saying anything as they mounted their horses and rode out of the yard of the crippled Swan. Their route took them northetly along the road to Gloucester to the only ferry crossing over the Severn river at Beachley.There a flat bottomed ferry pulled by ropes which wound round great tubs on either side of the river and were pulled by horses. Crossed the turbulant stream with people, horses goods and whatever wished to cross. This ferry had been in operation for many years and cut the jouney to Wales by two or three whole days ending up near Chepstow castle. Very rarely did it fail, though on occasion it had been known for tipsy waggon drivers to miss the flat bottomed craft and run their wagons into the river.

Eloner and Thomas led their horses onto the ferry and tethered them alongside others who were crossing at the same time. The ferry master gave a signal and the dripping hawser tautened and squeezed out water as the srtrain was taken up on it as the horses on the opposite bank started to pull the rope round the fixed tub.The ferry jerked forward but soon settled into its familiar rhythm as it crossed the Severn.Within half an hour they had disembarked and were trotting placidly up the hill into Chepstow. This strategic town at the confluence of the Wye and Severn was dominated by the grey stone castle that lowered over the river. Skirting the town the two of them wended their way slowly up and onto thetop and out towards the valley of the River wye that took them past the Abbey of Tintern and eventually to the small but thriving township of Monmouth.Their road led them close to the water's edge and Thomas could see trout and occasionally something bigger flashing silver in the slow moving waters. By late afternoon they were crossing the stone bridge into the town of Monmouth where they stayed that night leaving the next morning in the direction of Abergavenny and Hay on Wye. An uneventful day's travel brought them up past the isolated but beautiful Llananthony Abbey and down past Hay Bluff and so into the township of Hay. Familiar land marks were everywhere and Thomas spent much of the time pointing out places and buildings he knew. Elenor was fascinated to be so close to the home of the man she loved and she took in the information like a sponge, asking pertinant questions.Thomas was beginning to feel a building of excitement in the pit of his stomach. He wondered how Diccon had got on being in sole charge of Stapleton Castle whilst he was away. He had ultimate confidence in his squire and steward, but he knew what a huge task it was he had left him.

The travellers crossed the river Lugg on the edge of Presteigne and there ahead of them on the top of a steep hillside suddenly stood the stone keep of Stapleton Castle. A cobbled roadbed led up through a neatly cropped meadow.To one side a working quarry from which building stone was being hewn served as a defensive feature whilst ahead of them a wooden bridge spanned a deep defensive ditch that led through to the stone keep of the castle.Sitting at one end of the bridge with his ears gently blowing in the wind sat the dog Orrid.First he sniffed the air as he smelt the horses then with a great leaping bound and a roaring bellow of greeting he sprang forward.as he recognised who it was coming over the bridge home at last.. Wagging everything and whining and barking and jumping towards the horses. So much so that Thomas had to dismount to quieten him. Laughing and patting the dog he hugged the huge and unruly animal.

Diccon came through the gate drawn by the noise and with a look of incedulity on his face knelt in the dust and embraced Thomas.

"Oh, Sir Thomas and Lady Eloner welcome, welcome to your home. I felt it in my bones that you were not far off and how right I was."He smiled that well known smile that had charmed many a servnt girl and clapping hands he ordered wine to be brought to the weary but ultimately happy travellers.

Historical Note

The period of the Wars of the roses was a very confused time in the history of England. There was a civil war raging, but only in relatively narrow parts of the country. Whole swathes of the kingdom were to all intents and purposes at peace. The soldiers that fought mainly did so against their own wishes having been levied or arrayed by their lords and masters as a bounty extracted by the king. The vast majority of the population tried to keep its head down and get on with their difficult and hard working lives.

In this story certain people ex sted in history. Anyone mentioned by name existed in reality, most of them were beheaded however, the ficticious characters are Thomas of Lingen, Diccon of Knighton, Eloner Countess of Hambye, the three archers in the golden arrow competition Father Ignatious and PhillipeDe Peynil. Anyone else I may have left out is also fictional. All the villages towns and disrtricts mentioned exist and there is a map to show Thomas's journey through th great Kingdom of England.

The battles of Mortimer's Cross and Towton had a significant effect upon the history of The times. The former as it enabled Edward to gain the confidence to declare himself king, and the latter as more men were slain on the battlefield at Towton than lost their lives on the first day of the battle of the Somme 28000 by most accounts. In a country whose population had already been decimated by the Black Death only a few years before, this number of fatilities must have had a decided effect upon the demographic.

I hope you enjoyed this tale and be assured Thomas has more adventures to go through and more tasks to perform for his king.

Francis Lecane has had an abiding interest in history since he was a youngboy. He studied at Bristol University and taught english for a time. Most of his working life has been spent in the retail trade.

Now retired and living with his wife in the beautiful Marches countryside between England and Wales.